10/04   4.95

D1482105

On the Couch

On the Couch

Great American
Stories About *Therapy*

Edited and with an Introduction by
Erica Kates

The Atlantic Monthly Press
New York

Published simultaneously in Canada
Printed in the United States of America

FIRST EDITION

Library of Congress Cataloging-in-Publication Data
On the couch : great American stories about therapy / edited and with an
    introduction by Erica Kates. — 1st ed.
        p.   cm.
    ISBN 0–87113–662–7
    1. Psychotherapy—Fiction.   2. Psychological fiction, American.
3. Psychotherapy patients—Fiction.   4. Therapist and patient—
Fiction.   5. Short stories, American.   6. Mental illness—Fiction.
7. Psychiatrists—Fiction.   8. Mentally ill—Fiction.   I. Kates,
Erica.
PS648.P7706   1997
813'.0108356—dc20   96–24064

Design by Laura Hammond Hough

The Atlantic Monthly Press
841 Broadway
New York, NY 10003

10   9   8   7   6   5   4   3   2   1

Acknowledgments

For their help and encouragement, I'd like to thank Amanda Beesley, Daniel Menaker, Colin Dickerman, Sloan Harris, Arthur Brunwasser, Michael Freeman, Alisa Levine, and Sheldon Roth.

Contents

No therapy is comfortable, because it involves dealing with pain. But there's one comfortable thought: that two people sharing pain can bear it easier than one.

—Elvin Semrad, M.D.

Two in a deep-founded sheltering, friend and dear friend.

—Wallace Stevens, "The World as Meditation"

Introduction

Contemporary culture is fascinated with psychotherapy, but for most of us, what takes place during a typical session is a mystery. The therapist's office remains one of the few private places in our world, and consequently, perceptions of what happens there are often distorted. The media feeds on this distortion; the portrayals of therapists and patients on television and in recent films are overwhelmingly negative, as is the press's tendency to highlight cases of therapists' sexual misconduct. In addition, although there is an endless appeal to the expertise of therapists who appear on popular television talk shows, the time constraints posed by these commercial-laden programs prevent the therapists from providing wholly satisfying insights. None of these sources comes close to revealing the essence of the unique therapist-patient relationship—the exchange of a broad range of highly charged feelings.

In fiction we can find in-depth accounts of these exchanges. The stories in *On the Couch* provide a window into an intensely private world by disclosing both the therapist's and the patient's experience of the therapy—and of each other—in and out of the office. Although we can never observe the confidential exchange that takes place during another person's therapy session, in reading these stories we gain a sense of what such meetings are like. The writers' imaginations expand upon these encounters in diverse ways. Writers, like inquiring therapists, are drawn to the same mystery—how to fashion a coherent story out of the mass (or, mess) of human experience. The writer's wish to explore therapy may be likened to the wish to look inside this experience, to shape it, and to understand it. Part of fiction's appeal is that it provides us with greater access to the intimate details of other people's lives than even a therapist has: not only do we learn about the patient's intimate thoughts, we are privy to those belonging to the therapist as well.

Although these stories contain therapists and patients whose behavior toward each other is occasionally as unsettling as their film and TV counterparts, these written accounts present us with such poignant and wildly funny explanations of the characters' motivations that we cannot help but feel compassion for them. These stories show us how therapy alters the lives of its participants. As we read, we encounter patients whose expectations for their therapy are unrealistic; we observe the processes of transference and countertransference; we watch as therapists abuse their power; we learn about the role of responsibility in therapy; and we note the ingredients for a successful therapeutic experience. Even though each of these accounts is fictional, the consistencies in theme among such a wide range of voices and situations point to what are realistic experiences.

Further, these stories supplement one another in remarkably symmetrical ways. The works by Lynne Sharon Schwartz and John Updike, for example, present virtually identical depictions of patient dependence, and Charles Baxter and Francine Prose do the same for the experience of loss. Meanwhile, Lawrence Block and Stephen McCauley provide contrasting visions of what occurs when a patient lies compulsively. Daniel Menaker's fictional duo honor their ancestor in Peter Collier's work, an "unconscious homage" says the author, in reference to his portrayal of a therapist similar in both personality and background to the doctor in Collier's story. And a quick glance at the titles of these stories is telling in and of itself. In such words as "surprised," "changed," "transference," "mysterious," "crazy," and "imaginary" are woven foreshadowings of the mystery and magic to come.

Mirroring real-life therapy, every story here is concerned in some way with love and the difficulty of either attaining it or holding on to it. The therapist becomes the vehicle through which the patient can explore his feelings about love, and the object against which he measures those feelings. So, too, are their roles often reversed, and the patient acts as catalyst for the therapist's unresolved feelings and reactions. It is this remarkable interface that provides the foundation for the therapist's and the patient's work in real life, as well as in fiction.

Erica Kates
CAMBRIDGE, MA

I.
Loss

Though the experience of loss permeates all of the stories in this book, the ones in this section focus the most intensely on it. These stories explore what happens when various therapy patients are unable to recognize the extent of their own grief, and point to the necessity of finding an appropriate and effective way to mourn.

In the first three works, the therapist is able to set the patient's mourning process in motion by being simply a listener. In "If Only Bert Were Here," the death of a pet is used as a device that humorously illuminates the various distinct stages of mourning: "Anger, Denial, Bargaining, Häagen-Dazs, Rage." Only after the protagonist enters therapy and recounts her dead pet's "finer qualities and golden moments, his great sense of humor and witty high jinks," does she move past her sadness. This grieving, we learn, requires recounting the details.

In "Transference," these details are examined through the feelings exchanged between the therapist and patient. In a telling moment—an "auditory Freudian slip"—the patient realizes that the feelings he has for his therapist are actually those he harbors for his dead father.

"Slatland" contains two conflicting views of therapy. As in the two previous stories, the protagonist is encouraged by her therapist to mourn a loss; here, it is of her childhood innocence and happy family. Her peculiar therapist prompts her to visit Slatland, a magical place or mental state where she is able to "separate from the situation" once she can "literally rise above it," so as to view it with perspective. But her new objectivity and relief are accompanied by a detached loss of feeling. For the protagonist's foreigner fiancé, this feeling—though painful—is true and powerful, and therefore *should* be felt: "When a father leaves a child, the child feels sad. This seems right to me. This rising above, that is the problem. In fact, that is the problem of America." The therapist in this story, in being both an appealing and disturbing figure, embodies the story's ambivalence.

"Surprised by Joy" and "Imaginary Problems" present an even darker view of therapy. Though recounting the details of what they've lost is what ultimately helps the patients in these stories, it is not by the encouragement of their therapists that they do this. Though the therapists here suggest what may be legitimate solutions to remedy their patients' pain, they seem to possess a limited view of life experience and are unable to understand how deeply their patients are suffering. These therapists are more concerned with merely finding a speedy anesthetic, something that "helps." Their suggestions, which include keeping a journal, going on vacation, and taking up a primitive-style ritual, seem superficial. "How to explain why we're here," the protagonist in "Imaginary Problems" exclaims, "believing or at least pretending that the pain of loss . . . can be eased by mumbling some mumbo-jumbo and committing to earth a frozen rodent in an extra-large Ziploc bag?"

If Only Bert Were Here

Lorrie Moore

When the cat died, his ashes packed into a cheesy, pink-posied tin and placed high upon the mantel, the house seemed lonely and Aileen began to drink. She had lost all her ties to the animal world. She existed now in a solely man-made place: the couch was furless, the carpet dry and unmauled, the kitchen corner where the food dish had been no longer scabby with Mackerel Platter and hazardous for walking. *Oh, Bert!*

He had been a beautiful cat.

Her friends interpreted the duration and intensity of her sorrow as a sign of displaced mourning: her grief was for something larger, more appropriate—it was the impending death of her parents; it was the son she and Jack had never had (though wasn't three-year-old Sofie cute as a zipper?); it was this whole Bosnia, Cambodia, Somalia, Dinkins, Nafta thing.

No really, it was just Bert, Aileen insisted. It was just her sweet, handsome cat, her buddy of ten years. She had been with him longer than she had with either Jack or Sofie or half her friends, and he was such a smart funny guy—big and loyal and verbal as a dog.

"What do you mean, *verbal as a dog?*" Jack scowled.

"I swear it," she said.

"Get a grip," said Jack, eyeing her glass of blended malt. Puccini's "Humming Chorus," the Brahms "Alto Rhapsody," Samuel Barber's "Adagio for Strings" all murmured in succession from the stereo. He flicked off the dial. "You've got a daughter. There are holidays ahead. That damn cat wouldn't have shed one tear over you."

"I really don't think that's true," she said, a little wildly, perhaps with too much fire and malt in her voice. She now spoke that way sometimes, insisted on things, ventured out on a limb, lived dangerously. She had already—carefully, obediently— stepped through all the stages of bereavement: Anger, Denial, Bargaining, Häagen-Dazs, Rage. Anger to Rage—who said she wasn't making progress? She made a fist but hid it. She got headaches, mostly prickly ones, but sometimes the zigzag of a migraine made its way into her skull and sat like a cheap, crazy tie in her eye.

"Look, I'm sorry," said Jack. "Maybe he would have. Fund-raisers. Cards and letters. Who can say? You two were close, I know."

She ignored him. "Here," she said, pointing at her drink. "Have a little festive lift!" She sipped at the amber liquor; it stung her chapped lips.

"Dewar's," said Jack, looking with chagrin at the bottle.

"Well," she said defensively, sitting up straight and buttoning her sweater, "I suppose you're out of sympathy with Dewar's. I suppose you're more of a *Do-ee.*"

"That's right," said Jack, disgustedly. "That's right! And tomorrow I'm going to wake up and find I've been edged out by Truman!" He headed angrily up the stairs, while she listened for the final clomp of his steps and the cracking slam of the door.

Poor Jack: perhaps she had put him through too much. Just last spring, there had been her bunion situation—the limping, the crutch, and the big blue shoe. Then in September there had been Mimi Andersen's dinner party, where Jack, the only nonsmoker, had been asked to go out on the porch while everyone else stayed inside and lit up. And then, there had been Aileen's one-woman performance of "the housework version of *Lysistrata*," "No Sweepie, No Kissie," Jack had called it. But it had worked. Sort of. For about two weeks. (There was, finally, only so much one woman on the vast, wicked stage could do.)

"I'm worried about you," said Jack in bed. "I'm being earnest here. And not in the Hemingway sense, either." He screwed up his face. "You see how I'm talking? Things are wacko around here." Their bookcase headboard was so stacked with novels and sad memoirs it now resembled a library carrel more than a bed.

"You're fine. I'm fine. Everybody's fine," said Aileen. She tried to find his hand under the covers, then just gave up.

"You're someplace else," he said. "Where are you?"

The birds had become emboldened, slowly reclaiming the yard, filling up the branches, cheeping hungrily in the mornings from the sills and eaves. "What is that *shrieking*?" Aileen asked. The leaves had fallen, but now finches, ravens, and jays darkened the trees—some of them flying south, some of them staying on, pecking the hardening ground for seeds. Squirrels moved in, poking through the old apples that had dropped from the flowering crab. A possum made a home for himself under the porch, thumping and chewing. Raccoons had discovered Sophie's little gym set, and one morning Aileen looked out and saw two of them swinging on the swings. She'd wanted animal life? Here was animal life!

"Not this," she said. "None of this would be happening if Bert were still here." Bert had patrolled the place. Bert had kept things in line.

"Are you talking to me?" asked Jack.

"I guess not," she said.

Thanksgiving came and went in a mechanical way. They went out to a restaurant and ordered different things, as if they were strangers asserting their ornery tastes. Then they drove home. Only Sofie, who had ordered the child's Stuffed Squash, was somehow pleased, sitting in the back car seat and singing a Thanksgiving song she'd learned at Day Care. "Oh, a turkey's not a pig, you doink/He doesn't say *oink,*/he says *gobble, gobble, gobble.*"

Their last truly good time had been Halloween, when Bert was still alive and they had dressed him up as Jack. They'd then dressed Jack as Bert, Aileen as Sofie, and Sofie as Aileen. "Now, I'm you, Mommy," Sofie had said when Aileen had tied one of her kitchen aprons around her and pressed lipstick onto her mouth. Jack came up and rubbed his magic marker whiskers against Aileen, who giggled in her large, pink footie pajamas.

The only one who wasn't having that much fun was Bert himself, sporting one of Jack's ties and pawing at it to get it off. When he didn't succeed, he gamely dragged the tie around for a while, trying to ignore it. Then, cross and humiliated, he'd waddled over to the corner near the piano and lay there, annoyed. Remembering this, a week later—when Bert was dying in an oxygen tent at the vet's, heart failing, fluid around his lungs (though his ears still pricked up when she came to visit him; she wore perfume so he would know her smell, and hand-fed him cat snacks when no one else could get him to eat)—Aileen had felt overwhelmed with sorrow and regret.

"I think you should see someone," said Jack.

"Are we talking a psychiatrist or an affair?"

"An affair, of course." Jack scowled. "An *affair?*"

"I don't know." Aileen shrugged. Whiskey had caused her joints to swell, so that now when she lifted her shoulders they just kind of stayed like that, stiffly, up around her ears.

Jack rubbed her upper arm: either he loved her or he was wiping something off on her sleeve. Which could it be? "Life is a long journey across a wide country," he said. "Sometimes the weather's good. Sometimes it's bad. Sometimes it's so bad your car goes off the road."

"Really."

"Just go talk to someone," he said. "Our health plan will cover part."

"O.K.," she said. "O.K. Just—no more metaphors."

She got recommendations, made lists and appointments, conducted interviews. "I have a death-of-a-pet situation," she said. "How long does it take for you to do those?"

"I beg your pardon?"

"How long will it take you to get me over the death of my cat, and how much do you charge for it?"

Each of the psychiatrists, in turn, with their slightly different outfits, and slightly different potted plants, looked shocked.

"Look," Aileen said. "Forget Prozac. Forget Freud's Abandonment of the Seduction Theory. Forget Jeffrey Masson—or is it *Jackie* Mason? Whatever: The only thing that's going to revolutionize *this* profession is Bidding the Job!"

"I'm afraid we don't work that way," she was told, again and again—until finally, at last, she found someone who did.

"I specialize in Christmas," said the psychiatrist, a man named Sidney Poe, who wore an argyle sweater vest, a crisp bow tie, shiny black oxfords, and no socks. "Christmas specials. You feel better by Christmas, or your last session's free."

"I like the sound of that," said Aileen. It was already December 1. "I like the sound of that a lot."

"Good," he said, giving her a smile that, she had to admit, looked a little demented. "Now, what are we dealing with here, a cat or a dog?"

"A cat," she said.

"Whoa, boy." He wrote something down, muttered, looked dismayed.

"Can I ask you a question first?" asked Aileen.

"Certainly," he said.

"Do you offer Christmas specials because of the high suicide rates around Christmas?"

"The high suicide rates around Christmas." He sniffed in a bemused way. "That's a myth, the high suicide rates around Christmas. It's the *homicide* rate that's high. Holiday homicide. All that time the family gets to spend together, and then *bam,* that *eggnog.*"

"I see." She went to Sidney Poe on Thursdays—Advent Thursdays, she called them. She sat before him with a box of Kleenex on her lap, recalling Bert's finer qualities and golden moments, his great sense of humor and witty high jinks. "He used to try to talk on the phone, when *I* was on the phone. And once, when I was looking for my keys, I said aloud, *'Where's my keys?'* and he came running into the room, thinking I'd said, *'Where's my kitty.'* "

Only once did she actually have to slap Sidney awake—lightly. Mostly she could clap her hands once, and call his name—*Sid!*—and he would jerk upright in his psychiatrist's chair, staring wide. "In the Intensive Care Unit at the Animal Hospital," Aileen continued, "I saw a cat who'd been shot in the spine with a BB. I saw dogs recovering from jaw surgery. I saw a retriever who'd had a hip replacement come out into the lobby dragging a little cart behind him. He was so happy to see his owner. He dragged himself toward her and she knelt and spread her arms wide to greet him. She sang out to him and cried. It was the animal version of *Porgy and Bess.*" She paused. "It made me wonder what was going on in this country. It made me think that we should ask ourselves, 'What in hell's going on?' "

"I'm afraid we're over our time," said Sidney.

The next week she went to the mall first. She wandered in and out of the stores with their tinsel and treacly, Muzaked Christmas carols, which, she was embarrassed to admit, she sort of liked. But everywhere she went there were little cat Christmas books, cat Christmas cards, cat Christmas wrapping paper. She hated these cats. They were boring, dopey, insulting—not a patch on Bert.

"I had great hopes for Bert," she continued to Sidney. "They gave him all the procedures, all the medications—but the drugs knocked his kidneys out. When the doctor looked grim, I asked, 'Isn't there anything else we can do?' And you know what the doctor said? A thousand dollars later and he says, 'Yes. An autopsy.'"

"Eeeeyew," said Sid.

"A cashectomy," said Aileen. "They gave Bert a cashectomy!" And here she began to cry, thinking of the poor, sweet look on Bert's face in the oxygen tent, the bandaged tube in his paw, the wet fog in his eyes. It was not an animal's way to die like that, but she had subjected him to the full medical treatment, signed him up for all that metallic and fluorescent voodoo, not knowing what else to do.

"Tell me about Sofie."

Aileen sighed. Sofie was adorable. Sofie was terrific. "She's fine. She's great." Except Sofie was getting little notes sent home with her from Day Care. *Today, Sofie gave the teacher the finger—although it was her index finger.* Or, *Today, Sofie drew a mustache on her face.* Or, *Today, Sofie demanded to be called Walter.*

"Really."

"Our last really good event was Halloween. I took her trick-or-treating around the neighborhood, and she was so cute. It was only by the end of the night that she began to catch on to the whole concept of it. Most of the time she was so excited she'd ring the bell, and when someone came to the door, she'd thrust out her bag and say, 'Look! I've got treats for you!'"

"We've got to focus on Christmas here," said Sidney.

"Yes," said Aileen, despairingly. "We've only got one more week."

On the Thursday before Christmas, she felt flooded with memories: Bert as a kitten, Bert catching mice, Bert in the garden or on the couch taking a long nap. "He had limited sounds to communicate his limited needs," she said. "He had his 'food' mew—and I'd follow him to his dish. He had his 'out' mew and I'd follow him to the door. He had his 'brush' mew and I'd go with him to the cupboard where his brush was kept. And then he had his existential mew, where I'd follow him around the house as he wandered vaguely in and out of rooms, not knowing exactly what he wanted or why."

Sidney's eyes began to well. "I can see why you miss him," he said.

"You can?"

"Of course. But that's all I can leave you with."

"The Christmas Special's up."

"I'm afraid so," he said, standing. He reached out to shake her hand. "Call me after the holidays and let me know how you feel."

"All right," she said sadly. "I will."

She went home, poured herself a drink, stood by the mantel. She picked up the pink-posied tin and shook it, afraid she might hear the muffled banging of bones, but she heard nothing. "Are you sure it's even him?" Jack asked. "With animals they probably do mass incinerations. One scoop for cats, two for dogs."

"*Please,*" she said. At least she had not buried Bert in the local pet cemetery, with its intricate gravestones and maudlin inscriptions—*Beloved Rexie: I'll be joining you soon, boy.*

"I got the very last Christmas tree," said Jack, hopefully. "It was leaning against the shed wall with a broken high heel and a cigarette dangling from its mouth. I brought it home and fed it soup."

At least she had sought something more tasteful than the cemetery, the appropriate occasion to return Bert to earth and sky, get him down off the fireplace and out of the house in a meaningful way, though she'd yet to find the right moment. She had let him stay on the mantel and had mourned him deeply—it was only proper. You couldn't pretend you had lost nothing. A good cat had died—you had to begin there, not let your blood freeze over. If your heart turned away at this, it could turn away at something else, then more and more until your heart stayed averted, immobile, your imagination redistributed away from the world and back toward the bad maps of yourself—of pointlessness—the sour pools of your own pulse, your mean and watery wants. Stop here! Begin here! Begin here with Bert! Here's to Bert!

Early Christmas morning she woke Sofie and dressed her warmly in her snowsuit. There was a light snow on the ground and a wind blew powdery gusts around the yard. "We're going to say good-bye to Bert," said Aileen.

"Oh, Bert!" said Sofie, and she began to cry.

"No, it'll be happy!" said Aileen, feeling the pink-posied tin in her jacket pocket. "He wants to go out. Do you remember how he used to want to go out? How he would mee-ow at the door and then we would let him go?"

"Mee-ow, mee-ow," said Sofie.

"Right," said Aileen. "So that's what we're going to do now."

"Will he be with Santa Claus?"

"Yes! He'll be with Santa Claus!"

They stepped outside, down off the porch steps. Aileen pried open the tin: inside there was a small plastic bag and she ripped that open, too. Inside was Bert: a pebbly ash like the sand and ground shells of a beach. Summer in December! What was Christmas about if not a giant mixed metaphor, the mystery of inter-species love—God's for man! Love had sought a chasm to leap across and landed itself right here!—the Holy Ghost among the barn animals, the teacher's pet sent to be adored and then to die.

Aileen and Sofie each seized a fistful of Bert and ran around the yard, letting the wind take the ash and scatter it. Birds flew from the trees. Frightened squirrels headed for the yard next door. In freeing Bert, perhaps she and Sofie would become him a little: banish the interlopers, police the borders, go back inside and play with the decorations, claw at the gift wrap, eat the tasty headless bird.

"Merry Christmas to Bert!" Sofie shouted. The tin was now empty.

"Yes, Merry Christmas to Bert!" said Aileen. She shoved the container back into her pocket. Then she and Sofie raced back into the house to get warm.

Jack was in the kitchen, standing by the stove, still in his pajamas. He was pouring orange juice and heating buns.

"Daddy, Merry Christmas to Bert!" Sofie ripped open the snaps of her snowsuit.

"Yes," said Jack, turning. "Merry Christmas to Bert!"

He handed Sofie, then Aileen, some juice. But before she drank hers, Aileen waited for Jack to say something else. He stepped forward. He raised his glass. His wide, quizzical smile said, *This is a very weird family.* But instead he exclaimed, "Merry Christmas to everyone in the whole wide world!" and let it go at that.

Transference

Peter Collier

The first thing Adam looked for was the picture of Freud. He was surprised to find that it was still there, centered on the large beige wall as if parodying ancestor worship, framed in dime-store black, the glass microscopically specked by flies and their discontents. He had assumed as a matter of course that it would be gone, a victim of feminism's witch hunt against primal fathers. A reactionary part of him he usually didn't acknowledge was secretly pleased to see that Fuentes had held out.

He stood in front of the photo, blocking the window's glare with his head and shoulders. It was Freud near the end, baleful and defiant, angles of bone and sag casting shadows that ran down from the forehead to the straight, distasteful line of the mouth. This face had bothered him when he had come here during what he later thought of as his "neurotic period," almost as if he were an artist who had moved on to a more mature form of composition. Sitting in one of these same chairs, waiting for his name to be called, he had often found himself glancing up over the rim of a *New Yorker* to check on the photo, knowing he was like a character in one of the cartoons he had just been smiling at, but still half convinced that if he moved fast enough, he would catch Freud's somber features just finishing some mocking little gesture. Once when no other patients were here he had moved from one seat to another in all parts of the waiting room to see if that critical eye could follow him everywhere, as it had once been pointed out to him at Sunday School that the eyes of Jesus did in certain Presbyterian paintings. Twelve years ago the face had seemed tragic, portentous. But now it seemed diminished, the sort of face that might belong to a querulous old Jewish man just returned from an irritating conversation with God.

Adam remembered the time when his father had pronounced the name "Frood" in front of company and his mother had triumphantly corrected him. Later in the conversation his father tried to save face by making a pun on "id" and "yid," and so shocked himself by this silly anti-Semitism that he suddenly looked as if he would cry, shortly after finding an excuse to leave the room and go out to the garage workbench.

He also remembered the time after they had just met when his wife, Patsy, had asked him if he "believed in" Freud. He had always liked that formulation: there was an abundance of the revealed word and reports of many miracles, but no empirical proof. He had never been sure how much he had profited from his time here with Fuentes. The only true Freudian epiphany he ever experienced had come later on in his own kitchen, when his son, Matty, was about five and going through a period when he couldn't bear the sight of Adam. The boy had taunted him with his independence, and had devoted himself to possessing Patsy, tangling in her long legs during conversations or sitting on her lap and reaching up to center her face on his whenever she happened to break eye contact. Wounded by the rejection, Adam had tried to protect himself by remaining aloof and cynical. One night he had come home from work and seen the child scurry away from the door to go and hang on Patsy like an organ grinder's monkey. "Well, and how's my little Oedipus today?" He had reached behind her thigh to tousle the boy's hair. "I'm not *your* little Oedipus," Matty had sneered back at him. "I'm *Mommy's* little Oedipus."

Adam smiled grimly at the picture and whispered, "Thanks a lot, Frood," then turned and sat down on a plump chocolate-colored sofa.

The difficulty of love between the generations had been on his mind when he called Fuentes last night from Pasadena. He wanted to talk about it right then, but as the answering service patched him through to the residence and Fuentes came on the line, his agenda leaked away. Too formally he announced his name and was beginning to explain who he was when Fuentes interrupted, his voice still bearing trace elements of Spanish, "Yes, Mr. Marsden, I remember. What can I do for you?"

"Well, I don't know, really." He felt himself falling into one of his orgies of over-explanation. "The thing is that my father is dead. He just died. I don't mean that he died unexpectedly, but that he died just yesterday. I'm down here in Pasadena with my mother and sister, but I'll be back in Berkeley tomorrow. I'd like to have a talk with you." And then, inanely, he tried to prove that he wasn't so hysterical as he must have sounded. "I assume, by the way, that your warranty is still good."

"I stand behind my workmanship, yes," Fuentes's words were encoded with professional neutrality, and the leaves of his appointment book rustled audibly over the phone. "I could see you at three tomorrow afternoon."

Until a few months ago, it seemed impossible that he would ever return here. Sometimes complexities resisted his ingenuity and left him blue, but he had scorn for the professional patients who spent tens of thousands of dollars on the couch in narcissistic reverie and also for the amateurs who obsessively wrote down their dreams on waking each morning so they could relate them later in the day. He did not want to be one of that breed of moderns who have their emotions in the palms of their hands and work them over like jewelers staring through eyepieces. Therapy was like puberty: you went through it and looked back only to marvel that you ever survived it.

He had come to this waiting room almost an hour early on the day of his first appointment, squirming under Freud's harsh gaze and auditioning things to say. He planned to tell how he and Jane, whom he called Crazy Jane after the character in Yeats, slept together but never touched; and how that bisection of their conjugal bed really had nothing to do with some Wagnerian code of virtue or honor, unless it was a resolve to remain pure to hurt each other more effectively when sleeping with others. He planned to tell how he had thought he could match her infidelity for infidelity until a few weeks earlier, when he had begun to have a feeling that there was a gun barrel in his mouth, the snub nose of a pistol with a hair trigger capable of going off at any minute; and how a few days ago he had been driving up University Avenue and suddenly sighted down the hood ornament of his car at a light stanchion fifty feet away and bloodied his forehead when he hit it. He had all planned what he would say when his turn came.

Finally the door to Fuentes's inner office had opened and a woman came out holding a corsage of Kleenex to her nose and reaching for the knob of the front door as if it were a life preserver. All his plans had gone away, leaving him in panic. After waiting a few minutes, he had wandered in, noting the arrangement of the furniture, and the diplomas from the University of Mexico and Heidelberg on the wall as sounds of urination came from behind a closed door. When Fuentes emerged from the bathroom drying his hands, Adam had been looking out the sliding glass door onto the garden. After politely telling him to wait next time until his name was called, Fuentes had motioned for him to sit, then folded his compact body into a chair in a shadowy corner of the room. Adam had quickly tried to psych out the face—dark and square, a Zapata mustache curling down the sides of the mouth, eyes that glittered with an Aztec fierce-ness and black hair so shiny it looked like patent leather.

"You don't have to lie down or cry to participate here, do you?" Adam had tried for a tone of witty vulnerability in gesturing at the couch next to his chair and the box of Kleenex on the table.

"Do whatever is agreeable for you." Fuentes had flashed the noncommittal smile that made his face look like one of those figurines sold in Mexico City notions stores. "Just pay me at the beginning of each month and I'll be happy."

"Well, you can't tell the players without a program." Adam had begun by telling about each member of the family—the homosexual uncle Waldo; his unknown Jewish grandfather Myron; the paternal grandparents who had helped raise him. He told about his sister, Alison, and about his mother and fa-ther, and found himself yielding to the gravitational pull lead-ing toward their fights. He told of how he, perhaps five or six, had once walked from the darkened hallway as they fought furi-ously in the living room.

"Thinking back on it, I'd say my mother was like a good welterweight going up in class against a heavier opponent. She'd fly at him, banging away as hard as she could, working the body and then moving up to head-hunt, jumping up and down like a banty to equalize the height disadvantage. He was like one of those reluctant light-heavies, covering up on the ropes and try-ing to pick off the punches. This particular time he was cower-ing in a corner of the living room with one knee up in case she tried to kick him in the groin. Every once in a while, he'd sort of flick out a fist, almost as if by accident, and down she'd go to the floor, crying not because she was hurt but because she wasn't stronger."

Afraid that they would kill each other, he had gone to the medicine cabinet where he smeared shoe polish on his teary face and then ran into the living room, got down on one knee near their legs and began an imitation of Al Jolson doing "Swanee."

As he spoke he had been interrupted by a sudden smacking sound and had looked over to see Fuentes with a mocking smile making slightly obscene kissing noises with his puckered lips. "Oh, isn't that cute." The caustic intervention had shocked Adam. "The little Christ child taking others' sins onto himself, sacrificing his sanity to preserve the family. Marvelous! But you know what I think? That little Adam is a giant pain in the butt. Interfering with Mommy and Daddy's fun like that. For shame! And still doing it today with these self-pitying little replays. Still trying to use bad dreams as an excuse to get in bed with your parents and snuggle down there in all that erotic heat where you can make them jump apart with your cold feet. You little devil, you!"

"I don't get it." Adam had gotten to his feet he was so angry. "Are you an actor or something? Is this some kind of comedy routine? The picture of Freud out there is a joke?"

Fuentes leaned forward. "I'll be happy to sit back and look profound and be silent and brooding and Freudian if you've got about fifteen thousand dollars and a couple of years to spare. I thought by the look of you that you were a poor graduate student. But if you've got hidden assets, please say so. Nothing I'd like better than one of those long term doctor-patient relationships. Like the old saying: you got the money, honey, I got the time. I'd be happy to do some real *psychoanalysis* if you're up to it. I've got the credentials."

After a few minutes of petulant silence, Adam had begun speaking again, describing in a halting, earnest style how he and Jane had picked on people who would be easily dominated for their involvements. "She had this thing going with a high school kid in the office where she worked. A stock boy, I think. I found out because I saw his report cards in her purse. He gave them to her with little love notes—kind of a pathetic offering.

"I got even with her by starting up with this secretary named Arlene who worked in the English Department. She was a little older than me, tall and blond, one of those un-pretty women you describe as 'handsome' as a sort of consolation prize. I remember we went to see *Wild Strawberries,* and then to her apartment. We came to this rational decision that we should go to bed. She was self-conscious about the size of her breasts and sort of covered them up by crossing her arms. This made me curious. I looked at them and felt that in fact they did look strange—like tennis balls on that long torso of hers. After we were through she told me I was the first man she'd slept with. I couldn't believe it—she must have been twenty-six or twenty-seven years old. I asked her why. Know what she said? 'I've never gotten away from the habits of childhood.' It was very poignant. 'The habits of childhood': that phrase got to me. I felt a little queasy. I've always wondered . . .'"

Hearing a heavy intake of breath, Adam had looked down from his spot on the ceiling to see Fuentes's jaw become unhinged, the eyes show white, and the head flop as if on a broken neck. The loud snore froze his monologue. After a moment, Fuentes suddenly snapped to attention like an old man subliminally alerted to the fact that others were watching him sleep.

"What's the point?" Again Adam had been barely able to control his anger. "That I'm boring you?"

"Oh no," Fuentes smiled sweetly. "Whatever gave you that idea?" Then his face cleared of expression like a blackboard that had been erased. "Listen, instead of giving me these little canned speeches, these little bare stage readings of your graduate school version of *Who's Afraid of Virginia Woolf,* maybe you could just do a recording on a cassette and leave it under my door. I'll listen and grade it and send it back. We can do therapy by mail."

"You're trying to get at me." Adam was embarrassed by the petulance in his voice.

"Get at you?" Fuentes bent forward attentively. "Like your uncle, you mean?"

"So you have been listening."

"I got a few sentences here and there."

"What's the comment about my uncle supposed to mean?"

"Well, you said he was a homosexual, and that he made a pass at you when you were a boy. That also qualifies as trying to 'get at you.' You're just too sweet. My feeling is that you like being queer-bait. That's your racket: be sweet and nobody takes you seriously. But the problem is that if you're too sweet they might eat you up. In fact, I think you're trying to entrap me with these little moral tales you're telling. They have the quality of a calculated flirtation."

"I still don't get what you're driving at."

"Don't try too hard." Fuentes smiled and stood up. "Anyhow, that's all the time we have today. Let's get back to the gun in the mouth. I'd just like you to agree that you won't kill yourself or become a homosexual without giving this situation here a try for a couple of weeks."

"You think I'm a homosexual, then?"

"Funny." Fuentes got up and walked over to open the door in a gracious continental gesture and spoke as if to a third party. "He doesn't mind when I say no suicide. But I tell him no homosexuality, and he gets upset."

"You think I'm queer." Adam stood in the doorway.

"I think you're angry at your father—among other things for being so weak and feckless as not to protect you against his brother's advances. But no matter. You must excuse me now, I have another patient."

There had been days when he talked and talked, hopelessly trapped in the logic he saw himself fabricate and, like a blacksmith, pound into odd shapes; he looked at Fuentes to see signs that what he said was pleasing and tried to figure out ways to make him tell him what to do.

"I want a head-to-toe operation," he said, "a new me."

"You love the apocalyptic," said Fuentes, "the cosmic things you can't control. Start with the small things, like gripping the steering wheel in such a way that it doesn't run into things."

Adam told him about a fear he had. Since leaving Pasadena to come to Berkeley, he had sometimes had a powerful apprehension that disaster had overtaken one or more members of his family. It was one of those truthful insights like he imagined precognition to be. He would try to ride the feeling out, but always the fear would grow until he was compelled to call home on some flimsy pretext to find out if everyone was okay. He told Fuentes about this, imagining what ridicule he'd get in return, and told him also about a recurring dream that had plagued him since his junior year at college, before his marriage to Crazy Jane. Always the same: he was standing up in the mountains of Tilden Park, high above the city of Berkeley, looking down at the whole Bay Area. Suddenly there would be a flash and the skyline would light up with a putrid yellow glow. Mushroom clouds would form in rolling pillars somewhere in what he knew to be the southern part of the state. He would know that Los Angeles was dead; his mother and father and sister incinerated.

"Is that a death wish for them?"

"Oh, I suppose part of you probably wants to wipe the whole bunch of them out," Fuentes answered after a long silence. "But another part probably wants to be there with them when the attack comes—just like always, little Addie in the middle of everything."

"Here I am twenty-four years old and I feel still like I'm back with them. It's like a crucial part of me stopped developing from the age of five. I can't get any purchase on this part of my life. I feel it's guiding me by remote control."

"The family is involved in a basic tragedy that's almost Greek." The psychiatrist shrugged in non-disagreement.

"What's that?"

Adam saw the impatient look he came to recognize as a sign that Fuentes felt he had been manipulated into talking too much. "It's too complex. This will have to do for now: the family is built to fall apart. That's how you estimate its success—by the manner in which people leave it. Like the individuals who make it up, the family is born to die."

Adam had spent the first few weeks steering their talk in the direction of his father. "He had been married and divorced before. He had these other children he never saw. He had staked everything on the relationship with my mother. He was afraid to be a two-time loser; to wind up all alone. That's why he let her pussy-whip him all his life; that's why he made up to her every time they had a fight, even when he wasn't to blame. It was sort of disgusting, weak and effeminate."

"What would you have him do, knock her down and carry her back to the cave and whip her into submission with the Avenger here?" Fuentes had fingered the bulge near his fly.

"I'd have him hold his own. Why are you taking his part? Do you think I need to have the father image built up?"

"You're the one operating here. I'm just interested in the fact that you seem to have a need to justify your contempt for him. *Weak, effeminate*: those are attack words in your dictionary. The thing about your father that strikes me is that he's very average. He does the things that most men do. He sires children. He tries to have a relationship with his wife. He scratches out a living for his family in a mean world. He does okay. He sure doesn't need me or you to confer manhood on him."

After a while, he and Fuentes went through a period in which little things were suddenly terribly important. Adam would smoke his last cigarette or use his last match and then try to borrow one. "No, you bring your own," Fuentes would say. "I have a practice limited to psychiatry. This is no smoke shop." Adam would forget his checkbook on the last visit of the month and offer to send a check in the mail. "I'm not in the credit business," Fuentes would storm. "You've got this habit of ignoring your basic responsibilities to concentrate on what you think are the big deals of your emotional life. I don't have that luxury. I've got obligations to meet and a family to feed. Should I tell my kids that there's no frijoles tonight because I've got this prima donna patient who can't be bothered to pay his bills on time?" Adam would bring his checkbook but forget his pen and ask to use Fuentes's. "No, this one's mine. You're after your father's, and now mine. But even leaving aside the phallic implications of your wanting it, which of course we can't, I'd say that you didn't bring your pen because you still want to cheat me of the money you owe me. I refuse to be an accomplice in that crime of theft and fraud."

It was during this time that Adam met Patsy and began spending long periods of time at her apartment, always leaving after a week or so to go back home to Jane. At first he hid the affair from Fuentes, then told him about it and got the yawning response he had feared.

They were perfect antitypes. Patsy was long-legged, dark, languorous. Jane was short, compact, violent. They fought over him in his dreams, but Patsy always finally gave way as if admitting Jane's greater claim. The dreams would end with his following Jane, helpless and tragic, as Patsy receded into the distance.

"I want to go one way, but I can't," he told Fuentes. "It's that typical dreamwork horror when your feet have their own will, apart from your volition."

"Afraid to leave your Mommy?"

"I was right all along with my theory about this recip-
rocal neurosis, the fact that I made Jane into a maternal figure?"

"Right? Yes and no. Right for the wrong reasons,
maybe, right accidentally."

One morning after he had been seeing Fuentes for nearly
four months, he moved out of the house, packing a suitcase of
clothes and a box of books. He had passed Jane as he walked
toward the door. She smiled knowingly, and both of them
thought of the times he had tried to do it before, each time returning like a little boy who had unsuccessfully run away from
home. "Well, this is it," he had said standing in the doorway.
"Sure," she'd answered, not even looking up from the fingernail she was sculpting with an emery board.

When he saw Fuentes the next day he said, "Well, I've
left my Mommy."

"Really?" There had been a brief smile. "Maybe that's
because you've got another Mommy already lined up as a
replacement."

"You're not so proud of me then?"

"Oh, I suppose in the larger scheme of things it's better
to be with your good Mommy than with your bad Mommy."

As the war had heated up and Adam had become active
in the first Teach-Ins on the Berkeley campus, he also became
obsessed by the issue of whether or not Fuentes supported the
Johnson administration. He wheedled and accused, but Fuentes
refused to say one way or another. After seeing his name in a
news story about Bay Area backers of the UFW grape boycott,
Adam attacked him for nearly an hour as somebody who didn't
see the connection between the fate of the Vietnamese and the
farmworkers.

"By the way, is your father for the war?" Fuentes had
remarked with portentous casualness during a lull in the diatribe.

"That's a smooth transition," Adam replied sarcastically. "Yes he is. And I understand that you're accusing me of transference."

"Accusing? It's not really a crime, you know."

The last two words came out slurred with Mexican and sounding like "juno." Adam pounced on them homicidally. "What did you say?"

Fuentes cleared his throat wearily and started to repeat the entire sentence as he often did when he had rolled his r's or slurred his s's. Adam interrupted him. "No, I got what you said till the last couple of words. Sounded like you said *juno.*"

Fuentes paused for a moment then narrowed his eyes to peasant slits. "O, jou doan comprehend how I spic Eengleesh, verdad?"

"You're saying I'm a racist just because I didn't understand you?"

"Naturally. And also that you've got a stake in seeing your father as stupid, inferior to you and your morality. You don't want a penis, but you don't want him to have one either. You want to make him as powerless as a poor Mexican, put him down at the bottom of the ladder where us greasers live so he wouldn't think of taking the beautiful gringo Mommy away from you."

"That's all bullshit."

Fuentes replied with a burst of Spanish.

"What's that supposed to mean?"

"It so difficle." Fuentes waved his hands and smiled like the Frito Bandito. "I say no bullseet. Us cholos bin seein jou a long time now. We compredend de gringo by heart. Juno?"

Adam had almost fallen out of his chair from laughing so hard. As he laughed until the tears came, he realized he was thinking not only of Fuentes but of the few times he would remember when his father had cut loose from the daily cares

that bound him. On these rare times he would mimic Mortimer
Snerd or Kingfish, sing a comic version of the aria from *Pagliacci*,
or imitate Ted Lewis soft-shoeing "Me and My Shadow."

"You're not all that funny," Adam had said to Fuentes
as he gasped for breath and tried to fight the giggles that would
set him off again. "I'm not laughing just at you."

"I know," Fuentes replied.

Adam had stopped coming here the day Patsy found out that
she was pregnant. It was one of those fall afternoons when Berkeley seemed to defy nature by drawing summer out forever.
Fuentes had walked with him to the door after he announced
that he felt he didn't need to come anymore, shaking his hand
with a slight bow as if they were concluding a business deal. Since
then he had seen him only once—several years later in the men's
room during a recess of a Berkeley PTA meeting directed to the
issue of multi-racial classrooms. He had stood impassively before the urinal, looking over to acknowledge Adam with a nod.
Adam had been suddenly nervous and had trouble with his fly
at a moment when he wanted to look most capable of taking
care of business.

"Don't worry, Mr. Marsden." Fuentes had shuddered
and shanked it, then zipped up his pants and turned to the wash
basin. "We're all peers here."

Adam hadn't gotten it for a moment. Fuentes was almost out the door when he called after him. "*Peers*, you say. I
hope the pun is not intended."

"People in my business believe there are no accidents."
Fuentes had disappeared outside into the crowd.

Adam had not thought of him for years. But then came
the night three months ago when he got off the phone with his
father after worming the truth out of him that recent tests had
showed malignancies on both lungs and signs of metastasis

throughout the rest of his body. He remembered clearly that he had sat down after setting the telephone receiver back into its cradle with two thoughts on his mind: first that this event justified buying a pack of cigarettes and breaking his four-year abstinence; and second that he should call Fuentes.

His father's first radiation treatment was something like a family outing. The three of them were waiting for Adam as he deplaned into the PSA module, jumping up and down and waving as they had nearly twenty years earlier on his first trip home from college. His mother wore a gray suit that would have captured the effect of "smartness" she always strived for if the tint of her auburn hair had not been a shade or two toward pastel: when she hugged him he had felt the makeup on her cheek like a coating of warm clay. His father had put one of the white carnations he grew in the backyard into the buttonhole of his lapel; when Adam shook hands he had been hit by the flower's strong cinnamon and by the fact that the man looked as though he had been put in a dryer and shrunk. His sister, Ali, was there in the background, smiling and giving them all small pats on the shoulder, anxious as always for there to be peace, in between jobs, husbands, and apartments, she looked like someone on tour from the land of transition.

At the UCLA Medical Center, Adam played frisbee with her while their parents went to the radiology department. As he watched her go after the spinning disc, he thought he saw her character and destiny engraved in the effort: running long and hard and getting there when it didn't seem she would; having time in fact to get set while the frisbee spun lazily down to her hands; then dropping it and looking at him as if she would cry. Had he helped do this to her?

They went home after the treatment and his father made them all a Pink Lady. Then they dressed and went to Alfredo's, the small place in Hollywood where they had always celebrated birthdays. His mother talked about how arrogant the waiters had become, and how the quality of the food had gone down. Ali ate compulsively, picking hors d'oeuvres off the plate and tucking them in her mouth so slyly that Adam experienced a sudden moment of panic and began to eat quickly too for fear he would not get his share. His father sat back in his chair, teasing a slice of prosciutto, coughing politely into the starched napkin every now and then and covertly studying it for blood.

He had promised to fly down every other weekend to keep in touch with the illness. But he hadn't been able to force himself to make the trip after he found that his mother had begun driving the car and his father sat slumped at the passenger side. He stayed home and wrote long, witty letters to Pasadena on his lunch hour, continuing them after dinner and late into the night. At first they were clever notes explaining why he wouldn't be flying down soon—"guiltograms," Patsy called them. But then they became detailed, knotty tracts about being and nothingness which he wrote out in longhand and put into envelopes he had to seal with tape because they bulged so hugely. He threw the envelopes into the litter barrel beside the bus stop on his way to work each morning.

He could tell his father was getting worse by the sound of the voice over the phone—reedy, off-key, like a piano with flaccid wires. He stopped writing letters and began going to the movies, first a couple of times a week, and then every night, setting out right after dinner so he could catch a full double feature. At first Patsy had wanted to come with him, saying that he had the look about him of someone who might be molested. But then she saw that he wanted to go alone. Over breakfast she would scan the entertainment section, sometimes pausing with the coffee halfway to her mouth. "*Murmur of the Heart* is at the Northside, Adam. Tonight only. You'd better catch it now. Who knows when it will be here again?"

She thought that it was escape he needed. He didn't tell her that he didn't really watch the films, but used them as a sort of kinetic screen where he showed slides of his own from a past until then forgotten. His father with a BB gun shooting the pet hamster, Squeaking, which the cat Thomas had mangled, tears in his eyes as he put the barrel behind the tiny velvet ear and said: "Well, you can't let some poor dumb creature suffer a nasty lingering death." *Click.* His father coming into the house with a vast smile on his face and announcing that he had invented an improved cement block. *Click.* His father buying an organ and sitting in the playroom late at night teaching himself to play something that sounded like music until its components were analyzed. *Click.* His father waltzing with his mother after Arthur Murray lessons in solemn hop-step like Henry Fonda in *My Darling Clementine. Click.* The two of them touching hands in the front seat as the car radio played "Laura," which they had claimed as theirs back in that era when every couple had its song. *Click.*

During this time he had also oppressed his son with attention. He would sometimes come home from work early so that he could walk up to school and watch Matty playing at recess. He would go into his room at odd moments and make awkward conversation, cajole him into playing catch, take him to McDonald's. The boy got into the habit of coming home every afternoon and reporting to Adam, trying to demonstrate that he enjoyed the sudden comradeship. But at some point when they were together there would be a moment of silence and Matty would summon up what he thought was a tone of nonchalance. "I was thinking of going out to play with Jerry, Dad. Would you like to come? We're building a fort over in the lot behind the church. Maybe you could help?"

Adam and Patsy talked about the transference of love between the generations. "It's an awesome process," he said. "Yes," she answered, "like transporting nuclear materials over a bad road." He paused, then said: "That's right. Sometimes you get the feeling that love skips a generation—like baldness or some other genetic quirk."

He remembered the fury he had felt the night he called his father to tell him Matty had been born and named after him.

"There should always be a Matthew in the family." The words seemed to come from Iceland. "My uncle had that name and also my great-grandfather. The first Matthew Marsden I know of got off the boat in Charleston in 1773."

"It's your name, Dad." Adam strained to keep acid from eating the edges of his voice. "That's why it's important enough to give my son: because it's yours."

"And I appreciate it, Ad, I really do." The voice sounded like the one his father used at Christmas time to thank people who gave him socks and ties he really did appreciate but really didn't need.

Later on, in the course of the sessions with Fuentes, Adam realized that what stood between them that night had been his own desire to deliver up an apocalyptic gift, an offering that would reveal the inadequacy of his father's love for him. As it worked out, his father accepted a kind of stewardship for the boy and supplied a benign paternity Adam thought made up for his own lacks.

Over the years Adam had tried to reacquaint himself with his father, together with his son. The three of them went on fishing trips and spent time together. But Adam felt that he was squeezed in a generational vise, and that his presence made the other two more subdued and circumspect. He looked for opportunities to watch them when they didn't think they were being observed. His father would slouch among the marigolds and tomato vines in the backyard of Adam's Berkeley house, muttering about nematodes and grunting in response to Matty's chatter, dropping half-smoked Camels which the boy picked up and puffed on behind his back.

On the last visit before his cancer had been confirmed, the two of them had sat on the back steps as Adam watched unobserved from behind the one-way glare of the screen door. His son was playing with G.I. Joe in the jungle of a planter box. His father sat bent over his knees, inhaling deeply to catch his breath and spitting oysters of ochre mucus on the lawn. The subject of their desultory talk was life back on the homestead in Iowa.

"We had a sort of crawl space under the old house." He noticed that his father did not demand that Matty stop his military noises to indicate attention as he probably would have. "Rattlers would breed and live under there. My dad said we needed us a king snake. So me and my brother Waldo went out and caught this king and put him under the house. Waldo named him: Jasper. We'd feed him and play with him. Old Jasper would come right up to the vent space and wait for his supper. He wasn't big but was he mean. He cleaned them rattlers out and kept them out. Many's the time we saw him go after them. He'd sort of circle round them and then jump right up on some rattler's back and do him in with a bite right here. . . ."

At this point his father had made a pincer of thumb and forefinger and applied it on the ticklish neck just below the boy's ears with enough pressure to make him squeal and hunch his shoulders before collapsing in his lap. Separated from the two of them by the screen partition that had in that moment seemed like the Great Wall, seeing but not being seen, Adam heard the words so clearly that he could play them later in his mind like a taped encounter. Each time he did he felt a wrenching desire to have his father tell him such stories and to be able to touch his son without causing an inner flinch.

Adam tried for a time to take Matty with him to the movies. But it didn't work and so he went back to going alone, coming home late at night to find Patsy already in bed, wearing that look of faint amusement which was her sleep mask. Undressing in the dark, aroused by her smell, he would knead her torpid body awake, knowing that she was smiling with eyes closed as she kissed with gummy mouth, and pulled him above her by reflex. She was the fertile crescent where he sought to plant himself and germinate. "Let's have another baby," he whispered in her ear. As she wakened slightly, he would often pause, bemused, part of him still finishing the slide show. His father trying to invent the perfect bomb-shelter to save them from the Russians. *Click.* His father working two jobs during Christmas. *Click.* His father deciding to read every book Edgar Rice Burroughs had written. *Click.*

"You're like the rhino in the joke." She would nip at his ear. "The rhino who forgets what he's doing, dismounts in the middle of things, and goes off somewhere to graze."

Coming back to himself he would hold her so tight that he squeezed tears out of her eyes. "Dying, Egypt, dying," he would say.

Four nights ago, he had come home from *The Magnificent Ambersons* to find that the lights were still on. Patsy was sitting on the stairs in a nightgown, a dull, vacant look on her face, legs splayed apart like a washer woman sitting on a stoop. "Ali called about an hour ago," she said. "Your dad is in the hospital now and she says you'd better come quick."

He felt an odd relief, and whistled to himself as he went into the bathroom to shave and shower. He put on the old three-piece suit he had not worn since his wedding. Forbidding Patsy and the boy from coming with him lest they be contaminated with his own malignant karma and die in the air crash, he caught the red-eye to Los Angeles smelling of cologne. A single obsessive question wormed through his mind as he bolted two airborne martinis that sloshed his gut like moonshine: how shall I behave?

By the time he got there his mother and sister had already established camp in the hospital room. There were empty cans with fragments of sardine dorsal fin floating in oil and waxed paper with crumby remnants of Ritz crackers. He could tell his mother's plan: to provide insulation between his father and the people who might handle him without care. He watched her way of dealing with the nurses on that first graveyard shift: standing up when they entered and shadowing them in the room; putting the disgusting food tray outside the door like old shoes to be polished. She forced a chatter to buoy his father's spirits not by telling lies, but by showing that one could die within a matrix of normalcy even in this ugly place.

Around four o'clock in the morning, Adam took over while his mother and sister went to sleep in armchairs in an alcove outside the room. Transfixed by tubes and siphons like an experiment, his father lay in bed with his hair oiled and parted down the middle, and looked like a gigolo exhausted by too many parties. From where he sat, Adam could see the map of wrinkles on the back of his neck, lines so deep they looked like scars from slashings. When his father caught him looking, he said defensively, "I've had a good life, Ad."

He looked so small. Adam wanted to pick him up and cradle him, to kiss him and sing nonsense rhymes the way he had when Matty was a baby. He also wanted to talk metaphysics, to know what his father was feeling as he readied for takeoff. But they talked of small things, taxes instead of death. "I think it's the IRS that you've got to worry about, Ad," his father said in a raspy voice. "If there's going to be a gestapo in this country, it'll come from that direction instead of the FBI." There was a silence during which his father worked to clear his throat. "I hope you won't be insulted, or feel hurt. But I've left that little insurance policy to Ali. It's only four thousand. I guess you're pretty well able to make it on your own. I don't know about her. I suppose she'll get the nesting instinct again one of these days, but who knows if she'll ever find somebody who'll last?"

"That's all right, Dad, I understand." But even as he said the words, he felt the old question looming up: do you love her more than me?

They made small talk until nearly six o'clock, his father seeming to grow smaller and smaller, becoming more and more anxious for his morphine. When he drifted off to sleep, Adam sat back, exhausted from the effort, yet unable to sleep. He had the feeling that he was in the middle of something that should be a portentous ritual but was instead mundane, one of those things that just happens. When it began to get gray outside, the silence in the hospital yielded to the sound of breakfast trays being banged and orderlies shouting. His father awoke and rolled his eyes in wild narcosis. "This is the noisiest damned hotel I ever stayed in, Ad. We've got to find us another place to stay in tomorrow night."

After he fell back asleep, Adam went out into the hall laughing. His mother was sitting on the chair, her hair standing up in a caul. Smoothing the coat she'd used as a blanket, she asked what was wrong. "Dad thinks he's in a hotel," Adam giggled. She stood up and gestured at her chair. "Here, sit down and take a little nap." He snuggled into her barely relinquished warmth.

Each time his mother entered the room, his father followed her with his eyes, always seeming to incline toward her like a plant reacting phototropically. Adam realized that this synchronicity, this sense of matehood between them must always have been there, just beyond his view.

"They've been like ballet partners in a pas de deux." Ali talked to him about the past few weeks the second morning of their deathwatch as they sat in the empty commissary where inverted chairs perched atop tables as if in fright of mice. "The thing I've noticed is their efficiency. Dad worked at the office until about three weeks ago. He said he wanted every penny he could get because he knew the bastards wouldn't do much for Mom when he was gone. Then when he got too weak, he quit without giving notice. He laughed like hell when he told us— one of those small rebellions after a lifetime of eating shit. He concentrated on getting things done around the house—selling the second car, putting a new lock on the back door, changing all the washers on the faucets. Mom drove him around from store to store to get what he needed. When he was too weak to sit up, she made him a little bed in the back of the station wagon. They went to the lawyer, the tax guy, the insurance agent. All the time she'd be babbling her Christian Science nonsense, and all the time he'd be laughing at her and saying, 'Yes, Gracie; sure, Gracie,' in his George Burns voice."

As Ali spoke he could see that she was talking about something she had never had: a relationship presumed to be long-term. He looked through her yearning to try to determine if the scenes she described were true. Some of the things she described he couldn't see. But he could see his father lying in bed looking out onto the backyard at the peach tree he called his "old boy." Drooping when they'd bought the house thirty years earlier, the tree was now ancient, arthritic, and gnarled, growing almost perpendicular to the ground with a few wrinkled fruit appearing each spring like shrunken heads. Over the years his father had often spared the tree from death sentences decreed by his mother. During the last few weeks he had lain in bed watching it, occasionally joking about its outlasting him. "You're wrong, Matthew," his mother had said. "That ugly old thing will be firewood keeping us warm next winter." His father smiled and said, "Don't kid an old kidder, Ella."

He could see the two of them together in the bedroom, his father staring at his "old boy," and his mother sitting beside him reading from a Louis L'Amour novel, this in itself a sign of how much she loved and pitied him, since reading aloud was the one thing that gave away the fact that she had gone only as far as the ninth grade.

He could see the tableau that occurred when his mother and Ali returned from a brief trip to the market and found his father crumpled in the hall like a pile of dirty clothes, having fallen on the way back from the bathroom and then being unable to get up by himself. "Oh Matthew," his mother began to cry as she bent over him. "How could they do this to you?" That *they* was typical of her: blame the gods, the fates, the tax assessor, the bureaucracy, and the other faceless cowards responsible for this obscenity.

"She wanted him to die at home," Ali finished, sipping at the tepid form of instant coffee. "But he wouldn't go for it. I thought they'd have a fight about it, I really did, just like the old days. But he gave in and then yesterday morning while she was still sleeping he snuck out of bed and managed to get to the phone and call the ambulance. He woke her and told her to help him dress."

It was Adam's shift when his father died. It was Friday, April 1—Good Friday as he knew by the headline on the L.A. *Times.* He watched the man, searching the face for some final revelation, waiting for some kind of message. But there was nothing— just a staring up at the blank television set as if perhaps to replay there the crucial events of his life.

"What are you seeing, Dad?" he asked in a soft voice, drawing so close that he could smell his father's death. "Can you tell me?"

"Matty," the words crept out. "That marble. Don't. Let him swallow." Adam knew the reference: once his son had been playing with marbles and had suddenly popped one in his mouth. His father had stood up and walked over with forced calm to pry it out of his mouth, then gave Adam one of his rare adult lectures. "Don't you remember that time when you were a baby when you swallowed an ice cube and I had to claw it out to keep you from strangling? I tore your throat all to hell with my fingernails. You want to have to do that to Matty and maybe still not save him? Jesus, Adam!"

An hour later, his father opened his cracked lips and mimed one word: *sorry*. Then he fell silent. Adam wondered if he had been referring to his vow never to put them through this. During the first stages of his illness, after an exploratory operation, he had taken Adam into his room and shown him the sedatives he had stored up during his stay in the hospital, hiding them under his pillow each night. "I'm keeping these aside," he had said, "and when things get too bad I'll take them."

Adam found himself angry that he had not done it and saved them all this misery. "I'm sorry too," he whispered.

As a bubbling sound came from his father's chest, the sound of involuntary muscles beginning to spasm, Adam felt that he too was dying of strangulation. He took his own pulse and felt his heart skip and stutter. "Trachycardia," he said aloud as he counted eighty-three beats a minute.

He thought that he should go out and get his mother and sister, but he couldn't relinquish his proprietary hold. He felt that there might yet be some epiphany for his eyes only. As the noises of dying became louder and brown foam bubbled from one of his father's nostrils, he seized one of the cold hands and kissed it, rubbing the horny fingernails and knobbed knuckles on his cheek. He had to speak loudly to make himself heard over the hiss and rattle coming from the tarry lungs. "I love you, Dad, I love you, Dad, I love you. . . ." And then he saw something happen to his father's eyes, some congealing of pigment that made the pupil turn to isinglass. He felt something constricting his throat and he heard the words come out different then he intended. "Do you love me, Dad? Do you love me, Dad? Do you love me. . . ." His eyes felt like hot stones. He wanted to cry, but couldn't.

After a while he took one last look at the waxen face, the eyes half lidded and the jaw recessed. It was like a corpse in one of the old *Police Gazette* magazines his father used to bring home from the second-hand book stores. Then he went to wake the two women up. "Dad's gone," he said.

His mother started up at him with her fighter's pose and said, "Gone? Matthew dead? And I didn't get a chance to say good-bye? Why didn't you come and get me?" She took two steps toward him, and for a moment he feared she was going to hit him. But then she wilted slightly and stared at the floor. "Dead. Well then. Let me go in and see him one last time and then we'll go."

Driving home Adam told them that he felt like a child who wanted to cry to get pity and had tried to make the tears come but couldn't manage it. "Really?" Ali asked in such a way as to make him look over to the back seat of the car and see that she had been crying a small and steady stream for several minutes. When they got home his mother crawled into bed fully clothed and Ali turned on the television. Adam wandered through the house, ending up in the den where his father slept the last few weeks when he was getting up at odd hours to pad around gasping for air. He had a sudden impulse to rifle the dresser. In the top drawer, underneath the socks, he found an envelope sealed with tape and addressed to his mother. He had to fight the urge to open it himself. What does a dead man say to the woman he's lived with for forty years? He wanted to know because one day he would have to leave such a note for Patsy. Wasn't a father's duty to teach such lessons? But he mastered the urge and put it back, this thank you note meant for whatever dreary future day when she should take on the task of cleaning out his things.

In the second drawer, below the ironed jockey shorts, he found birthday and Father's Day cards from a time when he had still called himself Addie and signed his name in slanted caps. There was a pack of rubbers, and at the corner of the drawer one of those tiny keychain games once found in souvenir shops in the seedy parts of town. He looked down through the plastic dome and saw the face and body of a sumptuous blonde imprinted on the backing. A name appeared in red script above her hair: *Boobs Galore.* There were holes at the tips of the breasts into which you were supposed to try to roll the two tiny pink balls that would give her nipples. He remembered the time his father had brought the game home from Reno and allowed him to play with it until his mother began to raise hell. "Oh, Ella, it's a game of skill," his father had laughed, reluctantly taking it away from him. Adam slipped the game into his pocket, smiling that his father should have saved such a thing.

After a while he went into his mother's room and saw her rolled into a knot beneath the bedspread. He felt that they must find a way to punctuate this death or it would never end. It occurred to him that St. Bellarmine's would probably have late Mass for Good Friday. "Come on, Mom," he said and roused her by the shoulder. "Let's go to church."

The three of them sat through the service. He and his mother weren't able to bend Protestant knees to papist ritual, but Ali had. The two women cried quietly during the talk about rising and redemption. Adam sat there, feeling as though his heart had been removed. As they were walking out of the church, a boy Matty's age ran up and yelled that their car was burning. When Adam took off toward the parking lot, he heard the words behind him. "April Fool!" Ali looked up. "God, Good Friday and April Fool's Day both." His mother said, "Yes, something for everybody."

When he left this morning, his mother was out in the back wearing his father's old mackinaw with the sleeves rolled up, trying to chop the peach tree down with a double-bladed ax so large for her that she could only hit the trunk with helpless, glancing blows that chipped the bark. She hefted it like a child too young to swing a baseball bat. Watching her flail away, he felt embarrassed at the absurdity of the melodrama, yet oddly proud of the attempt to punish nature for its arrogance in winning the bet with his father.

"Well, I'm going, Mom." He stood in the middle of the patio, anxious to get away.

"Okay, honey," she replied without turning around. "I'd take you to the airport, but I've got to finish here. Take care."

He heard his name and opened his eyes in time to see the front door close. When he came into the inner office Fuentes was sitting in shadows as before, tucked into a chair that wrapped around him like a cocoon. Adam was struck by the changes that had come over the man. He was thinner. There were grayish pouches under his eyes that looked soft as deerskin, and the nose seemed somehow larger with age. The hair was thinning outward from a tonsure on the crown of the head and the mustache had bloomed to a full beard, thick as black steel wool.

"Rotating the crops, are you?"

"Pardon?" Fuentes stalled, not changing the faintly bemused smile which was his psychiatric mask.

"No aggression intended." Adam sat down. "Just noting that the hair is going and the beard had sprouted."

"The ravages of time." Fuentes shrugged. "You have changed quite a bit yourself."

Adam looked out the window onto the garden. There was an old Japanese gardener pruning a flowering cherry and humming a melody in a sing-song alto. Adam listened and watched him. He had wanted to be here badly, yet now he found himself feeling lazy. Words seemed boring, and speaking them too great an effort. He thought that it would be nice if thoughts could be instantaneously infused as in science fiction. "Thanks for seeing me," he said without looking at Fuentes. "It was short notice."

The gardener moved like a martial artist, stepping in to snip a branch, then quickly standing back as it fell. "I don't know where to begin." Adam was unable to bring himself to make eye contact. "My father's dead. What more is there to say?"

Fuentes shrugged. "You tell me."

"Same old situation here. Like playing tennis against a wall: the ball comes back at you just as hard as you hit it."

Fuentes lit a cigarette and reclined deeper in his chair, focusing on a spot somewhere near the center of the ceiling. "The game here is rigged against you. You know that."

"Tell me about it." Adam had trouble taking his eyes off the gardener. Finally he turned to face Fuentes. "Well, nature abhors a vacuum. I suppose I ought to try to get my money's worth."

"Might as well." Fuentes still watched the ceiling.

"I don't know what to say. I wanted to talk to you pretty bad last night. Now it all seems banal. My father's gone. This man I knew all my life. I don't seem to feel anything. What's wrong with me?"

"Wrong?" Fuentes's smile was doleful. "Your father died."

"You charge all this money to propound tautologies?" Adam rotated his neck to relieve vertebral pressure. "I saw Freud out in the waiting room. Don't the women patients give you hell?"

Fuentes allowed his mouth to dip at the corners in a small gesture of arrogance.

"Still macho?"

"Still trying." Fuentes raised his eyebrows like Groucho.

"Didn't Freud say that his father's dying was the worst thing that ever happened to him?" Adam asked.

"The most poignant loss of a man's life," Fuentes intoned as if quoting.

"What?"

"That's what he said. Preface to the second edition of *The Interpretation of Dreams.* Yet the death also seemed to liberate fantastic creative energy for him. Not long after he embarked on his self-analysis. Who's to say?"

"Hard to accomplish anything if you still have the child's fantasy that you'll live forever, and your father will protect you from everything." Adam felt he was making small talk. "Didn't he also say something about the exaggerated sense of grief he felt over his father's death coming from a homosexual cathexis?"

"Cathexis?" Fuentes swatted at the word. "Please, this is not a session of the American Psychiatric Association. Let's use real language."

"I guess the thing that surprised me most is how hard it is to die." Adam felt unable to make transitions between his thoughts. "I had this infantile notion that is like in the movies: one sweet little breath escapes, the head lolls over onto the pillow, and that's that. It took him a long time. It was like there was some invisible force pounding the life out of him."

Fuentes stubbed the cigarette out and lit another.

"You still do it?" Adam felt himself grow angry.

"Do what?"

"Smoke. It's so stupid. I can't believe it. You're supposed to be under control, and all that. Don't you know that cigarettes cause cancer?"

Fuentes inhaled deeply.

"Maybe they didn't tell you about cancer in your Mexican medical school." Adam felt his voice rising into octaves he rarely used. "They do study more than amoebic dysentery, don't they?"

Fuentes held the cigarette out at arm's length as if appraising it, then gave a broad grin that parodied the old television endorsements of tobacco and put it back in his mouth. "Tastes awful good," he said, gushing out a mouthful of smoke. "You get to my point in life and you sure do like your pleasures."

"You mean to say that you're aware of the risks and *choose* to take them," Adam said. "You convert to est or something? All the bullshit going down in this culture about taking responsibility is getting old fast. My father smoked and he got dead. Do you want that?"

"Some people live by the actuarial tables as if they were oracles," Fuentes said, dragging on the cigarette in another exaggerated mime of pleasure.

"You're supposed to be a role model," Adam persisted. "Isn't that the term? You're supposed to be in control of things. What would your friend Freud say?"

Fuentes turned slightly in his chair so that Adam could see his face more clearly. "Freud? You knew he smoked his cigars until the end, don't you? Cancer had eaten away his jaw and he'd gotten this grotesque prosthetic he had to pry open with his fingers so he could clamp the stogie in place." Here Fuentes mimed that cumbersome procedure with two hands, clamping down finally on his cigarette. "But he smoked like a chimney."

"My mother and father were like different people from how I remember them." Adam still felt as though he were flailing for something to say. "It's like I never imagined they had a relationship apart from me and Ali. It's like I belonged to them, but never really knew them. They did a good job of this."

"There is heroism in the ordinary we find as we grow older," Fuentes said.

Adam found he was swallowing rapidly the way his golden retriever Byron did just before vomiting. "My father never played for pity. The lights going out forever: obviously it's a temptation. He just went ahead and did it. One of those who goes into the gas chamber and breathes deeply instead of holding his breath for two or three minutes."

"Are you creating a new myth of your parents?" Fuentes asked with a casualness that seemed too intentional.

"Probably we've got to have myths to live by, don't we?" Adam could feel the self-control slipping. "I just feel that I should have done better by him."

"How so?"

"I went through it all like it was a movie. I mean it was theater to me. It was moving, but the way a film is. I felt like I was experiencing it all through gauze. It was like I kept watching myself watch him die. I was wondering how *I* was doing. Can you believe it? I kept checking myself, I guess to see if I was dying too."

"You can make book on it."

"What?"

"That you're dying."

"Yes I know." Adam noticed that his cheeks were itching. As he scratched, his fingernails came away wet from tears. "It's like he was the shield against my mortality. Maybe that's what he meant when he said he was sorry."

"Sorry?"

"The last word he said: 'sorry.' Maybe he was telling me that he was sorry for taking the shield away."

"Maybe."

Now Adam found himself crying so hard that he made a continual noise. He heard it almost as if it were another person keening beside him. "I'm crying," he said. His speech was now being directed by sobs. "I guess. I guess what gets me. Is. That my father died. Not knowing. How much I loved him."

"How could that be?" Fuentes's voice was low, perhaps sympathetic. "Do you think he was unable to feel?"

"But did he. Know? How much?" Adam felt that their words were silly, but that they were getting through to each other at some symbiotic level beyond language. "I spent my life. Trying to justify. This view I had of him. As small."

"Do you know how much your son loves you? Of course. Your father knew."

Adam felt as though his essence were pouring out of him. "I have this feeling of. Failing him. You know? In life. And death. I wasn't with him. I should. Have told him. I love you. Dad. I said it. But he was dead. Or almost. I love you Dad. Thanks Dad. For giving some of your life. To me. It's not too hard. To say that. Not hard."

"We always think of what to do when the time is passed." Fuentes's face suddenly looked worn. "But people understand. The message usually gets through despite the static."

Adam felt that his ears were blocked. It was like the tears had penetrated them and closed them along with his nose and throat so that the thoughts could no longer get out and ricocheted around his head. The tears were gushing out of him, and he couldn't make his breathing return to normal. He grasped sections of air like a crying child. He wiped his face on the sleeve of his jacket and the mucus marked the fabric like a snail trail. Fuentes was talking, but Adam had trouble following him. There was the Mexican accent and his own blocked air spaces. He caught the words "also dying of cancer" as a look of resignation and misery passed over Fuentes's face. Suddenly it all came together: the smoking, the melancholy look, the thinness. Fuentes was dying too. "No!" Adam shouted.

"Yes, that's right, me too," Fuentes said.

He was crying again, deep in hysteria now, falling from the chair onto the floor in a kind of genuflection. "Oh God, no." He didn't feel responsible for the words. "Not you too. How serious is it? Both lungs?"

Adam saw the astonished look on Fuentes's face, but couldn't stop himself from babbling: "You can't die. Not you. I won't let you!"

Fuentes was trying to control the amazement that had gotten by the professional mask. "That's very generous of you, Mr. Marsden, but I don't know what you're talking about. I don't know what you mean by my dying. Do you know something I don't?"

Adam had melted with sorrow. "Cancer. You said you had it too. Don't die."

Fuentes frowned, and then he shook his head with a look of infinite pity. "I was talking about my father. Didn't you hear me? I was saying that when he was in Mexico also dying of lung cancer I was in Germany studying. There was no money and I couldn't come home. I was saying that I know how you feel, that it had happened to me too."

Adam felt himself laughing as well as crying. "Oh. Not dying. Thank God. You're all right."

"I'm okay," Fuentes said, and gave a shy smile as he re-assembled his face. "You're okay."

Adam waited for a few minutes and his breathing regained its normal rhythm and his passages unblocked. The Japanese gardener had a way of humming that was able to bring loud notes out of soft: yin and yang. "Was this some sort of auditory Freudian slip?"

Fuentes picked at the corner of one eye and then the other as if trying to pick vagrant lashes. "Didn't we decide when you came here before that there are no accidents?"

"Oh, yes." Adam watched him light a cigarette and try to focus his stare at the ceiling.

They sat in silence for several minutes more. The gardener's shadow moved across the shaded part of the sliding glass door. The snipping of shears and the soft rattle of bamboo were percussion behind his humming. Adam looked at his watch and then at Fuentes, whose color was still bad. "I guess what I was really wondering was whether or not he loved me."

"As you may discover someday when you become an adult," Fuentes smiled, "you don't need to talk everything to death. Really, do you need to ask this question?"

They sat in silence again. Adam was ready to go, but didn't want to breach the etiquette of the fifty-minute hour. Then he looked at his watch again and rose. "Well, I guess it's time. No particular need for me to come back, is there?"

Fuentes stood too. "I don't know, is there?"

"Tennis against the backboard again. No, I guess not."

"All right then." Fuentes coughed into a cupped hand and pounded his chest. Seeing Adam's look he waved to ward off criticism. "Physician, heal thyself. I know, I know. Don't worry, I'm quitting when I finish this carton."

Adam opened the door and then reached for his wallet. "What's your fee now?"

"Sixty an hour."

"Jesus, that's almost double what it used to be."

"Inflation."

"How come doctors' inflation is always three times other people's?"

"Battle pay, hazard duty, call it what you will. You know what they say about psychiatrists being crazy."

"Well I don't have it with me, so I'll have to send a check." Adam had stepped forward with his wallet open to show the three ten dollar bills.

"No." Fuentes took a step backward and held up his hand like a traffic cop. "No, that's okay. This one's on the house."

"Really?" Adam was about to insist.

"Really." Fuentes's look kept him from making any gestures.

"Well then, okay. I probably won't be seeing you again." Adam moved out into the hall.

"That's okay." Fuentes moved backward into the shadows, his Indian eyes especially bright. "I'll live."

"I hope so."

"Good luck, Mr. Marsden." Fuentes offered a handshake that Adam noticed was not particularly firm.

"Same to you."

After an awkward moment, Adam gave a small salute and then turned toward the front door. He heard the office door close behind him.

Outside, he felt the same elation he had often experienced twelve years earlier, an emotion Fuentes once commented sourly was probably the result of having gotten through yet another session without saying what was on his mind. He nodded at the Japanese gardener, who bowed ceremoniously in turn. As he reached the rental car he'd picked up earlier at the San Francisco airport, he dredged his pocket and brought up a palm full of keys and coins. There was also the little game he had taken from his father's dresser. He tilted it until the tiny pink balls came to rest in their holes. Boobs Galore: it occurred to him that he'd share the game with Matty just to see the look on his face.

Slatland

Rebecca Lee

I went to Professor Pine for help twice in my life, once as a child and once as an adult. The first time, I was eleven and had fallen into an inexplicable depression. This happened in the spring of 1967, seemingly overnight, and for no reason. Any happiness in me just flew away, like birds up and out of a tree.

Until then I had been a normal, healthy child. My parents had never damaged me in any way. They had given me a dusty, simple childhood on the flatlands of Saskatchewan. I had two best friends—large, unselfish girls who were already gearing up for adolescence, sometimes laughing until they collapsed. I had a dog named Chest, who late at night brought me half-alive things in his teeth—bats with human faces, fluttering birds, speckled, choking mice.

My parents couldn't help noticing my sadness. They looked at me as if they were afraid of me. Sometimes at the dinner table the silence would be so deep that I felt compelled to reassure them. But when I tried to say that I was all right, my voice would crack and I would feel my face distorting, caving in. I would close my eyes then, and cry.

One night my parents came into my bedroom and sat down on my bed. "Honey," my father said, "your mother and

I have been thinking about you a lot lately. We were thinking that maybe you would consider talking to somebody—you know, a therapist—about what is the matter." My father was an earnest, cheerful man, a geologist with a brush cut and a big heart. I couldn't imagine that a therapist would solve my problems, but my father looked hopeful, his large hand tracing a ruffle around my bedspread.

Three days later we were standing outside an office on the fourth floor of the Humanities Building. My appointment was not with a true therapist but rather with a professor of child psychology at the university where my father taught.

We knocked, and a voice called from behind the door in a bit of a singsong, "Come in you, come in you." Of course he was expecting us, but this still seemed odd, as if he knew us very well or as if my father and I were both little children—or elves. The man sitting behind the desk when we entered was wearing a denim shirt, his blond hair slicked back like a rodent's. He looked surprised—a look that turned out to be permanent. He didn't stand up, just waved at us. From a cage in the corner three birds squawked. My father approached the desk and stuck out his hand. "Peter Bergen," my father said.

"Professor Roland Boland Pine," the man said, and then looked at me. "Hello, girlie."

Despite this, my father left me alone with him. Perhaps he just thought, as I did, that Professor Pine talked like this, in occasional baby words, because he wanted children to respond as if to other children. I sat in a black leather chair. The professor and I stared at each other for a while. I didn't know what to say, and he wasn't speaking either. It was easy to stare at him. As if I were staring at an animal, I felt no embarrassment.

"Well," he said at last, "your name is Margit?"

I nodded.

"How are you today, Margit?"

"I'm okay."

"Do you feel okay?"

"Yes. I feel okay."

"Do you go to school, Margit?"

"Yes."

"Do you like your teacher?"

"Not really."

"Do you hate him?"

"It's a her."

"Do you hate her?"

"No."

"Why are you here, Margit?"

"I don't know."

"Is everything at home okay?"

"Yes."

"Do you love your father?"

"Yes."

"Do you love your mother?" A long tic broke on his face, from the outer corner of his left eye all the way down to his neck.

"Yes."

"Is she a lumpy mother?"

"Pardon me?"

"Pardon me, Margit. I meant does your mother love you?"

"Yes."

"Does she love your father?"

I paused. "Yes."

"And does he love her?"

"I guess so."

"Margit, what is the matter?"

"Nothing. I just don't see why we're talking about my parents so much."

"Why don't they love each other?"

"They do—I said they do."

"Why can't you talk about this?"

"Because there's nothing to talk about."

"You can tell me the truth. Do they hurt each other? Lots of girls' parents hurt each other."

"No, they don't."

"Is one of them having an affair, maybe?"

I didn't say anything. "Maybe?" he repeated.

"Maybe," I said.

"Which one, Margit? Which one of the baby faces?"

I stared at him. Another tic passed over his face. "Pardon me, Margit. I meant which one of your parents is having the affair?"

"My dad. But I don't think he's actually having it. I just heard him tell my mom a few months ago that he was considering it."

"And do you think he is?"

"I don't know. A few weeks ago I picked up the phone and a woman was talking to my dad. She told him that she had to have her breasts removed and asked if that would make a difference."

"How difficult for you. How sad for the girlie-whirl." Another tic, like a fault line shifting. "Margit, may I tell you something from my own childhood?"

This worried me, but I said yes.

"When I was young, I loved my mother. She was a real lumper. Then one day, *kerpow*, she was dead." He held his forefinger to his head as if it were the barrel of a gun and stared at me for a few seconds without speaking. "It wasn't actually her, you see, but a woman of about her age who happened to be walking toward me on the sidewalk. A man came running and shot her. I was so devastated that I fell right on top of her. I didn't care if he shot me, too. I was only ten at the time, and my mother's death could have scarred me for life. But it didn't. And do you know how I got from that moment to this one—how I got from there to here, to sitting behind this desk now, talking to you?"

I shook my head. "How?"

"I rose above the situation. Literally I did. I felt my mind lift slightly out of my body, and I stared down at myself leaning over the bleeding woman. I said to myself, very calmly, there is little Roland from New Orleans, the little erky-terk, realizing that someday his mother will die."

He was looking at me so intently, and his birds were flapping in their cage with such fervor, that I felt I had to say something. "Wow," I said.

"I suggest you try it, Margit. For every situation there is a proper distance. Growing up is just a matter of gaining perspective. Sometimes you just need to jump up for a moment, a foot above the earth. And sometimes you need to jump very far. It is as if there are thin slats, footholds, from here to the sun, Margit, for the baby faces to step on. Do you understand?"

"Yes," I said.

"Slatland, flatland, mapland."

"Pardon me?"

"Pardon me, Margit. I know so many languages that sometimes I say words out of place."

At the end of the session I asked him when I should return. He told me that another visit wouldn't be necessary, that usually his therapy worked the first time.

I didn't in fact understand what he had said to me, but his theory seemed to help anyway, as if it were a medication that worked whether you understood it or not. That very evening I was having dinner with my parents. It started as the usual dinner—me staring at my plate, my parents staring at me as if I were about to break in two. But about halfway through the meal

I started feeling light-headed. Nothing frightening happened, but I did manage to lift slightly out of myself. I looked down at our tiny family. I saw my father from above, the deep map of his face. I understood in an instant that of course he was having an affair, and that he was torn between my mother and this other, distant woman. I saw my beautiful mother from above, and I could see how she must hate this other woman, yet sympathize as well, because this other woman was very ill. I understood how complicated it was to be an adult, and how haunting, and how lovely. I longed to be back in my body then, to be breathing and eating, straining toward maturity. And when I returned, one split second later, I hugged my parents, one after the other, with a spontaneity that a depressed person could never muster.

In the twenty years that passed between my first visit to Professor Pine and my second, from 1967 to 1987, I remained in the same city. I graduated from Massey and then from LeBoldus High and then from the University of Saskatchewan, with a degree in biology. As an adult, I worked as a soil consultant, traveling around the province to small satellite towns in a flatbed truck that I could sleep in, if necessary, on warm nights.

Bouts of the depression did return, but they never overwhelmed me. Perhaps my life was not the most rigorous testing ground for Professor Pine's technique, because my life was relatively free of tragedy. Most of my depression erupted out of nowhere. I'd be in the fields in the midst of a bright day, and a dreariness would mysteriously descend. I'd sink into it for a few minutes, but the lift would always come. I would take a step up, or two or three, and recognize how good life in fact was. From above, my job appeared to me excellent and strange. There I was, under a blazing sun, kneeling in a yellow expanse, weighing samples of earth. And later, with instruments as tiny and beautiful as jewelry, testing the dirt for traces of nitrogen and phosphorus, the gleam of potash.

One night, in the middle of the year 1985, I made the mistake of describing this technique to my fiancé, Rezvan Balescu, the Romanian liar. We had known each other for only two months at this point, but we were already engaged. We were standing on a small balcony outside my apartment. He was smoking, wearing pajamas under a down-filled jacket, and he was in the midst of one of his tirades on North America, which he loved and hated. "This place is so strange to me, so childish. You have so many problems that are not real, and you are so careful and serious about them. People discuss their feelings as if they were great works of art or literature that need to be analyzed and examined and passed on and on. In my country people love or they hate. They know that a human being is mysterious, and they live with that. The problems they have are real problems. If you do not eat, that's a problem. If you have no leg, that's a problem. If you are unhappy, that is not a problem to talk about."

"I think it is," I said.

"Exactly. That is because you are an American. For you, big things are small, and small things are big." Rezvan was always making these large declarations on America in a loud voice from our balcony.

"I bet you one million in money," Rezvan said as he blew out smoke, "that the number of hours Americans spend per week in these—what do you call them?—*therapy* offices is exactly the same number of hours Romanians spend in line for bread. And for what? Nothing. To make their problems bigger. They talk about them all day so at night they are even bigger."

"I don't agree. The reason why people talk about their problems is to get over them, get rid of them. I went to a therapist once and he was very helpful."

"You?" He lifted an eyebrow, took a drag.

"Yes, when I was eleven."

"Eleven? What could be the problem at eleven?"

"I was just sad. My parents were getting divorced, and I guess I could tell that my dad was about to leave."

"But isn't that the correct emotion—sadness when a father leaves? Can a therapist do anything to bring your father home?"

"No, but he gave me a way to deal with it."

"And what is that way? I would like to know."

"Well, just a way to separate from the situation."

"How do you separate from your own life?"

"Well, you rise above it. You gain some objectivity and perspective."

"But is this proper? If you have a real problem, should you rise above it? When a father leaves a child, the child feels sad. This seems right to me. This rising above, that is the problem. In fact, that is the problem of America. I cannot tell my family back home that if they are hungry or cold, they should just rise above it. I cannot say, 'Don't worry, go to the movies, go shop, here is ten dollars in money, go buy some candy. Rise above your situation.'"

"That's not what I mean. I mean you literally rise above it. Your mind hovers over your body, and you understand the situation from a higher perspective." I knew that if he pushed me far enough, this would end up sounding insane.

"So, this is what your man, your eleven-year-old therapist, teaches you: to separate your mind from your body, to become *unhinged*. This does not teach you to solve the problem; this teaches you to be a crazy person."

But already I was drifting up until I was watching us from the level of the roof. There she is, I thought, Margit Bergen, twenty-nine years old, in love with Rezvan of Romania, a defector who escaped political hardship to arrive first in a refugee camp in Austria and a year later in Regina, Saskatchewan, where he now stands on a balcony in the moonlight, hassling her about America, as if she contained all of it inside her.

I had met Rezvan in my father's lab at the university. Rezvan was a geologist, like my father. Technically, for grant reasons, he was a graduate student, but my father considered him a peer, because Rezvan had already worked for years as a geologist for the Romanian government.

Originally he had been a supporter of Ceausescu. In fact, his father, Andrei, had been a friend of Ceausescu's right up until the time Andrei died, in 1985. Rezvan, by his own account, stood by his father's deathbed as he died and held his father's hand, but both father and son refused to speak, because Rezvan had by then ceased to be loyal to Ceausescu.

In the two years that Rezvan and I lived together, I would often rise from sleep to find him hunched over his desk, the arm of his lamp reaching over him. He wrote long letters into the night, some in English and some in Romanian. The English ones, he said, were to various government officials, asking for help in getting his family over to Canada. The ones in Romanian were to his family, an assortment of aunts and uncles and cousins. He wrote quickly, as in a fever, and if I crept up on him and touched his back, he would jump and turn over his letters immediately before looking up at me in astonishment. At the time, I thought this was simply an old habit of fear, left over from living for so long in a police state.

Sometimes he said he could not forgive his country for keeping his family captive. He told what he called jokes—dark, labyrinthine stories that always ended with some cartoonish, undignified death for Ceausescu: his head in a toilet, his body flattened by a steamroller. Other times he spoke about his country with such longing—the wet mist of Transylvania, the dark tunnels beneath the streets of his town, the bookstores lined with propaganda that opened into small, dusty rooms in back filled with *real* books.

In this same way Rezvan loved and hated America. He would rant about it from the balcony, but then we would return to our bed and sit side by side, our backs to the wall, and watch the local and then the national news, where almost every night somebody would criticize the Prime Minister, Brian Mulroney. Rezvan could never get over this: men appearing on television to insult their leader night after night, and never getting pulled off the air. Sometimes we would turn to the news from the United States, which we received through a cable channel from Detroit. This was a real treat for Rezvan during the period of Reagan-bashing. "I love that man," he said to me one night.

"Reagan? You don't like Reagan."

"I know, but look at him now." They were showing a clip of Reagan waving. His face did look kind. His eyes were veering off, looking skyward. He looked like somebody's benevolent, faintly crazy grandfather.

"All day long people insult him and he doesn't kill any of them."

Rezvan sometimes skipped work and came with me to the fields. He'd ride in the back of the truck, standing up, so that his head was above the cab, the wind pouring over him. He wanted to know all the details of my job. He became better than I was at some things. He could spot poor field drainage from far away. He loved to point out the signs of it—the mint, the rushes, the wire grass, the willows.

For lunch we stopped in the towns along the way at small, fragrant home-style diners. Almost all of them were run by Ukrainian women. Each one adored Rezvan. He would kiss their hands and speak in his strange accent—part British, part Romanian—and they would serve him free platefuls of food, one after another, hovering over him as if he were a long-lost son from the old country.

One afternoon, while we were driving back to the city from a little town called Yellow Grass, I fell asleep at the wheel. I woke up after the crash to see Rezvan crumpled against the passenger door. I felt myself rising then, far above the car, far above even the treeline. From there I watched myself crawl out of the wreck and drag Rezvan out onto the grassy shoulder. And then, instead of watching my own body run down the long charcoal highway, I stayed above Rezvan. I watched the trees bow in the wind toward his body, listening for his heartbeat.

Later that night, when I entered his hospital room for the first time, I expected him to refuse to speak to me. Rezvan smiled, though. "In my country," he said, "you could work for Ceausescu. He has been trying to do this to me for years." I started apologizing then, over and over. Rezvan just motioned me toward the bed, and then put his arms around me. "It's okay, it's okay," he said. "Don't cry. This is America. This is what is supposed to happen. I will sue you, and your insurance will give us money, and we will go on a trip. To California, a vacation. I am so happy."

I wiped my eyes and looked at him. His head was cocked to the side. A thin white bandage was wrapped around his forehead, and blood was still matted in the black curls of his hair. One side of his face was torn apart. His leg was suspended in a sling. Still, he looked at me incredulously, wondering how I could be crying when this was such a stroke of luck.

For the next few months he had a cane, which he loved. He liked to point at things with it. The scars settled into faint but permanent tracks down the left side of his face. He liked that, too. We saw the movie *Scarface* over and over again. When he discarded the cane, he still walked with a slight limp, which gave his gait an easy rocking motion that seemed strangely to suit him. He never once blamed me; I don't think it ever crossed his mind.

Rezvan and I stayed engaged for two years. He seemed to think of engagement as an alternative to marriage rather than as a lead-up to it. I didn't mind, actually. I just wanted to be with him. Life with Rezvan had a sort of gloss to it always. He passed quickly from emotion to emotion, from sadness to gratitude to arrogance, but he never fell into depression, ever.

Perhaps because I was so happy with Rezvan, I did not notice what may have been obvious signs. But, oddly enough, the signs indicating that a man is in love with another woman are often similar to the signs of an immigrant in a new country, his heart torn in two. He wrote long letters home; he hesitated to talk about the future; during lonely nights he seemed to be murmuring as he fell asleep, but not to me.

Nearly a year passed before I even noticed anything, or admitted to myself that I noticed anything. Then one day Rezvan received a phone call at four in the morning. I didn't understand a word of it, since it was in Romanian, but in my half sleep I could hear him mutter the word *rila* again and again, sometimes insistently. And when he hung up, after about an hour and a half, he just sat there in the living room like a paralyzed man, the light slowly rising across his body. I asked him, "Rezvan, what does *rila* mean?" He told me that it meant "well-lit," as in a room.

Two days later, as I walked up our driveway in my house-coat, the mail in my hand, I glanced through the letters and noticed a thick letter from Rilia Balescu. *Rila* was Rilia, a person, a relative. When I walked in the door, Rezvan was standing in his striped pajamas drinking coffee, smoking, scratching his head. As I handed him the letter, I tried to read his face, but saw nothing. So I said, "Who is Rilia?"

"She is my sister, my baby sister. Gavrilia."

Does an extra beat pass before one tells a lie? This is what I had always believed, but Rezvan answered immediately. Perhaps he had been waiting for the question.

"I didn't know you had a sister."

"I don't like to talk about her. We disowned each other long ago. She follows Ceausescu still; she has pictures of him and his son on her wall as if they were rock stars. I am trying to bring her over, but she is stubborn. She would rather go to the Black Sea and vacation with her boys than come here and live with me."

"So why have you never told me about her?"

"Because it is not wise to speak aloud the one thing you want more than anything. You know that."

"No, I don't know that."

"It's true. Romanians have a word for it: *ghinion.* It means don't speak aloud what you want most. Otherwise it will not happen. You must have a word for this in English?"

"Jinx."

"Okay. I did not tell you about my sister because of jinx."

"Why did you tell me her name meant 'well-lit'?"

"Pardon?"

"The other day I asked you, and you said that 'Rilia' was the word for 'well-lit.'"

"No, no. *Rila* is the word for 'well-lit.' *Rilia* is my sister." He smiled and kissed my face. "We will have to work on your accent."

Over the next month we settled into a routine. When Rezvan finished writing his letters in the night, he padded down the driveway, set the letters in the mailbox, and lifted the tiny, stiff red flag so that our mailman would stop in the morning. And then, after Rezvan was asleep, I would rise out of bed and go to the mailbox myself, pick out the ones to Rilia, and slip them into the pocket of my housecoat. I did the same thing with the letters she sent him. I collected those in the morning.

At first it didn't feel like a strategy. But I was desperate to know if Rilia really was his sister or his wife—as if her handwriting would tell me. Rezvan left for work an hour before I did, and I opened the letters then. I sat on our bed, laying the pages in front of me, cross-referencing. Some of her passages were blacked out by censors. I found many names, but mostly two, Gheorghe and Florian, again and again. Gheorghe and Florian, Gheorghe and Florian, Gheorghe and Florian. I began to realize, very slowly, that these were probably their children.

On one of these mornings my mother showed up at my door to drop off a skirt she had sewed for me. "Good," she said, bustling in, "you're home. I wanted to drop this off." Already, as she said this, she was rapidly moving through the rooms of our apartment. My mother liked to do this, to catch me off guard and check all my rooms immediately for anything I might hide if given the time. "What is this?" she said, reaching the bedroom, where all the pages were strewn across the bed.

"Oh, that's just some stuff I'm reading for Rezvan. Proofreading."

She picked up a sheet. "Oh, so now you proofread in Romanian?"

I smiled weakly. She didn't pry, but for once I wished she would. What I wanted to do was tell her that this was my life spread across the bed, thin as paper, written in a language I could not understand, dotted with four names—Rezvan, Gavrilia, Gheorghe, Florian—but never my own. I wanted to ask her how she felt when my father was having an affair. And I wanted to ask what happened to the other woman. My father never married her, even after he and my mother split. Where had she drifted off to? Did she ever lose her breasts? Did she get well again? Was she happy somewhere now?

I didn't tell my mother anything, but when she left that day, she gestured toward the bedroom. "You know that you can find people at the university who will translate that for you."

I nodded, and stared at my feet.

"Maybe you don't really want them translated? Maybe you already know what they say?" She ducked her face under, so that she could look at my face. "It'll be okay," she said, "either way."

I stockpiled the letters for two months. I didn't intend to be malicious; I was just sitting on them until I could figure out what to do. Every night as I drove home from the fields, I thought, I will tell Rezvan tonight; I will say I know everything and I am leaving. But when dinner came, I could hardly speak. It was as if I were eleven all over again.

Even Rezvan was getting depressed. He said that his letters were turning out to be all in vain. Perhaps, he said, he would quit writing them altogether. One night he said, "Nothing gets through those bastards. Perhaps I will never see Rilia again." Then he limped to the sink, rocking back and forth, and filled his glass with water. He turned to me and said, "Why would they want to keep us apart, anyway?" His head was tilted to the side, and he looked like a child. He stared at me as he really expected me to answer.

"I don't know," I said. "I don't know about that stuff."

But of course I did. At the other end, across the ocean, men in uniforms were collecting letters and censoring them, blacking out whatever threatened them, and at this end I in my housecoat was doing the same thing.

I tried to rise above the situation, but that strategy didn't work at all. I was increasingly distressed at what I saw. I'd fly up and look down. There she is, I'd say, Margit Bergen of Saskatchewan. Who would have thought she'd grow up so crooked, crouched on her bed, obstructing love, hoarding it, tearing it apart with her own hands.

Until this point in my life I had always thought of myself as an open-minded person, able to step into another's shoes. But I could not picture this Rilia. Her face, and the faces of her children, were blank for me. I hoped that this inability, or unwillingness, to imagine another's face was not hatred, but I was deeply ashamed that it might be.

Finally, one windy night in November, as I cut into a roast, I said, "Rezvan, is Rilia your wife?"

"What do you know of Rilia? Has she called? Has she sent a letter?"

"No, not at all. I was just wondering."

"Tell me what you know."

"I don't know anything. I was just asking."

"Have you spoken to her on the phone?"

"No, I have not." I enunciated this very clearly. "Is she your wife, Rezvan?"

"I am not a liar," he said. "I will marry you to prove this. We will go to British Columbia and get married in the trees. Whenever you want. Tomorrow, if you want."

The next morning I put the letters in a bag and drove straight to the administrative offices at the university. A woman disap-

peared and reappeared with a list of professors who could translate Romanian for me. I had my choice of four. I glanced down
the list and there, at number three, was Professor Roland Pine.

I found him in the same office. He had aged well, his
hair now ash instead of blond, a few extra lines across his face.
When he stood up to greet me, I saw that I had grown to be
about half a foot taller than he was. His tic was still there,
flashing across his face every fifteen seconds or so. As I shook
his hand, I marveled that it had continued like this since the
last time I'd seen him, keeping time as faithfully as a clock.

"My name is Margit Bergen. I came to you once as a
child."

"Hello, Margit. It's nice to see you again. Was I helpful?"

"Yes, very. I've always been grateful."

"What was the problem in those days?"

"Just childhood depression, I guess. My parents were
splitting up."

He squinted at me, and turned his face slightly to the
side. "Oh, yes," he said. "That's right. Of course. Little Margit.
You were such a girlie-whirl. So sad. What did you become?"

"You mean in my life?"

"In your life. What did you become?"

"A soil consultant."

"What a good job for you." He gestured toward the
black leather chair. His birds fought in their high cages,
their wings tearing at each other. "Mortalhead. You be nice to
Eagerheart." He turned to me. "The kids love funny names, you
know. Mortalhead, Eagerheart, Quickeye."

I smiled and sat down in the chair, pulling a stack of
letters from my bag. "Professor Pine . . . ," I said.

"Call me Roland," he said. He leaned back. His face
cracked in a tic. "Roland Boland. Just think: little Roland and
little Margit, the professor and the soil consultant, back again,

sitting in a warm office surrounded by bird-people." He rolled his eyes and grinned, almost girlishly.

I didn't know what to say. "Yes, it's nice," I eventually said. "Actually, Roland, I was wondering if you could help me out with a problem I have."

"I thought I solved all your problems." He looked disappointed.

"You did. I mean, for twenty years you did."

"What could be the problem now?"

"I need you to translate these letters for me, from Romanian."

"Romanian?" He took the stack of letters from me, and began to leaf through them. "Is your name Rezvan?" he said.

"He's a friend of mine."

"Then you should not read his letters." He smiled.

"Professor Pine, I really need you to do this for me."

"Who is Rilia?"

"I don't know. Look, you don't even need to read them to me. Just read them to yourself and tell me if the people writing them are married."

"Why do you want to know?"

"That doesn't matter. I just do."

"Why?"

I didn't say anything.

"Are you being a dirty-girlie?" He smiled—and then a tic, as forked as lightning.

I sighed and looked over at his birds, who were cawing loudly. One was green with black wings, and it was flapping furiously, staring at the letters fluttering in Professor Pine's hand.

"Fine, Professor Pine. If you don't want to read them, I'll take them to somebody else." I reached for the letters.

He pulled them back, toward his chest. "Okay, okay, girlie," he said. "You are so stubborn, Margit."

He read softly, in a lilting voice, as if he were reading me a bedtime story. "Rilia says, Remember how tiny Florian was at his birth? Now he is forty-five kilos, the same as his brother. Rilia says, Remember the Black Sea, it is as blue as the first time we went to it. Rilia says that Rezvan must be lying when he says there is so much food that sometimes he tosses rotten fruit from the window."

I interrupted. "Do you think they are married?"

"Well, they are both Balescus."

"They could be brother and sister?"

He frowned, and leafed through the letters again. "But here she calls him darling. Darling, barling, starling."

He looked up then. "Oh, no," he said, "don't cry. Please don't cry." He jumped up, came around the side of the desk, and crouched beside my chair. He looked up at me. His face was close, and the next tic was like slow motion. I saw the path that it followed, curving and winding like a river down his face.

He sat back on the edge of his desk. "It's going to be okay," he said. "We just have to figure out what the girlie wants. If you want Rezvan, the liar face, you can have him. Is that what you want?"

"No, I don't think so. I mean, I do, but I can't. He has kids and everything."

"Then it sounds like you've made up your mind already."

"Not really," I said.

"Margit, you need some perspective."

"Perspective?"

"You know"—he rolled his eyes upward—"Slatland."

Slatland—I remembered that that was what he'd called it, the drifting up and looking down.

"I've tried Slatland. It didn't work," I said.

"Slatland always works. Just close your eyes, all right, girlie?"

I started to stand up. "Thanks for your help, Professor Pine. I really have to go now." But then I felt it, the lift, and my mind started rising, until the caws of Mortalhead and Eagerheart and Quickeye were far below me. I could see the yellow fields surrounding my town, and then even those went out of focus. I hurtled faster and faster until I finally stopped, what seemed like minutes later.

So this is Slatland, I thought. I looked down, and to my left I saw North America, large and jagged, flanked by oceans. Its face was beautiful—craggy, broken, lined with rivers. I found my part of the continent, a flat gold rectangle in the upper middle. I saw what my daily life looked like from this distance: my truck beetling through the prairies, dust rising off its wheels the way desire must rise, thousands of fragments of stone lifting off the earth. And when the truck stopped and I stepped out into the bright, empty fields, my loneliness looked extreme. I could almost *see* it, my longing and desire for Rezvan rising out of me the way a tree rises out of its trunk. I perceived, in an instant, exactly what I should do to keep him. I saw how simple it all would be, just to keep collecting the letters every morning, one by one, in order that what was between Rezvan and his wife would die slowly and easily and naturally, and what was between him and me would grow in exactly the same proportion.

If I had been able to climb down then, to drop out of Slatland at that moment, everything would have remained simple, and probably Rezvan and I would still be together. But Slatland seemed to have a will of its own. It would not let me go until I looked down to my right. If I was willing to see the simplicity, the purity, of my own desire, than I also had to see the entire landscape—the way desire rises from every corner and intersects, creates a wilderness over the earth.

I stood on Slatland a long time before I looked down to my right. There it was, Eastern Europe, floating above the

Mediterranean. I traced with my finger the outline of Romania. I squinted through the thick moss of trees, until I found her. She stood in a long line of people, her forty-five-kilo children hanging on her skirts. She bent to them and broke for them some bread as hard as stone. I hovered a few feet above her and watched. Even so, I might still have been able to return to my own life, my own province, unchanged if she hadn't turned her face upward right then, as if she had felt some rain, and looked directly at me.

This all happened very fast, in a blink of my eyes. When I opened them, Professor Pine was sitting on his desk, watching me. "You're a real erky-terk," he said, with a tic so extreme that it looked like it might swallow his face. He walked me to the door and handed me the letters, which later that night I would give to Rezvan. We would be standing on the balcony in the semidarkness of the moon, and I would be surprised at how easily they passed through my hands, as easily as water.

The birds shrieked. "Birdmen!" Professor Pine said. "Sometimes I feel like saluting them," he said to me. He shook my hand. "Good luck, girlie-whirl." Then he went up on his tiptoes and kissed me good-bye.

Surprised by Joy

Charles Baxter

1

Because their psychiatrist had recommended it, they both began to keep journals. Jeremy's was Woolworth-stationery drab, and Harriet's was sea-blue with the words "A Blank Book" printed in gold script in the upper right-hand corner. Thinking that pleasant images would relieve the tone of what was to follow, she sketched a wren in flight, a Victorian lamppost, and an ash tree on the first page. Then she changed her mind and blacked the drawings out. There weren't any drawings in the book Jeremy used. His writing was tiny and defiant. His first sentence, which was undated, read: "Benson told us it would help if we wrote down our thoughts, but I don't have any thoughts, and besides, the fact is that I don't feel like writing a goddamn thing." That was the end of the first entry.

One night Jeremy came home and found all the silver-ware—knives, forks, spoons, gravy bowls, and ladles—lined up according to type on the living-room carpet in front of the hide-a-bed sofa. Harriet said she wanted to do an inventory, to make sure the place settings were all present and accounted for. She threatened to count all the dishes, and all the books. A week later when he arrived home she was standing on her head with her legs crossed and her knees positioned against the wall. He put down his briefcase, hung up his coat, and sat in his chair. "So," he said. "What's this?"

"An article I read says it helps." Upside down, she attempted a smile.

"Standing on your head."

"Yeah. Think about it: the brain under stress needs more blood, the cerebral cortex especially. The article says that when you stand up you feel an instant of physical exhilaration." She closed her eyes. "The plumber came out this morning. The faucet's fixed."

"Physical exhilaration." He turned away from her to stare out at the street, where two children were roaring by on their Big Wheels.

"They say you'll feel better."

"Right. What article did you say this was?" He didn't wait for her to answer. "It sounds like *Parade* magazine. How much did the plumber charge? God, I could use a drink. I have the most amazing willpower." He glanced at her. "Did you cry a lot today?"

"No. Not much. Not like last week. I even did two full baskets of laundry. After lunch, when the plumber was gone, that was hard. For about ten minutes I couldn't help it and locked myself in the bathroom and then I wrote in the journal. Gretchen called and invited me into her weaving class. Do you think I should? It seems so dull and womanish. How was your day?" She tumbled backward, stood up, and looked at him with an unsteady, experimental smile.

"Do you feel exhilarated?" She shrugged. He said, "I feel the usual. Carrying around the black box." He rose, went to the kitchen for a beer, and clomped down the stairs to the basement, where he played his clarinet while watching television with the sound off. His music consisted of absentminded riffs in eerie unrelated keys.

They had brought their child home to a plain three-bedroom brick bungalow of the type referred to as a "starter house" for young married couples. Its distinguishing characteristics were those left by the previous owners. Jeremy and Harriet had never had time to redecorate it; as a result, their bedroom was covered with flocked jungle-orange wallpaper, the paint in Harriet's sewing room was oyster-gray, and the child's room had been painted blue, with two planets and four constellations mapped out on the ceiling with phosphorus dots and circles. At the time, their child was too little to notice such things: she gurgled at the trees outside and at the birds that sang in the shrubbery below her windowsill.

This child, Ellen, had been born after many difficulties. Harriet had had a series of ovarian cysts. She ovulated irregularly and only when provoked by certain powerful hormonal medications that left her so forgetful that she had to draw up hourly schedules for the day's tasks. She had the scars to prove that surgical procedures had been used to remove her enlarged ovaries piece by piece. The baby had been in a troublesome position, and Harriet had endured sixteen hours of labor, during which time she thrashed and groaned. Jeremy watched her lying in the hospital gown, his hands pressed against her lower back, while her breathing grew louder, hoarse and rhythmical. Their Lamaze lessons proved to be useless. The lights glared overhead in the prep room and could not be dimmed. In its labors her body heaved as if her reproductive system were choking in its efforts to expel the child. Her obstetrician was out of town on vacation in Puerto Vallarta, so the delivery was finally performed by a resident, a young woman who had a short hairdo and whose purple fingernail polish was visible through her surgical gloves.

✳ ✳ ✳

The oyster-gray paint and the phosphorus planets in the house suited Ellen, who, when she was old enough to toddle, would point at the stars on the ceiling and wave at them. At this time she could not pronounce her own name and referred to herself as "Ebbo" or, mysteriously, as "Purl." On a spring morning she climbed from the crib onto the windowsill in pursuit of a chickadee singing outside. Cheered by the sun, Harriet had left the window open to let the breeze in. Ellen pushed herself past the sill and managed to tumble out, breaking the screen. She landed on a soft newly filled flower bed next to a bush. When Harriet found her, she was tugging at flower shoots and looking pleased with herself. She said, "Purl drop." She shrugged her right shoulder and smiled.

They latched the screen onto a stronger frame and rushed around the house looking for hazards. They installed a lock on the basement door so she wouldn't tumble downstairs, and fastened shut the kitchen sink's lower cabinet so she wouldn't eat the ElectraSol. She lived one day past her third Christmas, when for the first time she knew what a Christmas tree was and could look forward to it with dazed anticipation. On Christmas Day she was buried up to her waist in presents: a knee-high table complete with cups and saucers, Bert and Ernie finger dolls, a plastic Fisher-Price phonograph, a stuffed brown bear that made wheezing sounds, a Swiss music box, a windup train that went around in a small circle, a yellow toy police car with a lady cop inside, and, in her stocking, pieces of candy, gum, a comb, and a red rubber ball her mother had bought at Kiddie Land for twenty-five cents.

On December 26, Jeremy and Harriet were slumped in the basement, watching Edmund Gwenn in *Miracle on 34th Street* for the eighth or ninth time, while Ellen played upstairs in her room. They went through three commercial breaks before Harriet decided to check on her. She hadn't been worried because she could hear the Fisher-Price phonograph playing a Sesame Street record. Harriet went down the hallway and turned the corner into Ellen's room. Her daughter was lying on the floor, on her side, her skin blue. She wasn't breathing. On her forehead was blood next to a bright cut. Harriet's first thought was that Ellen had somehow been knocked unconscious by an intruder. Then she was shouting for Jeremy, and crying, and touching Ellen's face with her fingers. She picked her up, pounded her back, and then felt the lump of the red rubber ball that Ellen had put in her mouth and that had lodged in her throat. She squeezed her chest and the ball came up into the child's mouth.

Jeremy rushed in behind her. He took Ellen away from Harriet and carried her into the living room, her arms hanging down, swinging. He shouted instructions at Harriet. Some made sense; others didn't. He gave Ellen mouth-to-mouth resuscitation and kept putting his hand against her heart, waiting for a pulse.

Later they understood that Ellen had panicked and had run into the edge of the open closet door. What with the movie and the new phonograph, they hadn't heard her. The edge of the door wasn't sharp, but she had run into it so blindly that the collision had dazed her. She had fallen and reached up to her forehead: a small amount of blood had dried on her hands. She had then reached for her stuffed raccoon; her left hand was gripping its leg. She was wearing, for all time, her yellow Dr. Denton pajamas. In the living room, waiting for the ambulance, Harriet clutched her own hands. Then she was drinking glass after glass of water in a white waiting room.

Their parents said, oh, they could have another, a child as beautiful as Ellen. Her doctors disagreed. Harriet's ovaries had been cut away until only a part of one of them remained. In any case, they didn't want replacements. The idea made no sense. What they thought of day and night was what had happened upstairs while they were watching television. Their imaginations put the scene on a film loop. Guiltily, they watched it until their mental screens began to wash the rest of the past away.

For the next two months they lived hour to hour. Every day became an epic of endurance, in which Harriet sat in chairs. Harriet's mother called every few days, offering excruciating maternal comfort. There were photographs, snapshots and studio portraits that neither of them could stand to remove. Nature became Harriet's enemy. She grew to hate the sun and its long lengthening arcs. When living trees broke open into pink and white blossoms in the spring, Harriet wanted to fling herself against them. She couldn't remember what it was about life that had ever interested her. The world began a vast and buzzing commentary to keep her in cramps, preoccupied with Ellen, who had irresistibly become Purl. The grass no longer grew up from the ground but instead stood as a witless metaphor of continuing life. Dishes and silverware upset her, unaccountably. She couldn't remember who her friends were and did not recognize them on the street. Every night the sky fell conclusively.

Jeremy had his job, but every evening, after seeing about Harriet, he went straight down to the basement where the television set was. He played his clarinet, drank beer, and watched *Hogan's Heroes* and the local news until it was time for dinner. He opened the twist-top beer bottles and drank the beer mechanically, as if acting on orders. After overhearing the music he played, Harriet began to call it "jazz from Mars," and Jeremy said, yes, that was probably where it came from. He paid attention to things at work; his music could afford to be inattentive.

He came upstairs when dinner was ready. This meal consisted of whatever food Harriet could think of buying and preparing. They didn't like to go out. They often ate hot dogs and A&P potato salad, or hamburger, or pizza delivered by the Domino's man in a green Gremlin. Jeremy sometimes fell asleep at the dinner table, his head tilted back at the top of the chair, and his mouth open, sucking in breaths. Harriet would drape one of his arms around her neck and lower him to the floor, so he wouldn't fall off the chair while asleep. They had talked about getting chairs with arms to prevent accidents of this kind; they both assumed they would spend the rest of their lives falling asleep at the table after dinner.

They started seeing Benson, the therapist, because of what happened with the Jehovah's Witnesses. In mid-May, the doorbell rang just after dinner. Jeremy, who this time was still awake, rose from the table to see who it was. Outside the screen door stood a red-haired man and a small red-haired boy, eight or nine years old, dressed in nearly identical gray coats and bow ties. The father was carrying a copy of *Awake!* and *The Watchtower*. The boy held a Bible, a children's edition with a crude painting of Jesus on the cover. Leaving the screen door shut, Jeremy asked them what they wanted.

"My son would like to read to you," the man said, glancing down at the boy. "Do you have time to listen for a minute?"

Jeremy said nothing.

Taking this as a sign of agreement, the man nodded at the boy, who pushed his glasses back, opened the Bible, and said, "Psalm forty-three." He swallowed, looked up at his father, who smiled, then pulled at the red silk bookmark he had inserted at the beginning of the psalm. He cleared his throat. "Give sentence with me, O God," he read, his finger trailing horizontally along the line of type, his voice quavering, "and defend my cause against the ungodly people; O deliver me from the deceitful and wicked man." He stumbled over "deceitful." The boy paused and looked through the screen at Jeremy. Jeremy was watching the boy with the same emptied expression he used when watching television. His father touched the boy on the shoulder and told him to continue. A bird was singing nearby. Jeremy looked up. It was a cardinal on a telephone wire.

"For thou art the God of my strength," the boy read. "Why hast thou put me from thee? and why go I so heavily, while the enemy oppresseth me?"

For the first time, Jeremy said something. He said, "I don't believe it. You can't be doing this." The father and the boy, however, didn't hear him. The boy continued.

"O send out thy light and thy truth, that they may lead me, and bring me unto thy holy hill, and to thy dwelling."

Jeremy said, "Who sent you here?" The father heard what he said, but his only reaction was to squint through the screen to see Jeremy better. He gave off a smell of cheap aftershave.

"And that I may go unto the altar of God," the boy read, "even unto the God of my joy and gladness; and upon the harp will I give thanks unto thee, O God, my God."

"You're contemptible," Jeremy said, "to use children. That's a low trick."

This time both the boy and his father stared in at him. Harriet had appeared and was standing behind Jeremy, pulling at his shirt and whispering instructions to him to thank them and send them on their merry way. The father, however, recovered himself, smiled, pointed at the Bible, and then touched his son on the head, as if pressing a button.

"Why art thou so heavy, O my soul?" the boy read, stuttering slightly. "And why art thou so disquieted within me?" "Stop it!" Jeremy shouted. "Please stop it! Stop it!" He opened the screen door and walked out to the front stoop so that he was just to the right of the father and his boy. Harriet crossed her arms but otherwise could not or did not move. Jeremy reached up and held on to the man's lapel. He didn't grab it but simply put it between his thumb and forefinger. He aimed his words directly into the center of the father's face. "Who sent you here?" he asked, his words thrown out like stones. "This was no accident. Don't tell me this was an accident, because I'd hate to think you were lying to me. Someone sent you here. Right? Who? How'd they ever think of using kids?" The bird was still singing, and when Jeremy stopped he heard it again, but hearing it only intensified his anger. "You want to sell me *The Watchtower?*" he asked, sinking toward inarticulateness. Then he recovered. "You want my money?" He let go of the man's lapel, reached into his pocket, and threw a handful of nickels and dimes to the ground. "Now go away and leave me alone."

The stranger was looking at Jeremy, and his mouth was opening. The boy was clutching his father's coat. One of the dimes was balanced on his left shoe.

"Go home," Jeremy said, "and never say another word about anything and don't ever again knock on my door." Jeremy was a lawyer. When speeches came to him, they came naturally. His face in its rage was as white as paper. He stopped, looked down, and hurriedly kissed the boy on the top of the head. As he straightened up, he said softly, "Don't mind me." Then, mobilized, Harriet rushed out onto the stoop and grabbed Jeremy's hand. She tried smiling.

"You see that my husband's upset," she said, pulling at him. "I think you should go now."

"Yes, all right," the father mumbled, blinking, taking the Bible from his son and closing it. The air thickened with the smell of his aftershave.

"We've had an accident recently," she explained. "We weren't prepared."

The man had his arm around his son's shoulders. They were starting down the walk to the driveway. "The Bible is a great comfort," the man said over his shoulder. "A help ever sure." He stopped to look back. "Trust in God," he said.

Jeremy made a roaring sound, somewhere between a shout and a bark, as Harriet hauled him back inside.

Benson's office was lodged on the twentieth floor of a steel-and-glass professional building called the Kelmer Tower. After passing through Benson's reception area, a space not much larger than a closet, the patient stepped into Benson's main office, where the sessions were actually conducted. It was decorated in therapeutic pastels, mostly off-whites and pale blues. Benson had set up bookshelves, several chairs, and a couch, and had positioned a rubber plant near the window. In front of the chairs was a coffee table on which was placed, not very originally, a small statue of a Minotaur. Benson's trimmed mustache and otherworldly air made him look like a wine steward. He had been recommended to them by their family doctor, who described Benson as a "very able man."

Harriet thought Benson was supposed to look interested; instead, he seemed bored to the point of stupefaction. He gave the appearance of thinking of something else: baseball, perhaps, or his golf game. Several times, when Jeremy was struggling to talk, Benson turned his face away and stared out the window. Harriet was afraid that he was going to start humming Irving Berlin songs. Instead, when Jeremy was finished, Benson looked at him and asked, "So. What are you going to do?"

"Do? Do about what?"

"Those feelings you've just described."

"Well, what am I supposed to do?"

"I don't think there's any thing you're supposed to do. It's a choice. If you want me to recommend something, I can recommend several things, among them that you keep a journal, a sort of record. But you don't have to."

"That's good." Jeremy looked down at the floor, where the slats of sunlight through the venetian blinds made a picket fence across his feet.

"If you don't want my help," Benson said, "you don't have to have it."

"At these prices," Jeremy said, "I want something."

"Writing in a journal can help," Benson continued, "because it makes us aware of our minds in a concrete way." Harriet cringed over Benson's use of the paternal first-person plural. She looked over at Jeremy. He was gritting his teeth. His jaw muscles were visible in his cheek. "Crying helps," Benson told them, and suddenly Harriet was reminded of the last five minutes of Captain Kangaroo, the advice part. "And," Benson said slowly, "it helps to get a change of scene. Once you're ready and have the strength and resources to do it, you might try going on a trip."

"Where?" Harriet asked.

"Where?" Benson looked puzzled. "Why, anywhere. Anywhere that doesn't look like this. Try going to someplace where the scenery is different. Nassau. Florida. Colorado."

"How about the Himalayas?" Jeremy asked.

"Yes," Benson said, not bothering to act annoyed. "That would do."

They both agreed that they might be able to handle it if it weren't for the dreams. Ellen appeared in them and insisted on talking.

In Jeremy's dreams, she talked about picnics and hot dogs, how she liked the catsup on the opposite side of the wiener from the mustard, and how she insisted on having someone toast the bun. The one sentence Jeremy remembered with total clarity when he woke up was: "Don't *like* soggy hot dogs." He wouldn't have remembered it if it hadn't sounded like her.

She was wearing a flannel shirt and jeans in Jeremy's dream; in Harriet's she had on a pink jumper that Harriet had bought for her second birthday. Harriet saw that she was outgrowing it. With a corkscrew feeling she saw that Ellen was wearing a small ivory cameo with her own—Harriet's—profile on it. She was also wearing a rain hat that Harriet couldn't remember from anywhere, and she was carrying a Polaroid photograph of her parents. Harriet wondered vaguely how dead children get their hands on such pictures. In this dream Harriet was standing on a street corner in a depopulated European city where the shutters were all closed tight over the windows. Near her, overhead in the intersection, the traffic light hanging from a thick cable turned from green to amber to red, red to green, green to amber to red. However, no cars charged through the intersection, and no cars were parked on the street. A rhythmic thud echoed in the streets. Leaves moldered in the gutters. Harriet knew that it was a bad city for tourists. In this place Ellen scampered toward her down the sidewalk, wearing the pink jumper and the rain hat, the photograph in her hand, the cameo pinned near her collar. She smiled. Harriet stumbled toward her, but Ellen held out her hand and said, "Can't hug." Harriet asked her about the hat, and Ellen said, "Going to rain." She looked up at the bleary sky, and, following her lead, so did Harriet. Flocks of birds flew from left to right across it in no special pattern, wing streaks of indecision. Clouds. Harriet gazed down at Ellen. "Are you okay?" Harriet asked. "Who's taking care of you?" Ellen was picking her nose. "Lots of people," she said, wiping her finger on her pant leg. "They're nice." "Are you all right?" Harriet asked again. Ellen lifted her right shoulder. "Yeah," she said. She looked up. "Miss you, Mommy," she said, and, against directions, Harriet bent down to kiss her, wanting the touch of her skin against her lips, but when she reached Ellen's face, Ellen giggled, looked around quickly as if she were being watched from behind the shuttered windows, reached both hands up to cover her mouth, and disappeared, leaving behind a faint odor of flowers.

"Such dreams are common," Benson said. "Very, very common."

"Tell me something else," Harriet said.

"What do you want me to tell you?"

"Something worth all the money we're paying you."

"You sound like Jeremy. What *would* be worth all the money you're paying me?"

"I have the feeling," Harriet said, "that you're playing a very elaborate game with us. And you have more practice at it than we do."

"If it's a game," Benson said, "then I do have more practice. But if it's not a game, I don't." He waited. Harriet stared at the giant leaves of the rubber plant, standing in the early-summer light, torpid and happy. Jeremy hadn't come with her this time. The Minotaur on the coffee table looked inquisitive. "What is the dream telling you about Ellen, do you think?"

"That she's all right?"

"Yes." Benson breathed out. "And what do you have to worry about?"

"Not Ellen."

"No, not Ellen. The dream doesn't say to worry about her. So what do you have to worry about?"

"Jeremy. I don't see him. And I have to worry about getting out of that city."

"Why should you worry about Jeremy?"

"I don't know," Harriet said. "He's hiding somewhere. I want to get us both out of that city. It gives me the creeps."

"Yes. And how are you going to get out of that city?"

"Run?" Harriet looked at Benson. "Can I run out of it?"

"If you want to." Benson thought for a moment. "If you want to, you will run out of it." He smoothed his tie. "But you can't run and pull Jeremy at the same time."

After Jeremy's dream, she no longer served hot dogs for dinner. That night she was serving pork chops, and when Jeremy came in, still in his vest but with his coat over his shoulder, she was seated at the table, looking through a set of brochures she had picked up at a travel agency down the block from Benson's office. After Jeremy had showered and changed his clothes, he was about to take a six-pack out of the refrigerator when he looked over at Harriet studying a glossy photograph of tourists riding mules on Molokai. "It says here," Harriet announced, "in this brochure, that Molokai is the flattest of all the islands and the one with the most agricultural activity."

"Are you going on a quiz show? Is that it?"

She stood up, walked around the dining-room table, then sat down on the other side. She had a fountain pen in her hand. "Now this," she said, pointing with the pen to another brochure, "this one is about New Mexico. I've never been to New Mexico. You haven't either, right?"

"No," Jeremy said. "Honey, what's this all about?"

"This," she said, "is all about what we're going to do during your two weeks off. I'll be damned if I'm going to sit here. Want to go to Santa Fe?"

Jeremy seemed itchy, as if he needed to go downstairs and play a few measures of jazz from Mars. "Sure, sure," he said. He rubbed his eyes suddenly. "Isn't it sort of hot that time of year?"

She shook her head. "It says here that the elevation's too high. You can stay in the mountains, and it's cool at night."

"Oh." Then, as an afterthought, he said, "Good."

She looked up at him. She stood and put her hand on his face, rubbing her thumb against his cheek. "How's the black box?" she asked. She had recently started to wear glasses and took them off now.

"How's the sky?" he asked. He turned around. "The black box is just fine. I move around it, but it's always there, right in front of me. It's hard to move with that damn thing in your head. I could write a book about it: how to live with a box and be a zombie." He reached for a beer and carried it to the basement. She could hear the television set being clicked on and the exhalation of the beer bottle when he opened it.

2

The flight to Albuquerque took four hours. Lunch was served halfway through: chicken in sauce. The stewardesses seemed proud of the meal and handed out the plastic trays with smug smiles. Jeremy had a copy of *Business Week* in his lap, which he dropped to the floor when the food arrived. For much of the four hours he sat back and dozed. Harriet was closer to the window and dutifully looked out whenever the captain announced that they were flying over a landmark.

In Albuquerque they rented a car and drove north toward Taos, the destination Harriet had decided upon, following the advice of the travel agent. They stopped at a Holiday Inn in Santa Fe for dinner. Appalled by the congestion and traffic, they set out after breakfast the next morning. As they approached the mountains, Jeremy, who was driving, said, "So this is the broom that sweeps the cobwebs away." He said it softly and with enough irony to make Harriet wince and to pull at her eyebrow, a recent nervous tic. The trip, it was now understood, had been her idea. She was responsible. She offered him a stick of gum and turned on the radio. They listened to Willie Nelson and Charlie Daniels until the mountains began to interfere with the reception.

In Taos they drove through the city until they found the Best Western motel, pale-yellow and built in quasi-adobe style. They took showers and then strolled toward the center of town, holding hands. The light was brilliant and the air seemingly without the humidity and torpor of the Midwest, but this atmosphere also had a kind of emptiness that Jeremy said he wasn't used to. In the vertical sun they could both feel their hair heating up. Harriet said she wanted a hat, and Jeremy nodded. He sniffed the air. They passed the Kit Carson museum, and Jeremy laughed to himself. "What is it?" Harriet asked, but he only shook his head. At the central square, the streets narrowed and the traffic backed up with motoring tourists. "Lots of art stores here," Harriet said, in a tone that suggested that Jeremy ought to be interested. She was gazing into a display window at a painting of what appeared to be a stick-figure man with a skull face dancing in a metallic, vulcanized landscape. She saw Jeremy's reflection in the window. He was peering at the stones on the sidewalk. Then she looked at herself: she was standing halfway in front of Jeremy, partially blocking his view.

They walked through the plaza, and Harriet went into a dime store to buy a hat. Jeremy sat outside on a bench in the

square, opposite a hotel that advertised a display of the paintings of D. H. Lawrence, banned in England, so it was claimed.
He turned away. An old man, an Indian with shoulder-length
gray hair, was crossing the plaza in front of him, murmuring an
atonal chant. The tourists stepped aside to let the man pass.
Jeremy glanced at the tree overhead, in whose shade he was sitting. He could not identify it. He exhaled and examined his
Seiko angrily. He gazed down at the second hand circling the
dial face once, then twice. He knew Harriet was approaching
when he saw out of the corner of his eye her white cotton pants
and her feet in their sandals.

"Do you like it?" she asked. He looked up. She had
bought a yellow cap with a visor and the word "Taos" sewn
into it. She was smiling, modeling it for him.

"Very nice," he said. She sat down next to him and
squeezed his arm. "What do people do in this town?" he asked.
"Look at vapor trails all day?"

"They walk around," she said. "They buy things." She
saw a couple dragging a protesting child into an art gallery.
"They bully their kids." She paused, then went on, "They eat."
She pointed to a restaurant, Casa Ogilvie's, on the east side of
the square with a balcony that looked down at the commerce
below. "Hungry?" He shrugged. "I sure am," she said. She took
his hand and led him across the square into the archway underneath the restaurant. There she stopped, turned, and put her arms
around him, leaning against him. She felt the sweat of his back
against her palms. "I'm so sorry," she said. Then they went up
the stairs and had lunch, two Margaritas each and enchiladas in
hot sauce. Sweating and drowsy, they strolled back to the motel,
not speaking.

They left the curtains of the front window open an inch or so
when they made love that afternoon. From the bed they could

see occasionally a thin strip of someone walking past. They made love to fill time, with an air of detachment, while the television set stayed on, showing a Lana Turner movie in which everyone's face was green at the edges and pink at the center. Jeremy and Harriet touched with the pleasure of being close to one familiar object in a setting crowded with strangers. Harriet reached her orgasm with her usual spasms of trembling, and when she cried out he lowered his head to the pillow on her right side, where he wouldn't see her face.

Thus began the pattern of the next three days: desultory shopping for knickknacks in the morning, followed by lunch, lovemaking and naps through the afternoon, during which time it usually rained for an hour or so. During their shopping trips they didn't buy very much: Jeremy said the art was mythic and lugubrious, and Harriet didn't like pottery. Jeremy bought a flashlight, in case, he said, the power went out, and Harriet purchased a keychain. All three days they went into Casa Ogilvie's at the same time and ordered the same meal, explaining to themselves that they didn't care to experiment with exotic regional food. On the third afternoon of this they woke up from their naps at about the same time with the totally clear unspoken understanding that they would not spend another day—or perhaps even another hour—in this manner.

Jeremy announced the problem by asking, "What do we do tomorrow?"

Harriet kicked her way out of bed and walked over to the television, on top of which she had placed a guide to the Southwest. "Well," she said, opening it up, "there *are* sights around here. We haven't been into the mountains north of here. There's a Kiowa Indian Pueblo just a mile away. There's a place called Arroyo Seco near here and—"

"What's that?"

"It means Dry Gulch." She waited. "There's the Taos Gorge Bridge." Jeremy shook his head quickly. "The D. H. Lawrence shrine is thirty minutes from here, and so is the Millicent A. Rogers Memorial Museum. There are, it says here, some trout streams. If it were winter, we could go skiing."

"It's summer," Jeremy said, closing his eyes and pulling the sheet up. "We can't ski. What about this shrine?"

She put the book on the bed near Jeremy and read the entry. "It says that Lawrence lived for eighteen months up there, and they've preserved his ranch. When he died, they brought his ashes back and there's a shrine or something. They *call* it a shrine. I'm only telling you what the book says."

"D. H. Lawrence?" Jeremy asked sleepily.

"You know," Harriet said. "*Lady Chatterley's Lover.*"

"Yes, I know." He smiled. "It wasn't the books I was asking about, it was the *quality* of the books, and therefore the necessity of making the trip."

"All I know is that it's visitable," she said, "and it's off State Highway Three, and it's something to do."

"Okay. I don't care what damn highway it's on," Jeremy said, reaching for the book and throwing it across the room. "Let's at least get into the car and go somewhere."

After breakfast they drove in the rented Pontiac out of town toward the Taos ski valley. They reached it after driving up fifteen miles of winding road through the mountains, following a stream of snow runoff, along which they counted a dozen fishermen. When they reached the valley, they admired the Sangre de Crísto Mountains but agreed it was summer and there was nothing to do in such a place. Neither blamed the other for acting upon an unproductive idea. They returned to the car and retraced their steps to the highway, which they followed for another fifteen miles until they reached the turn for the D. H. Lawrence shrine on the Kiowa Ranch Road. Jeremy stopped the car on the shoulder. "Well?" he asked.

"Why do we have to *decide* about everything?" Harriet said, looking straight ahead. "Why can't we just *do* it?"

He accelerated up the paved road, which climbed toward a plateau hidden in the mountains. They passed several farms where cattle were grazing on the thin grasses. The light made the land look varnished; even with sunglasses, Harriet squinted at the shimmering heat waves rising from the gravel.

Jeremy said, "What's here?"

"I told you. Anyhow, the description isn't much good. We'll find out. Maybe they'll have a tour of his inner sanctum or have his Nobel Prize up in a frame. The book says they have his actual typewriter."

Jeremy coughed. "He never won the Nobel Prize." Harriet looked over at him and noticed that his face was losing its internal structure and becoming puffy. Grief had added five years to his appearance. She saw, with disbelief, a new crease on his neck. Turning away, she glanced up at the sky: a hawk, cirrus clouds. The air conditioner was blowing a stream of cool air on her knees. Her gums ached.

"Only two more miles," Jeremy said, beginning now to hunch over the wheel slightly.

"I don't like this draft," she said, reaching over to snap off the air conditioner. She cranked down the window and let the breeze tangle her hair. They were still going uphill and had reached, a sign said, an elevation of nine thousand feet. Jeremy hummed Martian jazz as he drove, tapping the steering wheel. The little dirt road went past an open gate, divided in two, one fork going toward a conference center indicated by a road marker, the other toward the house and shrine. They came to a clearing. In front of them stood a two-story house looking a bit like an English country cottage, surrounded by a white picket fence, with a tire swing in the backyard, beyond which two horses were grazing. They were alone: there were no other cars in sight. Jeremy went up to the door of the house and knocked. A dog began barking angrily from inside, as if the knocks had interrupted its nap. "Look at this," Harriet said.

She had walked a few steps and was looking in the direction they had come from; in the clear air they could see down the mountain and across the valley for a distance of fifty miles or so. "It's beautiful," she said. Jeremy appeared from behind her, shielding his eyes although the sun was behind him. "What're you doing that for?" she asked.

"You have dark glasses. I don't."

"Where's the shrine?" she asked. "I don't see it anywhere."

"You have to turn around. Look." He pointed to the picket fence. At its north corner there was a sign that Harriet had missed.

SHRINE ☛

"That's very quaint," she said. "And what's this?" She walked toward the fence and picked a child's mitten off one of the posts. Mickey Mouse's face was printed on the front of the mitten, and one of his arms reached up over the thumb. She began laughing. "It doesn't say anything about Mickey Mouse in *Fodor's*. Do you think he's part of the shrine?"

Jeremy didn't answer. He had already started out ahead of her on a path indicated by the black pointing finger. Harriet followed him, panting from the altitude and the blistering heat, feeling her back begin to sweat as the light rained down on it. She felt the light on her legs and inside her head, on her eardrums. The path turned to the right and began a series of narrowing zigzags going up the side of a hill at the top of which stood the shrine, a small white boxlike building that, as they approached it, resembled a chapel, a mausoleum, or both. A granite phoenix glowered at the apex of the roof.

"The door's open," Jeremy said, twenty feet ahead of her, "and nobody's here." He was wearing heavy jeans, and his blue shirt was soaked with two wings of sweat. Harriet could hear the rhythmic pant of his breathing.

"Are there snakes out here?" she asked. "I hate snakes."

"Not in the shrine," he said. "I don't see any."

"What do you see?"

"A visitors' register." He had reached the door and had stepped inside. Then he came back out.

She was still ten feet away. "There must be more. You can't have a shrine without something in it."

"Well, there's this white thing outside," he said breathlessly. "Looks like a burial stone." She was now standing next to him. "Yes. This is where his wife is buried." They both looked at it. A small picture of Frieda was bolted into the stone.

"Well," Jeremy said, "now for the shrine." They shuffled inside. At the back was a small stained-glass window, a representation of the sun, thick literalized rays burning out from its center. To their left the visitors' register lay open on a high desk, and above it in a display case three graying documents asserted that the ashes stored here were authentically those of D. H. Lawrence, the author. The chapel's interior smelled of sage and cement. At the far side of the shrine, six feet away, was a roped-off area, and at the back an approximation of an altar, at whose base was a granite block with the letters DHL carved on it. "This is it?" Jeremy asked. "No wonder no one's here."

Harriet felt giddy from the altitude. "Should we pray?" she asked, but before Jeremy could answer, she said, "Well, good for him. He got himself a fine shrine. Maybe he deserves it. Goddamn, it's hot in here." She turned around and walked outside, still laughing in a broken series of almost inaudible chuckles. When she was back in the sun, she pointed her finger the way the sign had indicated and said, "Shrine."

Jeremy stepped close to her, and they both looked again at the mountains in the west. "I used to read him in college," Harriet said, "and in high school I had a copy of *The Rainbow* I hid under my pillow where my mother wouldn't find it. Jesus, it must be ninety-five degrees." She looked suddenly at Jeremy, sweat dripping into her eyes. "I used to have a lot of fantasies when I was a teenager," she said. He was wiping his face with a handkerchief. "Do you see anyone?" she asked.

"Do I see anybody? No. We would've heard a car coming up the road. Why?"

"Because I'm hot. I feel like doing something," Harriet said. "I mean, here we are at the D. H. Lawrence shrine." She was unbuttoning her blouse. "I just thought of this," she said, beginning to laugh again. She put her blouse on the ground and quickly unhooked her bra, dropping it on top of the blouse. "There," she said, sighing. "Now that's better." She turned to face the mountains. When Jeremy didn't say anything, she swung around to look at him. He was staring at her, at the brown circles of her nipples, and his face seemed stricken. She reached over and took his hand. "Oh, Jay, sweetie," she said, "no one will see us. Honey. What is it? Do you want me to get dressed?"

"That's not it." He was staring at her, as if she were not his wife.

"What? What is it?"

"You're free of it." He wiped his forehead.

"What?"

"You're free of it. You're leaving me alone here."

"Alone? Alone in what?"

"You know perfectly damn well," he said. "I'm alone back here." He tapped his head. "I don't know how you did it, but you did it. You broke free. You're gone." He bent down. "You don't know what I'm talking about."

"Yes, I do." She put her bra and blouse back on and turned toward him again. His face was a mixture of agony and rage, but in the huge sunlight these emotions diminished to small vestigial puffs of feeling. "It's a path," she said. "And then you're surprised. You get out. It'll happen to you. You'll see. Honestly."

She could see his legs shaking. His face was a barren but expressive landscape. "Okay," he said. "Talk all you want. I was just thinking . . ." He didn't finish the sentence.

"You'll be all right," she said, stroking his back.

"I don't *want* to be all right!" he said, his voice rising, a horrible smile appearing on his face: it was a devil's face, Harriet saw, and it was radiant and calm. Sweat poured off his forehead, and his skin had started to flush pink. "It's my pleasure not to be all right. Do you see that? My *pleasure*."

She wiped her hands on her cotton pants. A stain appeared, then vanished. "You want that? You want to be back there by yourself?"

"Yeah." He nodded. "You bet. I feel like an explorer. I feel like a fucking pioneer." He gave each one of the words a separate emphasis. Meanwhile, he had separated himself from her and was now tilting his head up toward the sky, letting the sun shine on his closed eyelids.

She looked at him. In the midst of the sunlight he was hugging his darkness. She stepped down the zigzag path to the car leaving him there, but he followed her. Once they were both in the car, the dog inside the ranch house began its frantic barking, but it stopped after a few seconds. She took Jeremy's hand

and scanned the clouds in the west, the Sangre de Crísto Mountains to the east, trying to see the sky, the beckoning clouds, the way he did, but she couldn't. All she could see was the land stretched out in front of her, and, far in the distance, all fifty miles away, a few thunderheads and a narrow curtain of rain, so thin that the light passed straight through it.

Imaginary Problems

Francine Prose

Doug (my wife calls her therapist Doug) says our family needs a mourning ritual, a formal rite to bring us together over what has been lost and what's left. Doug's office is full of primitive masks. I focused on a cone of ropy hair as he told us about the Amazonian tribe which, when too much went wrong, sent someone out to kill a jaguar and bury it under the headman's house. I said, "We can do in the hamster."

"Hamster?" said Doug.

"Murph," said Beth. "Buzzy's hamster." Doug looked reproachful, as if his not knowing about the hamster made him wonder what else she'd withheld.

Not long after, the hamster died of natural causes. I felt it was my fault.

If you were driving beside us, stalled at the entrance to the West Side Highway, it would never occur to you that in our trunk is a half-frozen hamster we are on our way to bury on my sister's farm. When you saw our quiet children, our twelve-year-old daughter, Holly, our six-year-old son, Buzzy, you would think they are better than your kids and wonder how we do it. How could you know that the children's silence scares us, though Beth—in that quiet voice, in which, from their infancy, she half pretended they couldn't hear—says, "Aren't the kids being great? They always come through when we need them." This is no more true than that the kids can't hear. Sometimes they come through, sometimes they don't. I have always been amazed by the places they could fight: crowded waiting rooms, the back seats of cars on icy drives. Now what we need from them is to fight as if nothing had happened, to bicker and scream like before.

So much has gone wrong, it seems gratuitous of Doug to trace it back so far: he says our problems began when I went alone to Jacksonville after my stepmother's death—that I was angry at Beth and the kids for not coming with me. I don't remember that. I remember it rained at La Guardia and later in Florida, too. Rain swept over the fuselage. I stayed in my seat in the warm bright plane, not wanting to ever get off—not stuck there, exactly, nothing like that, but just for the moment happy.

The road from the Jacksonville airport was half under water, and as the cab slowed down to part the oily floods, the driver said, "There's a funny thing about this town. Sometimes on summer nights when it rains, you see puddles on the city streets—hopping, hopping with frogs."

"Frogs?" I said. "From where?"

"The ocean," he said. "I don't know."

As my father and I drove through the rain to Paglio's Pizza, I mentioned this. He said frogs didn't hatch out of puddles. Already he'd found a restaurant where all the waitresses knew him. There was no real food in his house. My stepmother had cooked natural food, the kitchen was full of grains and rice, jars of apricots and cashews. She had many health theories, like seasonal migration to alternate wet climates with dry. The accident had happened on a dude ranch near Tucson. They had just gotten back from a hike. She took a sip of soda from a can into which a wasp had fallen; it stung her on the tongue, and ten minutes later she was dead.

I asked why the ranch didn't have a bee-sting kit. My father and I are both lawyers; we both knew he could have recovered the cost of a mini-ranch of his own. We didn't talk about that. The phone rang often. I knocked around the house. All day I put off calling Beth and the kids; once I did it, I couldn't look forward to it anymore. But when at last I talked to Beth, I was flipping through the Jacksonville phone book. The kids spoke too low or too fast, I couldn't hear, couldn't follow, couldn't imagine their faces. I couldn't wait to get off the phone.

The children know too much. That, too, is Doug's idea. He says we put Band-Aids on wounds that would heal faster in the air. It's strange, making Band-Aids sound so primitive and in the next breath praising people who bury jaguars under the headman's house. I remember Band-Aids with love—the little red string that opens the wrappers, the rubber-adhesive smell.

Somewhere the Palisades turn into the Thruway. I have lost track of time. Six weeks, two months ago, I sat in guilty silence while Beth told the children their father had fallen in love with someone else, but now he was home, that was over. The good news was that Beth was pregnant, they were going to have a baby brother or sister. Beth had cooked pasta and lemon veal. I'd thrown some asparagus on. I should have pared the asparagus bottoms. Holly peeled back the hard asparagus skin, curling it in strips. Buzzy said, "Hey, that's cool," and I thought he meant the baby. But he meant what Holly was doing, and then he did it, too. I said, "Don't play with your food."

Buzzy said, "We don't need another kid," as if we should all just change our minds and return it like the flannel sleepers Beth's parents still sometimes sent.

Two weeks later, Beth called me at work. I ran out and got a cab. Beth was waiting under the hospital awning. Her face was geisha-white. I couldn't believe the emergency room had just let her leave on her own. A lawsuit flashed through my mind and flashed out again. I thought of the ranch without the first aid to save my stepmother's life.

Beth slumped in the back of the cab. When we got home she went to bed. She said, "Martin, you tell the kids." The kids didn't seem to care about the baby; they were worried about Beth. I reassured them, thinking how much time had passed. I couldn't remember telling them how babies were born. Now clearly they knew how they weren't. Beth got her strength back soon, but she couldn't get over the miscarriage—she was just streaming grief. It was right after this that she got me to go to Doug's office, and Doug told us we needed a ritual.

We are not the same people we were. A year before, if I'd volunteered the hamster for ritual purposes, Beth would have burst out laughing. A year before, we would never have been in Doug's office, with its good rugs and well-lit niches housing statuettes of pre-Columbian birth goddesses. But so much had gone wrong, so much changed and unpredictably lost, everything felt up for grabs, ready and waiting for another wasp swimming furiously in its pitch-black Pepsi tea.

On the morning Buzzy ran into the living room and said Murph wasn't moving, Beth and I exchanged looks. It was the first time in months we'd looked at each other like that—a look that was like speech.

I said, "Isn't that strange? Remember, in Doug's office? You think Murph could have died for our sins?"

"Your sins," said Beth, and then, miraculously, laughed. We went into Buzzy's room. Beth said, "We can't just throw him out."

I said, "Okay, let's bury him under the headman's house."

"We should bury him *somewhere*," said Beth. "It's what families always did. We buried our goldfish in the back yard. Didn't you?"

I said, "My family didn't have a back yard. Nor, do I have to point out, do we."

Beth thought a minute. Then she said, "If you can believe you killed Murph by mentioning him in Doug's office, I can believe it would help us to bury him in the ground."

I told her I hadn't been serious about putting a jinx on Murph. Should I have tried harder to convince her? For a lawyer, I am surprisingly unlitigious. I am retained by a mega-construction firm that tears down large buildings and puts up larger ones; I am not paid to argue in court but to see that we never get there.

I said, "What we have here is city life. Where to bury the family pet?"

No one could see digging a grave in Central Park or some patch of Westchester woods. We thought of my sister's farm. I called Peg, who said come up, she'd love to see us, but her house was full of people two weekends in a row. I couldn't say it was urgent.

When Buzzy realized that Murph was really dead, he sat on his bed and wailed. We had the hamster in a shoe box on the fire escape. The weather was getting warmer. Beth said, "Let's put it in the freezer."

Beth told the children that night, gave them—as Doug suggested—a fully worked-out plan. In three weeks, we would go up to Peg's and bury Murph. The children said, "Fine." That they didn't seem to think it was strange was fairly strange in itself; they both have that overdeveloped child's sense of what is and isn't disgusting. Well, despite everything, we're their parents; you can't blame them for looking to us for guidance on what to do with the dead.

By then it was hard to feel Murph's loss. Not that I'd felt his presence much—he was mostly Buzzy and Beth's. Still, any death was a death, an absence in the house. Despite what

Doug thinks, I am not afraid of sadness—quite the contrary, I'd say. But once we had Murph in the freezer, loss became a joke, a sign of confusion and distance and change which I avoid with random thoughts of work or food or pure survival as I fight for a lane in the press toward the Bear Mountain exit.

Doug has told Beth that I did what I did because I had never grieved over my mother; my stepmother's death brought it back. He said I was out of touch with my feelings. He sent us an article, from a women's magazine, about a guy who was eating dinner one night and started hemorrhaging from the throat. Three operations, a repaired major blood vessel, and two years of therapy later, he realized that all his emotions had been locked there, in his throat. Now he expresses them more. When I read that, I thought: He was already expressing them in his own way. Am I wrong in thinking that a family has a language of its own, that I did not have to bleed all over the lemon veal and the tough asparagus, that everything was clear enough from the tone in which I told my children to stop playing with their food?

When I was a child there were toy steering wheels that attached to the back of the front seat. I wore out a dozen of them, oversteering wildly as my father drove and my sister lay flat on the ledge behind the seat and looked out the back window. That was before seat belts and child safety. For years before I could drive, I dreamed about driving as flight, as freedom, a way of being with girls, the car as an extension of my body. Beth used to have panic dreams in which she was driving before she knew how; I never had dreams like that. Doug doesn't approve of cars. He says they are bubbles that keep us apart, each in our own separate world. He thinks we were better off walking single file through the jungle. I have never been in the jungle, and neither, as far as I know, has Doug.

No one has spoken for thirty miles when Beth says, "Doug's thinking of giving up his practice and going to graduate school in anthropology."

I say, "He'll quit when he can't find a tribe to pay him a hundred an hour."

Doug was a mistake. It wasn't a time when any of us was thinking clearly. Beth knew something was wrong but not what, and I couldn't tell her. I asked a malpractice lawyer I knew. I said: Someone professional, not a crackpot, someone who won't convince her she's hated me all along. By accident, my friend and one of Beth's friends both gave us Doug's name; we mistook coincidence for consensus. I expected an elderly Viennese, not some guy with stringy hair and a necklace made of teeth.

Beth used to be funnier, used to talk more. Her hands flew around when she spoke. Now I reach out to touch Beth's hand, though that is no longer simple. When we met, I had an old Pontiac I drove with Beth practically in my lap. Now we have bucket seats. Couples who'd laugh at single beds have no problem with this. Beth doesn't see me reach for her hand, which is tucked in a corner of the armrest, so my groping for it has all the grace of wrestling a jacket off while you're driving.

We are sharp, realistic people. We have senses of humor, I think. Then how to explain why we're here, believing or at least pretending that the pain of loss, of adultery and miscarriage, can be eased by mumbling some mumbo-jumbo and committing to earth a frozen rodent in an extra-large Ziploc bag?

One morning last summer, a guy in my office said, "Guess who's coming to the Ninth Avenue site."

"Madonna," I said. I'd been corresponding with some people trying to pitch a rock video to Madonna—a video filmed at our site with lots of guys walking high steel.

"Better," he said. "Cookie the Clown."

"*The* Cookie?" I asked.

My supervisor was embarrassed when he told me I had to be there. He said, "If, God forbid, Cookie gets flattened, I need someone around I can count on. Come on, Martin. You'll be a hero to your kids."

A hero to my kids: Holly knew very well who Cookie was but pretended not to. Buzzy had only recently switched from clowns to baseball cards, but he hit his forehead with his palm and took an elaborate pratfall and shouted up from the ground: "Cookie the Clown? That's sick!"

This wasn't so long after my stepmother's death. I remember thinking that the steady drizzle falling on Cookie's set was the same rain that fell on Jacksonville. That day I saw it as Cookie's set, although it was our building.

The site was covered with puddles and mud. It wasn't raining too hard for the video crew to shoot, just hard enough to drench them. Cookie put on a slicker and explained to the boys and girls that work goes on in all weather. I was riveted, not by my job or the sight of Cookie in a bulldozer, but because I was standing next to a woman I desperately wanted to talk to. Her name was Marian. She was some kind of trouble-shooter from the show; she was the one who helped Cookie into his slicker. We'd said hello and discussed the rain, but I wanted to say something else. I kept looking up at the sky, rolling my eyes and shrugging.

I hung around till she'd packed everyone into the vans. By then we were totally soaked. We went to a hamburger joint. She asked about my job. I asked her what it was like working for Cookie the Clown. She said you had to be careful. It wouldn't look good for Cookie to sue or be sued.

I said, "There was one year when Holly was small, I don't think Buzzy was born yet; my wife used to say the two people

she hated most in the world were Richard Nixon and Cookie
the Clown." Marian laughed, but I got flustered, quoting Beth,
bringing in the kids. I felt I had ruined everything.

And that, more or less, was that. We said good-bye, we
shook hands. But I couldn't get her off my mind. I would walk
down the street, staring at strangers' faces, wondering how many
perfectly normal people were right at that moment obsessed
with someone they hardly knew and had chosen almost at random to fix on with what, for want of a better word, you might
as well call love. I felt like John Hinckley. I thought it would be
easier to shoot the President than to call her. But finally I called.
We met for lunch. She said that my calling had made her so
happy she was sure she'd be run over by a car on the way to
meet me.

I couldn't tell Beth. Of course she knew something was
wrong. I knew she was suffering, but couldn't explain—that was
the hardest part. I kept asking, Is it me? In fact, I had never
been so present. I had time and patience for everything—un-
raveling the children's shoelaces, settling their fights. I actually
talked to the children, though I can't now recall about what.

One day I persuaded Buzzy to watch Cookie the Clown
with me. He had, as I said, outgrown it. But he was so surprised
I asked, he agreed at once. Cookie was touring an underground
mushroom mine. The millions of fat white mushrooms waiting to be picked were a lovely sight, though not, I imagine, to
the women who worked there, day after day in the dark. One of
the workers told Cookie that each mushroom was different, like
snowflakes. "Like people," Cookie said, and she said, "Very
much like people." "Buzzy," I said, "mushrooms are *nothing* like
people."

Beth said her problems had nothing to do with me. She
felt that her sense of the world had gone sour—curdled, she
said, like milk. She woke me in the middle of the night to talk—

in a hot, dry, panicky voice. Some guy on the street had looked at her a second too long and she'd thought he was going to kill her. She began to hate going out. I said, Talk to someone. Some- one who isn't me.

I have to admit I was grateful at first, glad even for Doug's dental jewelry and Guatemalan poncho. I thought: They'll talk more about jaguar rites, less about me. Even when it struck me that my wife was telling him secrets she didn't tell me, I thought: Well, I deserve it.

Maybe I will never know why Beth decided to get pregnant. At the time I didn't ask; now I no longer can. I am sure it was a choice—we had been married fourteen years; both Holly and Buzzy were planned. For all I know, it was Doug's idea. Maybe Beth thought it would fix things, restore what had gone bad, like those cookbook tricks for fixing the spoiled hollandaise, the overthickened gravy.

And it did, it worked. As soon as Beth told me—as soon as it really sank in—images began streaming through my mind, pictures from our lives. One image stayed with me: when Buzzy was tiny, someone gave us a beanbag chair. Beth used to scoop him out a little hollow in the chair, and the two of them would lie there watching MTV. She'd said the videos were the perfect length for her and Buzzy's attention span. It's always the most trivial things that call us back to ourselves— never what you might expect. When I thought of that—Beth and Buzzy watching MTV—everything that had happened since seemed to dissolve, and I understood that my life with Beth and the children was my real life, and everything else was a dream.

That same night, I told Beth about Marian. I promised it was over. I called Marian and met her for lunch and told her

Beth was pregnant—that was the reason I gave. At first Marian couldn't see what difference it made. I couldn't really explain. Finally she smiled and said she'd learned her lesson from me. From now on, she was sticking to guys in clown noses and size-15 checkered shoes. That was my moment of sharpest regret; because, even then, we could still joke around. At home, nothing was funny.

That wasn't completely true. For that short time Beth was pregnant, something lightened; we could laugh about getting it right this time, or getting a child with all Buzzy's and Holly's worst faults. Then came the miscarriage. After that, we sat in Doug's office. I joked about Murph. I was the only one laughing.

When the traffic lets up, I say into my rearview mirror, "Nancy and Ronald Reagan go into a restaurant. Nancy says, 'I'll have the meat and potatoes.' 'And for the vegetable?' says the waiter. And Nancy says, 'He'll have the meat and potatoes, too.'"

Beth says, "Martin, that's awful." Buzzy bursts out laughing. Holly says, "Why are *you* laughing? I bet you don't even get it."

"Vegetable?" I say. "Ronald Reagan?"

"*I* get it," says Holly. "I think it's really mean."

"Toward Reagan?" I say. "Or toward vegetables in general?"

"I don't know," Holly says. "Toward both." Holly flips back and forth about us, always so as to find fault. Sometimes I'm too soft and sometimes I lack compassion. Sometimes we're too rich and sometimes too poor. Once, in fifth grade, Holly had to bring into school an anecdote from her very early childhood. It was a terrible moment: I couldn't remember one. Beth came up with something for her, but Holly stayed angry at me. I remember telling her that it wasn't a question of love or attention, but strictly a memory problem.

Doug says the whole point of ritual is remembering. He says they fix things in time, in the mind; they work like primitive record-keeping, tying knots in string. He says, "Time is the string, rituals the knots." That doesn't sound right to me. Anything worth its own ritual, you would remember without one. You'd know why you buried that jaguar under the headman's house.

Two exits from my sister's, I ask Beth how we should work this. Get out of the car and start digging a hole? Or wait, let Murph defrost? Sneak off on the sly? Invite everyone? Beth looks at me and blinks. The morning sun is harsh. She says, "Let's play it by ear."

In the uproar of arrival, Murph is forgotten. Buzzy jumps out and races in circles around the car with his cousin Jed. Holly heads across the field to toss sticks for Peg's dogs. My sister runs out and wraps her arms around me and squeezes. It's been so long since anyone hugged me that way, I decide to tell Peg everything, to get her alone and confess.

Eugene, Peg's husband, shakes my hand. His handshake matches the rest of him—bony and a bit stiff. Eugene is a semifamous painter with a reputation built on perfect hard-edge stripes. At least he and Beth can talk about paint. Once during each visit Eugene says you couldn't pay him to live in Manhattan now, he gets so sick of hearing everyone talk real estate. After that, it is impossible for me to mention my work.

When Eugene's paintings are selling, he drinks Mexican beer. When they aren't, it's Genesee. Everyone knows this, and, insofar as you can kid Eugene, we kid him about it. Now Beth and I get our choice of Tecate or Sol. We drink a couple of beers, then Eugene asks Beth to come see his studio. Before I can steer the conversation toward what's on my mind, Peg says,

"I need to talk to you about Dad." She's seen him more recently than I, three weeks ago; on the phone, she'd said he was fine.

Now she says, "Not *exactly* fine. I guess he's okay. But listen. I went into the bathroom, and when I closed the door this *thing* jumped at me from the back of the door, her dressing gown, silk, good lace, very Miss Havisham. It swung out from its hook, puffed a puff of lavender, then swung back."

I wonder why she's telling me this. "You think it was her ghost?"

"Ghost?" says Peg. "I think it was her dressing gown. It's been a year since she died."

"Maybe he's wearing it," I say, and we both start to laugh.

"That's disgusting," says Peg.

We fall silent, drinking our beer. Peg says, "You spend your life eating whole grains and nuts and you come back from a hike, take your first sip of Pepsi in thirty years, and bingo, good night, you're dead." There is an edge in her voice.

I say, "How are things going?" I hold up my Tecate can. "Looks like they're going okay."

"Terrible," she says. "Eugene is seeing someone. The thing is, it happened before, with this same woman. Two years ago."

"Really?" I'm horrified by how hopeful this makes me feel.

"Really," she says, and I understand I can't tell her. Eugene and I should be talking, Beth commiserating with Peg. Peg says, "How are things with you?"

"Fine," I say, and Peg says, "Sure. Beth looks completely zombified."

"Oh," I say, "you noticed. Well, the miscarriage . . ."

Beth and Eugene walk in. After an uneasy silence, Beth says, "It's wonderful. Eugene's doing something totally new." I think, That's not what *I* hear. But Eugene wasn't thinking that. When you talk to Eugene about his work, there are no double entendres, no subtexts.

Beth catches my eye and says, "We should get some stuff out of the car." I know she means Murph.

Beth turns to Peg and Eugene. "I hope this doesn't sound crazy to you," she says, "but Murph, Buzzy's hamster, died, and we needed somewhere to bury it, we brought it . . ."

Eugene looks pleased; the spectacle of city dwellers with nowhere to bury their dead confirms him. I search his face, but there is nothing for me there, no fellow-sinner recognition.

Peg says, "It's not crazy at all. Just bury it deep. Remember, Martin, we had that turtle that died and we just covered it with dirt, and the cat dug it up in the middle of the night and smeared turtle guts all over Mom's kitchen?"

"Where was I?" I ask.

Eugene says, "Let me get you a shovel." Beth and I go to the car. The children are playing in the field. I open the trunk. Murph is in an opaque white plastic shopping bag; his baggie is inside that.

Beth says, "Would you hold Murph a second?" She reaches into the trunk, gets another white plastic bag, and takes out a small container of strawberry yogurt.

"What's that?" I say. "Food for the dead? An afterlife snack for Murph?"

"It's the baby," she says. "The fetus. I saved it. I thought I was being crazy, but I discussed it with Doug. And he said I was right. I think we should bury it. Near Murph."

"You *were* being crazy," I said. "You are. You've gone totally around the bend. You've got a fetus in there? Are you kidding? Remember fifteen years ago we used to laugh at people eating the placenta after hippie communal births? What's gotten into you?"

Beth holds up the yogurt container. All I can think of is the Pepsi can that did my stepmother in. I imagine the interior of the yogurt carton, dim light straining in through the waxy white walls, streaks of tissue and blood. Then I picture the inside of the aluminum can: pitch black, metallic, buzzing.

Beth hands me the container. I don't want to take it, but I can't say no. It feels very light, it feels empty. I shake it, tentatively, tilt it back and forth. Then very slowly I open it. I look at Beth and she smiles at me, a smile I cannot read.

There is nothing inside.

II.
Secrets and Lies

"Keller's Therapy" and "The Whole Truth" each contain a patient-protagonist who lies obsessively to a therapist. In these stories, the patient perceives a danger in revealing the truth about himself. Interestingly, this danger is in merely acknowledging the truth, not in its outcome. The patients' fear is of admitting to *themselves* who they are. What binds these stories together so strikingly is that in both, the patients inadvertently reveal the truth, despite their efforts to hide it. Their therapists are invited to act as detectives, but only in "Keller's Therapy" does the doctor pick up on the clues. In both stories, however, the absence of mutual trust results in hopelessly failed treatments.

Keller's Therapy

Lawrence Block

"I had this dream," Keller said. "Matter of fact, I wrote it down, as you suggested."

"Good."

Before getting on the couch, Keller had removed his jacket and hung it on the back of a chair. He moved from the couch to retrieve his notebook from the jacket's inside breast pocket, then sat on the couch and found the page with the dream on it. He read through his notes rapidly, closed the book and sat there, uncertain of how to proceed.

"As you prefer," said Breen. "Sitting up or lying down, whichever is more comfortable."

"It doesn't matter?"

"Not to me."

And which was more comfortable? A seated posture seemed natural for conversation, while lying down on the couch had the weight of tradition on its side. Keller, who felt driven to give this his best shot, decided to go with tradition. He stretched out, put his feet up.

He said, "I'm living in a house, except it's almost like a castle. Endless passageways and dozens of rooms."

"Is it your house?"

"No, I just live here. In fact, I'm a kind of servant for the family that owns the house. They're almost like royalty."

"And you are a servant."

"Except I have very little to do and I'm treated like an equal. I play tennis with members of the family. There's this tennis court in the back."

"And this is your job? To play tennis?"

"No, that's an example of how they treat me as an equal. I eat at the same table with them, instead of with the servants. My job is the mice."

"The mice?"

"The house is infested with mice. I'm having dinner with the family, I've got a plate piled high with good food, and a waiter in black tie comes in and presents a covered dish. I lift the cover and there's a note on it, and it says, 'Mice.'"

"Just the single word?"

"That's all. I get up from the table and follow the waiter down a long hallway, and I wind up in an unfinished room in the attic. There are tiny mice all over the room—there must be twenty or thirty of them—and I have to kill them."

"How?"

"By crushing them underfoot. That's the quickest and most humane way, but it bothers me and I don't want to do it. But the sooner I finish, the sooner I can get back to my dinner, and I'm hungry."

"So you kill the mice?"

"Yes," Keller said. "One almost gets away, but I stomp on it just as it's running out the door. And then I'm back at the dinner table and everybody's eating and drinking and laughing, and my plate's been cleared away. Then there's a big fuss, and finally they bring back my plate from the kitchen, but it's not the same food as before. It's—"

"Yes?"

"Mice," Keller said. "They're skinned and cooked, but it's a plateful of mice."

"And you eat them?"

"That's when I woke up," Keller said. "And not a moment too soon, I'd say."

"Ah," Breen said. He was a tall man, long-limbed and gawky, wearing chinos, a dark-green shirt and a brown corduroy jacket. He looked to Keller like someone who had been a nerd in high school and who now managed to look distinguished in an eccentric sort of way. He said "Ah" again, folded his hands and asked Keller what he thought the dream meant.

"You're the doctor," Keller said.

"You think it means I'm the doctor?"

"No, I think you're the one who can say what it means. Maybe it just means I shouldn't eat Rocky Road ice cream right before I go to bed."

"Tell me what you think the dream means."

"Maybe I see myself as a cat."

"Or as an exterminator?"

Keller didn't say anything.

"Let's work with this dream on a superficial level," Breen said. "You're employed as a corporate troubleshooter, except that you use another word for it."

"They tend to call us expediters," Keller said, "but troubleshooter is what it amounts to."

"Most of the time there is nothing for you to do. You have considerable opportunity for recreation, for living the good life. For tennis, as it were, and for nourishing yourself at the table of the rich and powerful. Then mice are discovered, and it is at once clear that you are a servant with a job to do."

"I get it," Keller said.

"Go on, then. Explain it to me."

"Well, it's obvious, isn't it? There's a problem and I'm called in and I have to drop what I'm doing and go and deal with it. I have to take abrupt, arbitrary action, and that can involve firing people and closing out entire departments. I have to do it, but it's like stepping on mice. And when I'm back at the table and I want my food—I suppose that's my salary?"

"Your compensation, yes."

"And I get a plate of mice." Keller made a face. "In other words, what? My compensation comes from the destruction of the people I have to cut adrift. My sustenance comes at their expense. So it's a guilt dream?"

"What do you think?"

"I think it's guilt. My profit derives from the misfortunes of others, from the grief I bring to others. That's it, isn't it?"

"On the surface, yes. When we go deeper, perhaps we will begin to discover other connections. With your having chosen this job in the first place, perhaps, and with some aspects of your childhood." He interlaced his fingers and sat back in his chair. "Everything is of a piece, you know. Nothing exists alone and nothing is accidental. Not even your name."

"My name?"

"Peter Stone. Think about it, why don't you, between now and our next session."

"Think about my name?"

"About your name and how it suits you. And"—a reflexive glance at his wristwatch—"I'm afraid that our hour is up."

Jerrold Breen's office was on Central Park West at Ninety-fourth Street. Keller walked to Columbus Avenue, rode a bus five blocks, crossed the street and hailed a taxi. He had the driver go through Central Park, and by the time he got out of the cab at Fiftieth Street, he was reasonably certain he hadn't been followed. He bought coffee in a deli and stood on the sidewalk, keeping an eye open while he drank it. Then he walked to the building where he lived, on First Avenue between Forty-eighth and Forty-ninth. It was a prewar high-rise with an art deco lobby and an attended elevator. "Ah, Mr. Keller," the attendant said. "A beautiful day, yes?"

"Beautiful," Keller agreed.

Keller had a one-bedroom apartment on the nineteenth floor. He could look out his window and see the U.N. building, the East River, the borough of Queens. On the first Sunday in November he could watch the runners streaming across the Queensboro Bridge, just a couple of miles past the midpoint of the New York Marathon.

It was a spectacle Keller tried not to miss. He would sit at his window for hours while thousands of them passed through his field of vision, first the world-class runners, then the middle-of-the-pack plodders and finally the slowest of the slow, some walking, some hobbling. They started in Staten Island and finished in Central Park, and all he saw was a few hundred yards of their ordeal as they made their way over the bridge and into Manhattan. The sight always moved him to tears, though he could not have said why.

Maybe it was something to talk about with Breen.

It was a woman who had led him to the therapist's couch, an aerobics instructor named Donna. Keller had met her at the gym. They'd had a couple of dates and had been to bed a couple of times, enough to establish their sexual incompatibility. Keller still went to the same gym two or three times a week to raise and lower heavy metal objects, and when he ran into her, they were friendly.

One time, just back from a trip somewhere, he must have rattled on about what a nice town it was. "Keller," she said, "if there was ever a born New Yorker, you're it. You know that, don't you?"

"I suppose so."

"But you always have this fantasy of living the good life in Elephant, Montana. Every place you go, you dream up a whole life to go with it."

"Is that bad?"

"Who's saying it's bad? But I bet you could have fun with it in therapy."

"You think I need to be in therapy?"

"I think you'd get a lot out of therapy," she said. "Look, you come here, right? You climb the stair monster, you use the Nautilus."

"Mostly free weights."

"Whatever. You don't do this because you're a physical wreck."

"I do it to stay in shape. So?"

"So I see you as closed in and trying to reach out," she said. "Going all over the country, getting real estate agents to show you houses that you're not going to buy."

"That was only a couple of times. And what's so bad about it, anyway? It passes the time."

"You do these things and don't know why," she said. "You know what therapy is? It's an adventure, it's a voyage of discovery. And it's like going to the gym. Look, forget it. The whole thing's pointless unless you're interested."

"Maybe I'm interested," he said.

Donna, not surprisingly, was in therapy herself. But her therapist was a woman, and they agreed that he'd be more comfortable working with a man. Her ex-husband had been very fond of his therapist, a West Side psychologist named Breen. Donna had never met the man, and she wasn't on the best of terms with her ex, but . . .

"That's all right," Keller said. "I'll call him myself."

He'd called Breen, using Donna's ex-husband's name as a reference. "I doubt that he even knows me by name," Keller said. "We got to talking a while back at a party and I haven't seen him since. But something he said struck a chord with me and, well, I thought I ought to explore it."

"Intuition is always a powerful teacher," Breen said.

Keller made an appointment, giving his name as Peter Stone. In his first session he talked about his work for a large and unnamed conglomerate. "They're a little old-fashioned when it comes to psychotherapy," he told Breen. "So I'm not going to give you an address or telephone number, and I'll pay for each session in cash."

"Your life is filled with secrets," Breen said.

"I'm afraid it is. My work demands it."

"This is a place where you can be honest and open. The idea is to uncover the secrets you've been keeping from yourself. Here you are protected by the sanctity of the confessional, but it's not my task to grant absolution. Ultimately, you absolve yourself."

"Well," Keller said.

"Meanwhile, you have secrets to keep. I respect that. I won't need your address or telephone number unless I'm forced to cancel an appointment. I suggest you call to confirm your sessions an hour or two ahead of time, or you can take the chance of an occasional wasted trip. If you have to cancel an appointment, be sure to give twenty-four hours' notice. Or I'll have to charge you for the missed session."

"That's fair," Keller said.

He went twice a week. Mondays and Thursdays at two in the afternoon. It was hard to tell what they were accomplishing. Sometimes Keller relaxed completely on the sofa, talking freely and honestly about his childhood. Other times he expe-

rienced the fifty-minute session as a balancing act: He yearned
to tell everything and was compelled to keep it all a secret.

No one knew he was doing this. Once, when he ran into
Donna, she asked if he'd ever given the shrink a call, and he'd
shrugged sheepishly and said he hadn't. "I thought about it,"
he said, "but then somebody told me about this masseuse—she
does a combination of Swedish and shiatsu—and I have to tell
you, I think it does me more good than somebody poking and
probing at the inside of my head."

"Oh, Keller," she'd said, not without affection. "Don't
ever change."

It was on a Monday that he recounted the dream about the mice.
Wednesday morning his phone rang, and it was Dot. "He wants
to see you," she said.

"Be right out," he said.

He put on a tie and jacket and caught a cab to Grand
Central and a train to White Plains. There he caught another
cab and told the driver to head out Washington Boulevard and
to let him off at the corner of Norwalk. After the cab drove
off, he walked up Norwalk to Taunton Place and turned left.
The second house on the right was an old Victorian with a
wraparound porch. He rang the bell and Dot let him in.

"The upstairs den, Keller," she said. "He's expecting
you."

He went upstairs, and forty minutes later he came down
again. A young man named Louis drove him back to the station, and on the way they chatted about a recent boxing match
they'd both seen on ESPN. "What I wish," Louis said, "is that
they had, like, a mute button on the remote, except what it would
do is mute the announcers but you'd still hear the crowd noise
and the punches landing. What you wouldn't have is the con-

stant yammer-yammer-yammer in your ear." Keller wondered if they could do that. "I don't see why not," Louis said. "They can do everything else. If you can put a man on the moon, you ought to be able to shut up Al Bernstein."

Keller took a train back to New York and walked to his apartment. He made a couple of phone calls and packed a bag. At 3:30 he went downstairs, walked half a block, hailed a cab to JFK and picked up his boarding pass for American's 5:55 flight to Tucson.

In the departure lounge he remembered his appointment with Breen. He called to cancel the Thursday session. Since it was less than twenty-four hours away, Breen said, he'd have to charge him for the missed session, unless he was able to book someone else into the slot.

"Don't worry about it," Keller told him. "I hope I'll be back in time for my Monday appointment, but it's always hard to know how long these things are going to take. If I can't make it, I should at least be able to give you twenty-four hours' notice."

He changed planes in Dallas and got to Tucson shortly before midnight. He had no luggage aside from the piece he was carrying, but he went to the baggage-claim area anyway. A rail-thin man with a broad-brimmed straw hat held a hand-lettered sign that read NOSCAASI. Keller watched the man for a few minutes and observed that no one else was watching him. He went up to him and said, "You know, I was figuring it out the whole way to Dallas. What I came up with, it's Isaacson spelled backward."

"That's it," the man said. "That's exactly it." He seemed impressed, as if Keller had cracked the Japanese naval code. He said, "You didn't check a bag, did you? I didn't think so. The car's this way."

In the car the man showed Keller three photographs all of the same man, heavyset, dark, with glossy black hair and a greedy pig face. Bushy mustache, bushy eyebrows and enlarged pores on his nose.

"That's Rollie Vasquez," the man said. "Son of a bitch wouldn't exactly win a beauty contest, would he?"

"I guess not."

"Let's go," the man said. "Show you where he lives, where he eats, where he gets his ashes hauled. Rollie Vasquez, this is your life."

Two hours later, the man dropped Keller at a Ramada Inn and gave him a room key and a car key. "You're all checked in," he said. "Car's parked at the foot of the staircase closest to your room. She's a Mitsubishi Eclipse, pretty decent transportation. Color's supposed to be silver-blue, but she says gray on the papers. Registration's in the glove compartment."

"There was supposed to be something else."

"That's in the glove compartment, too. Locked, of course, but the one key fits the ignition and the glove compartment. And the doors and the trunk, too. And if you turn the key upside down, it'll still fit, because there's no up or down to it. You really got to hand it to those Japs."

"What'll they think of next?"

"Well, it may not seem like much," the man said, "but all the time you waste making sure you got the right key, then making sure you got the right side up—"

"It adds up."

"It does," the man said. "Now you have a full tank of gas. It takes regular, but what's in there's enough to take you upward of four hundred miles."

"How're the tires? Never mind. Just a joke."

"And a good one," the man said. "'How're the tires?' I like that."

* * *

The car was where it was supposed to be, and the glove compartment held the registration and a semiautomatic pistol, a .22-caliber Horstmann Sun Dog, loaded, with a spare clip lying alongside it. Keller slipped the gun and the spare clip into his carry-on, locked the car and went to his room without passing the front desk.

After a shower, he sat down and put his feet up on the coffee table. It was all arranged, and that made it simpler, but sometimes he liked it better the other way, when all he had was a name and address and no one to smooth the way for him. This was simple, all right, but who knew what traces were being left? Who knew what kind of history the gun had, or what the string bean with the NOSCAASI sign would say if the police picked him up and shook him?

All the more reason to do it quickly. He watched enough of an old movie on cable to ready him for sleep. When he woke up, he went out to the car and took his bag with him. He expected to return to his room, but if he didn't, he would be leaving nothing behind, not even a fingerprint.

He stopped at Denny's for breakfast. Around one he had lunch at a Mexican place on Figueroa. In the late afternoon he drove into the foothills north of the city, and he was still there when the sun went down. Then he drove back to the Ramada.

That was Thursday. Friday morning the phone rang while he was shaving. He let it ring. It rang again as he was showering. He let it ring. It rang again just as he was ready to leave. He didn't answer it this time, either, but went around wiping surfaces a second time with a hand towel. Then he went out to the car.

At two that afternoon he followed Rolando Vasquez into the men's room of the Saguaro Lanes bowling alley and shot him three times in the head. The little gun didn't make much noise, not even in the confines of the tiled lavatory. Earlier he had fashioned an improvised suppressor by wrapping the barrel of the gun with a space-age insulating material that muffled the gun's report without adding much weight or bulk. If you could do that, he thought, you ought to be able to shut up Al Bernstein.

He left Vasquez propped in a stall, left the gun in a storm drain half a mile away, left the car in the long-term lot at the airport. Flying home, he wondered why they had needed him in the first place. They'd supplied the car and the gun and the finger man. Why not do it themselves? Did they really need to bring him all the way from New York to step on the mouse?

"You said to think about my name," he told Breen. "The significance of it. But I don't see how it could have any significance. It's not as I chose it."

"Let me suggest something," Breen said. "There is a metaphysical principle which holds that we choose everything about our lives, that we select the parents we are born to, that everything which happens in our lives is a manifestation of our wills. Thus, there are no accidents, no coincidences."

"I don't know if I believe that."

"You don't have to. We'll just take it as a postulate. So assuming that you chose the name Peter Stone, what does your choice tell us?"

Keller, stretched full length upon the couch, was not enjoying this. "Well, a peter's a penis," he said reluctantly. "A stone peter would be an erection, wouldn't it?"

"Would it?"

"So I suppose a guy who decides to call himself Peter Stone would have something to prove. Anxiety about his virility. Is that what you want me to say?"

"I want you to say whatever you wish," Breen said. "Are you anxious about your virility?"

"I never thought I was," Keller said. "Of course, it's hard to say how much anxiety I might have had back before I was born, around the time I was picking my parents and deciding what name they should choose for me. At that age I probably had a certain amount of difficulty maintaining an erection, so I guess I had a lot to be anxious about."

"And now?"

"I don't have a performance problem, if that's the question. I'm not the way I was in my teens, ready to go three or four times a night, but then, who in his right mind would want to? I can generally get the job done."

"You get the job done."

"Right."

"You perform."

"Is there something wrong with that?"

"What do you think?"

"Don't do that," Keller said. "Don't answer a question with a question. If I ask a question and you don't want to respond, just leave it alone. But don't turn it back on me. It's irritating."

Breen said, "You perform, you get the job done. But what do you feel, Mr. Peter Stone?"

"Feel?"

"It is unquestionably true that peter is a colloquialism for the penis, but it has an earlier meaning. Do you recall Christ's words to Peter? 'Thou art Peter, and upon this rock I shall build my church.' Because Peter *means* rock. Our Lord was making a pun. So your first name means rock and your last name is Stone. What does that give us? Rock and stone. Hard, unyielding, obdurate. Insensitive. Unfeeling—"

"Stop," Keller said.

"In the dream, when you kill the mice, what do you feel?"

"Nothing. I just want to get the job done."

"Do you feel their pain? Do you feel pride in your accomplishment, satisfaction in a job well done? Do you feel a thrill, a sexual pleasure, in their deaths?"

"Nothing," Keller said. "I feel nothing. Could we stop for a moment?"

"What do you feel right now?"

"I'm just a little sick to my stomach, that's all."

"Do you want to use the bathroom? Shall I get you a glass of water?"

"No, I'm all right. It's better when I sit up. It'll pass. It's passing already."

Sitting at his window, watching not the marathoners but cars streaming over the Queensboro Bridge, Keller thought about names. What was particularly annoying, he thought, was that he didn't need to be under the care of a board-certified metaphysician to acknowledge the implications of the name Peter Stone. He had chosen it, but not in the manner of a soul deciding what parents to be born to and planting names in their heads. He had picked the name when he called to make his initial appointment with Jerrold Breen. "Name?" Breen had demanded. "Stone," he had replied. "Peter Stone."

Thing is, he wasn't stupid. Cold, unyielding, insensitive, but not stupid. If you wanted to play the name game, you didn't have to limit yourself to the alias he had selected. You could have plenty of fun with the name he'd had all his life.

His full name was John Paul Keller, but no one called him anything but Keller, and few people even knew his first and middle names. His apartment lease and most of the cards in his wallet showed his name as J. P. Keller. Just Plain Keller was what people called him, men and women alike. ("The upstairs den, Keller. He's expecting you." "Oh, Keller, don't ever change." "I don't know how to say this, Keller, but I'm simply not getting my needs met in this relationship.")

Keller. In German it meant cellar, or tavern. But the hell with that. You didn't need to know what it meant in a foreign language. Change a vowel. Killer.

Clear enough, wasn't it?

On the couch, eyes closed, Keller said, "I guess the therapy's working."

"Why do you say that?"

"I met a girl last night, bought her a couple of drinks and went home with her. We went to bed and I couldn't do anything."

"You couldn't do anything?"

"Well, if you want to be technical, there were things I could have done. I could have typed a letter or sent out for a pizza. I could have sung "Melancholy Baby." But I couldn't do what we'd both been hoping I would do, which was to have sex."

"You were impotent?"

"You know, you're very sharp. You never miss a trick."

"You blame me for your impotence," Breen said.

"Do I? I don't know about that. I'm not sure I even blame myself. To tell you the truth, I was more amused than devastated. And she wasn't upset, perhaps out of relief that I wasn't upset. But just so nothing like that happens again, I've decided to change my name to Dick Hardin."

"What was your father's name?"

"My father," Keller said. "Jesus, what a question. Where did that come from?"

Breen didn't say anything.

Neither, for several minutes, did Keller. Then, eyes closed, he said, "I never knew my father. He was a soldier. He was killed in action before I was born. Or he was shipped overseas before I was born and killed when I was a few months old. Or possibly he was home when I was born or came home on leave when I was small, and he held me on his knee and told me he was proud of me."

"You have such a memory?"

"No," Keller said. "The only memory I have is of my mother telling me about him, and that's the source of the confusion, because she told me different things at different times. Either he was killed before I was born or shortly after, and either he died without seeing me or he saw me one time and sat me on his knee. She was a good woman, but she was vague about a lot of things. The one thing she was completely clear on was that he was a soldier, and he was killed over there."

"And his name?"

Was Keller, he thought. "Same as mine," he said. "But forget the name, this is more important than the name. Listen to this. She had a picture of him, a head-and-shoulders shot, this good-looking young soldier in a uniform and wearing a cap, the kind that folds flat when you take it off. The picture was in a gold frame on her dresser when I was a little kid.

"And then one day the picture wasn't there anymore. 'It's gone,' she said. And that was all she would say on the subject. I was older then. I must have been seven or eight years old.

"Couple of years later I got a dog. I named him Soldier, after my father. Years after that, two things occurred to me. One, Soldier's a funny thing to call a dog. Two, whoever heard of naming a dog after his father? But at the time it didn't seem the least bit unusual to me."

"What happened to the dog?"

"He became impotent. Shut up, will you? What I'm getting to is a lot more important than the dog. When I was fourteen, fifteen years old, I used to work after school helping out this guy who did odd jobs in the neighborhood. Cleaning out basements and attics, hauling trash, that sort of thing. One time this notions store went out of business, the owner must have died, and we were cleaning out the basement for the new tenant. Boxes of junk all over the place, and we had to go through everything, because part of how this guy made his money was selling off the stuff he got paid to haul. But you couldn't go through all this crap too thoroughly or you were wasting time.

"I was checking out this one box, and what do I pull out but a framed picture of my father. The very same picture that sat on my mother's dresser, him in his uniform and his military cap, the picture that disappeared, it's even in the same frame, and what's it doing there?"

Not a word from Breen.

"I can still remember how I felt. Stunned, like *Twilight Zone* time. Then I reach back into the box and pull out the first thing I touch, and it's the same picture in the same frame.

"The box is full of framed pictures. About half of them are the solider, and the others are a fresh-faced blonde with her hair in a pageboy and a big smile on her face. It was a box of frames. They used to package inexpensive frames that way, with photos in them for display. For all I know they still do. My mother must have bought a frame in a five-and-dime and told me it was my father. Then when I got a little older, she got rid of it.

"I took one of the framed photos home with me. I didn't say anything to her. I didn't show it to her, but I kept it around for a while. I found out the photo dated from World War Two. In other words, it couldn't have been a picture of my father, because he would have been wearing a different uniform.

"By this time I think I already knew that the story she told me about my father was, well, a story. I don't believe she knew who my father was. I think she got drunk and went with somebody, or maybe there were several different men. What difference does it make? She moved to another town, she told people she was married, that her husband was in the service or that he was dead, whatever she told them."

"How do you feel about it?"

"How do I feel about it?" Keller shook his head. "If I slammed my hand in a cab door, you'd ask me how I felt about it."

"And you'd be stuck for an answer," Breen said. "Here's a question for you: Who was your father?"

"I just told you."

"But *someone* fathered you. Whether or not you knew him, whether or not your mother knew who he was, there was a particular man who planted the seed that grew into you. Unless you believe yourself to be the second coming of Christ."

"No," Keller said. "That's one delusion I've been spared."

"So tell me who he was, this man who spawned you. Not on the basis of what you were told or what you've managed to figure out. I'm not asking the part of you that thinks and reasons. I'm asking the part of you that simply knows. Who was your father? What was your father?"

"He was a soldier," Keller said.

Keller, walking uptown on Second Avenue, found himself standing in front of a pet shop, watching a couple of puppies cavorting in the window.

He went inside. One wall was given over to stacked cages of puppies and kittens. Keller felt his spirits sink as he looked into the cages. Waves of sadness rocked him.

He turned away and looked at the other pets. Birds in cages, gerbils and snakes in dry aquariums, tanks of tropical fish.

He felt all right about them; it was the puppies that he couldn't bear to look at.

He left the store. The next day he went to an animal shelter and walked past cages of dogs waiting to be adopted. This time the sadness was overwhelming, and he felt its physical pressure against his chest. Something must have shown on his face, because the young woman in charge asked him if he was all right.

"Just a dizzy spell," he said.

In the office she told him that they could probably accommodate him if he was especially interested in a particular breed. They could keep his name on file, and when a specimen of that breed became available . . .

"I don't think I can have a pet," he said. "I travel too much. I can't handle the responsibility." The woman didn't respond, and Keller's words echoed in her silence. "But I want to make a donation," he said. "I want to support the work you do."

He got out his wallet, pulled bills from it, handed them to her without counting them. "An anonymous donation," he said. "I don't want a receipt. I'm sorry for taking your time. I'm sorry I can't adopt a dog. Thank you. Thank you very much."

She was saying something, but he didn't listen. He hurried out of there.

"'I want to support the work you do.' That's what I told her, and then I rushed out of there because I didn't want her thanking me. Or asking questions."

"What would she ask?"

"I don't know," Keller said. He rolled over on the couch, facing away from Breen, facing the wall. "'I want to support the work you do.' But I don't know what their work is. They find homes for some animals, and what do they do with the others? Put them to sleep?"

"Perhaps."

"What do I want to support? The placement or the killing?"

"You tell me."

"I tell you too much as it is," Keller said.

"Or not enough."

Keller didn't say anything.

"Why did it sadden you to see the dogs in their cages?"

"I felt their sadness."

"One feels only one's own sadness. Why is it sad to you, a dog in a cage? Are you in a cage?"

"No."

"Your dog, Soldier. Tell me about him."

"All right," Keller said. "I guess I could do that."

A session or two later, Breen said, "You have never been married?"

"No."

"I was married."

"Oh?"

"For eight years. She was my receptionist. She booked my appointments, showed clients to the waiting room. Now I have no receptionist. A machine answers the phone. I check the machine between appointments and take and return calls at that time. If I had had a machine in the first place, I'd have been spared a lot of agony."

"It wasn't a good marriage?"

Breen didn't seem to have heard the question. "I wanted children. She had three abortions in eight years and never told me. Never said a word. Then one day she threw it in my face. I'd been to a doctor, I'd had tests and all indications were that I was fertile, with a high sperm count and extremely motile sperm. So I wanted her to see a doctor. 'You fool. I've killed three of your babies already, so why don't you leave me alone?' I told her I wanted a divorce. She said it would cost me."

"And?"

"We've been divorced for nine years. Every month I write an alimony check and put it in the mail. If it were up to me, I'd burn the money."

Breen fell silent. After a moment Keller said, "Why are you telling me all this?"

"No reason."

"Is it supposed to relate to something in my psyche? Am I supposed to make a connection, clap my hand to my forehead and say, 'Of course, of course! I've been so blind!'"

"You confide in me," Breen said. "It seems only fitting that I confide in you."

Dot called a couple of days later. Keller took a train to White Plains, where Louis met him at the station and drove him to the house on Taunton Place. Later, Louis drove him back to the train station and he returned to the city. He timed his call to Breen so that he got the man's machine. "This is Peter Stone," he said. "I'm flying to San Diego on business. I'll have to miss my next appointment and possibly the one after that. I'll try to let you know."

He hung up, packed a bag and rode the Amtrak to Philadelphia.

No one met his train. The man in White Plains had shown him a photograph and given him a slip of paper with a name and address on it. The man in question managed an adult bookstore a few blocks from Independence Hall. There was a tavern across the street, a perfect vantage point, but one look inside made it clear to Keller that he couldn't spend time there without calling attention to himself, not unless he first got rid of his tie and jacket and spent twenty minutes rolling around in the gutter.

Down the street Keller found a diner, and if he sat at the far end, he could keep an eye on the bookstore's mirrored front windows. He had a cup of coffee, then walked across the street to the bookstore, where two men were on duty. One was a sad-eyed youth from India or Pakistan, the other the jowly, slightly exophthalmic fellow in the photo Keller had seen in White Plains.

Keller walked past a wall of videocassettes and leafed through a display of magazines. He had been there for about fifteen minutes when the kid said he was going for his dinner. The older man said, "Oh, it's that time already, huh? O.K., but make sure you're back by seven for a change, will you?"

Keller looked at his watch. It was six o'clock. The only other customers were closeted in video booths in the back. Still, the kid had had a look at him, and what was the big hurry, anyway?

He grabbed a couple of magazines and paid for them. The jowly man bagged them and sealed the bag with a strip of tape. Keller stowed his purchase in his carry-on and went to find a hotel.

The next day he went to a museum and a movie and arrived at the bookstore at ten minutes after six. The young clerk was gone, presumably having a plate of curry somewhere. The jowly man was behind the counter and there were three customers in the store, two checking the video selections, one looking at the magazines.

Keller browsed, hoping they would clear out. At one point he was standing in front of a wall of videos and it turned into a wall of caged puppies. It was momentary, and he couldn't tell if it was a genuine hallucination or just some sort of flashback. Whatever it was, he didn't like it.

One customer left, but the other two lingered, and then someone new came in off the street. The Indian kid was due back in half an hour, and who knew if he would take his full hour, anyway?

Keller approached the counter, trying to look a little more nervous than he felt. Shifty eyes, furtive glances. Pitching his voice low, he said, "Talk to you in private?"

"About what?"

Eyes down, shoulders drawn in, he said, "Something special."

"If it's got to do with little kids," the man said, "no disrespect intended, but I don't know nothing about it, I don't want to know nothing about it and I wouldn't even know where to steer you."

"Nothing like that," Keller said.

They went into a room in back. The jowly man closed the door, and as he was turning around, Keller hit him with the edge of his hand at the juncture of his neck and shoulder. The man's knees buckled, and in an instant Keller had a loop of wire around his neck. In another minute he was out the door, and within the hour he was on the northbound Metroliner.

When he got home, he realized he still had the magazines in his bag. That was sloppy. He should have discarded them the previous night, but he'd simply forgotten them and never even unsealed the package.

Nor could he find a reason to unseal it now. He carried it down the hall and dropped it into the incinerator. Back in his apartment, he fixed himself a weak scotch and water and watched a documentary on the Discovery Channel. The vanishing rain forest, one more goddamned thing to worry about.

* * *

"Oedipus," Jerrold Breen said, holding his hands in front of his chest, his fingertips pressed together. "I presume you know the story. He killed his father and married his mother."

"Two pitfalls I've thus far managed to avoid."

"Indeed," Breen said. "But have you? When you fly off somewhere in your official capacity as corporate expediter, when you shoot trouble, as it were, what exactly are you doing? You fire people, you cashier divisions, close plants, rearrange lives. Is that a fair description?"

"I suppose so."

"There's an implied violence. Firing a man, terminating his career, is the symbolic equivalent of killing him. And he's a stranger, and I shouldn't doubt that the more important of these men are more often than not older than you, isn't that so?"

"What's the point?"

"When you do what you do, it's as if you are seeking out and killing your unknown father."

"I don't know," Keller said. "Isn't that a little far-fetched?"

"And your relationships with women," Breen went on, "have a strong Oedipal component. Your mother was a vague and unfocused woman, incompletely present in your life, incapable of connecting with others. Your own relationships with women are likewise out of focus. Your problems with impotence—"

"Once!"

"Are a natural consequence of this confusion. Your mother is dead now, isn't that so?"

"Yes."

"And your father is not to be found and almost certainly deceased. What's called for, Peter, is an act specifically designed to reverse this pattern on a symbolic level."

"I don't follow you."

"It's a subtle point," Breen admitted. He crossed his legs, propped an elbow on a knee, extended his thumb and rested his bony chin on it. Keller thought, not for the first time, that Breen must have been a stork in a prior life. "If there were a male figure in your life," Breen went on, "preferably at least a few years your senior, someone playing a paternal role vis-à-vis yourself, someone to whom you turn for advice and direction."

Keller thought of the man in White Plains.

"Instead of killing this man," Breen said, "symbolically, I am speaking symbolically throughout, but instead of killing him as you have done with father figures in the past, you might do something to *nourish* this man."

Cook a meal for the man in White Plains? Buy him a hamburger? Toss him a salad?

"Perhaps you could think of a way to use your talents to this man's benefit instead of to his detriment," Breen went on. He drew a handkerchief from his pocket and mopped his forehead. "Perhaps there is a woman in his life—your mother, symbolically—and perhaps she is a source of great pain to your father. So, instead of making love to her and slaying him, like Oedipus, you might reverse the usual things by, uh, showing love to him and slaying her."

"Oh," Keller said.

"Symbolically, that is to say."

"Symbolically," Keller said.

A week later Breen handed Keller a photograph. "This is called the thematic apperception test," Breen said. "You look at the photograph and make up a story about it."

"What kind of story?"

"Any kind at all," Breen said. "This is an exercise in imagination. You look at the subject of the photograph and imagine what sort of woman she is and what she is doing."

The photo was in color and showed a rather elegant brunette dressed in tailored clothing. She had a dog on a leash. The dog was medium-sized, with a chunky body and an alert expression. It was the color that dog people call blue and that everyone else calls gray.

"It's a woman and a dog," Keller said.

"Very good."

Keller took a breath. "The dog can talk," he said, "but he won't do it in front of other people. The woman made a fool of herself once when she tried to show him off. Now she knows better. When they're alone, he talks a blue streak, and the son of a bitch has an opinion on everything from the real cause of the Thirty Years' War to the best recipe for lasagna."

"He's quite a dog," Breen said.

"Yes, and now the woman doesn't want people to know he can talk, because she's afraid they might take him away from her. In this picture they're in a park. It looks like Central Park."

"Or perhaps Washington Square."

"It could be Washington Square," Keller agreed. "The woman is crazy about the dog. The dog's not so sure about the woman."

"And what do you think about the woman?"

"She's attractive," Keller said.

"On the surface," Breen said. "Underneath, it's another story, believe me. Where do you suppose she lives?"

Keller gave it some thought. "Cleveland," he said.

"Cleveland? Why Cleveland, for God's sake?"

"Everybody's got to be someplace."

"If I were taking this test," Breen said, "I'd probably imagine the woman living at the foot of Fifth Avenue, at Washington Square. I'd have her living at Number One Fifth Avenue, perhaps because I'm familiar with that building. You see, I once lived there."

"Oh?"

"In a spacious apartment on a high floor. And once a month," he continued, "I write an enormous check and mail it to that address, which used to be mine. So it's only natural that I would have this particular building in mind, especially when I look at this particular photo." His eyes met Keller's. "You have a question, don't you? Go ahead and ask it."

"What breed is the dog?"

"As it happens," Breen said, "it's an Australian cattle dog. Looks like a mongrel, doesn't it? Believe me, it doesn't talk. But why don't you hang on to that photograph?"

"All right."

"You're making really fine progress in therapy," Breen said. "I want to acknowledge you for the work you're doing. And I just know you'll do the right thing."

A few days later Keller was sitting on a park bench in Washington Square. He folded his newspaper and walked over to a dark-haired woman wearing a blazer and a beret. "Excuse me," he said, "but isn't that an Australian cattle dog?"

"That's right," she said.

"It's a handsome animal," he said. "You don't see many of them."

"Most people think he's a mutt. It's such an esoteric breed. Do you own one yourself?"

"I did. My ex-wife got custody."

"How sad for you."

"Sadder still for the dog. His name was Soldier. Is Soldier, unless she's changed it."

"This fellow's name is Nelson. That's his call name. Of course, the name on the papers is a real mouthful."

"Do you show him?"

"He's seen it all," she said. "You can't show him a thing."

"I went down to the Village last week," Keller said, "and the damnedest thing happened. I met a woman in the park."

"Is that the damnedest thing?"

"Well, it's unusual for me. I meet women at bars and parties, or someone introduces us. But we met and talked, and then I ran into her the following morning. I bought her a cappuccino."

"You just happened to run into her on two successive days."

"Yes."

"In the Village?"

"It's where I live."

Breen frowned. "You shouldn't be seen with her, should you?"

"Why not?"

"Don't you think it's dangerous?"

"All it's cost me so far," Keller said, "is the price of a cappuccino."

"I thought we had an understanding."

"An understanding?"

"You don't live in the Village," Breen said. "I know where you live. Don't look surprised. The first time you left here I watched you from the window. You behaved as though you were trying to avoid being followed. So I took my time, and when you stopped taking precautions, I followed you. It wasn't that difficult."

"Why follow me?"

"To find out who you are. Your name is Keller, you live at Eight-six-five First Avenue. I already knew what you were. Anybody might have known just from listening to your dreams. And paying in cash, and the sudden business trips. I still don't know who employs you, crime bosses or the government, but what difference does it make? Have you been to bed with my wife?"

"Your ex-wife?"

"Answer the question."

"Yes, I have."

"Jesus Christ. And were you able to perform?"

"Yes."

"Why the smile?"

"I was just thinking," Keller said, "that it was quite a performance."

Breen was silent for a long moment, his eyes fixed on a spot above and to the right of Keller's shoulder. Then he said, "This is profoundly disappointing. I hoped you would find the strength to transcend the Oedipal myth, not merely reenact it. You've had fun, haven't you? What a naughty boy you've been. What a triumph you've scored over your symbolic father. You've taken this woman to bed. No doubt you have visions of getting her pregnant, so that she can give you what she cruelly denied him. Eh?"

"Never occurred to me."

"It would, sooner or later." Breen leaned forward, concern showing on his face. "I hate to see you sabotaging your therapeutic progress this way," he said. "You were doing so *well.*"

From the bedroom window you could look down at Washington Square Park. There were plenty of dogs there now, but none were Australian cattle dogs.

"Some view," Keller said. "Some apartment."

"Believe me," she said, "I earned it. You're getting dressed. Are you going somewhere?"

"Just feeling a little restless. O.K. if I take Nelson for a walk?"

"You're spoiling him," she said. "You're spoiling both of us."

On a Wednesday morning, Keller took a cab to La Guardia and a plane to St. Louis. He had a cup of coffee with an associate of the man in White Plains and caught an evening flight back to New York. He took another cab directly to the apartment building at the foot of Fifth Avenue.

"I'm Peter Stone," he said to the doorman. "Mrs. Breen is expecting me."

The doorman stared.

"Mrs. Breen," Keller said. "In Seventeen-J."

"Jesus."

"Is something the matter?"

"I guess you haven't heard," the doorman said. "I wish it wasn't me who had to tell you."

"You killed her," he said.

"That's ridiculous," Breen told Keller. "She killed herself. She threw herself out the window. If you want my professional opinion, she was suffering from depression."

"If you want *my* professional opinion," Keller said, "she had help."

"I wouldn't advance that argument if I were you," Breen said. "If the police were to look for a murderer, they might look long and hard at Mr. Stone-hyphen-Keller, the stone killer. And I might have to tell them how the usual process of transference went awry, how you became obsessed with me and my personal life, how I couldn't dissuade you from some insane plan to reverse the Oedipus complex. And then

they might ask you why you employ an alias and just how you
make your living. Do you see why it might be best to let sleeping dogs lie?"

As if on cue, Nelson stepped out from behind the desk.
He caught sight of Keller and his tail began to wag.

"Sit," Breen said. "You see? He's well trained. You might
take a seat yourself?"

"I'll stand. You killed her and then you walked off with
the dog."

Breen sighed. "The police found the dog in the apartment, whimpering in front of the open window. After I identified the body and told them about her previous suicide attempts,
I volunteered to take the dog home with me. There was no one
else to look after him."

"I would have taken him," Keller said.

"But that won't be necessary, will it? You won't be called
upon to walk my dog or make love to my wife or bed down in
my apartment. Your services are no longer required." Breen
seemed to recoil at the harshness of his own words. His face
softened. "You'll be able to get back to the far more important
business of therapy. In fact"—he indicated the couch—"why
not stretch out right now?"

"That's not a bad idea. First, though, could you put the
dog in the other room?"

"Not afraid he'll interrupt, are you? Just a little joke. He
can wait in the outer office. There you go, Nelson. Good
dog . . . oh, no. How *dare* you bring a gun. Put that down
immediately."

"I don't think so."

"For God's sake, why kill me? I'm not your father, I'm
your therapist. It makes no sense for you to kill me. You have
nothing to gain and everything to lose. It's completely irrational. It's worse than that, it's neurotically self-destructive."

"I guess I'm not cured yet."

"What's that, gallows humor? It happens to be true. You're a long way from cured, my friend. As a matter of fact, I would say you're approaching a psychotherapeutic crisis. How will you get through it if you shoot me?"

Keller went to the window, flung it wide open. "I'm not going to shoot you," he said.

"I've never been the least bit suicidal," Breen said, pressing his back against a wall of bookshelves. "Never."

"You've grown despondent over the death of your ex-wife."

"That's sickening, just sickening. And who would believe it?"

"We'll see," Keller told him. "As far as the therapeutic crisis is concerned, well, we'll see about that, too. I'll think of something."

The woman at the animal shelter said, "Talk about coincidence. One day you come in and put your name down for an Australian cattle dog. You know, that's quite an uncommon breed in this country."

"You don't see many of them."

"And what came in this morning? A perfectly lovely Australian cattle dog. You could have knocked me over with a sledgehammer. Isn't he a beauty?"

"He certainly is."

"He's been whimpering ever since he got here. It's very sad. His owner died and there was nobody to keep him. My goodness, look how he went right to you. I think he likes you."

"I'd say we're made for each other."

"I believe it. His name is Nelson, but you can change it, of course."

"Nelson," he said. The dog's ears perked up. Keller reached to give him a scratch. "No, I don't think I'll have to change it. Who was Nelson, anyway? Some kind of English hero, wasn't he? A famous general or something?"

"I think an admiral."

"It rings a muted bell," he said. "Not a soldier but a sailor. Well, that's close enough, wouldn't you say? Now, I suppose there's an adoption fee and some papers to fill out."

When they handled that part she said, "I still can't get over it. The coincidence and all."

"I knew a man once," Keller said, "who insisted there was no such thing as a coincidence or an accident."

"Well, I wonder how he would explain this."

"I'd like to hear him try," Keller said. "Let's go, Nelson. Good boy."

The Whole Truth

Stephen McCauley

She told her psychiatrist she was happily married and had taken a lover only because she was afraid of being too close to her husband, whom she'd wed six years earlier. If she'd been more truthful, she'd have confessed that she'd begun her affair with the dentist, whose office was in the same medical building as her own, because she was bored with her husband, and that fear of intimacy with her lover had driven her to sleep with the carpenter who'd come to work on the front steps of the house late in the summer. But she hadn't told her psychiatrist about the carpenter at all, because her indiscretion with him struck her as slightly sordid, and her psychiatrist was a gentle, bald man who sucked on sour balls and nodded eagerly as she spoke and reminded her too much of her father. She thought he might be upset to hear she'd fallen into bed with a relative stranger. Mentioning her ongoing affair with the dentist was surely enough. Besides, the steps were long finished, and she was quite certain she'd never see the carpenter again, let alone sleep with him, even though, in truth, she still thought of him often.

To compensate for her omissions, she transposed her feelings as she spoke. Thus, whenever she wished to talk about her fear of getting too close to her lover, she pretended she was talking about her husband. And when she talked about the sexual excitement of her affair with the dentist, she was really describing her fantasies about the carpenter. If she wanted to discuss the exasperating boredom of her marriage, she talked about a brief, boring first marriage, which she'd invented during her second week of analysis. It wasn't hard to keep track once she had it all down. And, she assured herself, the essence of what she was saying was true; she simply toyed with the names. As long as she was able to keep it all straight in her mind, her analysis would have some value.

It was her husband, who was kind and bald and reminded her a little of her father—and now her psychiatrist—who'd first suggested she seek treatment. She'd confessed to him that she was unhappy, although she'd told him it was because, after all the years of school and training, she was bored with dentistry. She'd hinted, too, but only in the most gentle way, that she was having doubts about their marriage, which, in fact, she was not. She knew she was bored and that the marriage was simply a matter of convenience for her and dependency for her husband. What she was having doubts about was her affair. When her husband asked her, as he did from time to time, what she'd told her psychiatrist about their relationship, she'd report some of the things she'd actually said about him, even though they were, of course, things she really felt about her lover.

Despite what she'd told her husband, she enjoyed her profession and, after four years, had established a successful practice. She and her husband lived in a university town, and many of her patients were young professionals and academic wives, the kinds of people who usually didn't need major dental work but who came dutifully three times a year for a cleaning and a checkup. To please them, she'd decorated her waiting room with old black-and-white photographs she'd bought at antique stores and easy chairs draped with printed cloth imported from India. The decor had first struck her as homey, if a bit cluttered. Now, however, her waiting room had begun to look to her like a psychiatrist's office. She avoided subscribing to the predictable dentist-office publications and instead kept recent copies of literary journals on the table by the door. She'd bought a narrow pine bookcase in which she kept story collections by contemporary writers whom she admired, even though she didn't care much for short stories.

Most of her patients called her by her first name, and many felt to her like casual friends. A number of women always asked her about her husband, and as she worked on their teeth she'd talk about him amiably, describing a man made up of equal parts of her spouse, her lover, and her fantasies about the carpenter.

Her mother lived in Kentucky and was proud of her achievements. The only regret her mother ever expressed was that her husband had not lived to see their daughter graduate from dental school. She was close to her mother, and they talked on the phone once a week for at least an hour. Wanting desperately to tell her about her psychiatrist, but not wanting to alarm her, she told her mother that her husband, who was twelve years older than she was, had started seeing a therapist three times a week. Therapist sounded more benign than psychiatrist. She told her mother her husband was having a mid-life career crisis. Feeling daring, she hinted at suspicions that he was also having an affair. Her mother listened sympathetically and suggested that perhaps she and her husband should go to Bermuda together for a week and try to work things out. She reminded her mother that her husband's therapy appointments made such a vacation impossible. After she'd hung up, she went to her husband and told him she thought he should take a vacation, even though she wouldn't be able to go along.

Her lover was also married. He was severe and serious and driven by nervous intensity. He bit his fingernails and sometimes, after they'd made love, would take her in his arms and weep. He would divorce his wife if she would divorce her husband. The two of them would go off together, set up a practice in a different city, and start life all over. She explained to him that she was tempted, but could not make any moves until she had resolved some things in analysis. When her lover asked her if she was telling her psychiatrist how much they loved each other and the passionate nature of their sexual relationship, she told him that she was, even though when she described to her psychiatrist her longing for the dentist, she was thinking of the carpenter. And when she told her psychiatrist about her desire to leave her husband, she was really describing her desire to break off her affair with the dentist.

She feared that if she confessed to her psychiatrist that she'd been unable to tell her mother about him, his feelings would be hurt, and he would think she was resisting treatment. So instead she told him that she'd told her mother, and that her mother had been understanding and helpful. While she was on the subject, she told her psychiatrist that it was her mother who'd suggested her husband take a week in Bermuda on his own. She didn't want to sound manipulative by admitting she'd suggested it to her husband herself, and her mother had, after all, been the one to bring up the subject of a vacation.

In the middle of November her husband noticed that the floor of the porch on the back of the house was beginning to rot, and he called the carpenter. He told her this one night over dinner, and she felt her heart race and sink and race and sink in a peculiar way, almost as if she were running a fever. He told her that the carpenter would begin work in the middle of the next week, the very Wednesday, in fact, he was leaving for Bermuda. He apologized that he would not be there to oversee the job. She told him that the carpenter had impressed her as reliable and would probably need very little supervision, and she finished her dinner hastily.

The Monday before her husband left on his trip, she decided to test the waters. She told her psychiatrist that a young man would be working on their house that week, that she had met him when he'd come to estimate the cost of the job, and that she had found him attractive. She told him he was a crafts-man who painted walls with sponges so the finished surface looked like fine wallpaper. This skill, she felt, made the carpen-ter sound as sensitive and refined as she was certain he really must be. Her psychiatrist raised one eyebrow inquisitively when she told him this, a gesture that she took as a sign of disapproval. So she dropped the subject of the carpenter quickly, and told him, as if confessing it, that she was looking forward to her husband's departure so that she could spend more time with her lover, the dentist.

She canceled her appointments for Wednesday, drove her husband to the airport, and sped home in a state of con-fused anticipation. It was an oddly warm day, nearly eighty, and the November sky was blank and murky in the Indian-summer heat. She waited for the carpenter on the front steps of the house, dressed in a long skirt made of thin cotton and a baggy blouse, trying to read a collection of stories recommended to her by a patient.

When he finally arrived, she felt embarrassed, certain that he could read her anxiety and its source on her brow. She was only somewhat relieved to notice that he, too, seemed uncomfortable.

She stayed in the house all day, cleaning and arranging drawers and cautiously looking out the kitchen window to the porch where the carpenter was working. It wasn't until late in the afternoon, when he was sweeping up for the day, that she asked him inside and offered him a drink.

She called her receptionist the next morning and canceled her patients for the rest of the week. Then she called her lover and told him she'd decided to take advantage of her husband's absence by visiting her mother in Kentucky for a few days. She left a message on her psychiatrist's answering machine, explaining that she'd decided to go to Bermuda with her husband after all and would therefore miss her next two appointments.

The carpenter was five years younger than she was, dark-eyed and appealingly stocky. He wore blue jeans and a red T-shirt. He worked diligently on the porch for the next two days. Now and again he'd enter the house, and kiss her teasingly and tell her she was beautiful. When he finished work for the afternoon, he'd come inside, sweaty and exhausted, and they'd make love, though never, he insisted, in the bed she shared with her husband.

On Saturday night she prepared him an enormous, complicated dinner. After the meal, they lay together on the sofa in the living room with the curtains drawn and a light sheet pulled over their bodies. There had been a rainstorm that afternoon, and the weather had turned seasonably cool, though the rooms of the house were still warm. He told her he loved her, and she kissed him thankfully, even though she wasn't young or sentimental enough to believe he meant it.

He told her he was moving to Texas for the winter. He had friends there who had offered him a job for a few months; he'd put his books and his furniture into storage and drive south. He didn't really know how long he'd stay away. She was struck all at once by how wonderfully simple it sounded, by how unentangled and uncomplicated his life was compared with her own. It seemed pure, clean, and enviable. Jokingly, he asked her if she'd like to go with him. She told him she would in a soft, choking voice. She buried her face in his broad chest and began to laugh at the idea. Her laughter fed on itself until she lost control completely and discovered that she was weeping.

She rarely cried. She had cried only once in front of her psychiatrist. In response to something she'd said, he had asked her if she was happy, and, unaccountably, she had burst into tears.

Now she curled her body against the comfortable flesh of the carpenter's stomach and, as he stroked her hair, told him, in simple, flat sentences, the truth about her husband and her lover and her mother and her psychiatrist and the tangle of lies and the elaborate fabrications she had told each of them. She wept on and off as she spoke. Sometimes she would be struck by the awful humor of what she was saying, and she would start to laugh. When she finished, she looked at him and saw on his face a puzzled expression, as if he hadn't quite followed her story.

But perhaps it didn't matter whether he understood or not. It was enough that she had told him. She asked him to stay the night with her. He held her closely, kissed the top of her head tenderly, and told her he couldn't.

On Monday a different carpenter arrived at the door to finish the job. His partner, he explained, had had to leave town for a few days. She nodded and showed him to the porch, scorched by the obvious lie.

Her husband returned on Wednesday evening, and she picked him up at the airport. His skin was darker, and his bald head was shining, and he looked relaxed, as if he'd eaten and slept well. He told her about an old woman who'd sat next to him on the return flight, clicking rosary beads the whole way.

He asked her if she had missed him, and she said she had and told him that the work on the porch was finished.

She prepared chicken and rice and frozen peas, and they ate in silence.

On Thursday she decided that her analysis was getting her nowhere, largely because she had told so many lies. But she couldn't disappoint the bald, kind man with the sour balls who reminded her so much of her father and her husband by confessing that all of the work they'd done together for the past several months had been based on a network of half-truths. So she told him her husband had been transferred to Texas and that she was moving with him. She did love her husband, and the change of scene would be good for them: the trip to Bermuda alone had done wonders. They were moving next month, so she would have to leave treatment immediately. There was much organizing and packing she had to do.

She saw no point in telling her husband or her lover that she had stopped seeing her psychiatrist, since she certainly would not care to tell them the reasons why. And anyway, she had already made an appointment with a new doctor. It couldn't matter to them what her psychiatrist's name was, which, from their vantage point, would be the only visible change.

Her new psychiatrist was a towering man with bright eyes and a slight accent she couldn't place. He wasn't as kindly looking as her old psychiatrist, and she felt certain she would be able to tell him honestly about her husband and her lover and even the carpenter.

He asked her, as soon as she sat in the chair across from him, why she'd decided to terminate with her previous doctor. This question stunned her into silence, and she averted her eyes. If she told him the truth about that, he would probably begin to doubt everything else she told him, all of which, she had promised herself, would be true. So she told him instead that her old psychiatrist was quite old indeed, and that he had consistently confused the people she talked about, mistaking her lover for her husband, her husband for her father, and so on, until she herself had been confused. She hadn't seen the point in going on with him, much as she had liked him.

Her new psychiatrist listened sympathetically, nodded, and settled into his chair. She felt that he approved of her reasons for leaving her old psychiatrist and, reassured, she began to tell him the rest.

III.
Power and Dependence

The power of the therapist, real
or imagined, and the patient's response to it are issues explored
in most of the stories in this collection, particularly in those here.
"The Gentleman" explores the mysterious sexual power of the
therapist through the eyes of children, who view their mother's
therapist with idealized wonder. "I didn't know much about
God," the young narrator tells us, "but watching Anton appear,
I just thought about Him." In this story, which is saturated with
sensual imagery and—with the exception of two characters—
populated only by females, the idealization of the therapist by
both the adults and the children eventually leads to sexual abuse.

"The Fairy Godfathers" portrays two lovers whose passion requires the presence of their respective therapists, through
whom the couple relay their feelings for each other: "He loves
you"; "He thinks you're wonderful"; "He thinks you're beautiful." "The Age of Analysis," too, reveals a couple in a fragile
relationship, who are unable to communicate and function without first consulting each of their therapists. Here, though,
therapy becomes a substitute for real feelings. "I'll know better
how I feel," the mother in this story tells her son, "after I talk
to Dr. Steinberg tomorrow." In anarchistic fashion, "Crazy for

Loving You" mocks this notion of the all-powerful therapist
by demystifying him—"he could hold on for quite a long time,
but you could hear him breathing and shifting around and fidgeting"—and by suggesting that everyone is interchangeable;
anyone can be a therapist: one's doorman, a fellow patient, a lover.

Meanwhile, the therapists in "The Psychopathology of
Everyday Life" and "Samaritan" struggle to hold onto their
power, and what ensues is a form of battle between therapist
and patient. In the first story, a therapist whose marriage is
deteriorating finds himself "identifying with the mistreated
lovers of certain women patients" and soon embarks on a sexual
relationship with one of them. He and the patient struggle with
their simultaneous need for and desire to control each other.
The therapist comments, "If I didn't stop this affair, it was because I didn't want to stop, was getting something from it that
outweighed its disadvantages." In "Samaritan," the therapist
feels so threatened that his patient will usurp his power that he
turns to murder.

The Gentleman

Martha McPhee

Mom learned to fall backward into the arms of strangers without hesitating or looking over her shoulder. She learned to fall freely, with her muscles relaxed and her mind open, inhaling the bitterness of sweat along with stale cigarette smoke, inhaling the thought of freedom, with her hands by her sides, her fingertips clutching the fabric of her dress, her reddened lips turned up in a smile. At first she was afraid to fall. She wanted to look behind. She bent at the waist and fell awkwardly, buckling at the knees. But eventually she succeeded and fell freely into waiting arms which received her, catching her under the armpits, catching her with fingertips pressing into the soft flesh of her breasts. A human pillar, she fell and fell and fell, until she fell in love with Anton. Anton was her therapist.

Mom had curly hair, golden curls the color of sand. She was thin, with a big bust and a gap between her teeth and green, green eyes. She wore shiny taffeta dresses with big flowers and no sleeves. Some had matching jackets, some had matching sweaters. The colors were living colors that made me think about summer: peach, lemon, strawberry. Her skin was ivory and smooth and there was no hair on her legs or under her arms. It was comforting skin, the type that showed no signs of stress—

honest, sincere skin that wrapped her in an extra layer, protecting what was inside.

Mom did her falling with a group of other patients, in a barnlike old house, which she called "The Farm." Anton was an itinerant therapist of sorts who had come to our town to spread the Gestalt word and his idea of women's liberation. He started the local chapter of NOW and organized sit-ins in pubs that excluded women. But his specialty was lonely housewives. He taught them all to fall, and to him our mother fell.

We didn't meet Anton right away. We were on the outside, near the road, with a lemonade stand that Mom helped us set up so that we'd have something to do while we waited. We went there on Saturdays, arriving early, before the others. Mom left us with three crisp dollar bills and an old cigar case filled with shiny pennies and small bits of tobacco. The dollars were meant to appease us so that we wouldn't complain about bad business at the end of the morning, when she would emerge from Anton's with her face swollen with tears.

Daffodils and forsythia were in full bloom and the scent of the long oniongrass filled the air. A gentle mist lifted from the ground toward the sky and all around were trees. The house was gray and chipping paint, and it stood at the end of a short dirt driveway pocked with potholes. Ivy climbed up the walls, and the windowpanes were smoky with unpolished glass. One window was lit—a window on the second floor—by a blue light.

"He's a priest," Julia said. The words came from her mouth in a steam of warm breath. As she spoke her left eyebrow rose. Julia's hair curled like Mom's: small ringlets, sausages, that fell gently to just below her ears. Her dark-blue eyes gleamed. We stood by the lemonade stand, a little chilled, dressed alike in our yellow rain slickers and yellow boots, studying the blue light. A car rushed by on the road, blowing air over us. "A Jesuit priest."

I hadn't quite pictured him as a priest. A man dressed in a cope and cassock wasn't what came to mind when I tried to imagine Anton.

"He's not a priest anymore," Jane said. Her braids hung heavily, pulling her face long. The mist had left little beads of water glistening in her hair. "He's a Gestalt therapist now."

"*Deux trois*," Julia said, acting smart. She said she knew everything.

"Mom's falling in love with him," I said.

I didn't know what a Jesuit was then but I could tell by the way people looked when Mom told them he'd been a Jesuit that it was important. Awe seeped over their faces like a stain. I did the same with my face, pretending I understood. "Gestalt" was another one of those words that impressed people and that I didn't understand but used as if I did. I told teachers and classmates, anyone who'd listen, that he was a Jesuit and a Gestalt, and just using the words made me feel big.

"Gestalt therapist," Jane would correct.

We were serious, serious to the point of solemnity. The air was blue, wet and cold against my face, and suddenly I felt unusually clean. I thought of us as buttercups standing in the oniongrass in our yellow jackets and boots. We looked odd and out of place at the head of Anton's driveway. Odd because we were clean, as if there were something jarring and peculiar about being clean and being there. Everything about us was clean: behind our ears, the napes of our necks. We smelled of lemons and witch hazel, and our clothes smelled of bleach and starch. Our cotton bobby socks were clean, soft as feathers around our feet; our jumpers were clean; our shirts were clean; even the grosgrain ribbons tied around our hair were clean. I had the urge to run deep into the trees and roll around in the bitter and decaying leaves, and then I began to laugh. I pointed at the blue light. "Do you think they're fucking?" I said. Julia had taught me that word. I looked at Jane and Julia and they laughed. "Kaaate!" they said.

But we were bored. We laughed hard and loud, wheezing uncontrollably, and I worried that we would disturb Mom and Anton. Then I hoped that we would. I hoped that Anton would come to the window and tell us to be quiet, so that we could have a peek at him. I hoped he'd raise the window and rest his palms on the sill and call us each by name—Jane, Julia, Kate—and the sounds of our names would come to us with the warmth of his reprimanding words, making us want to obey him.

"He's a philosopher. And he's writing a book," Jane continued.

"He's got five children," Julia said.

"He's married," I blurted.

"Kate," they said. We weren't supposed to talk about that.

"He's a Texan and a poker player," Julia said. "And he's a big, big man with a big, big head." Her eyes widened and her nostrils flared. "And he's generous."

"And he likes to eat." Excitement flooded our voices.

"He earns over thirty thousand dollars a year playing cards," I said. I liked saying "cards" instead of "poker." It sounded more professional.

"How do you know that?" Julia snapped. She hated it when I knew something she didn't know.

But the image of Anton that I held and hoped for was the image of a distinguished man, tall and slender, with silver graying hair and long protective fingers, a gentle man.

The familiar coughing of a muffler warned us and Jane yelled for us to run. We darted through thistles, deep into the forsythia. Surges of panic excited us, shooting up our spines. We thought we could vanish. We thought the color of our raincoats would fuse together with the wilting flowers and blend us into hiding. Thickets and rough branches surrounded us and the ground was soft and gushy and speckled with the greens, whites, and yellows of ragweed and fallen blossoms.

Jane parted several branches so that we could spy on the people arriving at the house. First came Delilah, Anton's secretary. She didn't look much like a secretary, in her miniskirt and stovepipe patent-leather boots. Her hair was long and tangled, and it wrapped around her shoulders like a shawl and danced with the leather tassels of her jacket. She parked between the Cadillac and our station wagon and vanished into the house, like Mom.

"She's a hippie," Julia said.

Then the rest of the people came. There was something strange about them, though they weren't that different from Mom. I guess it was because they were all so similar. Their hair was nicely brushed and curled, held back with bows or bandeaux, coiffed. They wore wraparound skirts or slacks, and bright Argyle sweaters with initials embroidered on the side. On their feet were rain boots or loafers, and their gait was determined, emphatic. One by one they drove in, parking hurriedly, and rushed from their cars to the door as if pulled by some mysterious force. They were housewives, some of them the mothers of our friends. Mom had told us not to sell them lemonade. She said it might make them self-conscious to know that we knew they were in therapy.

We watched until the last car came and the last person went inside the house. Then we emerged from the forsythia, coming into a new space that was somehow larger than before, filled with new things. A telephone pole shot into the sky, blossoming into a network of black wires that webbed their way in and out of the trees. Planks of wood leaned against the side of the house, disorganized and ugly. I imagined rusty nails in hidden spots and thought about tetanus and rabies and lockjaw. Jane had read about lockjaw. Lockjaw from rusty nails, lockjaw from stepping in animal excrement, lockjaw from licking our dirty fingers. She told us to be careful. She warned us that lockjaw was easy to contract at a farm. She told us that our jaws would convulse and our muscles would spasm and our mouths would lock shut permanently.

"A car's coming! A car's coming!" Julia sang, running across the road. The first car to stop for us all morning, in fact the first car ever to stop for our lemonade. Julia's smile was electric and her cheeks were rosy. Her curls stuck in wisps to her forehead. As the car approached, she waved her hands furiously. Even when she was clumsy, she moved with grace. She threw off her rain jacket and rolled up her sleeves. I followed her, but Jane, who was the oldest, stayed behind. She was above selling lemonade. She said the only reason she came along was to baby-sit us. Ever since Dad left, she had pretended she was our mother.

Not so long before, Julia had made me her best sister. "This is a secret pact," she had warned. "Can't tell anyone. Specially Jane." We were sitting on the bathroom counter with our feet in the sinks, washing them before bed. The fluorescent light buzzed overhead, making the bathroom incredibly bright. In the mirror our skin was ugly, betrayed by the light, pasty and pale.

"I won't tell Jane," I promised. Jane and Julia fought a lot and I swung between them like a pendulum. I liked swinging between them. For the most part I always had someone on my side.

"Jane's a bitch," Julia said. "I'm the one who always does special things for you." Then Julia stuck me with a sewing needle, quickly, in the fingertip, and then stuck herself. Small beads of blood popped from our skin and she clamped our fingers together, mixing the blood, and pressing them hard until they turned purple. When I thought it was all over, she put my finger in her mouth and hers in mine. "We can become so close," she said. "By drinking each other's blood we can become each other."

A black Lincoln Continental approached. Dull and dirty. I stood on one side of the road and Julia on the other. The car slid quietly between us, as calmly as an ocean liner gliding through the sea. Julia disappeared and I heard the soft, mechanical murmur of an electric window going down. I waited.

"Kate! Kate!" Julia commanded suddenly, appearing at the front end of the car. "Get a cup of lemonade. This gentleman wants a cup of lemonade. He'll pay us twenty cents for a cup!" She looked at me from across the hood. "And he's gonna pay us to do him a favor. Get him a cup!" Her smile grew big.

She snatched the lemonade from my hand and passed it into the car. Her arm vanished for a second, and then reappeared with her fist clutching a dollar bill. I wanted to look in the car but she wouldn't move from the window. Hog, I thought.

"Look, Katy." She held the dollar up proudly. "He wants us to watch him change. He needs to fix his car and wants us to make sure that nobody peeks at him while he's changing into his old clothes." She spoke so fast, with assurance.

"Where do we have to go?" I said, suspiciously. I wasn't going into the woods with this man. Mom warned us about men that raped and killed. "Raped and killed": she said it a thousand times so we'd be careful. But Julia was older and knew everything. I watched the dollar in Julia's fist, wondering how much he'd pay us, hoping it would be more than just a dollar, thinking I'd bargain with him if he didn't offer more.

"Nowhere. Just here," she said. Then she grabbed my arm and pulled me near her, and together we leaned through the car window. She held my hand. I felt warm and special.

It was dark inside the car. A thick dust lay on the dashboard, broken with smudges and fingerprints. In several places stuffing poked from rips in the seat. The radio was turned on, and music struggled through static. Stacks of browned newspapers littered the back seat and plastic-foam coffee cups spilled from paper bags lying on the floor. I imagined there would be a lot of coins in that car.

The gentleman was oldish and the skin on his face was pulled taut, as if he'd been in the sun too much. He had very little hair, a halo of white fringe, and a large freckled bald spot. From his nose dangled something disgusting that I couldn't make out, and I thought I should tell him about it.

"This is my best sister. She's my very best sister and we are true blood sisters," Julia said, speaking as if she had found something great like a piece of blue sea glass on the beach. I knew I should feel privileged that she was including me.

"You have something coming out of your nose," I said.

"Kate!" Julia snapped. "Kate" really sounded a lot like "hate" when she said it that way. "She's just young," Julia apologized. I hated it when she said I was "just young." I didn't feel very young. I was eight.

"Uh-huh," the gentleman said, staring at me. The whites of his eyes were yellow and filmy. I thought he'd wipe his nose, but he didn't. He just left the thing there, as if he liked having something hanging from his nose. I couldn't look at his nose. "That's a . . . real nice, really quite nice," he said.

There was a strange smell in the car: a smell of old milk and smoke.

"It's a pleasure to meet you, little missy. You're just as charming as your sister." He reached for my hand and kissed it on the knuckles. His lips were wet and his whiskers pricked my skin. I was afraid the thing would fall onto my hand, but it didn't.

"Now, uh, yes, I could use another cup of this lemonade." His words drew out long and he stumbled over some of them. "How 'bout gettin' me another cup of this lemonade? Yeah . . . why don't you, uh, run along?" His eyes caught hold of mine again and he handed me the cup.

"But aren't we going to help you? Don't you need to fix your car?" I asked. The engine was still running and the car vibrated.

"When you return, pretty miss."

"Go on, Katy." Julia shoved me gently until I drew away from the car. I could imagine her saying, "You've gone and ruined everything and now I'll have to fix it." I was mad that I'd mentioned the nose.

I walked back across the road, leaving Julia with the gentleman. I wished I'd told him I thought it was snot coming from his nose. The only reason I didn't was because I was trying to be polite and the only other word for snot I could think of was "booger." My arms felt heavy swinging by my side—awkward and uncomfortable, as if I couldn't carry myself properly, and I was afraid that he'd be watching me. I could feel his eyes on my back and it made my legs twitch. Julia can get the gentleman a cup of lemonade, I thought. Julia can watch the gentleman change.

Jane picked forsythia, placing the boughs in her arms.

"Jane!" I yelled and she turned to me.

"What's wrong?" she asked, screwing up her eyes, confused. "Didn't you make a sale?" Her face was alert, ready to react.

"Julia's selfish," I said. That's what Mom said to us when we asked for too much.

"You're just figuring that out?" Jane said, relaxing. Her shoulders slumped forward. "I've been trying to tell you that for centuries."

I helped her pick forsythia, twisting the branches to break them off. They splintered into green and white flesh and I yanked and yanked. There was a difference between being with Julia and being with Jane. Jane was quiet and she didn't poke at me all the time and boss me around. Unless she was mad at you, she'd just let you be. Sometimes she'd speak and say something really smart, and you could tell she thought a lot. Nothing got by Jane. Sometimes I thought I'd rather be Julia and tried to be just like her. Other times it'd be Jane I imitated. Now I imitated Jane. I even put on her long face. But God, I wished I hadn't mentioned the nose.

Five, ten minutes passed. I looked at the car, feeling proud, glad to make Julia wait. It began to drizzle and the rain made sounds in the leaves. I practiced making long faces, stretching my mouth this way and that, raising my eyes.

"What are you doing with your face?"

"Nothing."

A car door slammed and wheels screeched, burning rubber, churning over pavement, and the Lincoln Continental vanished in a cloud of exhaust. We turned, knees trembling, afraid Julia would be gone. "Raped and killed" flashed across my mind. But she was standing where I had left her, frozen for a minute, with her hands in her hair. Slowly, she began to cross the road. Slowly, she leaned down for her ribbon, which lay on the road, and then she rose and erupted into tears.

Mom rushed from the house out onto the little front porch. She stood there for the instant it took Julia to run screaming from the road. Jane and I followed, stopping a little way back from the steps. Mom's taffeta dress was wrinkled at the waist and her lipstick was gone. Her arms opened for Julia and Julia collapsed into them. Mom's hand caressed the back of Julia's head. She looked past Julia's curls to Jane, slapping Jane with her eyes. Jane's face became long and she looked ugly.

Her eyes became big and dense, taking over her face until it seemed she just had two enormous brown eyes. The rain plastered her hair to her skull. Even her braids hung awkwardly, like two fraying ropes. The flowers drooped in her arms.

"Eve! Eve, is everything all right?" said voices from the upstairs window and then three women's faces appeared up there. Their hair wasn't so neat anymore. Their ribbons and bandeaux were gone. They smiled, panicky smiles, and one of the women's teeth sparkled silvery with braces. Their bodies smushed together at the window and I stared, hoping I'd recognize one of the mothers so that I could make her feel uncomfortable, but I didn't.

"Don't worry," Mom called. She tilted her head up to them. "It'll be all right. Jane wasn't watching the girls."

I wished I hadn't taken Jane's side. I was afraid I'd get the silent treatment, too, now, and Julia would be favored for days.

The screen door creaked open slowly and a man came out. Anton: as big as Julia had described him. Big round head. Big tall body. Big fingers. I thought about poker and the thirty thousand. Then I thought about God—I don't know why. Maybe because Julia had mentioned that he was a priest. I didn't know much about God. But watching Anton appear, I just thought about Him, and then the thought vanished and I felt spooked and smelled the stink of rotting toadstools that came from some old sycamores not far from the forsythia.

Anton squinted his eyes and a deep furrow ran across his brow, and he bent his knees to squat down next to Julia and Mom. I could hear his joints cracking. His hair was thin and graying. Thick sideburns striped his cheeks, and his shirt was an explosion of oranges, yellows, purples, and greens. The sleeves were pushed up to his elbows and he wore a pair of faded jeans that hung low on his hips.

"What's wrong, babe?" he asked. *What's wrong babe. Babe.* His words rushed through me. "Babe." Tender. He had a Southern accent that was somehow tough and strong yet protective. He bent down close to Julia and ran his fingers through her hair, patting her head. Her face was messy with tears and drool. Mom watched, pressing her thumbnail into her lip.

Anton's mouth touched Julia's ear and her crying stopped. His lips on her ear whispering into it. I felt as if his lips were touching my ear, wet and warm and soft, and I had that shivery feeling that a whisper sends through your entire body. All the way to your toes. Julia sank against him and he pulled her deeper into him. She was tiny in comparison. They whispered back and forth and I wished that I were her.

"It'll be all right," he said, rising. Anton loomed above us. His hand fanned out on top of Mom's head. On his ring finger there was an enormous turquoise ring. I thought of Julia's hand reaching inside the car. I thought of my hand with the whiskers pressing into it. I wanted to know what the gentleman had done. I wondered if he'd done something gross. I almost hoped he had, because I knew I'd hear about it in detail if he'd done something gross and if she learned something from it I knew she'd try to teach me. Anton noticed Jane and me. He winked. "It'll be all right," he repeated, a little louder, for us.

We fell quickly to Anton, more quickly than Mom. We were limber, falling freely and our world opened up, suddenly becoming brighter. Mom wanted it that way, the four of us as one, falling, falling freely. Mom said Anton would love us, promised to God it would be the truth. And we fell and fell and fell, for the pure sensation of it, trusting until later. We were still young enough not to hesitate or question, not to look behind.

The Fairy Godfathers
John Updike

"Oh, Pumpkin," Tod would say. "Nobody likes us."

"That's not quite true," she would answer, her lips going cloudy in that way they had when she thought.

They were lovers, so the smallest gesture of hers flooded his attention, making his blood heavy. He knew exactly whom she meant. He objected, "But they're paid to."

"I think they would anyway," she answered, again after thought. She added, "Oz *loves* you."

"He doesn't love me, he just thinks that my self-hatred is slightly excessive."

"He loves you."

Oz was his psychiatrist. Rhadamanthus was hers. Tod had met Rhadamanthus but once, in the grim avocado hall outside his office. Pumpkin had gone in, as usual, flustered and harried, self-doubting and guilty, and had emerged flushed and smoothed and cheerful. Behind her, on this one occasion, loomed a shadow, but a shadow Tod could no more contemplate than he could look directly into the sun. He knew that, via her discourse, he dwelt, session after session, within this shadow, and as he took the man's unenthusiastically offered hand Tod had

181

the strange sensation of reaching out and touching, in a sense, himself.

After her next session, Pumpkin said, "He wondered why you wouldn't look him in the eye."

"I couldn't. He's too wonderful."

"He thinks *you're* wonderful."

"The hell he does."

"He does. He loves what you're doing for me."

"I'm ruining your life."

"He thinks my life was very neurotic and I'm incredibly stupid to grieve the way I do."

"Life is grief," Tod said, tired of this conversation.

"He thinks my life was very neurotic," Pumpkin told him, "and I'm incredibly stupid to grieve."

"She repeats herself," Tod told Oz. Oz rustled in his chair and touched the fingertips of his right hand to his right temple. His every gesture, however small, won Tod's full attention. "That doesn't seem to me so very bad," the psychiatrist said, with the casual power of delivery attainable at only the highest, thinnest altitude of wisdom. It was like golf on the moon; even a chip shot sailed for miles. Oz's smile was a celestial event. "You spend so much of your own energy"—he smiled—"avoiding repeating yourself."

Tod wondered why Oz was so insistently Pumpkin's champion. Through the tangle of his patient's words, Oz seemed to see an ideal Pumpkin glowing. They looked rather alike: broad pale faces, silver hair, eyes the no-color of platinum. Unearthly personalities. Whereas Rhadamanthus, in Tod's sense of him, was subterranean in essence: there was something muddy and hearty and dark and directive about the man. Pumpkin would return from her sessions as from a cave, blinking and reborn. Whereas Tod descended from a session with Oz giddy and aerated, his blood full of bubbles, his brain intoxicated by its refreshed power to fantasize and hope. Oz was, Tod flattered himself, more purely Freudian than Rhadamanthus.

"Oz says," he would say, "I shouldn't mind your repeating yourself."

"Rhadamanthus says," was her answer, "I don't repeat myself. At least he's never noticed it."

"You trust him to hear you the first time," Tod theorized. "He's realer to you than I am. You repeat yourself with me because you doubt that I'm there."

"Where?"

"In the world your head makes. Don't be sad. Freud says I'm not really real to anybody." It was seldom out of Tod's mind that his name in German was the word for death. He had been forty before this had really sunk in.

In those days, their circumstances were reduced. He lived in a room in a city, and she would visit him. From the fourth-floor landing he would look down, having rung the buzzer of admission, and see her hand suddenly alight, like a butterfly in forest depths, on the stair railing far below. As she ascended, there was something sinister and inexorable in the way her hand gripped the bannister in steady upward hops. After the second-floor landing, her entire arm became visible—in fur or tweeds, in cotton sleeve or bare, depending on the season—and at the turn on the third landing she would gaze upward and smile, her face broad and luminous and lunar. She would be coming from a session with Rhadamanthus, and as he embraced her on the fourth-floor landing Tod could feel in the smoothness of her cheeks and the strength of her arms and the cloudy hunger of her lips the recent infusion of the wizard's blessing. She would go into his meagre room and kick off her shoes and tell him of the session.

"He was good," she would say, judiciously, as if each week she tasted a different wine.

"Did he say you should go back to Roger?"

"Of course not. He thinks that would be terribly neurotic. Why do you even ask? You're projecting. *You* want me to go back. Does Oz want me to go back, so you can go back? He hates me."

"He loves you. He says you've done wonders for my masculinity."

"So would weight-lifting."

He paused to laugh, then continued to grope after the shadow of himself that lived in the magic cave of her sessions with Rhadamanthus. He flitted about in there, he felt, as a being semi-sublime, finer even than any of the approbation Pumpkin reported. "He thinks," she would say, wearily, "one of my problems is I've gone from one extreme to the other. You sound just utterly lovely to him, in the way you treat me, your children, Lulu . . ."

The mention of Lulu did bad things to him. "I am *not* utterly lovely," he protested. "I can be quite cruel. Here, I'll show you." And he seized Pumpkin's bare foot as it reposed before him and twisted until she screamed and fell to the floor with a thump.

"I think it was her foot I chose," Tod told Oz the next Tuesday, "rather than twisting her arm or pulling her hair, say, because her feet are especially freighted for me with erotic import. The first time I was vividly conscious of wanting to, you know, *have* her, I had dropped over at their house on a Saturday afternoon to return a set of ratchet wrenches of Roger's I had borrowed, and while I was standing there in the hall she came up from the cellar in bare feet. I thought to myself, Goes into the cellar barefoot—that's great. The only other woman I knew who went barefoot everywhere was my wife. Lulu even plays tennis barefoot, and leaves little toe marks all over the clay. Then, about Pumpkin, at these meetings of the Recorder Society she would wear those dumb sort of wooden sandals that are supposed to be good for your arches, and during the rests of the tenor part I could see underneath the music sheet her little pink toes beating time for the soprano, very fast and fluttery—eighth notes. Soprano parts tend to have eighth notes. And then, the first time we spent the whole night together, coming back from the bathroom, with her still asleep and feeling sort of strange—me, I mean—here she was asleep with this wonderful one foot stuck out from beneath the blankets. She loves to have her toes sucked."

It seemed to Tod that Oz shifted uneasily in his chair; there was a creak that could be leather or a furtive noise of digestion. Tod's weekly appointment came after the lunch hour, and he had a sensation, sometimes, of being engorged by the psychiatrist, of dissolving, attacked by enzymes of analysis. Tod persisted with his pedal theme. "The winter before last, I just remembered, Lulu took the wrong Wellington boots away from the carol sing, and they turned out to be *her* boots, and they were too big for Lulu, which is surprising, since Lulu is taller. *Her* feet, I should say, Lulu's, are quite high-arched, almost like hooves, which is why they leave such marks on the tennis court. When I met her at college, the soles were so tough she could stamp out cigarettes barefoot, as a trick. The third and fourth toes aren't divided all the way down, and she used to hate to have me mention this. Or anything about her feet, for that matter. Yet she never wore shoes if she could help it, and when we'd walk on the beach she'd always admire her own prints in the sand. For the gap where the arch was." Suddenly the theme was exhausted. "What do you make of it?" Tod asked weakly.

Oz sighed. His platinum eyes seemed to be watering. Tod felt that Oz, gazing at him, saw a deep, though fathomable, well of sorrow—sorrow and narcissistic muddle. "It's a paradox," the psychiatrist said, sadly.

Lulu's attitude toward her own feet, he must mean. Tod went on, "After they swapped the right boots back, Pumpkin said to me at a party that Lulu's had pinched, and I had this odd wish to defend Lulu, as if she had been insulted. Even now, I keep wanting to defend Lulu. Against you, for example. I feel you've undermined her, by giving some sort of silent approval to my leaving her. Everybody else is horrified. Everybody else likes Lulu. So do I. She's very likable."

Oz sighed in the special way that signaled the end of a session. "What's that old saying?" he asked, casually. "If the shoe fits . . ."

"What did he say?" Pumpkin asked anxiously, over the telephone. She had had a bad day, of crying children and unpayable bills. Roger was bombarding her with affidavits and depositions.

"Oz attacked Lulu," Tod told her. "He implied she was a shoe I should stop wearing."

"That's not an attack, it's a possibility," Pumpkin said. "I'm not sure you're quite sane, on the subject of Lulu."

"I'm as sane as you are on the subject of Roger."

"I'm quite sane on the subject of Roger. Rhadamanthus says I was all along, only I doubted my own perceptions."

"I've always liked Roger. He's always been very sweet to me."

"That's one of his poses."

"He loaned me his ratchet wrenches."

"You should hear him go on about those ratchet wrenches now. He calls them 'those wretched ratchet wrenches.'"

"Who do you trust more on the subject of Roger—me who's met him or Rhadamanthus who hasn't? I say he is *sweet.*" Whence this irritability and unreason? Tod couldn't understand himself. Once, when Pumpkin had wavered and it seemed she might go back to her husband, he had been in agony. His heart had turned over and over in jealousy like a lump of meat in a cauldron of stew.

"Rhadamanthus," Pumpkin answered, to a question he had forgotten asking.

"He thinks you're his princess," Tod snapped. "He thinks I sully you, no doubt."

"He thinks you're *beautiful*," she said, infuriatingly.

"Who *are* these men anyway," Tod countered, "to run our lives? What do we know about *them*? Are *their* marriages so great, that they should put ours down? From the way Oz's stomach burbles I think he has an ulcer. As to your guy, I didn't like the shifty way he shambled out the door that time. He wouldn't look me in the eye. What do you two *do* in there anyway?"

Pumpkin was crying. "Go back," she said. "That's what you're saying to me you want to do. Go back to Lulu and have pinchy feet." She hung up.

But the next time he saw her, after her Thursday session with Rhadamanthus, the psychiatrist had told her that wasn't what Tod had meant at all; he meant that in truth he loved her very much, and she loved him. She felt all smooth and plumped-up on the fourth-floor landing, and inside his room she kicked off her shoes and told all that had been disclosed in the cave of knowing.

They seemed, sometimes, as they moved about the city enacting their romance, gloves on the hands of giants, embodiments of others' hopes. They had no friends. They had children, but these they had wounded. Tears glistened about them like the lights of the city seen reflected in the square pool beside the round white table of an outdoor restaurant. In museums, tall stainless-steel constructs probed space to no clear purpose, and great striped canvases rewarded their respectful stares with a gaudy blankness. In movie houses, her hair tickled his ear as pink limbs intertwined or Sherlock Holmes stalked through the artificial mist of a Hollywood heath. They liked revivals; Esther Williams smiled triumphantly underwater, and Judy Garland, young again, hit the high note. Outside, under the glitter of the marquee, ice glistened on the brick pavements, and chandeliers warmed the bay windows of apartments whose floors and furniture they would never see. They were happy in limbo. At night, sirens wailed lullabies of disasters that kept their distance. Traffic licked the streets. Airplanes tugged snug the blanket of sky. They awoke to find it had snowed through all their dreaming, and the street was as hushed as a print by Currier & Ives—the same street where in spring magnolias bloomed first on the sunny side and then, weeks later, on the side of constant shade. They walked enchanted, scared, unknown but for the unseen counsellors whose blessings fed the night like the breathing of stars. Then the world rotated; the children stopped crying, the pace of legal actions slowed, the city lights faded behind them. They bought a house. He built bookshelves, she raised flowers. For economy's sake, they stopped seeing psychiatrists. Now when she said to him, "You're beautiful," it came solely from her, and when he answered, "So are you," it was to quell the terror that visited them, stark as daylight, plain as the mailman. For Tod was death and Pumpkin was hollow and the fairy godfathers had vanished, taking with them the lovers' best selves.

The Age of Analysis

Lynne Sharon Schwartz

Paul had always had an analyst, ever since he could remember. It began long ago, when, after several days of kicking, screaming, and gobbling handfuls of soil from his mother's potted plants, he was carried by his parents, working in tandem, into the car and on to Dr. Trowbridge's office in a tall building on North Michigan. How old he was then—eight, ten, six—Paul couldn't recall precisely. But he did remember quite clearly that first sight of the analyst.

Dr. Trowbridge struck him as a comfortable, grandmotherly woman. She sat calmly in a leather chair behind a formidable wooden desk, smiling a friendly greeting as his parents dragged him in. She had short wavy gray hair, plump cheeks, and very thick glasses with pale-pink frames; she wore a cotton print dress with short sleeves. It must have been summer. He remembered they had no coats. Later on, in their private sessions, when she used to come out from behind her desk to stroll around the green-carpeted office, he noticed that she wore black oxford shoes with laces, old-lady shoes. Her ankles were thick.

Once he was in the office that seminal afternoon, he ceased his kicking and screaming. No one knew exactly why. He was distracted, perhaps, by the new surroundings, by the abstract mobile of colorful shapes hanging from the low ceiling, by the soft artificial light and the numerous framed documents on the paneled walls. He caught his breath and shut up, impressed that he had driven them to do something about him at last, to stop him, as if he were a runaway windup toy on which they had placed an overdue restraining hand. And what they had done was this relaxed elderly woman who smoked with a slender black cigarette holder, something he had never seen before.

He grew very fond of her and she allowed this fondness. Now, at fifteen, Paul didn't remember much of what they had done or said together except for the mazes. Dr. Trowbridge was very keen on maze games. She produced a new one almost every time Paul came. They bored him, but he felt it would sound impolite or ungrateful to tell her that, particularly as she appeared to enjoy them so. As time passed, he graduated from large wooden block mazes to small cardboard or plastic structures, to dittoed sheets, the most abstract. (Yes, she said, when he remarked on the dittos, she had other young patients. This bothered him, the idea of other children bending their heads with her over the same dittoed sheets, basking in her endless, soothing calm, especially since he never saw them in the small waiting room that hummed with white noise. But as they talked it over he came to accept a nonexclusive relationship.) He hadn't understood the purpose of mazes at first, and performed aimlessly, until Dr. Trowbridge explained that the purpose was to find the most direct way out. Even then they didn't make much sense—why not linger, he thought, on the intricate paths—but he tried to be cooperative. She taught him to work backwards from the goal. Dr. Trowbridge didn't take things as seriously as his parents, nor was she appalled by his lapses into violence. And as she listened and nodded in her quiet way, it began to seem that there was space in him to absorb still another shaming incident with a bit of compassion. This lack of seriousness in her puzzled him, though, for he knew what her purpose was. She was hired specifically to take him seriously, to find out what made him so difficult. She was a superior being who lived above the fray. At least that was what he inferred. Her office was hushed like a holy place. With her he was not difficult.

Then, one nasty day, she announced that he was getting too old for her. She was a child psychiatrist, she explained, and he at thirteen was no longer a child. He was ready to move on to a specialist on adolescence. Paul made a scene, of course; it was the least he could do to preserve his self-respect. He ripped the mobile from the ceiling, tangling and cutting his fingers in the wires, and shouted bitter accusations, which she sat through quietly as if she had expected them.

"I know how you feel," she said. "Separation anxiety." That phrase from the occult language was a further betrayal, and sent him further into rage. He was heading for the curtains, the blood pounding in his head, lunging to fling them down, when she said, "Please, Paul. It's so hard to get curtains. They have to come and measure, and bring samples of fabric. It takes weeks. Please." She smiled mildly, and he stopped.

By now he had forgiven her and thought about her with gentle nostalgia, since he was fairly well settled in with Dr. Crewes, whose office was just off Lake Shore Drive. Dr. Crewes was not like Dr. Trowbridge, either in spirit or in appearance. She was much younger, for one thing, maybe thirty or thirty-five, he guessed. Sometimes he thought she was smarter, too; she sounded smarter, in any case. She chain-smoked and fiddled with things on her desk and had a sharp, knifelike voice that sometimes echoed gratingly in his ears hours after he left her. She wasn't easygoing, but to compensate, there was a shimmering excitement in talking to her. Lately a pleasant sexual buzz hovered around him when he sat opposite Dr. Crewes. They talked about it, naturally, and she said evenly that it was quite all right. It was to be expected. She smiled and showed two perfect rows of small sharp teeth. Dr. Crewes had a broad face, wide green eyes, and shoulder-length straight brown hair that she dashed nervously off her forehead. She never removed her very large round tinted glasses. Usually she wore pants suits with soft sweaters and odd loops of beads. Once, on a rainy day, she had worn blue jeans. Paul encountered her sometimes in his dreams wearing a succession of bizarre costumes, but he never touched her. Either he was afraid, or she drifted away when he reached out.

With the professional help of Drs. Trowbridge and Crewes, Paul had inched his way through youth as through a mined field. He had reached his second year of high school, a better than average student, though there had been months now and then of neglecting his studies and becoming obsessed by games—first backgammon, then chess, most recently horse racing. He won $150 at the track last summer, which he never told his parents about, but he told Dr. Crewes. She seemed proud of his skill in calculating odds, and made clever, provocative analogies between games of chance and real-life situations. Paul told her everything. Even the things he deliberately planned not to tell—in bouts of resistance—she somehow got out of him, or else once they passed by undiscussed, they came to seem insignificant.

Now, Monday, he had made a special appointment with her, apart from his scheduled Thursdays and Saturdays, to discuss the calamity. His parents, after nearly two decades of marriage, were, incredibly, intolerably, separating. Immediately. His father had told him only last night. There had been a vicious scene, during which his mother retreated to the bedroom while he and his father shouted at each other. She was the one being left. His father was going to live with a woman about ten years older than Paul. The very thought of her was intolerable.

His father was a psychoanalyst, his mother was a psychotherapist, and his father's girlfriend was a psychiatric social worker in training, who had first appeared as his student in a seminar. Paul did not have the naive illusion that the membership of all three parties in what his parents called "the helping professions" was any guarantee against emotional upheaval. No. He had matured that much since Dr. Trowbridge. The wretched triangle of experts did not strike him as bizarre, any more than the fact that each of them continued daily to counsel others in torment. He had more than once overheard his parents remark on how the prolonged work of clearing the treacherous paths of the self disposes one to instability. Just like coal miners get black lung, thought Paul.

Indeed, among their friends, largely pairs of analysts, therapists, and social workers, Paul had already witnessed suicide, alcoholism, recurrent infidelity, breakdowns, and violence. So the source of his feeling of utter shock was merely that he had always believed Richard and Nan perfectly matched.

This was what he sullenly told Dr. Crewes now, after which she asked in cool tones, "How does it make you feel?"

He replied by resting his head on her desk and weeping. The sounds of his sobs were ugly to him, great gasping noises like the screeching of gears in an immense and overloaded machine.

Dr. Crewes played with the button of a ballpoint pen lying on her desk while she waited. "It's terrible for you, I can see, especially after all the progress we've made."

"I can't understand it," Paul wept. He blew his nose and tried to control the trembling of his shoulders. "The worst thing is that I can't believe it. How could he go and do this to us, after all those years? How could he? I'd like to . . ." His bony boy's fingers locked and tugged and twisted like an interpreter's making signs for a deaf-mute. "I could tear him to pieces."

"You seem to be identifying strongly with your mother."

"Well, for Christ's sake," said Paul, "it's not a question of identifying. I mean, look what he's doing to me! Shit, I didn't do anything to him except get born, and now . . . I don't know, maybe it *is* me. Maybe he can't put up with me anymore."

"Ah," said Dr. Crewes. "You see, your guilt is coming out. What did I do to deserve this, and so forth. You did nothing. You have to separate that out. What exactly did he say to you?"

"After dinner last night he said he had to have a talk with me. So we sat down. He said he was leaving right away, and he couldn't really explain but it was no longer possible— that's what he said, no longer possible, get that—for him to go on living with my mother. Then he said he was in love. In love! At his age!"

"And what did you say?"

"Nothing. Not until he started on the piano. I was being very quiet. I couldn't say anything, I was so shocked. And at that point my mother was puttering around the dining room table, clearing the dishes away like she just worked there or something. I didn't want to give him the satisfaction of answering. But then he got started on the piano. Which was right there, too, staring us in the face. Well, you know about the piano."

The baby grand piano had been a joint acquisition. Paul and his father both played extremely well. They had shopped for it together two years ago to replace an old upright, when it became obvious that Paul's was no ordinary talent. Paul still remembered what a good time they had had in the showrooms, trying out all the models with snatches of sonatas and popular tunes. Finally they settled on a large black Steinway. Paul cared for it like an attentive parent, cleaning its keys and polishing its glossy surface. He was as fussy about his piano, his father used to joke, as Nan was about her expensive carpeting.

"So he says"—and here Paul mimicked his father's thin raspy voice and ponderous delivery—"'Paul, I know this will seem unfair to you, but I have to have the piano.' 'Over my dead body,' I said. Then he started yelling and running around the room, about how he's tired of giving and has to start taking for himself. And then . . ."

"Well?"

"Well, I sort of got hysterical and tore the place up." Paul grinned, a tentative flicker of light, then his mouth set sullenly again. He stared at the harsh Van Gogh print of sunflowers above Dr. Crewes' head, which often had a semihypnotic effect on him.

"You look proud of yourself."

"Well, then to calm me down, I guess, he said okay, he'd leave the piano. Then a minute later, no, he'd take it. Meanwhile my mother went off to their room. She said she was tired and going to sleep, and he could handle this scene since the whole thing was his idea anyway, and he should have given me more time to adjust to the change. Honestly, by the time it was all over I swear I didn't know if he was taking it or leaving it."

"What about your mother's going off to her room? How did you feel about that?"

"What? Hell, I don't know. I guess I thought she could have stuck up for me more. But she's got her problems too. Listen, I'd like to kill the both of them. What the fuck am I going to do?"

"You're filled with rage and guilt, Paul. As is to be expected. You have to understand that, and that's what we'll have to work on, whatever happens. We'll have to deal with your rage and guilt."

"Deal with! Deal with!" Paul leaped up, his thick gray sweater hanging loosely from his shoulders as he waved his arms violently in the air. He was a tall, sandy-haired boy with gaunt cheeks and a wide mouth. He had ice-blue eyes that in moments of excitement became flecked with pale-green flamelike shapes. "Is all of life one long process of dealing with things? Is that all there is to it? Hell!"

Dr. Crewes flashed her teeth in one of her courteous, enigmatic smiles. With a familiar final gesture, she reached for her appointment book. The fifty-minute hour was over.

"Thanks," said Paul. "I must say I expected more sympathy from you. I mean, simply as a human being. You've known me all these years."

"Yes," she said, "you're disappointed. I can see that. But if I gave you the sympathy you want, it wouldn't help the treatment. I understand how you feel—we'll have to deal with that too."

He set out to walk the mile home, though the cold winds off the lake were fierce. Night was falling. The sky was a dull gray. He had heavy schoolbooks to carry and his bus was right at the corner. But he felt like walking, masochistic or not. Thinking, out in the cold. He was disturbed at how he hadn't been able to get across to Dr. Crewes that his reaction was not yet loss or sadness but only shock. It was inconceivable that they were not happy with each other. He had thought of them, sometimes with mild sarcasm, as practicing experts in marital happiness.

They left for work together in the morning—his father would drop his mother off at the Carl Rogers Institute, loosely connected with the university—leaving Paul alone to clear the breakfast dishes. Often, calling good-bye from the kitchen as he heard the door click open, he had felt like the parent, sending the youngsters off to school with a sense of release. Then his father picked her up at five-thirty. Sometimes they stopped to shop on the way home. They cooked dinner together—Nan was a meticulous and inventive cook—while talking over their cases. The last year or two, Paul had found the daily progress of these cases rather tedious, so he had taken to staying in his room until they called him to the table. But they seemed to enjoy it, that was the crucial point. Finally at dinner they would ask, "And how are things going with you, Paul? Everything under control at school?"

It was beginning to rain. Little pellets of ice hit his face and clung to his eyelashes. He trudged along Fifty-fifth Street, thinking. Once a week his father went out again in the evening to give a seminar to social work trainees. Paul turned a windy corner, winced with pain and cold as a fluttering twig blew at his cheek. As he blinked, he could see some faceless dark feline creature leering at his father, raising her hand often to impress him with pretentious answers, luring him away from home, where he belonged. He was not going to think about that part of it.

They had been happy—he had watched them for years at it, and if he couldn't trust what he saw anymore, then what could he rely on? In school they were learning about a dead philosopher called Berkeley, who said that nothing we see is really there. Of course Paul had thought it was pure nonsense, but maybe Berkeley was right. Maybe everything in the world was deceptive, his parents included.

Richard and Nan generally did not go out on week nights since they got up so early every morning. They read side by side, or else his mother made phone calls to her friends while his father did paper work at the small desk in the living room. Occasionally people dropped over, therapists who talked about their cases. Paul would greet them—they liked to scrutinize him; he had something of a reputation for his violent tendencies, and he rather enjoyed their veiled curiosity. He might listen to them talk for a while, then go to his room. They did not stay late. But weekends were another matter entirely, devoted to pleasure. Nan and Richard would wake early as usual, and as soon as the few chores were done, take off in their shorts and running shoes along the Midway—weather permitting, as they said. In the winter it was swimming in the university pool. They seemed to have a passion for rhythmic movement which Paul did not share. When he was twelve he had rebelled, declaring that he no longer wished to accompany their leisure-time rounds like a pet—their five-mile runs, their serious movies on social themes, their bargain-hunting expeditions, their drawn-out dinners in foreign restaurants, their eternal Sunday afternoons at friends' houses, drinking cocktails and eating through numberless bowls of salted nuts. His mother was hurt, but his father smoothed it over. "Typical of adolescence. He's finding his own style. It's natural that he should be bored with us. Let him alone." "All right, Paul," Nan said, in a voice straining not to sound resentful. "From now on you can make your own plans. You have your keys to come and go."

Of course they were happy, thought Paul, wiping the wetness from his face with his glove. It was unmistakable. Sometimes they seemed such a closed, snug unit that he felt like an intruder. They had spent years alone together before he was born, and he suspected that they had never grown used to the fact of his presence, or sensed quite what to do about it. One evening last fall he was studying in his room and didn't come out to greet them when they returned from work. When he finally emerged at seven o'clock they were busy in the kitchen, earnestly reconsidering one of his mother's drug addicts. "Why,

Paul, my goodness, I forgot all about you," his mother said, and rushed over to kiss his cheek. "You must be starving. Here, have some crackers while we finish getting dinner ready."

The only times he didn't feel like an intruder, but like the very whirling axis of their lives, were the times he got into trouble and caused them trouble. When it was found in his freshman year at U High that he had been cutting classes for weeks, when it came out a year later that he was the mysterious decimator of the school library, with a cache of unstamped books on the floor of his closet, when it was discovered that he was the founder and guiding genius of the widespread and lucrative football pool the school principal had been trying in vain to stamp out, then their evenings turned into long tearful family confrontations. What Nan and Richard said during these sessions was confusing: at first they threatened to stop paying for his analysis if he didn't give up his antisocial behavior. But at the end, at the reconciliation, they said he needed more intensive treatment, and that they would all go together to talk to Dr. Crewes. Those discussions caused him pain and anger and remorse, yet when they were over Paul felt a satisfactory sense of wholeness. He pulsed with energy and appetite; while his parents crept to bed weary and enervated, Paul would fix himself a triple-decker sandwich and a glass of milk, and eat voraciously. Then he rested, complacent in the knowledge that thoughts of him would keep them lying awake for hours.

Still, despite the trouble he used to cause them (he had been somewhat better lately—the result of good treatment, his father claimed as he puffed on his pipe), he knew they were happy. It was a quiet life, but they appeared to thrive on it. A quiet life indeed; a year ago he used to rage over it in his sessions with Dr. Crewes, caricaturing it with contempt as a suffocating, middle-class, middle-of-the-road, mediocre dead life. But Dr. Crewes had helped him deal with those feelings of rage and rebellion. When he was grown, Dr. Crewes said, he could lead whatever sort of life he chose. Meanwhile, in their home, he must have some respect for their preferences, which were in fact his parents' ways of dealing with their own needs and hostilities and fears. Paul was stunned by that profound insight. He glimpsed a baffling world where every attitude was a way of dealing with the attitude beneath it; as time passed, attitudes heaped up in stratified layers like geological formations. Social criticism had no place in the analyst's office. Gradually he gave up his scorn. To understand all is to forgive all, somebody once said. They seemed so happy and settled, it was uselessly cruel to keep battering at the walls of their comfort. They called each other dear and darling and did small favors for each other like making cups of tea or fetching newspapers, with glowing benign faces that seemed to portray an utter and wholesome rightness. They had found their center, he thought, borrowing Dr. Crewes' phrase. They were all center, no movable electrons.

Then this mad dash to the periphery, this flying apart, must be some form of illness, like a virus, that could attack and disjoint the entire system. But like a virus it could go away just as mysteriously as it had come. As he walked and mulled it over, stepping carefully on the slippery sheet of ice underfoot, Paul became fervently convinced it would go away. It was some sort of emotional disruption in his father, certainly, and it would have to be dealt with, but it was not anything that came from the center.

He entered his apartment building with relief, chilled to the bone. His lips were stiff and chapped. It must be below twenty degrees out there, and God knows what with the wind-chill factor. Perhaps he should have taken the bus. But at least he had thought things through a little. He had faith now that it would all work out eventually. Just a half hour ago he had imagined the session with Dr. Crewes was a waste of time, yet after going over the facts he felt much better. He recalled some of the things Dr. Crewes had said, and they seemed quite perceptive. Very often, in his long experience, the sessions did seem a waste of time, and then later he would realize how much had actually been accomplished. The sessions had a delayed effect, like some medications. It was all very intriguing. Maybe he would study medicine after all and go into psychiatry rather than music. With his background he had a head start.

He was almost smiling as he got off the elevator. He walked briskly, stuffing his damp gloves in his pockets and looking forward to a hot dinner. It might not work out right away, he mustn't expect miracles, but he couldn't be deceived by the happy tableau they had presented for so long. Berkeley was absurd, as he had thought at the beginning. What you see, you see because it is there. Meanwhile he thought to comfort his mother and explain things to her. Caution her about trying to rush things one way or the other. Nan was like that. Once a decision was made she immediately had to do tangible acts to verify it, as if it might slip through her fingers. He remembered how, when she and Richard decided last September to go to Barbados over Christmas, she had rushed out to buy new luggage. Paul unlocked the door and stepped into the hall. It was dark.

"Mom?"

"Yes. I'm in here, Paul."

He flicked the hall switch—a warm glow of light filled the tidy narrow space. Nan was curled up on the living room couch, doing nothing, not even reading the paper that lay spread out in her lap. She was tall and dark blond, rather like Dr. Crewes, but older and fairer in complexion. She had a pleasant, squarish face with thin lines of anxiety around the eyes and the small mouth. She could look quite attractive, Paul always imagined, if she wore clothes with some dash. But as though unaware of the passage of time, Nan wore the placid styles of her youth two decades ago, shirtwaist dresses, pleated skirts, and shoes with high thin heels. She wore pearls and clip-on earrings and used hair spray. Still, he thought uncomfortably, she was not the kind of woman to drive a man away. She was warm and capable and easy to be with. If he were his father, he would think he hadn't done so badly after all those years.

"Hi," he said. "Why are you sitting here in the dark?" He turned on another light, then followed her fixed stare across the large room.

Stunned, Paul saw why she wasn't speaking. There was a huge nude space in the corner near the window where the piano should have been. Three hollows in the rug where the legs had rested.

"Shit!" he screamed. He tore off his coat, threw it onto the floor with his books, and rushed to the space as if the piano could spring back, conjured by the pressure of his lanky body. "Shit! He can't do that!" And he let out a long howl. He could feel the blood rushing and pounding in his chest, his face growing unbearably hot. This was how it always happened, starting with the rush of blood. There were no words for this storming bloody torrent. He thrashed around looking for objects to attack and hurl.

"Paul," his mother said quietly. She didn't sound restraining, only tired. "Paul, don't, please don't go into that. I'm too worn out. I couldn't stand it."

He stood quivering like a besieged animal.

"Thank you. Come here and sit down by me." She patted the cushion next to her. "Can you?"

He obeyed, sat down next to her on the couch, and sobbed loudly again.

"Paul, I am so sorry. Really I am. I am so sorry for what this is doing to you."

"What about you? What are you going to do about it?"

"I don't know," she said in a high voice. She ran both hands through her fine hair, pulling it all back from her face so that for an instant she looked austere. "I've been thinking that I'll go back into treatment. I could go back to Dr. Steinberg. He was always very supportive." She pressed the fingertips of both hands together, forming a little spired temple. "To find out what I've done, why this is happening. I'm totally in the dark. Oh, I know I've made a lot of mistakes, that I have certain ways. . . . I'm sure some things must have driven him crazy. But still—"

"I meant," he cried, "what are you going to do about the piano?"

"Oh, the piano. I don't know. What can I do? He did it while we were both out. I came home a little while ago and found it gone. He took all his clothes too." She spoke calmly, as if from a vacant space inside.

"I have to get the piano back. Where is it?"

"In his apartment, I guess."

"What apartment?"

"Didn't he tell you? He's got an apartment with this Cheryl, on Dorchester. He arranged it all last month, before we knew."

Paul hung his head over his knees. "He can't get away with this," he mumbled.

"Would you like some dinner?"

"I don't know. I don't feel like eating anymore."

"I'll make something anyway. You've got to try."

It was odd seeing her in the tiny kitchen by herself. They had always done their fancy dishes together. Paul watched from the living room. Nan moved in slow motion, opening cabinets with faltering hands and a vague air, very slowly taking cans and boxes off the shelves and staring at their labels for long moments as if she had never seen them before. Then she opened the refrigerator door and stood looking inside it for a long time. Paul stared at her back; her shoulders began to shake as though she had opened the door onto a pathetic scene.

"Oh, forget it, you don't have to cook."

She finally removed something wrapped in aluminum foil and let go of the door. "No, it's all right. I've got to get used to it. This is some chicken Kiev left from yesterday. He made it, actually. You see—" and she tossed her head archly—"he leaves something of himself with us."

"How long have you known?" he asked her while they ate.

"A week. I wanted him to tell you before, to give you some time, but he said no. He insisted. A clean swift break was what he wanted. It's been absolute hell, knowing all week and not being able to tell you. He's not himself, Paul, this cruelty, this coldness. That bothers me more than anything else. It's like a sickness. I think he's psychotic. I really do. I think he's sick. It has to do with his mother. He needs help."

The food was sticking in his throat. Everything he ate felt dry and scratchy as straw. He kept taking gulps of milk to wash it down, but he could still feel the lumps lying heavily in his chest. "I'm going over there tomorrow to get the piano back. You'll give me the address."

His mother pushed her plate away and got up. "I'm going to call him." She brushed a few crumbs off her blouse and caught them in the palm of her hand. Paul realized how wan and weary she looked. Her face was shiny, her lipstick faded, and her skirt wrinkled as though it had been crushed underfoot. "I can't just let it fall apart like this. It's too hasty. It doesn't make any sense. Maybe I can talk to him about it." Nan went to the phone.

"Wait. What if she answers?"

"Her?" His mother smiled wryly. "I don't care a thing about her. As far as I'm concerned, she doesn't exist. I've met her, you know, around the university. We once discussed Karen Horney. Isn't that funny? She's nothing at all. Just young."

"So why . . . ?"

Nan tilted her head and gave him a peculiar look that he couldn't decipher, almost a grin, as she raised the receiver. She took a folded piece of paper from her pocket. "His number. How do you like that? I've got to consult a scrap of paper to telephone your father."

Evidently the girl didn't answer, since his mother began talking right away. "Richard, it's me. Look, Richard . . ." Her voice was shaking, cajoling and vulnerable. Paul felt flushed; he began clearing the table noisily to drown out her words, while his ears strained to hear above the clatter. Nan waved her hand at him to be quiet.

"Richard, look, I'm not calling to pester you or whine, believe me. I want what's best for you. I mean, whatever you think is right for your particular needs. But I think, I've been thinking, this has all been too fast—I mean, I can't absorb it. Can't we get together and talk about it, just so it isn't so abrupt? Maybe," she added timidly, "even see someone about it, together?"

A very short silence. His mother sat down quickly, perched on a hard chair. Paul scraped the leavings of the two plates into the garbage can.

"All right. But, Richard, can I tell you one thing? Before you get all involved in your—your new life, as you call it, Richard, think about what you're doing. It isn't so simple. You have a . . . a problem, this is an emotional crisis. Try to see it that way, Richard. I think you need help. Maybe you should go back to see Dr. Jonas alone, have a consultation."

Another silence. Her lips twitched. "You've never talked like that. That's what makes me think——"

Then, after a dead pause. "All right, if that's how you've decided it's going to be, I'll call a lawyer in the morning." She hung up.

Paul was holding a pot half-filled with reheated rice. He walked slowly into the living room. "But you didn't mention the piano!"

"He's really finished. He said . . . incredible things."

"The piano!" he shrieked.

"The piano," she repeated, as if it were an unfamiliar word. "Oh, the piano. I'm sorry."

He dumped the rice on the carpet, at her feet, and slammed the pot down after it. Then he grabbed his coat. As he went out the door he glimpsed Nan sinking slowly to her knees and scooping up handfuls of rice.

He skipped school the next day and walked all the way to the Point and back. There had been a thaw after yesterday's rain, so that the gutters were running with slush. At about seven he went to his father's place. It was a sleek new apartment building, steel and glass. The doorman stopped him to ask his name and destination, and Paul laughed curtly as he replied. When he got up to the sixth floor his father was at the apartment door, waiting.

"Paul."

"I came for the piano."

"Paul, you can't carry it away."

"Aren't you going to let me in? I'm kind of cold."

His father stepped aside. The girl was sitting cross-legged on the floor, leaning against a pile of crammed cartons.

They were apparently in the middle of their dinner, which was Kentucky Fried Chicken. A large paper bucket bearing the face of the jovial colonel lay on its side, spewing out chicken parts and discarded bones. They were drinking wine out of paper cups, Bolla Soave, the same kind his father and Nan drank at home. The girl was pretty much what Paul had expected. It was reassuring yet eerie to see his banal predictions verified. She had short straight black hair that fell in bangs to her green-shadowed eyelids, and she wore a long red and green flowered gypsy dress with a round neck. Silver earrings dangled nearly to her shoulders. Her bare feet, sticking out from under the dress, were very small and delicate. But she was plumper than Paul had envisioned. She had enormous breasts. Paul imagined his father's head nuzzling the huge breasts while the girl lay naked on the bare wood floor, her legs raised and parted. She wiped the chicken grease off her lips and hands and stood up.

"Cheryl, my son Paul."

Cheryl came toward him smiling, extending a hand. Paul turned away from her. "I want to talk to you."

"Cheryl, would you mind?" It was a disgrace—he was apologetic.

Cheryl went into another room and closed the door behind her. Paul hadn't heard the sound of her voice.

The apartment was cluttered yet looked bare and unlived in—it could be adapted to any pattern of life his father and this Cheryl fell into. Odd pieces of furniture, cartons, shopping bags, a broom and dustpan, were placed haphazardly, like litter. Looking around, Paul recognized with a slight shock two bridge chairs, a brass magazine rack, a straw wastebasket.

"Where is it?"

Richard finally shut the front door. "Where is what?"

"You know, the piano."

208 Lynne Sharon Schwartz

"Oh, in the living room. This way."

It stood alone in a large room that was empty except for a cream-colored shag rug on the floor and two more bridge chairs from home.

"Didn't she bring any bridge chairs of her own?"

Richard cleared his throat and patted his graying hair. "Look, believe me, I know this confrontation is very difficult for you."

"Oh, never mind that crap. I really didn't think you'd do it. I didn't realize what a bastard you were underneath."

Richard paled. "Well," he said coldly, "take it. No one's stopping you."

"Don't worry. I'll have a mover here tomorrow. I'm taking the day off from school."

"Paul." His father motioned to one of the bridge chairs. "Let's start again. Sit down. Please." Richard sat. His stomach, as he settled in the small chair, sagged with flab, despite all his running. He was so pathetic that finally Paul sat down too.

Richard's thinning hair was tousled. Paul wondered if she had rumpled it in a moment of affection. In his white shirt, dark trousers, and silver-rimmed glasses, his father resembled the benevolent village druggist Paul had often seen advertising toothpaste on television.

"I think I'm going to laugh," said Paul. "You and her." He motioned with a flip of his hand toward the door where Cheryl had disappeared. He expected, hoped, his father would respond angrily again, but Richard only nodded, as if it were the most natural coupling in the world.

"Are you feeling all right, Paul? Have you talked it over with Dr. Crewes? Don't hold anything back. Tell her what it's doing to you. It's best to get it out, you know that. You think I'm a bastard, fine, tell her. Say anything. She'll help you deal with it." His mother was right. Richard spoke in a tinny mechanical way, as if his real self were elsewhere. Once again Paul was forced to think he must be sick.

With pity he went over to Richard and put a hand on his shoulder. "What is it that's making you do this to us?" he asked kindly.

It was past eleven when Paul left for home. They had had a long and, he felt, meaningful talk. They both cried, Paul copiously, Richard joining in as one might to be sociable. At around nine Cheryl had padded into the room tentatively, but Paul shook his head, no, so Richard motioned her away. About an hour later they moved into the other room, where at Richard's suggestion Paul ate some cold Kentucky Fried Chicken. Then Cheryl, who must have entered the living room by another route, began playing a Scarlatti sonata on the piano. Richard closed the door.

"She's very good," he said. "She never could afford a piano of her own before. It makes her very happy."

Paul felt much better when he left. He understood, at least partially, why his father had done this shocking thing. According to Richard, the root cause was that he had smothered his rage at Nan's compulsiveness and rigidity for many long years. Now it had finally erupted, as it had to someday, in this form. Also, according to Richard, he was not sick but healthy for the first time in his life. His pathology, he outlined carefully in simplified terms that Paul could understand, had been in submitting to Nan's rigid controls. Now, with maybe twenty or more years ahead of him, he was going to start a new life and integrate his personality. It would be, he said, a voyage of self-discovery. He swallowed some wine as he talked of self-discovery, and in his eagerness to explain, a few drops dribbled along his chin. He had had trouble with women, he said, ever since boyhood—his mother got him off on the wrong track, as mothers tend to do (they both smiled knowingly), and as a result his whole marital relationship with Nan had been an unconscious working out of unresolved hostility toward his mother. He sucked deeply on his pipe amid pained reminiscences of his mother. This revelation surprised Paul slightly. His grandmother was a kindly, frail old woman with an unexpected and remarkable sense of humor; true, he thought, she did have a tendency to shower them with food and gifts on the rare occasions when they visited, but he had never realized, until Richard told him, just how controlling she was. As for Nan, Paul knew of course that Nan kept the house neat and worried excessively about getting places on time, but he had never dreamed of the tortuous ramifications these failings might have had in Richard's mind.

"We'll see each other often, Paul," Richard said as he was leaving. "We'll have an even better relationship, now we can be more open with each other."

Paul was relieved to find Nan wasn't waiting up for him. He felt funny—no, he could recognize and accurately name the sensation now, thanks to Dr. Crewes—ambivalent about telling Nan of his visit. He was filled with elation at the true communication he and Richard had achieved, and what he craved more than anything else was to share that elation with someone close. Yet that person couldn't be Nan since, in some complicated way, it had been achieved at her expense. He had to hide it from her, to protect her from more pain. Paul couldn't be angry with Nan for her pathology— with his background in treatment he knew better than that; he could only be sad at how it had wrecked the family. With the dim light of the hall behind him he looked in on her from her bedroom door. She was wearing a faded blue flannel nightgown and sleeping discreetly on her side of the big bed, her thumb touching her lips. He pitied her.

He didn't get up at the usual time the next morning. When Nan finally came to awaken him he said he had a bad cold and wouldn't be going to school. He was planning to surprise her with the piano.

"I'm sorry you're sick. It's all that walking in the rain. Can I get you some aspirins? A cup of tea?"

"No, I don't have any fever."

"You were out late again last night. With friends?"

"Yes."

"Well," she sighed, gazing sleepily around the room, "I'd better run. I've got my battered wives group coming first thing in the morning, then I'm taking a couple of hours off, first to see the lawyer, and then I'm seeing Dr. Steinberg for a consultation. I've got to get this thing straightened out in my head so I can start dealing with it realistically. I'm just not able to function this way. Patients talk to me at work and I drift off, I just can't concentrate."

"Well, maybe he can help you."

"You don't have an appointment with Dr. Crewes today, do you?"

"No, tomorrow."

"Okay, take care of yourself. I'll phone later to see how you are. You're sure it's nothing more than a cold? Does your throat hurt?"

"No, I'm sure. So long."

As soon as she was gone he leaped out of bed and telephoned the moving company around the corner. He had worked there last summer, so they knew him well. They would do it on short notice if he offered to help.

When all the arrangements were made he had a sudden doubt—maybe he had better call his father. In the elation of last night he had forgotten to remind Richard to leave his key with the superintendent. Cheryl might not be in, and even if she was, he didn't feel up to dealing with her yet.

Richard was with a patient, the secretary said.

"This is his son. It's urgent."

"What is it, Paul?" Richard's voice came across anxiously. "Are you all right? Is Mother?"

"Yes, yes, we're fine. It's about the piano. I wanted to get you early. Could you have your super let the movers in? I'm not sure what time. Sometime between one and five, they said."

"But, Paul, I don't remember saying anything about the piano."

"But—I told you I was coming today. Don't you remember? And then we talked, and—"

"Paul, I'm sorry, I'm with a patient and I can't talk. There's been a misunderstanding. Can I call you back in half an hour?"

"The piano!" Paul screamed, frantically winding the cord of the phone around his arm and stamping his foot. "You've got to give back the piano!"

"Paul, please calm yourself. I can't talk now. Paul?"

"You shit, you fucker, you motherfucking lying bastard, I'm going to kill you—"

"Paul, if you don't stop I'll call Dr. Crewes and have her come over and give you something." In a quieter, muffled tone, "Excuse me, Mrs. Reed, I'm sorry for this interruption—an emergency. Paul, are you there? We must talk this over calmly, don't do anything violent. Paul?"

Paul tore the cord out of the wall and hurled the phone to the floor.

In half an hour he was at the door of his father's new apartment, breathing hard. He knocked quietly, so as not to alarm her. Paul had it all planned. This time he hadn't broken his mother's dishes or uprooted her plants. He had controlled himself with effort, hoarded it for the explosion. It was a new experience for him, dressing swiftly with deft hands, plotting and savoring his vengeance. His excitement was so strong, seething and boiling in his thighs, that it felt almost like physical pleasure. It was uncanny—as he left the building he had an erection.

"Who is it?" A high young voice. She pronounced the phrase with a rising and falling melody.

"Paul, Richard's son."

"Oh." The door opened. In jeans, a navy-blue turtle-neck sweater, and high boots she looked completely different, swinging and competent and held together. She wasn't as plump, either, as she had appeared last night in her long dress. She wore horn-rimmed glasses that made her face serious and purposeful. Her skin was bright with morning. "Hello, Paul. I was just on my way out. Your father's gone to his office already. Would you like to call him?"

"I didn't come for him."

"Oh, me?" She was bewildered for an instant, then masked it quickly with politeness. "Why, sure. Come in. Have you had breakfast?"

He shoved past her. It was difficult to keep his arms from flying at the cartons and ripping them apart, but he wanted to carry this out perfectly, according to plan. He had a goal. He went to the living room. The bridge chairs were still close together, facing each other for intimate talk, as he and Richard had left them last night.

"Do you want to hear me play something?"

"Well . . . sure. Go ahead," she said.

He plunged into a flamboyant, racing Beethoven Rondo. His fingers recoiled instantly, for she had gotten the keys dirty with her chicken grease. But he kept on playing.

"You're terrific. Listen, please come over and play it whenever—"

"You like Scarlatti, right? Bach? That's your sort of thing?" He didn't need an answer. Her music was right on the rack. Grinding his teeth together till they ached, he tore the first thin book through. She reached out to stop him, shrieking with disbelief, but he waved her off with a long arm, hitting her on the shoulder so that she stumbled a few steps away. Then he did the other books, one by one, systematically. She looked on in silence.

Then she said, "Those can be replaced, you know."

He shredded every page of her music till the room was scattered with scraps, black notes strewn on the bare floor like trampled insects.

"Look, I understand your rage. It's separation anxiety, very common, very normal. Can't we talk about it?"

Paul laughed. "Do you want to deal with it too?"

He came toward her.

"Paul, you're upset, you need help. What—"

She was at the wall, one shoulder tensed and huddled against it. Her hands flew to her chest in a crossed, protective gesture. He liked that sight of her in dread, liked it so much that he paused, relishing it like the taste of something tart on his tongue.

"Paul, please, I didn't do anything to you. Listen, my parents were divorced too. I know how you—"

He hit her across her open mouth and stepped back. At last he felt some small relief from his seething. He was overheated, and took off his heavy jacket.

"Don't. Don't do anything! Please!" It was a little girl's voice now.

He laughed again. It made him feel years older to think she was afraid of that. "Stand up straight and look at me."

She obeyed.

"I'm not going to do that. You think I'd do that? You're crazy. You think I want to be where he's been, in that filthy hole?"

He hit her across the face four or five times until he felt satisfied. She tried to fight back, but she was so much smaller and weaker that he could restrain both her wrists with one hand. She kicked at him, aiming for the groin, but he kicked back, flicking her feet away as he might throw off an overeager dog. Her glasses lay smashed on the floor. Then he dragged her through the rooms until he found one with a double-bed mattress on the floor. He pushed her down on it.

"There. That's all. Aren't you relieved? And don't forget to tell him, when he comes back, that I want the piano."

He had planned to do more, to hit her harder and longer and all over, but he had lost the will. It was not the pleasure he had anticipated. He was stretched out on the couch when his mother came home.

"Paul, are you feeling any better? I called twice but you didn't answer. Were you asleep?" She set down her packages and came over to feel his forehead. "You feel cool. You don't look too well, though. Listen," she went on, "I brought home some Kentucky Fried Chicken for us. I know it's kind of tacky, but I just couldn't face cooking. Dr. Steinberg said I shouldn't try to do everything, just take things slowly, one at a time. Not push myself. I know you could use a decent meal, but— Paul? Are you there?"

"It's okay. Actually I adore Kentucky Fried Chicken."

"I'll make you some tea with it." She started toward the kitchen. At the threshold the telephone lay in parts at her feet. "Oh, no . . . This is your work, I take it?"

"Elves."

"Oh, Paul. Paul, honestly, I'm not in any state to deal with this now. I swear I don't know what to say. I didn't need this. I didn't need this at all," she muttered.

"They'll come to replace it if you call your business office. You can use the extension meanwhile."

"But why?"

"He's not returning the piano. His little pussycat plays it too. She's very talented."

"Oh, God. The rotten bastard. It doesn't excuse this mess, though. Pick it up, for heaven's sake. And will you call the phone company in the morning? You have to learn to take the consequences of your actions."

"Sure," said Paul. "No sweat."

She served the chicken and mashed potatoes on their bone china plates, and opened a bottle of Bolla Soave for herself, pouring it into a wine goblet. Nan had her hair pulled back in a bun, which made her seem older. He saw her as she would be in twenty years, her parched remains. They ate silently for a while, and then abruptly Nan put down her fork and began to speak, her eyes fixed on a point beyond Paul.

"I had a good session with Dr. Steinberg today. He's very supportive. God knows I can use some support in this. He says there are whole areas of pathology that I've repressed completely, that I must bring out in the open if I want to be in touch with reality. I'll have a lot to do. But first, he says, I have to deal with the real feelings of loss and jealousy and fear and all that, that I'm feeling. But I haven't seemed to be feeling them, have I?"

Paul shrugged. "How do I know what you're feeling?"

"That's the trouble. Neither do I."

She drank, gulped, and began to sob loudly over her goblet of wine. "Oh, God, why did this have to happen! We were happy, weren't we? We seemed all right, didn't we? I don't know anything anymore. I can't even remember, it's all gone. I know I'm compulsive in some ways, but I never thought—" She pounded her fist on the table. "Why is he so hateful to me? I'd like to kill him. And I'm terrified. Terrified."

"Is that what you're supposed to do when you deal with your feelings?" Paul inquired as he continued to eat. "It didn't sound quite right."

She groaned and shuddered, hiding her face. "You're right, you're right. I'm totally out of touch. I can't even convince myself."

"I'm sorry. I didn't mean it. I shouldn't have said that."

Nan wiped her eyes with her linen napkin. "I have a patient whose husband beats her," she said dully. "She comes in and talks about it. And I think, while I listen, that's better than this—this screen between us. I haven't known him for years. It's been like a play."

He led her to the couch and sat next to her. She seemed genuinely present for the first time in days—it made him want to talk, to seize the opportunity. "Mom? Do you know what I did today?"

Immediately he regretted his words. Nan raised her head with a start; the familiar shadow of dread crossed her face, and her eyes closed.

"What?"

"Oh, nothing. I mean, I just slept the whole day. I guess I was that wrung out."

"Oh, Paul, it must be hell for you, and neither of us is doing you much good. You've got to rely on Dr. Crewes. She'll help you, she knows you, and she can be objective about the situation. That's what you need. You're seeing her tomorrow, aren't you? You'll be well enough to go out tomorrow."

The next morning the phone, the extension in the master bedroom, rang before eight, as Paul was dressing. This was nothing unusual; the phone had been ringing steadily ever since his father left—friends calling daily for reports on his mother's emotional condition. Several called quite early so as to be undistracted, before leaving for tightly scheduled days at the office. Paul ignored it and began getting his books together. In two days he had completely forgotten what was happening in school, that world having flicked off like a light bulb. He even had to check his program card to remind himself which class to report to first. He was trying to fix his thoughts on the day ahead when, passing by his parents' bedroom on his way out, he saw Nan sitting on the edge of the bed with the phone at her ear, listening, not whispering rapidly as she usually did. As she listened, tears ran down her face, which she wiped carelessly with the belt of her coarse woolen bathrobe. Paul stopped in the doorway to watch.

"Yes, yes, of course I will. I know." Her voice was gentle, lower and more intimate than he had ever heard it. He was embarrassed, as if he were surprising her naked. Her whole body seemed to have softened and relaxed; her face was somber but live with emotion. "It's all right," she was saying. "You know I do. I can. I'll do anything." She hadn't yet combed her hair, and it hung in soft pale clumps over her forehead and cheeks and neck. Her words came out husky with sleep and tears. She held her unbelted robe loosely around her body with one arm, while she stretched her long bare legs in front of her, as though feeling their weight and mass after long disuse. "No, no, I'm not crying. I'll be right there. Don't do anything. I have to finish dressing." Paul reddened and turned away.

"That was him," she came to tell Paul, tying the robe quickly. She looked haggard now. He noticed how much weight she had lost over the week. "He wants me to come to his office right away. He had a fight with her last night, and he realized he can't stay with her. Paul, I'm worried. But relieved, in a way. He says he suddenly sees that this is all some kind of pathological outburst, that he's having a sort of breakdown. He's canceled all his patients. I'd better get over there."

"And you think . . . something may work out?"

"I don't know. But he turned to me—that's a good sign. He sounded more like himself, except weak. Like he was . . . in need. Oh, Paul, I hope we can . . . God knows I'll do anything."

She rushed off to dress.

Paul didn't go to school after all, but instead walked the streaming slushy Hyde Park streets most of the day. That afternoon he told Dr. Crewes that he had beaten up Cheryl.

"Did you want to rape her too?"

"Oh, no, I don't think I'm ready for rape yet. I'm only fifteen, you know. Don't rush things."

"You can be funny if you want to, but you know it's just avoidance, Paul. Resistance."

"Okay, okay. No, I didn't want to rape her. I'm not even sure how to go about raping someone, but I think if I wanted to I could have done it. You know I don't have the proper inner restraints. That's my problem, right, what we're supposed to be dealing with?"

"Maybe you were afraid you couldn't measure up to your father?"

"Huh?"

"And now you're worried that you may not be punished for it. Your father hasn't called or come around to express his disapproval, has he? So you may in effect be rewarded for what you did, if your parents do get back together. You would then see this violence as having a positive effect. Which would be very confusing."

He tried in vain to follow her path of reasoning. "I never thought of that."

"There are a lot of things you haven't thought of. Now, what do you feel about your parents seeing each other today?"

"Good. I mean, anything but this hell. It can't get worse, can it? They were happy, you know. Oh, sure, pathologies, repressions, all that shit, but they were okay."

"Do you really think so, or do you just want very much to believe it?"

"Well . . . it's funny you should say that. See, we were reading this eighteenth-century philosopher in school and—"

"Wait a minute. Let's not get into philosophy. Let that rest a minute. What were you really feeling when you hit that young woman?"

"It was terrific. Like, sexy. Like jerking off."

"You see, even your imagery—"

"Oh, I'm teasing you." He laughed. "You're playing right into my hands. What's wrong with you today, Claudie? Is something bothering you?" Her name was Claudia. He used it sometimes with joking bravado, and she didn't seem to mind, in fact he suspected that she liked it. But she hated his diminutive version; it worked every time.

Dr. Crewes started to put a cigarette between her lips but it slipped out of her grasp and rolled along the waxed floor. Paul retrieved it for her. "It seems to me," she said, holding the burning match, "that your one 'success,' as it were, in overpowering a woman has made you very . . . skittish, so to speak, and your attitude—toward me, for example—is colored by it."

"Okay, you know you turn me on. I've told you that before. What does it have to do with anything? Listen—my family is living through this—this nightmare. Are you going to help me or aren't you?"

Dr. Crewes puffed and blew smoke at the ceiling with apparent concentration. "I'm trying to, Paul. All right, let's get back to the violence. After your phone conversation with your father about the piano, did any alternatives occur to you, any possible responses other than going to his apartment and attacking his mistress?"

"Mistress! Jesus, I thought that was only in books." He reflected, and answered thoughtfully. "The way I saw it, it was going to be the piano or her that got it. Something had to get it. But I realized that if I broke up the piano I'd be sorry later. Self-defeating. You see, I thought it out logically. So it had to be her. Now, considering everything we've been dealing with all these years, I think that was progress. Don't you?"

She stubbed out the cigarette with sharp taps of annoyance.

Paul arrived home before his mother that afternoon, feeling almost lighthearted. Certainly he had been flippant during the session, but maybe that was a good sign. There was reason to hope. He was impatient to hear how things had gone between them. He was also starving, he had realized on the way home, and so he stopped to buy a real dinner: two large steaks, a box of spaghetti and a can of clam sauce, a head of lettuce and two ripe tomatoes. He had the water boiling for the spaghetti and was trimming the steaks when his mother entered. Paul rushed to the door, the carving knife still in his hand.

"Well, how was he? What happened?"

Nan squeezed his hand with her chilly gloved fingers. "Oh, Paul. Oh, so much happened. Let me get my coat off. Would you make me a strong Scotch? I'm worn out."

She collapsed in the nearest chair, Richard's leather recliner.

"Well, tell me, for Christ's sake."

"First of all, he's sending back the piano tomorrow. I wanted you to know that right off. He realized how horrid and selfish he's been about that."

"Great, but I mean what really happened?"

"I thought you'd be so excited about the piano. He told me, by the way, how much it meant to you. That is, precisely how far you would go. . . ." She frowned for an instant. She was looking more like herself, Paul noticed. "But we won't go into that now. No more guilt and recriminations. I guess we've all been overwrought and irrational. Still, Paul, really! . . . Well, anyway, he's sick, as I thought. He's a man who's sick and needs help badly. While I was there I made an appointment for him with Dr. Jonas for tomorrow morning."

"But what happened, about you and him?"

"Shh. Don't yell. And don't wave the knife around like that, you'll hurt yourself. This whole Cheryl episode was the working out of a psychosis. I'm mixed in, his mother, the works. Classic."

Groaning with impatience, Paul went to the kitchen and got out the Scotch and ice cubes.

"Anyway," she went on, "we talked and cried, and he was different. Like he used to be, not with that cold surface. Oh, Paul." Her face eased for a moment. "I wasn't wrong all those years, was I? I mean, we loved each other, didn't we?"

"I thought so. Here's your Scotch."

"Thanks." Nan took a short swift drink, tossing her head back expertly. "Ah, that's good. He was heartbroken at what he's made us all go through. He said he was even afraid to call, he was afraid I wouldn't want to see him. Of course I'd see him, no matter what. He's totally bewildered and mixed up. But I think he's past the worst."

"How about you?"

"I don't know. I'm glad, I'm hopeful. Anxious, too. I'll know better how I feel after I talk to Dr. Steinberg tomorrow, and hear what happens with Dad and Dr. Jonas. Meanwhile we'll just have to wait. How did it go with Dr. Crewes today?"

"The usual. I'm cooking steaks. We'll celebrate."

"Oh, Paul, that's sweet of you. For the first time in a week I feel like eating."

"Will he be home for dinner?" he asked hesitantly.

"Oh, no, not yet. We're not ready to face that yet. We're both still too—too sore. It's better to wait a few days till we figure out what to do. Maybe he'll come Saturday. But don't count on it. Don't count on anything."

"Oh. I guess I had this silly idea that it would all straighten out overnight."

She came over and stroked his head. "No. It's not that simple. There's still a lot of struggle and pain ahead. We'll have to change the whole structure of our relationship. Everything out in the open." Nan drank some more, her eyes bright with zeal. "I'm going to change. It won't be easy, but—"

"All right, all right. Let me get back to the kitchen."

He went to bed peaceful, with only a few nagging doubts that mutated into strange dreams in which a pack of women chased him up and down a beach, half threatening, half in play. He raced up and down the concrete path bordering the shore of the lake, darting into a grove of trees to elude them, enjoying the game, but afraid too. Then he found that if they got too close all he had to do was wave his erect penis at them and they retreated in a tight cluster, backing off with round gazing eyes. He awoke suddenly on sticky damp sheets. Claudia would love this one, he thought, as he rolled over to a dry part of the bed.

He rushed directly home the next day, Friday, to see if it had arrived. School hadn't been too painful. Refreshing, almost. He had forgotten the minor comfort of having a warm, predictable place to go each day. Of course there were problems, as he had expected. For one thing, Paul was informed that he was failing American History because he had handed in no work for two weeks. A failure would mean being dropped from the basketball team, unless he had a very good excuse. Also, the teachers were waiting for the spring term's program choices: if he really wanted medicine later on, maybe he should take chemistry now and drop music. This was a decision he wanted to talk over with Richard and Nan. He hoped desperately that Richard would come to dinner tomorrow. They would all sit in the living room and discuss things calmly and peacefully, as they used to. He would have to tell them how he hadn't been in school—they would find out sooner or later. His homeroom teacher, naturally, was demanding an explanation of his absence all week. Nan and Richard would ask where he had been. On the streets. But then again they might be too preoccupied even to ask.

He paused before opening the door, trembling. Then he rushed in. The piano was home, back in place, where it should be. Tears of relief came to his eyes at the sight of it. So it was all right to have trusted them, this time. He touched the keys hesitantly, awkwardly, as if he hadn't touched them for weeks, then wiped them off with a damp rag. He took out his Beethoven, his Joplin, his folk song books, and rearranged them on the rack where they belonged. Then he played till Nan returned, running through nearly every piece he knew, one after the other. It was the beginning of good times again. For they had been good—he hadn't appreciated his life before. Even Nan's and Richard's old, dull, suffocating ways would be welcome now, anything after this week.

"Oh, I see it's back," Nan called from the hall. "I'm glad." She came over and kissed Paul. "At least one thing is in place again." She was almost in place again too, Paul saw. That brisk, self-assured everyday coping, Nan's distinctive note, was returning. He watched as she stepped into the kitchen, where she washed her hands and immediately began to slice onions for her special chili with avocado and sour cream. She seemed to know exactly what to do; it was a relief. Still, it was odd how he missed the wan, weepy Nan, strung out on the taut threads of her agony, or that other strange, sensual Nan, with the night-time voice and undone hair.

"I called him today," she chattered from the kitchen, "and asked how it went with Jonas, and he said all right. That was all he said about it. I think we should relax for a couple of days and let things take their course. Oh, he will be here for dinner tomorrow night after all. Sort of a phased re-entry." She slid the onions into a frying pan and a hot sizzle arose, like the sizzle of Nan's energy returning. "He asked about you. Also, I saw Dr. Steinberg again this morning."

"Oh. What did he have to say?"

"Well, for one thing, he said to act spontaneously, out of feeling, not from a predetermined script, you know, with built-in expectations. Why don't you play something till it's ready, Paul?"

He chose ragtime, an ironic beat. His father would be home tomorrow night; that was all that mattered. The rest of it was puzzling. He clung to the one stable fact: Richard would come tomorrow; they would talk calmly about his problems in school; things would be normal again.

Paul went out early next morning while Nan was still asleep, leaving a note saying he would be at the library. He had phoned to cancel his eleven o'clock Saturday morning appointment with Dr. Crewes, explaining to her tape machine that he had urgent schoolwork to make up. Restless with energy, lying sleepless in bed as a gray light dawned, he had formulated a practical plan. He could work all day, getting as much of the history done as possible, and hand it in Monday along with a note from one of his parents pleading family difficulties, some crisis or other. They would know what to say. With luck he would catch the teacher in a sympathetic mood; then he could remain on the basketball team.

He sat over his books for hours, surprised that he was able to concentrate. Throughout, the prospect that Richard would be there at night sustained him like a snug life jacket. By five o'clock he was weary and pleased with himself. When he got in from the bitter cold, he saw Nan's coat thrown carelessly over a chair, her open pocketbook hanging by its strap from a doorknob. A half-empty coffee cup rested on the carpet near the couch. That was unlike her. Paul hoped she wasn't sick. Nothing could go wrong tonight. He had been through enough— it had to end now. His back and chest broke out in a cold sweat. He had done all that homework; he had controlled himself; now he needed to talk to them. As he turned the lights on he felt a twinge of pain and remembered one more detail that demanded attention: the school nurse had told him last Friday that he might need glasses; the glare of the fluorescent bulbs hurt his eyes. This week they had been aching more than ever, especially today in the library. Paul had felt the pain but not registered it as a discrete fact, it had been so merged in the larger pain.

There was no answer when he called out, so he knocked on Nan's bedroom door, then opened it. She was lying fully dressed on the bed, one arm shielding her eyes.

"Mom, are you sleeping?"

"Paul?" She raised her head. "No. I didn't hear you come in. What time is it?"

"Twenty after five. Are you sick?"

"No. I'm not sick."

He had never heard that voice before. It was low, not sensual but vacant, and sounded like it came from the marrow of her bones. He rushed over. "What's the matter with you?"

"He called this morning. He's decided after seeing Dr. Jonas, the high priest, that what he needs is a complete separation, even though he's not going back to his girlfriend." Her face was totally motionless except for her lips, which barely moved as she spoke.

Paul sat down on the bed. He hardly grasped the sense of her words, so stunned was he by this new, hollow voice coming out of her. It must be Nan, he thought wildly, yet it was not Nan. In panic, he hunched his shoulders and made a supreme effort to sit still and speak quietly.

"He's not coming back?"

"No. I told you. He's—uh, let me see, what does he have now? Oh, it's a midlife crisis, the doctor said. It's so hard to keep up with the diagnoses."

"Are you being funny?"

"Yes, I think so. Isn't it funny?" She didn't laugh or smile, though. "He wants control over his own life, he wants—um, let's see, what else—he wants to change his patterns of response." She spoke in a dull, singsong manner, almost demented, almost like a chant. "There is allegedly a whole phase of early development he never went through. And of course he needs to get in touch with his true feelings. That, by all means. Who could quarrel with that?"

"Mom, should I call a doctor for you? I mean, a regular doctor?"

"No. I'm quite well. I am in touch with my feelings at last. I have no feelings."

"Please!" he shrieked, his voice cracking high like a much younger boy's. "Stop it!"

"Sorry," she said in the same flat way. "That wasn't true. The truth is—what is the truth? Can you believe, I think I love him. But how can I love that bastard? It's an obscenity."

He got up. His veins were throbbing with blood again. It was himself he would hurl this time, knock himself out cold to lose consciousness. Bang his head on the wall till it broke open and spilled like a coconut oozing milk. The roots of his hair prickled; he felt a falling, thudding drop in his intestines.

She half sat up, leaning on her elbows, and gave him a stabbing, menacing look. "If you do that," she said slowly in her hollow tone, "if you throw anything or touch anything, I swear I will tear you to shreds." Her fingers bent stiffly and curled up.

She was hypnotic. He wished he could go to her and cry on her breast, but she had become too awesome for that, a terrible, mythical creature.

"Thank you," she said, relapsing into herself, and lay back again.

Paul went to his room, sat on the bed, and shook. Everything shook, inside and out. He watched the shaking hands with a removed fascination. Soon he heard a key in the lock and he jumped to his feet. The door opened and closed, then a shuffling sound, then the bumping of wooden hangers in the front closet.

"Paul? Are you home?"

He tried to answer but nothing came out of his throat, which had locked shut. He walked to the living room.

"Hello, Paul. I wanted to see you," his father said. His suit was creased. His striped shirt was wrinkled, too. He lit a cigarette.

"I . . ." Paul tried to say, but only a crackling sound came. Tears filled his eyes. He feared that he was going to collapse into his father's arms and cry like a child. He didn't want to do that, but he felt it was going to happen anyway. Then he heard the soft padding sounds of his mother's slippered feet and he waited, gripped with curiosity to see who she would be this time. Nan was simply herself, worn, gray-faced, smoothing her dress and brushing the hair out of her eyes.

"Richard? I wasn't expecting you."

"Hello, Nan. I thought I was coming for dinner. Or do I have the wrong night?"

"Dinner?" she whispered.

"Dinner. What's the matter? Are you sick or something?"

Nan leaned on the kitchen doorframe. "Richard, I assumed after you called this morning that you weren't coming."

Paul rolled his aching eyes from one to the other. It was like a play, just as she had said.

"Oh, did I say that? I don't remember. I wanted to see Paul. Nan, we can still see each other, after all—"

"Richard, you're insane." It was that voice again.

"Now let's not get started like that. Can't we even meet without accusations? Always the same old story. God, how did I ever put up with it for so long," he grumbled bitterly, turning away and walking to the window with his hands thrust in his pockets.

Nan straightened up. "All right. Dinner." Her voice was charged now with an eerie brightness. "What's for dinner? Anyone have any ideas? What can we serve on short notice for our distinguished guest?"

"I'll get dinner," said Paul.

They stared at him in surprise, as if they had forgotten he was there.

"I'll get dinner," he repeated in a loud, hoarse voice. Paul shoved past Nan into the kitchen. His hands were shaking again. He yanked open a drawer and took out the carving knife. Clutching its handle tightly to steady the trembling, he held it out straight in front of him and returned to the doorway. He looked from one to the other. They were standing in the same places, Nan slumped against the doorframe and Richard farther away, at the window, hands in his pockets. They didn't know yet. Nan was not looking at him but at Richard.

His father noticed him first. "Paul?" he said quietly, and started toward him. Then Nan saw too and gasped. Her hand jerked up to her mouth.

"Don't come near me," said Paul. Nan stepped aside, but Richard moved closer to grab his wrist. Paul flicked the knife upward so it grazed the sleeve of Richard's jacket.

"I'm going to solve all your problems for you," Paul said.

"Paul, no, put it down, please," said Nan. He ignored her. Richard was affecting nonchalance now, standing nearby in a relaxed pose, waiting for Paul to lose his nerve and drop the knife.

Paul imagined the thrust, how hard and deep he would have to push, the resistance of the flesh and then the crowning surge of warm blood. It would be the greatest release of his life, a great flow, a torrent. He stepped toward Nan, who cringed, then he stepped back. He moved toward Richard, who inched back cautiously. To Nan again. Then Richard. Then Nan. They were holding their breath, terrified of him. Whose blood? The question darted through his head, in and out of turns and dark corridors, a maze with no exit, and then suddenly balked, up against a flat wall of flaming red, he swiveled the knife and sliced inside his own wrist. A path opened, a thin red line, then an ooze, a stream, dripping from his trembling arm onto the green carpet. He dropped the knife. They were upon him, Nan whimpering and rocking to and fro, Richard embracing him and sobbing. Nan ran for a dish towel and bound it tightly around his wrist.

"Quick, let's get him into the car," she cried. "Get his coat."

Richard stood sobbing in choking gulps. "Oh my God. Oh my God."

Nan threw a coat over Paul's shoulders and pushed them both toward the door. She was swift and efficient.

"I did this," moaned Richard. "This is my doing."

She had a moment, at the elevator, to place a hand on his shoulder and lean against him. "Oh, Richard," she said gently in a soft wail, "you can't leave now. Oh, you can't. You see how much he needs you."

Richard nodded again and again, wiping his eyes with his fist.

The towel was sopping with blood, but luckily Nan had remembered to bring along extras. She changed the bandage and dropped the dripping red towel in a trash can outside the front door.

"Poor child," she murmured. "Oh, my poor baby."

"I'll do anything for him now," said Richard. He had stopped crying and was slamming the car door shut and starting the engine. "He'll need more intensive treatment. I'll have a consultation with Dr. Crewes. Can you stand to have me—"

"We'll work everything out, everything. Just so long as he's all right," said Nan from the back seat, where she sat cradling Paul's head in her lap.

Crazy for Loving You

Notes from Week One of the Psychiatrists' Strike

James Gorman

Monday: Came in today needing to talk. I was very antsy. I had that pressured speech you hear from schizophrenics. Not that I'm schizy. Sure, I'm on medication. I'm a pharmacological construct like everyone else. But it's nothing heavy—an anti-depressant, a little lithium, sometimes a tad of something from the benzodiazepine family to take the edge off. So who do I find filling in for Stanley because of the strike? Enid, the agoraphobe. Only now she doesn't mind leaving home like this because not only the shrinks but the doormen and the elevator operators are on strike. Enid is also afraid of elevators and doormen.

I lie down on the couch and I tell her my dream. It has to do with this enormous tree, something like a redwood, and a guy in a dark hat with a beard, kind of Chassidic-looking, carrying an axe. I didn't actually have this dream, but I want to test her on something easy before I give her real material. She does pretty well. She knows that Stanley is Jewish, as was Freud, and she quickly pegs the guy with the axe as a mohel, which of course explains the tree.

What really surprises me is that she actually seems concerned about me—not something I ever noticed in Stanley. This, after all, is a woman who understands fear. Castration, wide-open spaces, elevators—what's the difference? We are discussing ways to bolster our courage—real support-group stuff, not the sort of thing Stanley charges a hundred and seventy-five dollars an hour for—when my time runs out. I suggest she skip her next patient so we can have a cup of coffee together. She agrees. Since she is not in fact a shrink, we figure there is no ethical conflict.

Tuesday: Jack, the depressive, is Shrink-for-a-Day. Jack is the patient Enid canceled yesterday. He is wearing a dark three-piece suit and pointy-toed wing tips. He has a pad in his lap, and he is grinding his teeth while he sharpens a pencil with a small custom-made penknife.

Immediately I start to have associations that I am not willing to disclose to a layman. I have only met Jack once, when all Stanley's patients got together to figure out a schedule during the strike, and I'm sure you can imagine the things I'm thinking. A depressed guy, with a pathetic stub of a pencil, whittling it down even smaller? With analysts like this, who needs dreams?

I must say, however, that Jack does the silence very well. In my experience this is one of the tough moves for shrinks. Stanley was all right at the silence, he could hold on for quite a long time, but you could hear him breathing and shifting around and fidgeting. That always reassured me. I can't hear a thing from Jack. It comes to me with some force that I am lying down, in a very vulnerable position, and that behind me, where I can't see him, is a mental patient with a knife. Am I crazy?

Finally Jack breaks the silence.

"What's the thought, Ted?" Boy, you can tell one of Stanley's protégés a mile away. What's the thought, indeed.

"I was just wondering what you do, Jack—you know, regularly?"

"I'm a doorman."

"Oh."

Wednesday: My day. Jack turns out to be not such a bad guy after all—some fairly sticky psychosexual conflicts, and not a lot of ego strength, but not a bad sort. The standard approach with a patient like this is to support the defenses, not to probe too far too fast. I notice that Jack is still sharpening the pencil—it's down to paper-clip size, just about—but I don't challenge him on it. We talk about superficial issues mostly— how the doormen's strike threatens his sense of self, and how betrayed he feels that just when he needs Stanley most Stanley has abandoned him. I point out that Stanley may feel the same way about his doorman.

None of the other patients are much of a challenge either: Ellen is a copy editor at an electrical-engineering journal. Her presenting problem is difficulty concentrating on her work. My diagnosis: absence of castration anxiety. Thomas is on the rebound from a therapist who freed his inner child, thus causing him to move all his capital from biotechnology to toys, just before the Gulf War. Now he hopes to make a killing on his Schwarzkopf action figure. Obviously Oedipal. Gary, who has questions about his sexual identity, clearly suffers from a full-blown narcissistic personality disorder. He takes all strikes personally. Striking screenwriters are depriving him of movies. When the sanitation men went out it was because they hated his garbage. Gary has been through quite a number of psychiatrists and is convinced that his dreams alone have caused them to walk. With Enid, I decide to attack her agoraphobia with something unconventional: I take her to an Imax film about the

Grand Canyon. Breakthrough! Afterward we go to her apartment for tea and Tylenol.

It is Florence who causes me the most difficulty. She enters the office slowly, looking straight at me with a smoky gaze. My first impression is of a young woman in black net stockings, with psychosexual conflicts. I cannot help noticing her full red lips (wet look) and firm and shapely breasts. Indeed, Florence is in therapy because she acts out sexually and has poor impulse control. Countertransference sets in immediately. I know, of course, that, if I, as her analyst, fall prey to her charms, as so many other men have, rather than remaining concerned and helpful at a distance, I will be doing her no good. On the other hand, I'm not actually her analyst.

Thursday: Off day. I meet Enid at her place. She says she is not coming out anymore, ever again. Apparently she has found out about me and Florence, whom she refers to as a decompensating tramp. I point out that (a) although Florence may have some sexual issues to work through, she is not a tramp; (b) as a friend of mine, and nothing more than that yet, Enid has no business diagnosing my other acquaintances; (c) as a sometime analyst of mine she has no business making value judgments and directive comments about my sex life; (d) as my patient it's none of her business.

Friday: Florence's day. Enid stays home. Jack, encountered at the end of his hour, looks happier than usual. For me countertransference and transference have become inextricably entangled. I ask Florence if the same sort of thing goes on with all her patients.

"What's the thought?" she says.

I am beginning to suffer from confusion. Wednesday I was a shrink. Last night I was a doorman. Tomorrow I'm a porter. People I hardly know ask me if I live in my own building. Every day I have a different analyst. They all seem to think I suffer from hidden sexual conflicts.

On my way out, I see Stanley in the elevator, operating it. The encounter is awkward for both of us. I thank him for letting us continue to use his office during the strike, and I compliment him on how close the elevator and the lobby floor line up when he stops. I can see him formulating a question, some probe, some pipe-munching aperçu, and then stopping himself, abruptly, as if this would violate the passenger-operator relationship. It's a sad moment.

"Watch your step," he says.

"Thanks," I say. "See you next week."

The Psychopathology
of Everyday Life
Jonathan Baumbach

As my marriage deteriorated, I became increasingly distracted with my patients, drifting off into fantasy, confusing details and names, falling into private obsession. I found myself identifying with the mistreated lovers of certain women patients. One, in particular.

There was an untherapeutic harshness in my voice as I pointed out to Melinda Goldhart that her behavior toward the boyfriend she complained endlessly about was provocative and self-fulfilling. —Don't you see, I threw at her like stones, the man behaves badly because you want him to behave badly.

She shook loose a tear. I was supposed to feel sorry for mistreating her. Instead, I felt annoyance, wanted to shake some real tears out of that calculating soul. I was also aware—dimly—that these feelings were inappropriate, that I was behaving unprofessionally, that I was out of control.

Why do I go on like this?

This not a confession but an investigation into feeling. I am imperfect.

Melinda's parents had refused all authority, had pretended to Melinda that she could do anything she liked. They had offered her a world without boundaries, a dazzling chaos. Every step was a step off a precipice into space. The simplest act for Melinda engendered paralyzing anxieties.

When Melinda first went into treatment with me she rarely talked during the therapy session. She withheld speech willfully, talked to me in her head, as she later reported, but could barely articulate a complex sentence in my presence. She was afraid of exposing her secrets, she said. We tried different arrangements to make her feel less vulnerable. For a while we sat with the backs of our chairs together. She worried when she couldn't see that I had gone away, or was reading a book, or had gone to sleep.

What are you doing now? She would ask from time to time.

Why don't you turn around and see for yourself? I said.

She sometimes turned, sometimes didn't.

The same or almost the same conversation repeated like an echo. The repetition seemed to comfort her like the routine of a game. I know it lulled me into a sense of false comfort. The routines we established between us broke down the feelings of strangeness, created a bond of familiarity.

We moved our chairs into a whole range of configurations. That too was part of the game. We could do or say anything in my office, I wanted her to see, without real danger.

If I was Melinda's parent in the sense that she imagined me as a parent, I was also much of the time a fellow child with her.

When Melinda began to talk in our sessions she talked nonstop, the words coming out in barrages like machine-gun fire. She alternated between silence and prattle, the talk a disguised form of silence.

She sometimes talked to me as if she were talking out loud to herself.

In most of her relationships, Melinda felt herself to be the victim though in fact she tended to be the controlling one. She rarely allowed herself, despite her pretense that it was otherwise, to be not in control. A way to control situations, while at the same time not feeling responsible for her life, was to make herself appear to be a victim.

A victim needs a victimizer to complete the circle.

Melinda had been dating the same man for five years—she was twenty-three when she came to me—a man she complained about whenever his name came up in the conversation. He was insensitive to her feelings. She was repelled by much of his behavior and—this a recurrent obsession—his odor. The repulsion was uncharacteristic. Melinda was not ordinarily squeamish and was subject to few sexual taboos.

Why did she continue to see him if he repelled her?

She tended to ignore questions in areas of confusion or ambivalence, would take recourse in silence. It embarrassed her to admit that there was any question she couldn't answer.

On the evidence it appeared that she continued to see the man in order to complain of his failings. He was her occasion for grievance.

Sometimes she would say no more than a dozen words in an entire fifty minute session.

I didn't urge her to speak, not at first, not directly. I knew from our first meeting that to ask something directly of Melinda was to be denied. Why did I know that?

I want to be part of your life, she told me on one occasion. I want you to think of me when I'm not here.

Sometimes I do, I said. I think of all my patients.

She mumbled something.

What? . . . What?

It's cold in here, Yuri. Would you turn off the air-conditioning please. I'd appreciate it if you would consider my comfort once in a while.

You sound as if you're talking to a servant, I said.

I don't think you like me, she said. She had a sly smile on her face.

If you don't think I like you, why are you smiling?

Melinda pushed the corners of her lips down with her fingers. —Am I ugly? she asked with a slight stammer.

You haven't told me why you were smiling, I said.

I wasn't, she said, covering her mouth with her hand. When she took her hand away her tongue shot out at me. —Are you angry? I don't want you to be angry with me. She raised her eyes which had been averted.

You're a tease, Melinda, I said. That makes people angry.

Fuck you, she said, shouted it at me.

Her outburst, because it seemed so uncharacteristic— she had always been exceedingly polite in our sessions—shocked me. My first impulse was to order her out of my office—I wanted to punish her for offending me. —Fuck you, I said in return.

Her face broke. —I won't be talked to that way, she said. You have no right to say that to me.

You handled that very well, Melinda, I said.

She smiled joyously through her tears, wiped her cheeks with the back of her hand like a child. —Oh thank you, she said.

We moved in these sessions between war and seduction, different faces of the same aggression.

Her accounts of experiences with the man she referred to as her boyfriend were unvaryingly unpleasant. It worried me that I was encouraging her to disparage him, that I had a personal stake in her negative feelings toward other men.

* * *

I mention my difficulties with Melinda to Adrienne who says, under her breath, that my misunderstanding of the girl is symptomatic.

I ask her to explain this unflattering description but she is in another room, her attention focused elsewhere. When I persist she says, What do you really want?

Human contact, I say.

Adrienne laughs without amusement, laughs wryly, laughs with some measure of disdain.

Melinda protested again and again that I didn't like her, that it was only because I wanted her money that I continued to see her.

I tried different responses, admitted on one occasion that I sometimes found her unbearable. My remark brought a smile to her face, a look of triumph.

She denied that she was smiling.

We were facing each other that day at my insistence. The denied smile persisted brazenly.

Did I say that Melinda was seductive? Have I mentioned it anywhere?

I wish I had a mirror so that I could show you your face, I said. You continue to smile.

You too, she said, her smile opening like a blossom.

I traced my lips with an imaginary finger. It was possible that our unacknowledged smiles mirrored one another.

I felt the strongest impulse to say something hurtful to her. My feelings must have expressed themselves in my face because she blanched, seemed almost to tremble.

I have the feeling, she said, that this is the beginning of the end of our relationship.

I was trembling, though I didn't know why, did and didn't. I was conscious of wanting to assure her that I had no intention of dropping her as a patient and conscious of withholding such assurance out of anger.

She turned her chair halfway around. —You want to be rid of me, she said.

I'm your therapist not your lover, I said.

I had a dream about Melinda, a seemingly literal dream, not all of which I remembered. I wrote it down as soon as I awoke in a notebook I used to keep at bedside for just that purpose.

There is, I discover, only one chair in my office. The other chair, the patient's chair, is at some shop being reupholstered. Why hasn't it been returned? Melinda comes in conspicuously late, and asks indignantly where she is supposed to sit.

I offer her my seat. She remarks that I am still in it.

It surprises me to discover that what she says is true. I am sitting in the very seat I offer her. It is wide enough for two, I say. At this moment I'm not sure whether the ostensible patient is Melinda or Adrienne. She shakes her head coyly. I beckon to her with a finger. We are both standing. The chair is between us. It is not my office any longer but a bedroom, a room I had as a child. I point out the view from the window. The overgrown garden, the porcelain cupids, the huge cherry tree just coming into blossom.

She says she admires the tree, though she is unable to believe that it actually produces cherries. Her breasts press against my back as she makes this announcement.

She says that the nipples of her breasts are real cherry buds.

I am leaning out the window trying to find a bud on the cherry tree to prove the tree's identity. There are no buds, only faded blossoms.

I bring in a handful of crushed petals. These are cherry blossoms, I say. Melinda giggles, says not really.

Just take my word for it, I say. This is a cherry tree. It produces sour cherries. I take a bud from the tree and hold it out to her.

She puts my fingers to her lips, says poor man. I notice that there is a red stain on the back of my hand.

I've always wanted to taste your blood, she says.

You're a liar, I rage. That's your blood. That's female blood.

Today was the first time Melinda talked about her boyfriend, Phillip, by name.

She valued Phillip most when he ceased to be available. It was the pattern of their relationship. Melinda would mistreat Phillip, would reject and torment him until, provoked beyond endurance, he would stop seeing her. At that point she would decide that she was in love with him and plot obsessively to get him back.

When Phillip would return to her, as he did, she would feel contempt for him again as if such yielding were a failure of character. Any man foolish enough to love her was unworthy of her love.

I pointed this out to her, but for the longest time she refused to acknowledge it.

I tended to respond to Melinda's complaints about Phillip as if they were complaints about me.

As an aspect of this identification, I found myself intensely attracted to her. Was this counter-transference or something else?

* * *

Melinda told me of a dream in which I appeared in the guise of a teddy bear named Swoosh whom she held in her arms while she slept. That's all she offered of the dream.

I said the best way to remember dreams was to write them down as soon as she woke.

She pouted, said that most of her dreams were crazy and that it embarrassed her to think about them. The first three buttons of her gauzy blouse were open and I could see the lacy top of her pink undershirt. My impulse was to look away, but I didn't. I was almost certain she wasn't wearing a bra.

I don't have to tell you my dreams if I don't want to, she said. I have a right to privacy. Do you tell everything? I don't know anything about you, do I? She turned her chair halfway around to offer me a view of only half her face.

Her gesture enraged me out of all proportion. —I'm not going to let you do that, I said, getting to my feet.

Don't you dare touch me, she said.

When I stood up she gasped as if in fright and shifted her chair part of the way back toward its original position.

Put your chair back the way it was or I'm going to discontinue the session, I said.

She grudgingly moved her chair back into position, sulked.

I returned to my seat with an assumption of dignity, felt relieved that she hadn't tested me further.

Though I don't like it, Yuri, it's good for me to be treated that way.

How do you feel I treated you?

Your face is flushed, she said. Are you blushing?

I repeated my question, had to repeat it several times to get a response.

I don't understand what you're asking, she said.

Tell me what's so funny, I said.

I can't, she whispered, lowering her eyes. —I'll tell you when I know you better.

Our sessions had the quality on occasion of lovers' quarrels.

When I finally went to see Leo Pizzicati after several months of procrastination I was in a state of intractable depression.

I sat down, somewhat disoriented, thinking myself in the wrong seat.

Adrienne won't sleep with me, was the first thing I said, which was interesting because it was not what I had planned to say.

Leo seemed pained on my account, profoundly sad, which I immediately recognized as a projection.

I have the sense that I am making this up, recreating a scene out of a mix of memory and imagination. The ugly paintings on the wall, the tacky plastic furniture, the refusal to lay claim to style. There are a few inconsequential changes in his office (or maybe it's just a lapse of memory) but in matters that count nothing has changed.

I talk about Adrienne despite my intention to avoid that subject, get lost in a maze of evasion.

I came to talk to you about a counter-transference problem I'm having with a woman patient, I say with about ten minutes left in the session.

Are you fucking this patient? he asks.

I laugh nervously at this abrupt perception, I feel exposed and defensive. —I'm not fucking anyone, I say.

Are you feeling sorry for yourself?

I am close to tears, though unaware of feeling sad. —She wants me to fuck her, I say.

And you can't turn her down? he asks. Does she have a name, this patient? Yuri, you look as if you want to cry.

I deny it, but the tears come in the wake of my denial. I refuse to cry, cover my face with my left hand, feel the tears prick my fingers. Just a minute, I hear myself say.

I've never fully worked through the feeling that it is unmanly to cry so suffer embarrassment at breaking down. I remove my hand as if to say it's really nothing, a momentary aberration, but the crying continues and I am unable to speak.

When the fit is over, when I come back to myself, I begin to talk to Leo about my mother, though I have no new insights into that relationship. —What's the point of my telling you this? I ask him.

He removes his pipe, says nothing, puffs coded messages in smoke.

I know the answer. My relationship with my mother is a paradigm of my relationship with all women. —My mother thinks I'm perfect, I say.

I should say something about that, not so much what I said to Leo which is in a certain context, within a shared realm of assumptions, but say something about my mother, what she's like, how I experience her. Last week I lost her at the Metropolitan Museum of Art, couldn't find her for almost two hours. It is symptomatic. She had ways when I was a child of being there and not there. When she was missing we split up to search for her—Adrienne and Rebecca taking the first floor while I went upstairs. It was as if she had been claimed by some black hole. When she finally made herself available—she just seemed to appear—my mother refused to acknowledge that she had been lost. What I didn't mention to Leo was that while I was searching for her, I had the urge to take off and leave her to her disappearance. I felt—how should I put it?—burdened by the pressure of her absence.

Two facts. My mother lost in the Egyptian tombs of the Metropolitan Museum. Melinda sitting with her back to me.

Sometimes in bed in the morning Adrienne would see something in my face and say, What?

I am wary these days with Melinda, take a distant and paternal tone in our sessions. She comments on my apparent disaffection, says it hurts her that I no longer care for her.

Her left breast is slightly higher than the right, I notice. The disparity touches me, takes my breath away.

Her new phase is less confrontational. She seems to court my sympathy, wants me to be pleased by the progress she is making.

Am I getting ahead of myself? I have fallen into disorder, have lost the thread of events.

It is another time. The question comes up at an unexpected moment. —Do you find me attractive? she asks, looking sagely skeptical, aware of performance.

What did I tell you the last time you asked? I say.

I can't trust your answer, she says, looking up shyly under hooded eyes. —How could you say no? I mean, you're trying to build up my sense of self-worth.

It is not what she says (do I even remember it as precisely as I pretend?), but the unspoken context we share.

I ask her if there's some way I can prove to her that I find her attractive.

The question enlists a sly smile and a delayed shrug. There are six minutes left in our fifty-minute hour. I know that the next time we meet, which is two days from now, we will fuck. I have made an oblique offer and she has given oblique acceptance.

Reading over what I have written, I can see how melodramatic, even pathological, this all sounds. I knew what I was about to do was unethical and at the same time I felt driven to do it, I felt the need to bust loose, to take what I had previously considered unacceptable risks. And maybe, said arrogance, in its nasty whisper, it would do us both some good.

I was resolved that it would happen once and once only, a demonstration of my attraction to her, and then we would use it as an area of exploration in her therapy. I have a predilection for being defensive so I will stop myself here to say that whatever the extenuating circumstances—I am imperfect, I am human—I am fully responsible for what happened with Melinda.

Outside of my professional commitments, I am a man of obsessive urges, sudden fixations, deep pockets of need. I have never learned to put off having the things I want. My tolerance for frustration is small. I sometimes, out of the blue, ache with undefined longing. Unaccountable things fill me with desire, present themselves as unavoidable needs.

I barely slept the night before, was in a revved-up state the next morning. Rebecca took note of it, said, Daddy's in a silly teasing. You used to be funnier, she said, withdrawing herself, fading out of the picture.

Having decided on a course of action, I gave my attention to logistics, the where and how of the matter. The idea of making love to her in my office, on the couch or on the rug, gave me pause. Yet I couldn't very well take her to a hotel without trashing the therapeutic situation altogether.

And then just before she was scheduled to arrive, I had a change of heart, decided not to pursue the matter further.

When she didn't show up on time—she was not usually late—I assumed she wasn't coming, assumed further that she had decided to break off treatment with me. I felt rueful.

I am not very observant as to what women wear—it is the effect rather than the details that catch my attention—but I was aware that Melinda, when she made her belated entrance, was wearing a red dress with black trim. She didn't sit down, stood alongside her chair as if keeping it company. My sense of her was that she was glowing, that she was absolutely radiant.

I disguised my anxiety in exquisite self-possession. Her reality testing may have been weak in other circumstances, but Melinda understood my intentions in the full flower of their confusion.

There is no point in going on with this, in recounting how we got from here to there.

We used the seldom-used analytic couch for our transaction—I was glad to find some service for it—then spent what remained of the hour talking about what it was like.

It was like: good for me. Like that.

I remember her saying this much: I feel, you know, that I've corrupted you.

With the putting on of my pants, I moved back into the role of therapist. —What makes you think you're so powerful, I said.

I can get any man I want, she said, blushing. I got you, didn't I?

Is that how it feels to you?

I feel used, she said. I feel that you've taken advantage of me. I feel that you don't really like me. Not *really* like me. I feel that you shouldn't have done what you did. I feel that I've ruined everything. I'll never get well after this. Her eyes filled with tears.

I maintained an appropriate distance, performed my role as it suited me to perceive it.

The next three sessions followed a similar pattern. Melinda would arrive late, offer a perfunctory greeting, then lie down on the couch with her skirt above her knees. Although it had been my conscious intent not to continue the physical relationship, I had no heart to deny either of us its melodrama. The sex was unexceptional, took place, we pretended, for the sake of the discussion in its wake.

What feelings did it excite? For me, it excited a sense of shame, a moderate, not unbearable sense of shame. For Melinda: I no longer thought of Melinda's feelings as apart from mine.

I was collaborating with Melinda's fantasy, proving to her that she was capable of winning her therapist's (and father's) love. Can that be right? I am something of a literalist. I was not, despite the evidence of my behavior, lost to blind urge.

If I didn't stop this affair, it is because I didn't want to stop, was getting something from it that outweighed its disadvantages. It gave me a sense perhaps of power and accomplishment. Is that it?

I have the illusion that if I can say the right thing to Adrienne, she can't help but love me again or recognize (in that vast backwater of repressed feelings) that she hadn't stopped loving me. The words don't come, refuse to announce themselves, though the illusion itself sustains me.

I feel surges of passion for Melinda when she isn't there, particularly when she isn't there, my need for her complicated by her actual presence.

Melinda misses her appointment, leaves a garbled message with my answering service about some prior commitment. I feel vaguely needy the rest of the day, lack energy, doze during one of my sessions at the hospital. My inattention seems to go unnoticed. The patient, a lingerie fetishist, is so self-absorbed that I could put a mannequin in the room with him and he would go on with his obsessive story.

Peter told me when he had an affair with a patient he felt so guilty he expected to be pulled out of his bed at night—he once actually heard footsteps—and be carted off to jail.

I have a dream the next night of dying, wake in a state of grinding anxiety, barely able to breathe. I haven't felt this vulnerable since the early days of analysis—my first analysis. (First analysis = first love.)

Melinda comes in, coughing, huddled over, removes her scarf and coat and without acknowledgement of me, begins to talk about an experience with her boyfriend, Phillip. No reference is made to what's gone on the past three—three or four—sessions with us. It's as if I'm hardly in the room with her, as if she's talking in a dream.

I listen to her in an analytic way, try to pick up the real issue of the monologue. She is putting me in an intricate double bind. If I admit to feeling jealous, I lack the appropriate distance to deal with her problems, disqualify myself as her therapist. If I am not jealous, it indicates that I don't care for her sufficiently. My impulse is to pull down my pants and take her on the floor while she babbles on about Phillip's fear of making commitments.

Why are you telling me this? I ask.

She blinks her eyes with mock innocence. —What do you mean, Yuri. I don't understand what you're asking.

You know very well what I'm asking, I say. Something is going on with us that you're conspicuously avoiding.

She pouts childishly, flutters her hands. —Are you saying that all I can talk about here is you?

Melinda, why did you miss our last session?

I was sick, she says. You'll say it's hysterical. I know, but the fact is I had a splitting headache. I almost didn't come today—I had to drag myself here. I just don't know what I'm doing here.

Why did you come today?

She shrugs, starts to say something and doesn't. Because I'm in love with you, she whispers.

Leo has no answers for me, refuses to give advice, though I can tell from his face that he is worried about me. I can tell from the sorrowful pinch at the corner of his eyes that he suspects I am lost. I grieve for the person he sees.

Another therapist couldn't have helped her as much as I have, I say.

His mouth moves into a smile that is gone the moment I perceive it. —You see the sex, do you, as part of a therapeutic program?

I no longer believe in therapy, I shout at him. If I had my courage, I'd give it up and do something more honorable.

Yes? What would you do? What is this honorable profession you have in mind for yourself?

If I gave up therapy, I say, I think I'd give up psychology altogether.

If you do, you do, he says, as if my defection from the science of the soul were not a serious issue.

Leo is unimpressed with my threat to give up the faith, and I am disappointed that he has no solace for me, come away from the session unimproved.

He doesn't tell me, as he might, that I am making a serious mistake. It is what I want from him and what he refuses to give me.

UPTOWN SHRINK CAUGHT WITH PANTS DOWN
(Headline in the *New York Post*.)

I was having difficulty sleeping through the night. I would wake periodically and look at Adrienne asleep or pretending to be asleep, turning in her sleep. I would move from back to side, from side to back, hoping to send tremors of my presence to her, to wake her to affection after this long sleep of rejection and denial. When I moved she also moved. When I turned toward her she would turn away as if there was some mechanism between us that had gone awry.

I looked at her sleeping form (her feigned sleep perhaps) and thought of the things I might do to her, was unable to separate the sexual from the violent. Pain short-circuited awareness. The moment I got in touch I was out of touch, lost to feeling, dead to myself. I imagined Adrienne in a fatal car crash, or crushed by the wheels of a train, or snuffed by a sniper's bullet, or falling from a high window. I suffered her loss, mourned her death as she slept next to me (or pretended to sleep) blissfully unaware. I was in a fever of madness.

I feel myself in some kind of helpless limbo, some deadly inertia. I talk to myself as though I were a robot. Move, I say. Sit. Eat. Stand. Right. Left. Turn. Move. Do something. Why aren't you moving? The answer is: I am. From outside and only from an exterior vantage is there the illusion of paralysis.

I go alone to the Virgin Islands for a week, a way of getting myself together, lie impatiently in the sun. I read detective stories and psychology journals, keep a fragmented record of my thoughts and feelings, interior dialogues, the story of my soul. It worries me that for seven days not once do I concern myself with the well-being of my patients. Melinda barely touches my consciousness. I consider at times not returning, going somewhere else, starting over. The truth is, I am homesick.

When I get back, Adrienne and Rebecca embrace me like a returning hero.

I feel a constant buzz of irritation in her presence as if faced by unwanted news. We talk only to transact the business of the house, act as if the other were a moving shadow, a false image.

Melinda comes for another week, for two weeks, for three, seems eager to please, talks of the improvements in her life. I suggest she see another therapist and, to my surprise and disappointment, she agrees, without further discussion.

It is the same thing, the same experience, the same silent presence, the same oppressive house, the same feeling of hopelessness. Despite appearances, despite the extent of our dislocation, I am convinced that the deepest ties of feeling between us remain unbroken.

I decided to put down the story of my marriage as a means of investigating its peculiarly contemporary neurotic pattern.

For months after Melinda leaves treatment with me, I feel the pull of her attraction—a tug on the sleeve of feelings from an invisible hand.

I made arrangements for her to see someone else, a therapist I knew only by reputation. She refused my choice.

After that she isn't available when I want her, except on rare occasions when she is, Melinda choosing the occasions. And then not at all. My need for her when she is not available is twice (is ten times) what it was when she was there for me.

She tells me in a letter that I was the best therapist she ever had. I am both amused and made anxious by the implications of the pun.

Samaritan

Steven Barthelme

America was full of fat people taking baths. I was watching them with binoculars from a large seventh-floor office in a new professional building in a good section.

My patient Mr. R comes each Monday, Wednesday, and Friday and spends the day in the chair. He does not like to lie down. Mr. R thinks I am a psychiatrist. He is wrong, of course; Mr. R is wrong about everything.

Mr. R is a heavyset male, about six feet, with slightly wavy slightly long blond hair, who wears shades when the sun is very bright.

"She said my eyes looked bad. She said the evil showed in my eyes—"

"Nancy?" I said. Nancy is Mr. R's wife. Nancy R.

"No," he said. "My mother. My mother told me that when I was eighteen."

"What was the evil she was talking about?"

"I was screwing some sweet little thing. It was obvious somehow."

"You're twenty-seven years old."

"God, I know. Do you think I can get back into law school?"

"I don't think it would be healthy. Why do you remember at this time something your mother said to you almost ten years ago?"

"I don't know," he said. "I mean, I'm not sure." Mr. R is leaning a little forward in the armchair. He is thinking. "Are you directive?"

"No."

"I think I said it because I talked to her last week. On the telephone. She's in Santa Barbara." Mr. R cannot help indicating the direction of Santa Barbara by gesture. "She asked me if she had done it to me, fucked up my life. She said she had done her best, the best she knew. She wanted me to tell her if it was her fault."

"If what was her fault?"

"Me—me—if I . . . if my problems were her fault. What could I say?"

"No."

"That's what I said. Sort of."

I glanced at the clock on my desk; it was late. White numerals. "It's near twelve," I said. "Let's break for lunch. Be back here at one-thirty."

Mr. R was very thankful, for the morning. That's normal. Mr. R is usually thankful for the morning. In the afternoon he is often angry, I think because he glimpses that his problems are very involved and complex and may well take a very long time to resolve in an acceptable way. In the morning he is usually thankful because he knows that if he is not I will punish him during the afternoon.

During lunch Mr. R drives home and takes a bath, eats whatever Nancy (Nancy!) has prepared for him, reads, returns, and waits in the outer office. I am there the whole time, with the binoculars, eating fitfully at the sliced barbecue which I have paid for with Mr. R's money, and taking a Valium, 20 mg. If when he returns R parks in the west lot, I can pick him up as he turns off Thirty-fourth, the perfect swing of the Lincoln into a parking space, the expression on his face as he gets out, the strong stride toward the building. He looks healthy. I can imagine what it's like talking to crazy people all day long. I much prefer the sane sober ones like Mr. R, and the state wants you to have a license. Mr. R has bought up all my Mondays, Wednesdays, and Fridays for over a year and there is no sense taking the risks involved in seeing other patients. I am not greedy. I congratulate myself on my sensible attitude.

At two o'clock Miss Davies (Brenda!) tells me that he is back. He has been back for half an hour. Sweet Brenda and I are finishing up. Trading off on the binoculars. Interplay. Balling seven stories in the air, looking at each other and at the wildly potent city through the large bluish sheets of plate glass. "Think of me as a doctor." And she does. She makes phone calls while we're making it, in the old style. She pretends disinterest. Pauses. Sweet Brenda is a lover, and a lover of irony with a degree in psychology. Silver buttons all down her back.

I can appreciate it. How fresh Mr. R looks when he returns for the afternoon. A clean shirt (R has a great many). A shave. The Valium is spinning around in my brain and I can appreciate practically anything. At three-thirty, Stelazine. At five, a Triavil 4-10 so I don't fall asleep on the way home. I bathe, and at six-thirty show up at Lisa's for dinner. All my early life I spent working toward a lady named Lisa. And, for the most part, she has made good, although in a somewhat different way than expected. All that time in Mass General, where when we got the brain in view, I could never figure out what was what.

And God, it was nauseating. You can't imagine how disgusting the naked brain. But I never vomited. I mean you get in there, and you can't tell which is which and what the grease does. ("Doctor, what's that yellowish stuff . . . No, no, the grease over he—" He hit my hand.) I didn't last.

At Lisa's there is booze, a drink and then dinner. She can cook. She is civilized, sweet and civilized. She has a second-story place, two paneled rooms with a kitchen and a flat roof where you can fuck in the wind. There is also a lake, water through the trees. Whoever is up can watch the water if she or he wants. On the roof, super natural. Lying back, looking at the sky, and it's cold in the fall. In the winter you freeze, so we stay inside. Sometimes it rains. Lisa loves me. I worked long and hard to get where I am.

Mr. R looks fresh and clean at two when I step to the door of the waiting room and nod slightly toward him, wait, then turn and follow him down the hallway and into my office, like his father. I seat myself behind the desk while he is still standing. Mr. R has a fetish about this; he must always be the last to sit down. He is a large man, several years younger than I, but filled out as in maturity in a politician. In fact, I think he is a lawyer, has a firm, real estate, oil, other interests. Friendly with the great and powerful. Once I was afraid of Mr. R, but I have come a long way, and I have shown him—rather, pointed at him—the Smith & Wesson, and the dominance situation has been clearly understood ever since.

Finally he sits down, relaxes back into the big chair which situates him most nearly opposite the door, lays his filterless Chesterfields and matches on the glass table. He tightens a little and leans forward in the chair. Rearranges the cigarettes a little farther away from the pot which holds the plastic plant. The walls are wood. We are subdued.

"You were speaking about your eyes . . ."

He remembered the morning's session. "Oh my God, can we talk about something else?"

"Surely," I said. "But there seems to be some energy here and we might be able to make use of it."

"Okay," he said. "Okay." He takes a Chesterfield out, effortlessly, without moving the pack. For a moment, I hate his guts. But the feeling never makes it to my face and I cover easily by beginning to speak.

"Your eyes?"

"Oh yeah." He takes a long first drag on the cigarette and drops his hand. "Well, it wasn't much, it was just something my mother said to me when I was graduating from high school—"

"Do you know why you are reluctant to talk about it?"

"I'm not. I mean not really. I'm reluctant to talk about my mother, really."

"Were you close to your mother?"

"Yeah, I guess, close enough. Up until high school. You know, I started getting laid. I started exaggerating, you know, lying. I started sucking up to the other kids instead."

"Instead of . . ."

"Instead of to them."

"I would say that what you describe is a fairly common process. Your family was well-to-do?"

"Yeah, well enough. My old man runs a mud company."

Mr. R has made a joke. "A mud company?"

"Yeah, yeah, he sells mud. They shove it down oil wells. Keeps the drill bits cool."

"Did you get along with him?"

He hesitates. "Yeah, we got along pretty well. We used to go hunting. We had a dog, a shepherd named King, and I wanted to take him hunting but Dad said we couldn't. He had a lot of reasons, good reasons, he was right."

Mr. R stops and gets himself another cigarette, slowly. He looks as if he can't decide whether or not to light it. "He got hit by a car. King. One Sunday he got hit. I found him up against the gate, whimpering, there was a lot of blood on the walk. We rushed him to the vet, carried him in and laid him on this stainless steel table. He was every once in a while raising his head, swinging it up a little and kind of whimpering to me, but mostly he just lay there. The vet stuck a needle in him. King just lay there on the table, and then he shook a little, shuddered, and all this blood and crap started coming out, blood out of his mouth and crap falling out of his ass and he was still in it, and didn't move. I helped the vet put him into a big black plastic bag and he tied it up and we carried it out to the back and put it inside a freezer with some others. Then we left. My old man had to drive the car, but I just sat there on the front seat and didn't have anything to do. And, you know what was funny about it?" he said. "What was funny about the whole thing?"

"What?"

"—That week . . . my only reaction to all that, was one night I broke up, crying and sobbing and choking and all that shit, and the only thing that came to my mind was 'He was just a dog. He was just a goddamned dog . . .'" Mr. R is looking at me asking some question.

"Because he was not responsible . . . didn't deserve . . .."

"Yeah, yeah! Like he wasn't responsible for anything because he was just a goddamn dog, he didn't do anything that justified getting mauled that way. So I went out and started digging up the street with a pick. I was digging a rut across it in front of the house so you'd have to drive real slow. But my old lady saw me and said a lot of stuff about how I'd cause a wreck and somebody might get killed and the street wasn't ours, so I stopped. She was right. I started hating the dog."

He was making me nervous, moving around too much, making gestures which were unusually harsh. "Let's quit for the afternoon," I said. "I don't think we can get anything more done this afternoon."

"Okay," he said. "Okay." Relaxing back into the chair. "That's crazy, isn't it?"

"I think your behavior was normal, under the circumstances. I don't see anything else you could have done. Everyone uses unusual methods when put into strong stress situations."

"No, no, I mean about the dog. I mean *hating the dog* . . ."

"That is what I was talking about," I said. "Let's quit for today."

After he left I got another Valium and asked Brenda to transcribe the tapes before she went home. At street level I went into a telephone booth and called Lisa at work.

"Hey, lady, you've got the afternoon off."

"I can't . . ."

"Oh yeah you can; you've got to see a doctor. He's liable to die if you don't. Pick you up in twenty minutes . . ."

Then I dialed Nancy.

"Chico, is that you?"

"Yeah, just thought I'd call. He's coming at you."

"Why, what for? You get tired of hearing him whine?"

"Sweet young thing, aren't you?"

"Speaking of which, how's that tanned little number in your office?"

"Look, Nancy, he's coming home, just thought I'd alert you. Broaden your awareness a little."

"What happened? Why so early?"

"A . . . well, he started telling me about this dog he had when he was a kid . . . Oh God. He ever tell you about that?"

"About 'King.' About 'King' getting run over?"

"Yeah. He started— What are you laughing at? What's so fucking funny?"

"Did he get any? Get into your pants?"

"I think I've got the wrong number."

"Listen, honey, he made himself king of the Phi Delts with that story."

"Yeah, well, what were you going to be when you grew up? Hey, look, I'm not gonna make it tomorrow. I've got too much to do. Next week, okay?"

"Finally," she said.

"Finally what?"

"Finally we get to the purpose of this call."

"Only to hear the soothing sweetness of your voice."

I left, picked up Lisa at her office and asked Brenda to call R and tell him that his Friday appointment was postponed. On Saturday Lisa went to the grocery store. On Sunday we turned the lights back on.

"God, it's bright in here."

"Where's the *TV Guide*?" she said, in a long brown gown. She turned off some lights. "I threw it on the floor . . . here it is." She picked it up. White sun-colored hair, nothing so sweet in this whole world as a rich girl.

"Hey, lady, come lie down so's I can disrobe you . . . Is that right? Can I 'disrobe' you? Sounds disgusting."

"How about Tony Franciosa and Dean Martin?"

"Wonderful. C'mon and lie down. What's it called?"

"*Career.* Chico, I've been lying down for *four days.*"

"Wanna go for the record?"

"God, Chico, where'd you get to be so *quick.* Quicker than a speeding—"

"Yeah, well, I used to be quick. But you know, an agile mind's . . ."

"What is the matter with you?" She looked at me.

"I had a bad week. But if you'll lie your slinky body down right here . . ."

"That's lay."

I looked at her.

"Don't say it," she said.

Monday morning, Mr. R came in and worried about his daughter, seven. Brenda worried about her boyfriend. I took a few of these and a few of those and didn't worry. I was all right. Happy, perhaps.

By eleven-thirty, I felt that the whole daughter thing was getting silly, and so I provided a solution, a temporary one. Most solutions are.

"Look, how old is she?"

"Seven," he said.

"All right, then, you've got five or six years before it really becomes a problem, right? Right now her problems are on about the *doll* scale. I can't see any advantage in rushing it. Perhaps she'll be ugly." An insensitive remark.

"Look," he said.

"Mr. R," I said. "If you're not willing to deal in the general area . . . I would be curious to know what connection there is between your child's future sexual adjustment, a problem that is in large measure several years off, and the matters we have been discussing these last few months."

"Yeah, yeah. I'm sorry. I've got a lot of things on my mind. I wasn't thinking." He was smoking and standing up. He was leaving.

"I realize that it is important, but it seems that, for our purposes, the time could be better spent, and that we might be discussing this to avoid discussing something else. Anyway, why don't we try again this afternoon?" This jargo-spanking made us both unhappy. I felt incautious. He was taking everything much too seriously.

At lunch Brenda attacked with questions about Mr. R. She is taking her second degree, and doing very well. She has a healthy natural curiosity. A rare thing in a healthy girl. I do my best. Slate black hair and deep green eyes.

"How would you characterize his case?" she said.

"His case. Yes, well, I would say that R's problem has something to do with the fact the he's just like everybody else. Success is his problem. No, that's wrong. R's problem is that he is just like everybody else and *he doesn't like it.*"

"He can't adjust?" she said.

"Adjustment," I said. "Adjustment is precisely the problem. It doesn't work."

"For very long. It's not permanent."

"Exactly, beautiful. *You* have hit on it. And somehow Mr. R was convinced by something or someone that adjustment was, in fact, permanent. And past that, that it worked. A cruel joke on him, but a bit of good luck for you and me."

"Isn't it a little dishonest?" she said.

"Yes. A little. But you know, so is bowling. One does better not to worry too heavily about his honesty. One tends to discover that all his crimes are petty ones. Okay?"

"I know what you mean," she said.

"That makes one of us," I said. "Could I have one last taste of that there?"

At one-thirty R came back, sweating. At two, he came into my office and sat down. Then stood up. We talked for about half an hour. He walked around the office, smoking, picking things up to look at them. He talked. And finally he sat down, as if very tired, and was silent for a long time, perhaps ten minutes.

"Doctor. You were asking, last week, about what I wanted to do with analysis . . ."

"I don't think I quite understand."

He settles on the forward part of the big armchair. "I mean you asked me what I wanted ultimately to achieve, through being here, through seeing you." Massive, blond.

"Yes."

"Well, I don't think I'm going to make it. I don't think I'm going to be able to do it." He tightened a fist and stared down at it. Quiet.

Then he began again. "I saw this movie on television. Did you ever see that Zapata movie? With Marlon Brando?" He was leaning forward; I slid the desk drawer open.

I nodded. "I've seen it . . ."

"*That's* who I want to be!" he says. Falls back into the chair, relaxing; he has gotten a clear statement of purpose out.

Watching this bizarre performance, easy and uneasy.

"Like in the scene," he says, "where they're bringing him in—Brando—and all the peons are there, crouched over, and they start clapping the stones together until all you can hear are the horses' hooves and the stones clapping . . .

"Or, oh God!" he says, "the best scene—the scene where the soldiers—"

"Diaz's army . . ."

"Yeah, or whoever they are, they're riding in this double column with Zapata on foot in the middle, and one of them has—"

Staring at a circular glass ashtray to the left on my desk which cost eighteen dollars.

"—this rope which is around his neck, and they're riding down this narrow road through some hills dragging him along with his hands tied behind him, and down from the hillsides come the peons in the white pants and white shirts, and they're only carrying machetes while the soldiers have rifles, but they just keep coming, walking alongside the columns of soldiers, until there're about a hundred of them, and there's only about fifteen or twenty soldiers, and the soldiers are still riding along just real slow like they have been the whole time, not even looking at the peons with their machetes . . ."

I cured him. It was easy. I just opened the drawer, took the .38 out, aimed at his forehead, and blew a big hole in it, a little right of center.

He was so wound up, so oblivious to everything, that it was really quite simple to get the gun out of the drawer and squeeze off a loud and easy shot into his brain before he said, or thought of, whatever it was he was going to say, eventually.

IV.
Limitations

The three stories in this section deal with the variety of limitations present in the therapist-patient relationship. In "The Mysterious Case of R," it is suggested that the artist and the process of artistic creation are too mysterious for even a therapist to understand. "The artist who works without inspiration creates a dead child," the knowing writer-patient tells his therapist, and "the sensation of all one's work and love going into something not alive . . . is very much the same sensation you would feel if a patient you had worked your painstaking, dedicated work with for years, and come to love, were suddenly to raise his hand in the air, snap his fingers, and disappear." Here, the therapist realizes that the only factor he can ever control is that he will be paid.

"Psychoanalysis Changed My Life" points to the time constraints inherent in the therapeutic process. Therapy requires time, but for the impatient, elderly therapist in this story, there isn't enough of it. Acting as fairy godmother to her patient's Cinderella, this therapist suggests "the name of a good masseuse, an expert hair colorist, and a store that specialized in narrow-width Swiss shoes," all of which are preparations to ready this patient for her prince. Finding a man for her patient seems a speedy solution that serves both of their needs, as the prince the therapist chooses is her own son. In addition, the therapist allows herself to be cared for, or repaid, by her patient. Was her "illness" merely a ploy to beat the therapeutic timeclock? We are left to wonder.

"Basil from Her Garden" points to another kind of limitation inherent in this relationship. Here, the consequences of violating therapeutic boundaries are explored. The therapist finds himself so "feverishly interested" in his patient's questions and discussion on the topic of adultery that a disturbing role reversal results between them. The therapist is left feeling like a tremendously anxious patient, full of questions.

The Mysterious
Case of R

Frank Conroy

DEAR COLLEAGUE,

Despite the obvious hazards of disclosure, I can no longer keep silent, as I have these many years, about the strange occurrences surrounding the case of R, one of my first patients when I took up practice in this country during the war. Those were lean years, as you doubtless recall, and I did not question R's assertion that he had picked my name at random from the *Journal of the American Psychoanalytic Association* in the public library. In fact I counted myself lucky, since he estimated his wealth as somewhere between twenty and twenty-five million dollars, and insisted, with the sort of idiosyncratic behavior toward money so common among the rich, on paying in cash at the end of each session. It was perhaps wrong of me to allow this arrangement. Nor did I examine closely enough my own slightly fugued state—a vague sense of well being—when, at ten minutes to four every weekday for almost three years a crisp one-hundred-dollar bill was removed from an elegant ostrich leather billfold and placed on the corner of my desk. The regularity of the ritual was enormously reassuring—far more, indeed, than I allowed myself to realize at the time. At any rate (correction—at that rate) allow it I did, and subsequent events suggest that it made no difference to R, while at the same time it enabled me to take on B, the penniless Armenian composer with the shrinking genitals syndrome whose cure did so much to establish me in those circles in which I now move.

R was a particularly charming boy of twenty-seven, intelligent, articulate, and talented. He was the author, despite his youth, of two well-known novels (published under a pseudonym) remarkable for their poetic style and purity of conception. As an artist he strove for only the highest aesthetic accomplishment, never compromising, never losing sight of his goal, which was, in his own words, "the creation of an art which both contains and transcends life." He entered analysis as the result of an acute anxiety attack precipitated by six months of continuous drinking and indiscriminate drug usage. His history—orphaned at two, reared by professional nannies hired by the executor of his estate—in conjunction with his symptoms—recurrent anxiety, suicidal tendencies, somatization—and his first dreams indicated classical therapy, which commenced immediately.

He responded well. The more powerful of his self-destructive behavior cycles broke apart quickly, and as anxiety abated he moved into the familiar stage of object hunger, specifically focused, in his case, on a desire to make love to beautiful women. But after a fast initial year analysis slowed down gradually, in exact parallel to a smaller and smaller output of prose from his pen, and in direct relation to his voracious sexual appetite, the size of which was one of the first clues as to the extent of childhood deprivation experienced by this sensitive boy. It was clear that a brilliant career lay before R, and I felt it my duty, not only to him but to society at large, to get him out of bed and at his desk. Further, since work provided the only extra-analytical continuity in his life which could possibly contain his energies, analysis could not end until a life style based on work had been firmly established. Therefore, in the third year, I began, very gently, to push him in that direction. To my complete surprise, and for the first time in his analysis, I met total resistance.

You are aware of the work I have done with artists. Three quarters of my patients have been artists. I have learned more about the relationship of the conscious to the subconscious, more about the dynamics of that quintessential mystery from my artists than from the literature of our own field. I have analyzed the leading poet, four of our best novelists, two painters, two composers besides the Armenian, a sculptor, and half a dozen actors. I am familiar with the special problems of creative people, and as you know from my published papers, I would be the last to insinuate myself into the mysteries of creation. Contrary to the opinions of some of our colleagues (most specifically that group over on the West Side, what's-his-name's group) I assume that the reluctance of artist-analysands to delve too deeply into their work is entirely appropriate. The unconscious cannot be taken apart like a watch and spread out in so many shiny pieces on a table. The artists are correct—the source is unknown and will forever remain unknown. You can imagine, then, the extreme care with which I introduced the subject. R resisted every step of the way. After explaining that I was well aware of the dangers of any attempt to analyze the creative source, I suggested that he might not have been working because he was using all his energy in bed. He denied any connection, maintaining that he was not working because, at that moment in his life, there was nothing to work on. The girls were simply to pass the time until inspiration returned. He spoke of the Muse as an actual being, and diverted the rest of the hour into a lengthy free associative screen about certain rhapsodic sexual events recent in his life.

During subsequent weeks I became obsessed with R's case. I know now that it was all carefully planned. He was, I should be ashamed to admit, my favorite patient. Indeed, he still is. You cannot imagine how charming he was, or what a tonic it was for me that first year, to see him respond precisely the way patients are supposed to respond, making me the father he never had, his ego growing, strength and confidence building in him daily, guilt and anxiety draining away. Every analyst should have a patient like R once in his life. I was led into loving him, and as it turned out, that was the point.

On Tuesday, September the fourth, I used (for the last time in an analytic situation) the expression "writer's block," hoping it would lead to something. R laughed aloud, clapping his hands smartly in the air as was his wont when something amusing occurred (he was refreshingly at ease on the couch, having developed a whole set of gestures with which, although supine, he could express himself) and said there was no such thing as "writer's block." There were assuredly writers who, at certain times, could not write, but that was as it should be and was due to the intercedence of particular Gods whose special interest was the prevention of bad prose on earth. This seemed to me a significant fantasy, and I drew him out. To write without authentic inspiration, he said, was hubris, hubris in the original sense, a sin against the Gods. A somewhat confused dialogue followed, during which it gradually became clear to me that R was not speaking metaphorically. He meant every word. At the end of the hour he announced that he was an angel, rose from the couch, put a hundred-dollar bill on the corner of the desk, and left.

I ask you, Doctor, to put yourself in my place. The rest of Tuesday and the beginning of Wednesday were a nightmare. I dealt with my other patients as if in a dream. How was it possible? After almost three years of analysis during which R showed not one schizoid symptom, not one single delusion, he seemed suddenly on the brink of disintegration. An angel! Had the ease with which we dealt with his neuroses been nothing more than an unimaginably elaborate schizophrenic ploy? Had I ever really known R?

I concealed my emotions during the Wednesday hour. Despite the danger of driving him deeper into his angel role I was determined to discover if it had been my insistence on discussing his work habits which got him there in the first place. Accordingly, he associated to his inability to start the next novel. He explained that he could not write because he was disharmoniously placed in relation to the Muse. I suggested that he might begin working nevertheless, in hopes that the Muse, and her favors, might somehow be attracted. At that point the following extraordinary events took place.

R announced that the Gods were pleased with my work with artists, whom they loved above all mortals, and that he, R, had been sent to dramatize the point, in the clearest possible terms, that I would otherwise have known only abstractly. It is right, he said, to help them collect their energies for art. It is right to clear away whatever stands between them and the full use of their talents. But it was wrong to suggest that they work in order to attract the Muse, not only because it displeases her to be called, but because such work tends to destroy the artists who create it. You must never forget, he said, and after this hour you never will, that the artist who works without inspiration creates a dead child, a child he nevertheless loves as he would a living one, and that the sensation of all one's work and love going into something not alive, as nothing can be alive without the Muse, is very much the same sensation you would feel if a patient you had worked your painstaking, dedicated work with for years, and come to love, were suddenly to raise his hand in the air, snap his fingers, and disappear. So saying, he raised his hand in the air, snapped his fingers, and disappeared. Eventually I got up and examined the couch, which was empty except for a crisp hundred-dollar bill where his head had been.

I write this to you now, Doctor, without further comment. As you know, since my retirement, I have devoted myself to the study of Ancient Greek culture and religion. I grow old. I may be seeing R in the near future and I want to be able to say I had the courage to tell someone.

Yours,

HERMAN FRIMMLE, M.D.

Psychoanalysis Changed My Life

Amy Bloom

For three weeks, four days a week, Marianne told her dreams to Dr. Zurmer. Fat, naked women handed her bouquets of tiger lilies; incomprehensible signs and directories punctuated silent gray corridors; bodiless penises spewed azalea blossoms in great pink and purple arcs. She also talked about her marriage, her divorce, and her parents. Behind her, Dr. Zurmer nodded and took notes and occasionally slipped her knotted, elderly feet out of elegant black velvet flats, wiggling her toes until she could feel her blood begin to move. Marianne could hear her even and attentive breathing, could hear the occasional light scratch of her cigarlike fountain pen.

At the end of another long dream, in which Marianne's father frantically attempted to reach Marianne through steadily drifting petals, Dr. Zurmer put down her pen.

"Why don't you sit up, Dr. Loewe?"

Marianne didn't move, still thinking of the soft drifts and the few white petals that had clung to her father's beard as he struggled toward her. Dr. Zurmer thought she had shocked her patient into immobility.

"After all, there are two of us in the room. Why should we pretend that only one of us is real, that only one of us is present?"

Marianne sat up.

"All these white flower dreams," Dr. Zurmer said, "what are they about?"

"I'm sure they're about my mother. I don't know if you remember, my mother's name was Lily. And she was like a white flower, thin, pale, graceful. Just wafting around, not a solid person at all. Just a little bit of everything, you know, real estate, house painting, for a while she read tea leaves in some fake Gypsy restaurant. I mean, now she's a business-woman, but then . . . My father was the stable one, but she drove him away."

Dr. Zurmer said, "He was stable, but he disappeared. You say she was 'wafting around,' but she never left you. And she always made a living, yes?"

"He didn't disappear. My mother was having an affair, one of many, I'm sure, she was such a fucking belle of the ball, and he couldn't stand it and he left." Marianne was glad that she could say "fucking."

"It's understandable that he would choose to end the marriage. Not everyone would, but it's understandable. But why did he stop seeing you?"

"He didn't really have much choice. She got custody somehow, and then he moved to California for his work. I went to California once, for about a week, but then, I don't know, he remarried, and then he died in a car accident." Marianne started to cry and wished she were back on the couch, invisible.

"How old were you when you went to California?"

"Nine."

"How did you get there?"

"My mother took me by plane."

"Your mother took you by plane to California so you could visit your father?"

"Sometimes she was overprotective. I remember he said that when I was old enough to take the plane by myself I could come out there. I thought nine was old enough, but my mother took me."

"Of course. Why would you send a nine-year-old three thousand miles away by herself, unless it was an emergency?"

"Lots of people do."

"Lots of people behave selfishly and irresponsibly. It doesn't seem that your father thought nine was really old enough either. He, however, was willing to wait another year or two before you saw each other."

"It wasn't like that."

"I think it was. You are almost forty now. I am almost eighty-five. We are not going to have time for a long analysis, Dr. Loewe, which is just as well. I will tell you what I see, when I see something, but you have to be willing to look. Your mother knew how important your father was to you, and even though your father had left her, she was willing to take the time and money to make sure that you saw him, even in the face of his indifference. You must think about why you need your father to be the hero of this story. Tomorrow, yes?"

Marianne went home, less happy than she had been the first time they met. Three weeks ago, walking into that gray-carpeted waiting room, with its two black-and-white Sierra Club photographs and the dusty mahogany coffee table offering only last week's *Paris-Match* and last year's *New Yorkers*, Marianne knew that she was in sure and authentic hands. Despite an unexpected penchant for bright, bulky sweaters, made charming and European by carefully embroidered flowers on the pockets, Dr. Zurmer was just what Marianne had hoped for.

On Tuesday, Dr. Zurmer interrupted Marianne's memory of her grandfather shaving with an old-fashioned straight razor to tell her that beige was not her color.

"Beige is for redheads, for certain blondes. Not for you. My hair was the same color fifty years ago. *Chatin.* Ahh, chestnut. A lovely color, even with the gray. You would look very nice in green, all different greens, like spring leaves. Maybe a ring or a bracelet, as well, to call attention to your pretty hands."

Marianne looked at Dr. Zurmer, and Dr. Zurmer smiled back.

"We must stop for today. Tomorrow, Dr. Loewe."

Marianne went home and fed her cat, and as she put on her navy bathrobe and her backless slippers, she watched herself in the mirror.

During the next week's sessions, Dr. Zurmer gave Marianne the name of a good masseuse, an expert hair colorist, and a store that specialized in narrow-width Swiss shoes, which turned out to be perfect for Marianne's feet and sensibilities. At the end of Thursday's session, Dr. Zurmer suggested that Marianne focus less on the past and more on the present.

"Your mother invites you to her beach house every weekend, Dr. Loewe. Why not go? I don't think she wants to devour you or humiliate you. I think she wants to show off her brilliant daughter to her friends and she wants you to appreciate the life she's made for herself—beach house and catering business and so on. This is no small potatoes for a woman of her background, for the delicate flower you say she is. Life is short, Dr. Loewe. Go visit your mother and see what is really there. At the very worst, you will have escaped this dreadful heat and you will return to tell me that my notions are all wet."

Charmed by Dr. Zurmer's archaic Americanisms and the vision of herself and her mother walking on the beach at sunset, their identical short, strong legs and narrow feet skimming through the sand, Marianne rose to leave, not waiting for Dr. Zurmer's dismissal.

Dr. Zurmer began to rise and could not. Her head fell forward, and her half-moon glasses, which made her look so severe and so kind, landed on the floor.

Marianne crouched beside Dr. Zurmer's chair and put just her fingertips on Dr. Zurmer's shoulder. Dr. Zurmer did not lift her head.

"Please take me home. I am not well."

"Should I call your doctor? Or an ambulance? They can bring you to the hospital."

"I am not going to a hospital. Please take me home." Dr. Zurmer raised her head, and without her glasses she looked extremely vulnerable and reptilian, an ancient turtle, arrogant in its longevity, resigned to its fate.

Terrified, Marianne drove Dr. Zurmer home, regretting the Kleenex and Heath Bar wrappers in the backseat, where Dr. Zurmer lay, pain dampening and distorting the matte, powdery surface of her fine old skin. When they approached a small Spanish-style house with ivy reaching up to the red tile roof and slightly weedy marigolds lining the front walk, Dr. Zurmer indicated that Marianne should pull into the driveway. Marianne could not imagine carrying Dr. Zurmer up the walk, although she was probably capable of lifting her, but she didn't think Dr. Zurmer could make the hundred yards on her own.

"Is someone home? I can go let them know that you're here, and they can give us a hand."

Dr. Zurmer nodded twice, and her head sagged back against the seat.

A thin old man, shorter than Marianne and leaning hard on a rubber-tipped cane, opened the door. Marianne explained what had happened, even mentioning that she was Dr. Zurmer's patient, which was a weird and embarrassing thing to have to say to the man who was obviously her analyst's husband. He nodded and followed Marianne out to the car. It was clear to Marianne that this little old man was in no position to carry his wife to the house, and that she, Marianne, would have to stick around for a few more minutes and take Dr. Zurmer in, probably to her bedroom, perhaps to her bathroom, which was not a pleasant thought.

"Otto," was all Dr. Zurmer said.

They spoke softly in Russian, and Marianne gently pulled Dr. Zurmer from the backseat, handing her briefcase to the husband, half carrying, half dragging Dr. Zurmer up the walk under his critical, anxious eye. Dr. Zurmer's husband seemed not to speak English, or not to speak to people other than his wife.

Marianne was so focused on not dropping Dr. Zurmer and following Mr. or Dr. Zurmer's hand signals that she barely saw her analyst's house, although she had wondered about it, with occasional, pleasurable intensity, in the last three weeks. Dr. Zurmer slipped out of Marianne's arms onto a large bed covered with a white lace spread and said thank you and good-bye. Marianne, who had not wanted to come and had not wanted to stay, felt that this was a little abrupt, even ungracious, but she was polite and said it was no trouble and that she would find her own way out so that they would not be disturbed. The old man had lain down next to his wife and was wiping her damp face with his handkerchief.

Marianne walked down the narrow, turning staircase, noticing the scratched brass rods that anchored the faded green carpeting, and looking into the faces in the framed photographs that dotted the wall beside her like dark windows. Two skinny boys in baggy dark trunks are building a huge, turreted sand castle trimmed with seashells, twigs, and the remains of horseshoe crabs, surrounded by a moat that reaches up to the knees of a younger, taller Otto Zurmer. In another, the two skinny boys are now skinny teenagers sitting on a stone wall, back to back like bookends, in matching sunglasses, matching bare chests, and matching fearless and immortal grins.

Marianne was conscious of lingering, of trespassing, in fact, and she only took one quick look at the photograph that interested her the most. Dr. Zurmer, whose first name, Anya, Marianne had read on the brass plaque of her office door, is sitting in a velvet armchair, legs stretched sideways and crossed at the slender white silk ankles. She cannot be more than twenty, and she looks pampered, with her lace-trimmed dress and carefully curled hair, and she looks beautiful; she peers uncertainly at the viewer, eager and afraid.

Marianne spent the next week working harder on the book she was trying to write, staking the tomato plants in her small yard, and getting her hair colored. It came out eye-catching and rich, the color of fine luggage, the color of expensive brandy, the kind drunk only by handsome old men sitting in wing armchairs by their early-evening fires. Marianne was tempted to wear a scarf until the color faded, but she could not bear to cover it up, and at night she fanned it out on her pillow and admired what she could see of the fine, gleaming strands.

She waited to hear from Dr. Zurmer and decided that if she didn't get word from her by Friday, she would leave a message with the answering service. On Friday, Dr. Zurmer called. She told Marianne that she was not yet well enough to return to the office but could see her for a session at home. She did not ask Marianne how she felt about meeting with her therapist, in her therapist's home, with little Dr./Mr. Zurmer running in and out, she simply inquired whether Monday at nine would suit her. That was their usual time, and Marianne said yes and hung up the phone quickly so as not to tire Dr. Zurmer, who sounded terrible.

Dr. Zurmer's husband let Marianne in silently, but when she was fully through the door he took her hand in both of his and thanked her, in perfectly good English.

"Please call me Otto," he said. His smile was very kind, and Marianne said her name and was pleased with them both.

Dr. Zurmer sat in bed, propped up by dozens of large and small Battenberg lace pillows, her silver hair brushed, neat and sleek as mink. She wore a remarkably businesslike gray satin bed jacket. Marianne couldn't tell if Dr. Zurmer's face was slightly longer and looser than before or if she had forgotten, in a week, exactly what Dr. Zurmer looked like.

"I feel much better today. A very tiny stroke, my doctor said. And no harm done, apparently. Thank you, Dr. Loewe. So, I will lie down during our sessions and you will sit up."

Marianne began by telling Dr. Zurmer her latest flower dream but wrapped it up quickly in order to talk about the photograph of Dr. Zurmer, not mentioning the boys; and she sat back in the little brocade chair, looking at the ceiling, in order to talk about the dislocating, fascinating oddness of being in Dr. Zurmer's house. Dr. Zurmer smiled, shaking her head sympathetically, and fell asleep. Marianne sat quietly, only a little insulted, and watched Dr. Zurmer breathe. At her elbow was a mahogany dresser laid over with embroidered, crocheted runners, four small photographs in silver frames and three perfume bottles of striped Murano glass sitting on top. The little gold-tipped bottles were almost empty. One photograph, as Marianne expected, shows the two young men from the stone wall and the beach, a good bit older, both in suits. They are clearly at a wedding, with linen-covered tables and gladioli behind them, although there is no bride in sight. Another shows Dr. Zurmer and Otto, their arms around each other, in front of the lighthouse at Gay Head, and the picture is not unlike one of Marianne and her ex-husband, at that same spot, during the brief, good time of their marriage. The other two photographs are of a dark-skinned woman in a bathrobe, holding what must be a baby wrapped in a blue and white blanket, and finally, a very little boy with black curls, jug ears, and the same slightly slant, long-lashed eyes as the woman.

As Marianne reached the front door, Otto clumped toward her.

"Tea?" he said, waving his cane toward the back of the house.

Marianne said no and went home to look up the phone numbers of other psychoanalysts.

On Thursday, Otto called. "Please come today," he said. "She wants to see you."

Marianne had already set up a consultation with another analyst, a middle-aged man with a good reputation and an office overlooking the river, but she went.

Dr. Zurmer was sitting up again, her bed jacket open over a flannel nightgown and her hair tufted in downy silver puffs. She stretched out her hand for Marianne's and held onto it as Marianne sat down, much closer than planned.

"It seems that I am not well enough to be your analyst after all. But I don't think we should let that stop us from enjoying each other's company, do you? You come and visit, and we'll have tea."

Marianne could not imagine why Dr. Zurmer wanted her to visit.

"Why not? You're smart, a very kind person, you have a wonderful imagination and sense of humor—I see that in your dreams—why shouldn't I want you to visit me? Otto will bring us tea. Sit."

Over pale green tea swarming with brown bits of leaf, Marianne and Dr. Zurmer smiled at each other.

"I was very interested in the photographs on your dresser," Marianne said.

"What about them interests you?"

"This is just a visit, remember? Tea and conversation."

Dr. Zurmer pretended to slap her own wrist and smiled broadly at Marianne, her cheeks folding up like silk ruching.

"Touché," she said. "Bring the photos over here, please. And there's an album in the magazine rack there.

"Oh, look at this, little Alexei. Everyone has these bathtub photographs tucked away. And this is Alexei in Cub Scouts, I think that lasted for six months. He loved the uniform, but he was not, not Scout material. And this is him with his brother, Robert. You saw some of these on the wall, I think. At Martha's Vineyard. We used to stay at a little farmhouse, two bedrooms and a tiny kitchen. Friends of Otto's lent it to us every summer. Otto designed their house, the big house in the background here, and their house, I forget, in the suburbs of Boston. We were the house pets, but it was wonderful for the children. This is Robert's college graduation. I can't remember what all the armbands represent, he protested everything. Unfortunately for him, we were liberals, so it was difficult to disturb us. He did become a banker, there was that. And here is Alexei graduating, no armbands, just the hair. But it was such beautiful hair, I wanted him to keep it long, I thought he looked like Apollo. And here are the wedding pictures, Alexei and his wife, Naria. Lebanese. They met in graduate school. And this is my only

grandson, Lee. As beautiful as the day. As good as he is beautiful. Very bright child. Alexei is a wonderful father, father and
mother both. This big one is Lee last year, on his fourth birthday. That's his favorite bear, I don't remember now, the train
station name."

"Padding. He's lovely. Lee is just lovely."

"Naria left them almost two years ago. She has a narcissistic personality disorder. She simply could not mother.
People cannot do what they are not equipped to do. So, she's
gone, back to Lebanon. Also, very self-destructive, to return to
a place like Lebanon, divorced, a mother, clearly not a virgin.
She will care for her father, in his home, for the rest of her life.
Who can say? Perhaps that was her wish."

Dr. Zurmer said "narcissistic personality disorder" the
way you'd say "terminal cancer," and Marianne nodded, understanding that Naria was gone from this earth.

"And this is a picture Alexei took of me and Otto two
years ago. Those two lovers, the gods made them into trees, or
bushes? Philomena? So that they might never part. We look like
that, yes? Already beginning to merge with the earth."

Dr. Zurmer lay back, and the album slid between them.

"I cannot really speak of loving him anymore. Does one
love the brain, or the heart? Does one appreciate one's blood?
We have kept each other from the worst loneliness, and we listen to each other. We don't say anything very interesting anymore, we talk of Lee, of Alexei, we remember Robert . . ."

Marianne waited for the terrible story.

"He died in a car accident, right after the wedding. I
am still grieving and I am still angry. He was drinking too much,
that was something he did. Alexei, never. My bad Russian genes.
He left nothing behind, an apartment full of junk, a job he disliked, debts. I thought perhaps a pregnant girlfriend would

emerge, but that didn't happen. I would have made it so, if I could have. I have to rest, my dear."

Dr. Zurmer sank back into her pillows and asked Marianne to go into the bottom drawer of the mahogany dresser. Marianne brought her the only thing in it, a bolt of green satin, thick and cool, rippling in her hands like something alive. Dr. Zurmer tied it around her waist, turning Marianne's white shirt and khaki slacks into something dashing, exotic, and slightly, delightfully androgynous.

"Just so. When you leave, please say good-bye to Otto. He likes you so much. 'Such a luffly girl,'" she said, mimicking Otto's accent, which was, if anything, less noticeable, less guttural, than her own. "If he's not in the kitchen, just wait a minute. He's probably getting the newspaper, going for his constitutional. Be well, Marianne. Come again soon."

The man sitting at the kitchen table was so clearly the slightly bigger boy from the photographs, the bearded groom, that Marianne smiled at him familiarly, filled with tenderness and receptivity, as though her pores were steaming open. He stared back at her and then, with great, courtly gestures, folded the newspaper and slid it behind the toaster.

"You must be Marianne."

"Yes. I just wanted to say good-bye to your father, I'm on my way home," she said.

"That will please him. I'm Alex Zurmer. I don't know where Pop is." He looked at her again, at her deep brown eyes and long neck, his own sweet baby giraffe, and watched her blunt, bony fingers playing with the fringe of the glimmering green sash. Alex shrugged, lifting his palms heavenward, as awestruck and grateful as Noah, knowing that he had been selected for survival and the arrival of doves. He watched Marianne's restless, slightly bitten fingers twisting in and out of the thick tasseled ends, and he could feel them touching his face, lifting his hair.

"Let's have tea while we wait. Marianne," he said, and he rose to pull out her chair, and she very deliberately laid her hand next to his on the back of the chair.

"Let's," said Marianne. "Let's put out a few cookies too. If you use loose tea, I'll read the leaves."

Basil from Her Garden

Donald Barthelme

A—In the dream, my father was playing the piano, a Beethoven something, in a large concert hall that was filled with people. I was in the audience and I was reading a book. I suddenly realized that this was the wrong thing to do when my father was performing, so I sat up and paid attention. He was playing very well, I thought. Suddenly the conductor stopped the performance and began to sing a passage for my father, a passage that my father had evidently botched. My father listened attentively, smiling at the conductor.

Q—Does your father play? In actuality?

A—Not a note.

Q—Did the conductor resemble anyone you know?

A—He looked a bit like Althea. The same cheekbones and the same chin.

Q—Who is Althea?

A—Someone I know.

Q—What do you do, after work, in the evenings or on weekends?

A—Just ordinary things.

Q—No special interests?

A—I'm very interested in bow hunting. These new bows they have now, what they call a compound bow. Also, I'm a member of the Galapagos Society, we work for the environment, it's really a very effective—

Q—And what else?

A—Well, adultery. I would say that's how I spend most of my free time. In adultery.

Q—You mean regular adultery.

A—Yes. Sleeping with people to whom one is not legally bound.

Q—These are women.

A—Invariably.

Q—And so that's what you do, in the evenings or on weekends.

A—I had this kind of strange experience. Today is Saturday, right? I called up this haircutter that I go to, her name is Ruth, and asked for an appointment. I needed a haircut. So she says she has openings at ten, ten-thirty, eleven, eleven-thirty, twelve, twelve-thirty— On a Saturday. Do you think the world knows something I don't know?

Q—It's possible.

A—What if she stabs me in the ear with the scissors?

Q—Unlikely, I would think.

A—Well, she's a good soul. She's had several husbands. They've all been master sergeants, in the Army. She seems to gravitate toward NCO clubs. Have you noticed all these little black bugs flying around here? I don't know where they come from.

Q—They're very small, they're like gnats.

A—They come in clouds, then they go away.

A—I sometimes think of myself as a person who, you know what I mean, could have done something else, it doesn't matter what particularly. Just something else. I saw an ad in the Sunday paper for the CIA, a recruiting ad, maybe a quarter of a page, and I suddenly thought, It might be interesting to do that. Even though I've always been opposed to the CIA, when they were trying to bring Cuba down, the stuff with Lumumba in Africa, the stuff in Central America. . . . Then here is this ad, perfectly straightforward, "where your career is America's strength" or something like that, "aptitude for learning a foreign language is a plus" or something like that. I've always been good at languages, and I'm sitting there thinking about how my résumé might look to them, starting completely over in something completely new, changing the very sort of person I am, and there was an attraction, a definite attraction. Of course the maximum age was thirty-five. I guess they want them more malleable.

Q—So, in the evenings or on weekends—

A—Not every night or every weekend. I mean, this depends on the circumstances. Sometimes my wife and I go to dinner with people, or watch television—

Q—But in the main—

A—It's not that often. It's once in a while.

Q—Adultery is a sin.

A—It is classified as a sin, yes. Absolutely.

Q—The Seventh Commandment says—

A—I know what it says. I was raised on the Seventh Commandment. But.

Q—But what?

A—The Seventh Commandment is wrong.

Q—It's wrong?

A—Some outfits call it the Sixth and others the Seventh. It's wrong.

Q—The whole Commandment?

A—I don't know how it happened, whether it's a mistranslation from the Aramaic or whatever, it may not even have been Aramaic, I don't know, I certainly do not pretend to scholarship in this area, but my sense of the matter is that the Seventh Commandment is an error.

Q—Well if that was true it would change quite a lot of things, wouldn't it?

A—Take the pressure off, a bit.

Q—Have you told your wife?

A—Yes, Grete knows.

Q—How'd she take it?

A—Well, she *liked* the Seventh Commandment. You could reason that it was in her interest to support the Seventh Commandment for the preservation of the family unit and this sort of thing but to reason that way is, I would say, to take an extremely narrow view of Grete, of what she thinks. She's not predictable. She once told me that she didn't want me, she wanted a suite of husbands, ten or twenty—

Q—What did you say?

A—I said, Go to it.

Q—Well, how does it make you feel? Adultery.

A—There's a certain amount of guilt attached. I feel guilty. But I feel guilty even without adultery. I exist in a morass of guilt. There's maybe a little additional wallop of guilt but I already feel so guilty that I hardly notice it.

Q—Where does all this guilt come from? The extra-adulterous guilt?

A—I keep wondering if, say, there is intelligent life on other planets, the scientists argue that something like two percent of the other planets have the conditions, the physical conditions, to support life in the way it happened here, did Christ visit each and every planet, go through the same routine, the Agony in the Garden, the Crucifixion, and so on. . . . And these guys on these other planets, these life forms, maybe they look like boll weevils or something, on a much larger scale of course, were they told that they shouldn't go to bed with other attractive six-foot boll weevils arrayed in silver and gold and with little squirts of Opium behind the ears? Doesn't make sense. But of course our human understanding is imperfect.

Q—You haven't answered me. This general guilt—

A—Yes, that's the interesting thing. I hazard that it is not guilt so much as it is inadequacy. I feel that everything is being nibbled away, because I can't *get it right*—

Q—Would you like to be able to fly?

A—It's crossed my mind.

Q—Myself, I think about being just sort of a regular person, one who worries about cancer a lot, every little thing a prediction of cancer, no I don't want to go for my every-two-years checkup because what if they find something? I wonder what will kill me and when it will happen and how it will happen, and I wonder about my parents, who are still alive, and what will happen to them. This seems to be a proper set of things to worry about. Last things.

A—I don't think God gives a snap about adultery. This is just an opinion, of course.

Q—So how do you, how shall I put it, pursue—

A—You think about this staggering concept, the mind of God, and then you think He's sitting around worrying about this guy and this woman at the Beechnut TraveLodge? I think not.

Q—Well He doesn't have to think about every particular instance, He just sort of laid out the general principles—

A—He also created creatures who, with a single powerful glance—

Q—The eyes burn.

A—They do.

Q—The heart leaps.

A—Like a terrapin.

Q—Stupid youth returns.

A—Like hockey sticks falling out of a long-shut closet.

Q—Do you play?

A—I did. Many years ago.

Q—Who is Althea?

A—Someone I know.

Q—We're basically talking about Althea.

A—Yes. I thought you understood that.

Q—We're not talking about wholesale—

A—Oh Lord no. Who has the strength?

Q—What's she like?

A—She's I guess you'd say a little on the boring side. To the innocent eye.

Q—She appears to be a contained, controlled person, free of raging internal fires.

A—But my eye is not innocent. To the already corrupted eye, she's—

Q—I don't want to question you too closely on this. I don't want to strain your powers of—

A—Well, no, I don't mind talking about it. It fell on me like a ton of bricks. I was walking in the park one day.

Q—Which park?

A—That big park over by—

Q—Yeah, I know the one.

A—This woman was sitting there.

Q—They sit in parks a lot, I've noticed that. Especially when they're angry. The solitary bench. Shoulders raised, legs kicking—

A—I've crossed both major oceans by ship—the Pacific twice, on troopships, the Atlantic once, on a passenger liner. You stand out there, at the rail, at dusk, and the sea is limitless, water in every direction, never ending, you think *water forever*, the movement of the ship seems slow but also seems inexorable, you feel you will be moving this way forever, the Pacific is about seventy million square miles, about one-third of the earth's surface, the ship might be making twenty knots, I'm eating oranges because that's all I can keep down, twelve days of it with thousands of young soldiers all around, half of them seasick— On the Queen Mary, in tourist class, we got rather good food, there was a guy assigned to our table who had known Paderewski, the great pianist who was also prime minister of Poland, he talked about Paderewski for four days, an ocean of anecdotes—

Q—When I was first married, when I was twenty, I didn't know where the clitoris was. I didn't know there was such a thing. Shouldn't somebody have told me?
A—Perhaps your wife?
Q—Of course, she was too shy. In those days people didn't go around saying, This is the clitoris and this is what its proper function is and this is what you can do to help out. I finally found it. In a book.
A—German?
Q—Dutch.

A—A dead bear in a blue dress, face down on the kitchen floor. I trip over it, in the dark, when I get up at 2 A.M. to see if there's anything to eat in the refrigerator. It's an architectural problem, marriage. If we could live in separate houses, and visit each other when we felt particularly gay— It would be expensive, yes. But as it is she has to endure me in all my worst manifestations, early in the morning and late at night and in the nutsy obsessed noontimes. When I wake up from my nap you don't *get* the laughing cavalier, you get a rank pigfooted belching blunderer. I knew this one guy who built a wall down the middle of his apartment. An impenetrable wall. He had a very big apartment. It worked out very well. Concrete block, basically, with fiberglass insulation on top of that and Sheetrock on top of that—

Q—What about coveting your neighbor's wife?

A—Well on one side there are no wives, strictly speaking, there are two floors and two male couples, all very nice people. On the other side, Bill and Rachel have the whole house. I like Rachel but I don't covet her. I could covet her, she's covetable, quite lovely and spirited, but in point of fact our relationship is that of neighborliness. I jump-start her car when her battery is dead, she gives me basil from her garden, she's got acres of basil, not literally acres but— Anyhow, I don't think that's much of a problem, coveting your neighbor's wife. Just speaking administratively, I don't see why there's an entire Commandment devoted to it. It's a mental exercise, coveting. To covet is not necessarily to take action.

Q—I covet my neighbor's leaf blower. It has this neat Vari-Flo deal that lets you—

A—I can see that.

Q—I am feverishly interested in these questions.

Q—Ethics has always been where my heart is.

Q—Moral precepting stings the dull mind into attentiveness.

Q—I'm only a bit depressed, only a bit.

Q—A new arrangement of ideas, based upon the best thinking, would produce a more humane moral order, which we need.

Q—Apple honey, disposed upon the sexual parts, is not an index of decadence. Decadence itself is not as bad as it's been painted.

Q—That he watched his father play the piano when his father could not play the piano and that he was reading a book while his father played the piano in a very large hall before a very large audience only means that he finds his roots, as it were, untrustworthy. The father imagined as a root. That's not unusual.

Q—As for myself, I am content with too little, I know this about myself and I do not commend myself for it and perhaps one day I shall be able to change myself into a hungrier being. Probably not.

Q—The leaf blower, for example.

A—I see Althea now and then, not often enough. We sigh together in a particular bar, it's almost always empty. She tells me about her kids and I tell her about my kids. I obey the Commandments, the sensible ones. Where they don't know what they're talking about I ignore them. I keep thinking about the story of the two old women in church listening to the priest discoursing on the dynamics of the married state. At the end of the sermon one turns to the other and says, "I wish I knew as little about it as he does."

Q—He critiques us, we critique Him. Does Grete also engage in dalliance?

A—How quaint you are. I think she has friends whom she sees now and then.

Q—How does that make you feel?

A—I wish her well.

Q—What's in your wallet?

A—The usual. Credit cards, pictures of the children, driver's license, forty dollars in cash, Amex receipts—

Q—I sometimes imagine that I am in Pest Control. I have a small white truck with a red diamond-shaped emblem on the door and a white jumpsuit with the same emblem on the breast pocket. I park the truck in front of a subscriber's neat three-hundred-thousand-dollar home, extract the silver cannister of deadly pest killer from the back of the truck, and walk up the brick sidewalk to the house's front door. Chimes ring, the door swings open, a young wife in jeans and a pink flannel shirt worn outside the jeans is standing there. "Pest Control," I say. She smiles at me, I smile back and move past her into the house, into the handsomely appointed kitchen. The cannister is suspended by a sling from my right shoulder, and, pumping the mechanism occasionally with my right hand, I point the nozzle of the hose at the baseboards and begin to spray. I spray alongside the refrigerator, alongside the gas range, under the sink, and behind the kitchen table. Next, I move to the bathrooms, pumping and spraying. The young wife is in another room, waiting for me to finish. I walk into the main sitting room and spray discreetly behind the largest pieces of furniture, an oak sideboard, a red plush Victorian couch, and along the inside of the fireplace. I do the study, spraying the *Columbia Encyclopedia*, he's been looking up the Seven Years' War, 1756–63, yellow highlighting there, and behind the forty-five-inch RCA television. The master bedroom requires just touches, short bursts in her closet which must avoid the two dozen pairs of shoes there and in his closet which contains six to eight long guns in canvas cases. Finally I spray the laundry room with its big white washer and dryer, and behind the folding table stacked with sheets and towels already folded. Who folds? I surmise that she folds. Unless one of the older children, pressed into service, folds. In my experience they are unlikely to fold. Maybe the au pair. Finished, I tear a properly made out receipt from my receipt book and present it to the young wife. She scribbles her name in the appropriate space and hands it back to me. The house now stinks quite palpably but I know and she knows that the stench will dissipate in two to four hours. The young wife escorts me to the door, and, in parting, pins a silver medal on my chest and kisses me on both cheeks. Pest Control!

A—Yes, one could fit in in that way. It's finally a matter, perhaps, of fit. Appropriateness. Fit in a stately or sometimes hectic dance with nonfit. What we have to worry about.

Q—It seems to me that we have quite a great deal to worry about. Does the radish worry about itself in this way? Yet the radish is a living thing. Until it's cooked.

A—Grete is mad for radishes, can't get enough. I like frozen Mexican dinners, Patio, I have them for breakfast, the freezer is stacked with them—

Q—Transcendence is possible.

A—Yes.

Q—Is it possible?

A—Not out of the question.

Q—Is it really possible?

A—Yes. Believe me.

V.
Love

Though issues related to loving are woven throughout this book, the inability to love is the central problem faced by the male protagonists in "The Patient" and in the pair of stories by Daniel Menaker, "I'm Rubber, You're Glue" and "Influenza." In each of these tales, the patient and therapist battle, often shouting at each other "like grade-schoolers in a playground." But these patients also internalize the voices of their therapists, and it becomes evident that each fiery interaction is actually a battle between the patient's neurotic tendencies and his desire to change his life. As in the stories contained in "Secrets and Lies," what the patient reveals is not a fear of relaying his thoughts to his therapist but a fear that these thoughts will be revealed at all. As the unswerving therapist in "I'm Rubber, You're Glue" points out during one exchange of sparring, "You force me to interrogate you, so that you can express the shock that you feel toward yourself." In all three stories, the therapist remains a catalyst for the patient's self-discovery. Though present and active, the therapist remains nevertheless a mysterious kind of mirror.

"Influenza" closes this book. Here, the protagonist surrenders to his therapist and lets go of his past fears and projections, a release signified by his orgasm, with which the story ends. In a revelatory moment with his lover, who unwittingly acts in conjunction with his therapist, this man at last understands what it means to love. "You have to take care of sick children even when you're sick yourself," he remarks. "That's love," his lover tells him, "—it's different." Perhaps her words speak to the nature of good psychotherapy, as well.

The Patient

Barbara Lawrence

To Alexander's surprise, Dr. Kahmstetter did not pay much attention to the problem of his nose. He was more interested, it seemed, in the kind of people Alexander knew.

Alexander began by describing the Ones. These were the gapers, he said. He found them staring at his nose on buses and trains, their faces unembarrassed and greedy for signs of aberration. They did not bother him particularly. Did not bother him at all, in fact. If they were his only problem, he would not have come to a doctor. Even the Twos were not exactly what he would call a problem—more disturbing than the Ones, to be sure, since their covert, embarrassed observation carried with it a certain sensitivity. But it was nothing that he could not deal with. Had dealt with quite successfully for years. No, it was neither the Ones nor the Twos. It was the Threes who had finally made his position unendurable.

"The Threes?" said Dr. Kahmstetter.

"The Threes," Alexander explained, "realize that my nose is growing larger, but they never even look at it. They look at *me*."

"Well?" said the Doctor.

"Well," Alexander told him in an anguished voice, "I am so amazed at their kindness that when I am with them I tremble and behave in such a peculiar way that they cannot possibly enjoy my company. You see," he continued, suddenly avoiding the Doctor's eyes, "I know now that I must solve the problem of my nose or I shall never win the love of the Threes."

"And in the meantime who are your friends?" Dr. Kahmstetter asked him.

"People I detest." Alexander sighed. "The Fours. They pretend to have all the qualities of the Threes and actually have none."

"Ah," said the Doctor.

During his first weeks of treatment, at the suggestion of Dr. Kahmstetter, Alexander stopped measuring his nose and scrutinizing it each morning in a magnifying mirror, and tried instead to take only cursory glances at himself in large, full-length mirrors. It was during this period that he discovered the existence of other patients, most of whom seemed to be Twos and Fours. Some of these, he learned, came to doctors because, like himself, they believed their noses were growing larger. Others came because of a fear that their noses were growing smaller. And still others, with undeniably enormous or infinitesimal noses, were taking treatments to persuade themselves that their condition did not matter.

"You see," Dr. Kahmstetter remarked one day, "it isn't so much the nose but why the nose should be this important to anyone. Many people, after all, have far worse problems than an imagined—or even a *really*—large nose, but this does not prevent them from living."

"I am aware of that," Alexander said, making a secret, burning note that the Doctor apparently considered his problem imaginary. "Quite aware of it," he added sharply, for he had begun to suspect Dr. Kahmstetter of seriously underestimating his intelligence.

"I mention it," the Doctor said, "only because you yourself have talked of almost nothing else."

"The fact that I have *talked* about my nose," said Alexander, "doesn't necessarily mean it's my most serious problem."

"But isn't that exactly what I was just saying?"

Alexander searched without success for a glimmer of malice or triumph in this remark.

"Isn't that what we have to examine?" Dr. Kahmstetter added.

Alexander declined to answer.

The more he declined to answer Dr. Kahmstetter, the more time Alexander seemed to spend discussing his problems with other patients. They, he was gratified to learn, were not too disturbed about their condition. Most of them, in fact, considered themselves in a better position than people who were not patients. This was a point of view he took pleasure in expounding to certain Fours, who smiled uneasily as he did so or sometimes stared pointedly and tastelessly at his nose.

"Let us assume, for example," he said one afternoon to a young Four with a rather small nose, "that somebody imagines his nose is growing larger." He paused and looked carefully over the Four's head. "Or perhaps someone imagines that his nose is growing smaller." The Four winced slightly. "There *are* people, you know, who believe that their noses are disappearing."

"Really?" she exclaimed with a bright, fixed smile.

"Yes," Alexander said. "I have known people to be so obsessed with ideas of this kind that they have gone to doctors for years and years."

"How astonishing," the Four said.

"Well, actually," Alexander told her, "it's not astonishing at all. The astonishing thing is that anyone could get that upset about a nose." He raised his head, and his eyes took on the unfocused look of a public speaker. "After all, lots of us may imagine we have something wrong with our nose—may really *have* something wrong, for that matter—but it doesn't prevent us from living."

There was a flicker of recognition behind the Four's bright smile.

"The important thing," Alexander continued, "is to try to find out why people get so upset about their nose."

"How long have you been taking treatments?" the Four asked suddenly, with such unstudied interest that Alexander's head swung toward her like a falling weight. "I ask," she said, "because you've changed so much in the past few months. You seem less guarded. I have the feeling," she added shyly, "that you don't secretly dislike everyone quite so much anymore."

Was it possible, Alexander asked himself when he was alone again, that the Fours had always been aware of his secret contempt for them? This could hardly be the case, he reasoned, for it was their *unawareness*, after all, that he hated. But suppose that their unawareness had never existed; what was it, then, that he had been hating?

"Could it be something in yourself that you have been hating?" Dr. Kahmstetter suggested. The Doctor's observations sometimes struck Alexander as unbearably stereotyped.

Out on the street, he held an imaginary conversation with the Doctor. "If the object of my hatred is myself and not the Fours," he said with elaborate dignity, "does this mean that the Fours are lovable or not lovable?" The fantasy Dr. Kahmstetter seemed to wilt under his scrutiny. "If they are *not* lovable," Alexander continued, "then there is a reason for my not *loving* them. On the other hand, if they *are* lovable, why haven't I loved *them* as I have always loved the Threes?" A faintly perceptible smile played around his mouth as he walked away from the inarticulate Doctor.

That evening, at a supper party, as he tried to catch a glimpse of himself in a full-length mirror, Alexander discovered that he was wearing the same fixed, hypocritical smile he detested in the Fours. He turned to the Four with the small nose, who was standing a short distance away and was watching him with interest.

"The trouble with most people," he said rather loudly, "is that they condemn in others what they are really guilty of themselves." The Four's puzzled expression made him feel a little ridiculous, and he gave her a piercing glance. "You, for example, have a habit of diagnosing people. You told me the other day that I secretly disliked everyone."

"I said you *seemed* to dislike people before your treatments," the Four protested mildly.

"Has it ever occurred to you that perhaps it is really *you* who secretly dislike everyone?" Alexander said with a twinge of pain, for he was beginning to get a headache.

The Four laid her hand on his shoulder with such delicate compassion that he knew she must have copied the gesture from a Three. "I've never seen you so upset before," she said.

"I should say it was very interesting—very interesting indeed," Alexander told Dr. Kahmstetter the next day, "that a friend who has known me for several years took pains to tell me last night that she had never seen me in worse condition."

"It is interesting," said the Doctor, "but not quite so interesting as the elation that such a depressing statement apparently causes you."

"But I *am* depressed," Alexander said. He was very depressed, he assured the Doctor—by this and several other things. People no longer admired him as they once had. He was losing the wit and authority that had made the Fours seek him out. His nose was just as large as it had ever been. He still had not found a Three to love him, and he had paid nine hundred and ninety-five dollars for treatments since the beginning of the year.

His accusations made only small soundless ripples in the deep well of the Doctor's patience. Might it not be wiser, Dr. Kahmstetter suggested, to try to understand why it troubled him so to be unpopular with people he professed to despise? Or better still, to concentrate on the *nature* of his hatred for the Fours. Had he any special feeling about this hatred? Had he ever been close enough to it to see what it was like?

He had never actually seen his hatred, Alexander said, but he had felt it often enough. It was a small, sharp stone in his chest. Dr. Kahmstetter seemed especially pleased with this reply.

For the next few weeks, without telling Dr. Kahmstetter, Alexander spent his time trying to examine the stone of his hatred. It was extremely difficult to touch the stone, he found. Occasionally even the thought of touching it caused his chest to contract in a way that made the effort impossible. The best time to approach the task was when he cared least about succeeding. After a particularly concentrated effort had failed and he was on the point of giving up the whole business in disgust, his chest sometimes relaxed and the stone was miraculously available to him. At last, although each movement filled his body with a thousand shocks, he managed to loosen the stone sufficiently to put one finger behind a corner of it. What he felt there when he did so made him scream with fright.

The stone, he announced, trembling and defiant, when he reached Dr. Kahmstetter's office, was attached to the right side of his heart.

"But how can you possibly say such a thing?" the Doctor asked, with the slightest trace of impatience. Alexander's contention that he *felt* it there did not impress Dr. Kahmstetter. That was just a way of refusing to examine the stone, he said.

"But suppose that the stone *is* attached to my heart and that dislodging it will cost me my life," Alexander insisted.

"In that case," said the Doctor matter-of-factly, "I can be of no help to you."

Alexander had such a glaring pain in his head when he left Dr. Kahmstetter's office that day that he could not remember a word they had said to each other. When he reached home, he went immediately to the telephone and called the Four with the small nose to apologize for his conduct at the supper party.

It was perfectly all right, she told him. She knew how irritable a headache made one feel and, actually, after thinking it over, she had decided there was some truth in what he had said about her secretly disliking everybody.

It occurred to Alexander as he hung up the phone that he might be falling in love with the young Four.

"It's the first time, of course, that I've ever felt this way about anyone who wasn't a Three," he told Dr. Kahmstetter at his next session, pretending not to notice the Doctor's veiled, approving glance.

"Perhaps you are discovering that people cannot be divided into categories, after all," the Doctor said with the suggestion of a smile.

Alexander kept remembering Dr. Kahmstetter's smile and his veiled, approving glance. Once or twice, he even found himself smiling in this same way at the Fours. When he did so, the Fours' fixed, bright faces became more fixed than ever, but their eyes shot him looks of loneliness and longing that amazed him. On a bus one afternoon, he smiled at a Two who was secretly study-ing the reflection of his nose in the window. The look that crossed the Two's face was almost identical with what he had seen in the eyes of the Fours.

Was it possible that the glances he had found so threat-ening were not really threatening at all? Could all these differ-ent faces conceal the same expression? How strange that this had never occurred to him before. The Fours, he remembered suddenly, had never said that they *disliked* his nose. Even the Twos had never looked at his nose with actual malice. Even the Ones, in their numb, fettered way, perhaps yearned to look beyond his nose. And as final, incontestable proof, there was the young Four herself, whose eyes and voice and smile and hands were as sensitive and comprehending as any Three's.

"Perhaps," Alexander said to himself, "you are discov-ering that people are not divided into categories, after all."

It was five months after their marriage—a year after he had stopped seeing Dr. Kahmstetter—that the young Four made her startling revelation to Alexander. She was extremely casual about it. That was one of the hardest things to forgive her for, really—her total failure to understand his feelings in the matter.

"The trouble with most people," he was saying when it happened, "is that they live by categories."

The young Four seemed rather abstracted, and Alexander went further than he had intended, to capture her attention.

"I myself believed in them once, you know. There was even a time when I would not have married you unless you had been a Three."

"But my darling," his wife said then, smiling in affec-tionate protest, her voice gentle and amused, "I *am* a Three."

Knowing how little importance he attached to catego-ries, she could not believe that she had shocked him. Nor could she believe that this aspect of her identity, or the circumstances which explained it, could really fascinate him. One of the things she had always loved most about him, in fact, was his indifference to such matters.

Alexander went immediately to call on Dr. Kahmstetter.

"My wife is a Three. Has been all the time," he said, fighting to control his voice, as he entered the Doctor's office.

"Yes?" said Dr. Kahmstetter.

"But I don't know what to do."

"Do? Why should you do anything?" the Doctor asked.

Alexander's chest contracted in such a strange way at that moment that he could not utter a word.

"This is exactly what you have always wanted," Dr. Kahmstetter continued in his kind, cheerful voice. "If I can help you," he added as Alexander walked mutely to the door, "please don't hesitate to call on me."

For several weeks it seemed as if Alexander might never recover the power of speech. And, indeed, this could very well have been the case had he not taken his measuring tape and magnifying mirror one day and discovered beyond any shadow of doubt that his nose was a sixteenth of an inch longer.

"The trouble with most people," he said then, with a buoyancy that quite amazed his wife, "is that they don't trust the evidence of their own senses."

I'm Rubber, You're Glue

Daniel Menaker

In 1977, after a year of psychoanalysis at the rough hands of
Dr. Ernesto Morales—the short, bald, muscular black-bearded
Catholic Hispanic tyrant-genius of East Ninety-third Street—
I could have written a case study about *him*. About how his
habitual throat-clearing became downright bronchitic when he
was bored, about how he chronically expressed pity for the rich
and famous, about how his voice grew cloyingly sweet when he
asked me about sex, about how as he was charging at my character with lance leveled I could unhorse him by raising the
conversational shield of investments. If I'd mentioned these
observations to him, he would have replied, "Ahem! Respec-
tively, your interest in my cough betrays on your part a repressed
preoccupation with bodily functions, your envy of celebrities
demonstrates a lack of self-respect, the lubricity you hear in my
voice tells us more about your inhibitions than about my voyeurism, and you think I am obsessed with money because you
earn so little."

At this same one-year mark, I told him that I'd passed
up a chance to sleep with a woman because she smelled funny.
This sexual near-miss was the closest I'd come to any sort of
intimacy with anyone in a long, long time. He said, "Now, Mr.

314

Singer, as you should perhaps know by now, this was your own odor that you detected. I do not refer to the odor of your body but to the way in which you transformed your disgust with your sexual appetites into a physical stench and then attributed this stench to this woman." Dr. Morales's Cuban accent, thick to begin with, stiffened further as he whipped it with the extra enthusiasm of an interpretation he found especially impressive. It wouldn't have surprised me to see the "r"s in "refer" roll past the couch I was lying on.

"I didn't say 'stench,'" I said. "I didn't say she smelled bad, just a bit odd."

"'A bit odd,' 'a bit odd,'" said Dr. Morales. "Why have you not told me this before that you are actually British and not American?"

That skirmish later developed into a separate war, over Dr. Morales's assertion that I held his English in contempt. I did not. His English was far superior to that of most of my colleagues in the English Department of the Coventry Preparatory School for Boys—to say nothing of that of my students. Superior in clarity, grammar, and economy—to say nothing of forcefulness of expression. Much later in what he called "our work," I was able to say calmly to Dr. Morales that it was his own insecurity that led him to make such an accusation against me, but at this point I was just beginning to learn his tricks, and it was only with agitation that I started to suggest that I wasn't the only one in that office at the rear of the top floor of a brownstone just off Fifth Avenue who was capable, on a Monday, Wednesday, or Friday morning from seven-thirty to eight-twenty, of tarring himself with his own brush.

Samira laughed. I was walking around in my bathrobe, doing an imitation of Dr. Morales touting triple-tax-free municipals—

"Eet ees as eef the government were eesuing to you licenses wheech permeet you to rob eet"—and she was lying in bed, now wearing, unbuttoned, the white shirt that, along with slacks and a sports coat, I'd hung over the back of a chair for my appointment with Morales on Monday morning. "Speaking of money, how can you afford to see an analyst three times a week?" Samira asked in her slow, dreamy, quiet voice. "I mean, on a schoolteacher's salary and all."

"I can't afford it. Except I can, in a way. This place is rent-controlled, for one thing, and also I've been living like a monk. Well, until tonight, ha-ha. I do a lot of tutoring in the summers, and I have this small trust fund that I could use that my mother left me when she died. And even though my father and I don't get along, I guess I could always go to him."

"You know, you don't have to be so nervous," Samira said. "Why do you go on seeing this shrink if he's so weird?"

"I don't know. It's as if I have to keep going back to make sure he's real."

"Is he helping you?"

"It's hard to tell."

"I feel like I'm talking to the Invisible Man or something," Samira said. "Come back over here where I can at least see you."

She raised herself up on her elbows, and the shirt fell open. Blue-white light from the street lamp outside my window on West End Avenue fell across her.

"Oh, Jake, please don't look at me," she said, laughing again.

"But you're beautiful," I said.

"But one of my breasts is a little larger than the other."

"Terrible!"

"And they're both too big. You know—the pill and all."

"One outrage after another," I said.

"I really think you can relax now." She got up, took the shirt off, and let it drop to the floor. "By the way, do you have any cake or cookies or anything around here?"

"I'm afraid not," I said.

"Nothing to be afraid of," she said. She sat down on the edge of the bed. "I'll manage."

I went and stood in front of her. She reached up and pushed the robe off my shoulders. "Tell him about this," she said.

"And why are you smiling so broadly this morning, Mr. Singer?" Dr. Morales asked the next day as I stretched out on the gray leatherette couch with the gray leatherette jellyroll head-rest. He had ushered me in with his own customary grin and his ironical-looking demi-bow and had then sat down in the gray leatherette chair, where he started fiddling with his answering machine. There we were, washed up again on those two tiny barren sister atolls, about to cast our lines into the Great Sea of the Unconscious.

"Well, I met someone over the weekend," I said. "She's very nice."

"Good," Dr. Morales said. Silence. "Did you fuck her?" The question had the honeyed tone characteristic of his sexual interrogations.

"I beg your pardon?"

"Please take your penis out from under the English bowling hat, Mr. Singer," Dr. Morales said tiredly. He was still fussing with the machine, which suddenly emitted five seconds' worth of backward Chipmunkese. "Did you fuck her?"

"Bowler," I said, "and as a matter of fact I did."

"And did you as a matter of fact enjoy it?"

"Greatly."

"Greatly."

"Is there an echo in here? What's wrong with 'greatly,' for Christ's sake? I enjoyed it a lot."

"Better. How many times did you fuck her?"

"Two or three. I don't know. Don't you even want to know her name? Don't you—"

"All in good time, Mr. Singer. You and I are not on a date at the opera. Here we do not have to comment on how very like a camel is the cloud overhead or raise our pinkie when we drink our tea. Did she have a climax?"

"I don't know. She said she did. Jesus, this is like a high-school locker room."

"Precisely. It is lamentable but true that that is the last time for many people to discuss these important matters. Now, what kinds of noises did she make?"

"What?"

"Perhaps you do not know because you have these episodes of deafness."

"Now, listen. You can't—"

"No, *you* listen. Mr. Singer. It is *you* who cannot. You cannot bring yourself to acknowledge that you think in such terms and to speak frankly to me about this sexual experience. You are ashamed, and so you force me to interrogate you, so that you can express the shock that you feel toward yourself. Not only do you claim that you do not have to sit down to move your bowels like the rest of us poor mortals, you claim not to move them at all, and then you react with disgust after compelling me to move them for you."

"A neat trick, you must admit."

"And now we have swimming into the session the red herring of your alleged humor."

We sparred a little longer, and then Dr. Morales resumed his extraction of graphic details. After the most unusual of these specifics, which he received in reverential silence, I added, "And she told me to make sure to tell you about it."

Dr. Morales awoke from his trance with conviction renewed. "You see, you see," he said. "She knows what is important. She and I are on the same frequency." He added, forlornly, "So you have discussed our work with this woman. Later, we shall have to analyze why you have broken our agreement." He was always doing this—adding another waltz to our therapeutic dance card, as if he wanted the music never to end. "Now, would you tell me what positions you used?"

I left the session feeling like a potboiler thumbed through by some creep in search of the good parts.

Samira had sat down at a table with me in the cafeteria of the Metropolitan Museum. It was a mild, dreary November Sunday, with wind-driven rain streaming out of the sky over Central Park. The weather had herded thousands into the museum. The hubbub depressed me even more than waiting out the afternoon with the N.F.L. in my apartment would have, and it was a measure of my mood that I didn't notice the small, beautiful olive-skinned girl with a sketch pad sitting nearby until she asked me to pass her the sugar.

"Oh, please, don't watch," she said. "I have an awful sweet tooth. I could probably grow crystals in this stuff." Her speech was soft and languid, as if the words themselves were coalescing one at a time.

"Yeah, well," I said. I looked up. "As a matter of fact I have a sweet tooth, myself." *The clam opens his shell, eh, Mr. Singer?*

"Small world," she said dreamily, and she gave me a solar smile.

320   Daniel Menaker

A regular museum pickup, as I recalled such things—
except that she started it off, and her conversation's veil of pretense was ultra-thin. What did you come to see, she asked me.
I don't know—nothing in particular. The Vermeers look good
on a day like this—all that sunlight pouring in the windows.
But it's so calm and buttoned up, don't you think, she said.
The baroque stuff here isn't that great, but still at least there's
passion and movement. But it's pretty theatrical, I said. *Now you
are throwing her out of the bed even before she is in it and feels your chilly feet.*

And so it went. Her name was Samira Khoury. She had
been born in Lebanon and was brought here when she was six.
Her family was Christian in background, but they lived in a
Muslim neighborhood in Beirut, and she couldn't say which was
worse—the cold, eyes-averted hatred of their adult neighbors
or the stones and curses of the children. I wondered later if living through such hostility as a child hadn't helped her become
the bemused, often nearly detached person she seemed to me in
the brief glimpse I had of her. I also imagined that so much
early disorder might have steered her toward art. And it was
private disorder as well as public. Samira's father, a wealthy
doctor in Beirut, anticipated the chaos that was lying in wait
for his country and uprooted himself and his family and fled to
the United States. But he hadn't anticipated and couldn't handle
the despair that lies in wait for all émigrés. He got a job as a lab
technician here and stayed in it, and he and Samira's mother
lived their lives—demolished lives, I gathered from Samira's
tone—in Wayne, New Jersey, in a tract house.

This city, Cuban psychoanalysts, pompous Scottish
headmasters, Hungarian superintendents too busy polishing
the brass to fix the boiler, fierce-looking mustachioed Afghans
running grimy delis on Tenth Avenue, Senegalese street-corner
umbrella sellers, British TV-commercial directors, island girls
in the parks playing sweetly with the children and despising the

parents, Sikh cab drivers short on English, old Yiddishers inching along the streets carrying plastic bags with cut-rate bruised fruit in them. Sexually intrepid Lebanese-born artists.

Samira must have been talented—four years on scholarship at Carnegie Mellon—but when I asked if I could see her drawings (*Ah, we are back in business, Mr. Singer*) she said, "Oh, please don't even ask. I'd be too embarrassed." Very demure she was in her manner, and very alluring in her black skirt and sweater and red tights. She was doing freelance catalog work for Honeybee, and she lived in Chelsea with another hopeful artist—from Turkey, of all places—and her roommate's boyfriend, a musician from Rio. She was going to take a course at the Art Students League at night, starting in January, if her father could lend her the money.

When she said no about the sketch pad, I said, "Well, then, would you have dinner with me instead?" *Olé, Mr. Singer!*

I never got the chance to tell the real Dr. Morales any of this. He missed his chance to cough through a description of walking back through the Park with Samira, of how lively she seemed in the sharp rain and among the fallen leaves and dutiful dog walkers. He lost the opportunity to needle me about my relentlessly self-deprecating dinner conversation when we met at a restaurant on Broadway in the evening, and about how I tried not to hear her when she said she didn't really want to go back to her place afterward. Didn't I mention that my apartment was right around the corner on West End?

No building of narrative tension for you, Dr. Morales, from Samira's telling me that she found me very attractive. No trembling like a pointer when she adds that I can easily find out *how* attractive, as she is wearing nothing under her cute short tan suede skirt. She said all this as pleasantly and informatively as an exotic stewardess offering in-flight services on an excellent Pacific Rim airline.

No, he missed all that, and I never got a chance to fill him in on it. The affair was a short one, and Dr. Morales and I spent the remainder of it shouting at each other like grade-schoolers in a playground. I'm rubber, you're glue. Whatever you say bounces off me and sticks to you.

On the Tuesday after I first met Samira at the museum, I took her to a Coventry football game up at Baker Field, at the northern tip of Manhattan. It's Columbia's football field, and they let Coventry use it for weekday games. The rain that had been falling since Sunday let up as we arrived, and a wind not yet cold but promising winter started blowing out of the northwest. Pewter clouds raced along below the leaden sky. I could hear the water coursing through Spuyten Duyvil, and the Henry Hudson Bridge vibrated with heavy traffic to and from the Bronx. Like so many ordinary activities in New York, the football game seemed to me dwarfed, improbable, and precarious, as if the skies might open and a Jehovian hand reach down and pluck us all up, a huge wave might crash in from the river, the bridge fall down.

"Would you look at their *be*hinds!" Samira muttered. We were standing on the sidelines and watching the boys flop around happily in the mud. "They're so beautiful," she sighed. She took my arm and adhered to my side. The question of how fully dressed she might be drove anomie from my mind. "I don't think I could ever be a teacher with kids like that. Or maybe when I was sixty-five." The Coventry student spectators, for their part, kept sidling up to us on one pretext or another, for a closer examination of this chick, and a teacher of theirs in the unfamiliar role of human being. I ended up enjoying myself.

On the way back downtown, we stopped at a Middle Eastern grocery. Then Samira went back with me to my apartment and cooked couscous and lamb stew for us. In the kitchen she was careful and neat. I helped her a little, and we kept on bumping or backing into each other. "Sorry." "Excuse me." The meal was excellent, but we got up from the table in the middle of it, and by the time we might have gone back, the food would have been long since cold.

"Do you want to talk while we're waiting?" Samira asked. She was sitting up and gazing out the window as the dark gathered and the street lamp on West End waxed full. I lay beside her.

"You're a good cook," I said. "Who does the cooking in your family?"

"My father now. My mother used to, in Beirut, but here he has so much time on his hands."

"He isn't trying to get accredited as a doctor?"

"I think he has given up. It's so sad. I hate to go home at all anymore. Maybe you and I are birds of a feather. It must be hard for you, with no mother and being on such bad terms with your father."

"It is," I said. "Morales must have done it—passed some test or something to be a doctor here—but then he's a maniac."

"Morales, Morales."

"You're right. I won't get started."

"You know, I had to call my father yesterday, because the first payment for that course I wanted to take is due soon. He doesn't have the money and he was ashamed to tell me."

"That's very sad. Is this teacher really that good?"

"He is very good, and he also happens to be very attractive. I'm going to seduce him, if I ever take his class."

"Sex, sex."

"Everyone has their own way of changing the subject, I guess. Sometimes I think that painting and sex are all I let myself care about."

"And sweets," I said. "Which reminds me." From under the bed I brought out a package of chocolate cookies.

"Oo, look," Samira said. "How nice of you."

"You know, I could lend you that money," I said.

"Oh, no. I couldn't accept that. You hardly even know me."

"I know you well enough so that I can't see you skipping town exactly," I said. "It's only a loan. I have to go into my trust soon anyway, for Morales. All it will take is a little juggling, and Morales will just have to wait a couple of extra days for his fee. I think he'll understand."

"Of course I understand," Dr. Morales said the next morning when, about fifteen minutes into the session, I told him I had lent Samira some money and wouldn't have his payment until Friday. "I understand that you had to pay your whore."

"Hey, hold on a second. I can't believe—"

"I am on the moon, Mr. Singer. I am on the moon—"

"I'll say," I muttered.

"What?"

"Nothing."

"I am on the moon looking at the earth through my shiny new telescope. I e-zoom in on New York City and then on the West Side. What do I see? What do I see? I see a man having sex with a woman. And then in the morning through my telescope I see the man giving the woman a check as she is leaving. Now, you must tell me what interpretation I am to put on these events?"

"But this is nutty. You're not on the moon. You're here, in this office with me, and I'm telling you it wasn't like that at all. There was no arrangement about money or anything like that."

"Did she know you had any money, Mr. Singer?"

"No. Yes, actually. She asked how I could be a school-teacher and pay for psychoanalysis at the same time, but—"

"So she established that you had at least some money. There are all kinds of whores, Mr. Singer, including those who do not know that they are whores."

"Whores don't give back the money they're paid."

"You are so certain that this woman will repay this money?"

"Of course she will."

"I wish I could share your confidence. Perhaps you would like to discuss why you are so offended by the suggestion that you might have paid for sex. It has happened once or twice in the world before, you know, without this sort of anger and shame."

"No, damn it—*you* are the one who is angry," I said. I didn't know where the idea had come from, and I wasn't even sure what I meant.

"And so now you put on the harmor of rage in order to resist the—"

"*You* are the one who is enraged, and *you* are the one who feels like a whore. I pay you, your patients pay you, for this kind of relationship. Now I come and tell you for the first time in more than a year that I'll be two days late with your goddamn fee because I lent money to someone else, and you get so angry that you construe my relationship with this person—the first nice thing that has happened to me in quite a while, I might add—the same way you secretly construe your patients' relationships with you. Angry and *jealous*, I might add—you are jealous. The money is only the paper on the surface. You know I'm responsible about your fee. You've been *slighted*. Your customer has put someone else before you."

There was a long silence, after which Dr. Morales, sounding incredibly distant—sepulchral, as if he'd passed over and were trying to communicate with the living—said, "In my judgment, Mr. Singer, you are projecting your view of me as a prostitute onto me, because you wish to disown it. No, I am sorry. I am lower than a prostitute. For you have paid the prostitute. That is my judgment, which, of course, you have already made sure to dismiss if not ridicule, this morning and frequently in our work together. But let us assume, for the sake of argument, which is after all what you so often desire to substitute for analysis—let us assume that you are correct, and that it is I who is angry and jealous, that it is I who is trying to disavow his feelings of defilement. Let us assume that you are right. Then my question is: Of what benefit is your triumph to you? What sort of ground have you gained with this counteroffensive, as you no doubt view it?"

Silence again.

"I shall tell you what you gain by such measures," Dr. Morales went on. "You become impervious to change. If you confront me, you do not have to suffer the pain of confronting yourself. This is *your* analysis, not mine, but your knowledge of your conflicts and your mastery of them will grow by neither an inch nor an ounce if you pursue these tactics. If you busy your mind with a war against me, you will never make peace with yourself."

"Well, then, if I'm incapable of doing analysis, of making any headway here, then maybe—"

"I did not say that, Mr. Singer. Perhaps saddest of all, and most insulting and demeaning to me, is that you refuse to admit the value of what you have managed despite yourself to accomplish here. Your failure to pay my fee on time is one aspect of denial."

"And your rigidity about the money shows a pretty shaky sense of self-respect," I said. "Am I catching on? Listen. I'll cash in one of the C.D.s after school today and pay you on Friday. I'm sorry I missed the payment, but I don't really see that it's—"

"And the last thing you will admit is that this new sexual liaison of yours, whatever its nature, would have been out of the question for you when we started our work."

"You're taking the credit?"

"How did it come about?"

"You were too preoccupied with the endocrinology of it to find out."

"Please try not to be a smart-alex, Mr. Singer. How did it come about?"

"Aleck. I met her in the museum on Sunday and asked her out to dinner."

"Would you have asked her out to dinner under the same circumstances a year ago? You do not see that— Why must you cash in a C.D.? You will lose some of the interest." Dr. Morales's voice had suddenly lost its otherworldliness.

"The trust fund is in C.D.s. Five of them, ten thousand dollars each."

"And what other instruments do you have?"

"Instruments? Investments? None. I've told you before. It's all in C.D.s."

"Surely you are joking! For how many years has it been this way?"

"Ten—since I turned twenty-one. I just roll them over."

"Now, really, Mr. Singer, you must diversify. Do you have any idea how much money you have already lost? Perhaps we may talk about this in the next session. Our time is up for today."

And a good thing, too. I might have got up and hit him if it had gone on a second longer. Next session next life, I said to myself as I walked out.

I asked Samira if she had ever been with women. Yes, she said with a drowsy laugh. Why did I want to know? A man and a woman, I asked. Yes, but they hadn't done much more than fool around. Older men? Yes, she said—you. She turned over to face me. I guess she thought I was taking a straightforward midnight sexual history, as new lovers often do. But in fact the sordidness of the session with Morales in the morning had been working within me like slow-acting venom.

"Have you ever been with two men?" I asked.

"One time."

"Did you ever have sex in front of other people?"

"Yes, once, when I was seventeen. But, really, we were just kids."

I went on for a few more minutes. The intimacy in Samira's voice gave way to puzzlement and then anxiety. I began to feel as Morales must when he roasted his patients on the spit of his own prurience. Finally Samira had enough. "I don't do those things anymore," she said. "And I don't want to talk about them anymore. This is mean."

In my mind, I said, *No, of course you do not wish to continue our discussion of the way you have chosen this unbridled sexual behavior to punish your father for his failure.* The idea made me feel brilliant, and horribly lonely.

After a tense silence, Samira asked me, as if in contrition, whether we could spend the weekend together. She seemed now not even faintly a gift from sex heaven or a member of some serene rescue squad or exactly what I'd been waiting for but thoroughly and alarmingly human. I said I was going to have a lot of papers to grade, and I would call her. I didn't get to sleep until just before dawn. I'd be surprised if Samira got any sleep at all.

When the alarm went off, I heard Samira moving around in the kitchen. I went to the closet and put on my bathrobe, and when I turned around she was standing there, dressed, holding her bright-red parka. "That was too weird last night," she said. "What happened?"

"I'm not awake yet," I said. "I don't know what to say."

"That's exactly right," Samira said, with tears now in her eyes. "And when you figure it out it will probably be too late. You could be so nice, you know?" She turned and left, and the small sounds of the apartment—the ticking of a clock, the frigid wind sighing at the windows, the hiss of the radiators, a siren from the street—came back as if they'd been switched on.

I stumbled into the kitchen. On the counter next to the stove, on top of a paper napkin with doodles on it, I found the check I'd given her, ripped into small pieces. I threw the check away and noticed that the doodles on the napkin were not doodles but a drawing. A drawing of me—almost but not quite a caricature. It showed a rail-thin young man with coarse straight black hair like a shoebrush, a big straight nose, big circles under his eyes, standing in front of a blackboard and gesturing expansively, almost frantically, with both hands. In the foreground was a row of ovals—the backs of kids' heads in a classroom, like eggs in a carton except for a cowlick here and there and one oval leaning over at a seventy-degree angle: asleep. It was a wonderful piece of work for something so offhand. Every line showed energy and discipline and wit. It was affectionate, in contrast to the figure it depicted, who looked as if he couldn't care about much more than the sound of his own words.

With dismay, I found myself rehearsing what I might say to Morales about the rejected check: See? So much for your commercial theory. Or did it prove him right? And the drawing. I held it in my hands and imagined myself showing it to him. See? See? And so, I realized, I would be going back to him after all. Evidently, it was still him or nobody.

Influenza

Daniel Menaker

I – Poison

It was a New York I'd never seen at close range before. I'd
known it only through the squibs in the papers, which repro-
duced what I imagined attending society events must have been
like: a background blur out of which emerged one rich or
famous mug after another. The pictures that floated out of the
inky blackness above these name blurts always made the people
look abnormal—prognathous, narcoleptic, Tourretic, or as
vacant as unlaid storm-drain pipes. This was strange, because
when some of these same people drove in their limos or 190
SLs over to the West Side, to drop their sons off at the Coventry
School, they were handsome and cheerful, the dads in slim business suits, the moms in pricey jeans and burgundy or winter-
green sweaters or sweatshirts. Every head of hair with a suave
streak or swath of gray; good skin, with crinkles instead of
wrinkles; amphitheatrically perfect white teeth. Maybe the combination of dusk and engraved invitations threw them into gar-
goyle phase. I taught English in the Upper School at Coventry
in the late sixties and seventies, and for the first three of those
years, when I was in neurotic despair and was on the outs with

the school's autocratic headmaster, W. C. H. Proctor—a socialite not only because of his capital-campaign obligations but out of native hobnobbery—the world of penthouses and summers at Niantic or Hyannis or Bar Harbor and of dressage and mixed doubles and poached salmon and charity bashes seemed as distant to me as a cloud to a clam.

In the early spring of my fourth year at Coventry, my gloom began to lighten. I'd tried to stop a fight in the locker room and got knifed, and Proctor saw it as some kind of courageous act. He began to call me "Jake" instead of "Singer" or "you." As time went on, he put me on this committee and that committee, and asked me to speak on behalf of the school to parents and prospective parents and groups of alumni. I found it uncomfortable under his wing, but I also began to feel more present in my life, at least my professional life, as if some psychic clutch had finally engaged and the neurasthenic idling—

Now, really, Mr. Singer—it is most embarrassing to listen to this narrative masturbation. I know that you had a good rhythm going as you flipped through the pages of your dictionary to find all your impressive words, and I'm so sorry to interrupt, but perhaps you could try a little harder to get to the point!

This would be the voice of Dr. Ernesto Morales, the psychoanalyst I saw three times a week for all but the first of my seven years as a teacher. I internalized his Spanish accent and speech patterns and the machete-like sarcasm that he wielded in the slash-and-burn process he tried to pass off as "interpretation," and I guess such internalization is part of the point of analysis. It's true that life improved for me as I went to him, but whether if I could do it all over again I would actually choose to have the homunculus of an insane, bodybuilding, black-bearded Cuban Catholic Freudian shouting at me from inside my own head I am not sure.

Dr. M. (clearing his throat, his audible for boredom): *Please let me know when you are sure of something, Mr. Singer.*

Me: *Sorry.*

Dr. M.: *I'm surprised that you didn't say that you guessed you were sorry.*

Me: *Sorry.*

Dr. M.: (Silence).

Me: *What's wrong now, for Christ's sake? I said I was getting better—you should take it as a compliment.*

Dr. M.: *So you ask me to kiss your ass in gratitude as you waste my time with this interminable prehahmble? Even an analyst's patience has—*

Me: *Preamble.*

Dr. M.: *Pree-ahmble. Even an analyst's patience has some limit, Mr. Singer.*

Me: *O.K., O.K.*

So anyway, at school, things were going well. I gave these talks to groups of parents who were considering Coventry for their boys, and I seemed to be convincing a lot of them. Of course, I'd be so nervous I'd spend a half hour on the shitter before hand, but—

Dr. M.: *Ah, honesty. It is always so refreshing, like a breeze through the palmettos in Havana. It is a pity we are still ninety miles off the shore of your subject.*

Anyway, there was a day in the middle of April when the air in New York was as cool and clear as—

Dr. M.: *And now we have the weather report! Isn't the news supposed to come first, Mr. Singer?*

As a day in October, while—

DR. M.: *What about the rich and famous people?*

ME: *I'm getting there. I'm just setting this up, trying to give the whole picture.*

DR. M.: *This giving of the entire picture, as you say, is your characteristic way of putting painful matters on the shelf for a while longer, preferably until they are stale and unappetizing. I would wager that you wish to speak of the problems that brought you to me in the first place—your rage at your mother for dying when you were six years old, the fact that months and months elapsed when no woman even so much as glimpsed your penis, the estrangement between you and your father, the compromises involved in your profession. Here they all are, still preying on your mind as if they were the eagle at the livers of Prometheus, no? This is what happens when a patient terminates the treatment before he should.*

ME: *But——*

DR. M.: *But most of all you wish to avoid the recognition of the crucial role I played in your life. You cling still to the belief—no, the delusion—that one can be his own man, create himself, and as it were have no parent of any sort.*

ME: *But that's what this is about. If you'd just give me a chance to get started, you'd——*

DR. M.: *Mr. Singer, you would put off the sunrise if you were not quite ready for breakfast.*

ME: *But——*

DR. M.: *But if we could not make progress in this area in our real work together, what chance is there, I ask you, of our getting anywhere in this absurd imaginary dialogue of yours? So proceed with your meteorology, if you feel that you must, but you must also forgive me if I catch forty huinks while you do.*

There was a Sunday in the middle of April when the air in New York was as cool and clear as it is in late October. The trees in Central Park had gone blurry with buds, the Great Lawn had begun to lose the look of an old blanket thrown down to protect the earth, and the water in the Reservoir had a fine chop, like a miniature sea. A few people—the avant-garde of the jogging movement—beetled around the gravel path. It was all down there and I was up here, fifteen stories above Fifth Avenue, on the terrace of an apartment that occupied the top two floors of a magnificent Deco building between Eighty-third and Eighty-fourth Streets. To my left, in his usual blue blazer and gray slacks, stood Coventry's headmaster, nautical in appearance and demeanor.

"Ah, fresh air, Jake," Proctor said, putting his hand on my shoulder. Fresh air was his universal restorative. "There's nothing like it, even in New York City."

To my right stood Allegra Marshall, the hostess of this Coventry fund-raising lunch. Luncheon. My first point-blank encounter with the Manhattan of pure wealth and glamour. Five round tables of eight in a huge dining room with wainscoting and a *Close Encounters* chandelier. White maids in black uniforms and white, lace-edged aprons. Cutlery, linen, chased silver. Not a bell-bottom in sight, no ankhs, no zoris, no peasant blouses. It could have been the fifties. It could have been now.

Before I escaped to the terrace, one sleek fellow, the grandfather of a student of mine, asked me where I was going over spring break, and I said, "Nowhere," and he said, "Well, what a good idea!" He and I then discussed the Yankees' prospects for the coming season, and he pointed out a relative of Jacob Rupert's across the vast living room or parlor or whatever it was. "This is a man who won't touch a drop of anything," the sleek fellow said. "I've heard that he's ashamed of his fortune." My other conversation was with the mother of one of my advanced placement seniors who simply could not get *over* how wonderfully *detailed* my comments were on her son's papers.

When Proctor and I arrived, Mrs. Marshall gave me an automatic smile but a firm handshake—the kind that a girl's rich, manly dad or independent-minded mom tries to install at an early age. She was wearing a short black dress and a black wristband. Her husband—Coventry '59—had died, of cancer, on New Year's Day, leaving her with a six-year-old son—in first grade at the school—an infant daughter, and his millions to add to hers. The apartment was beautiful and tasteful to the point of hilarity, and its mistress, with her tall, willowy stature, pale complexion, bright-blue eyes, and long, dark, ironed-looking hair, and her aristocratic imperfection of feature—a real nose with a real bump on it, one very white front tooth slightly overlapping the other—also seemed comically perfect for her role of young society personage gamely pressing on. Now, out on the terrace, in the presence of Proctor and his bromides, she seemed sad, and her perfection looked frayed at the edges, and after a fellow-blazer-and-gray-flannelsman hailed the headmaster back inside, I thought I saw her roll her eyes.

"Sometimes I think he'd make a better admiral than a headmaster," I said. "Do you ever see any muggings down there?"

"You're Mr. Springer?" she asked.

"Singer. Jake Singer."

"You're the one who is going to do the sales pitch."

"Yes. I've done something like this three or four times now, but I keep getting stagefright. Especially here. I mean, I feel sort of out of place. And it's for money this time, not just to try to get people to send their kids."

"Proctor says you do it very well. When we set this thing up, he told me the applications pour in after you talk."

"You know, a year ago he was barely speaking to me."

"Why?"

"Oh, I was always arguing with him, always mouthing off. Nothing better to do, I guess."

"What do you mean?"

"You know, just trouble with authority."

"But he certainly likes you now."

"I just calmed down, I suppose."

"Just like that?"

"No, it probably has something to do with being in analysis, though I'm not supposed to talk about it and I don't like to give my lunatic analyst any credit."

"I'm in it, too, so you're safe."

"But you have a real reason, not just the vapors, like me. Anyway, one thing I am sure of is that it isn't Proctor who changed. He'd prescribe fresh air for you if your husband had died." Good work, Jake. "Oh, Mrs. Marshall, I'm so sorry. What an idiot I am."

"It's all right. I've discovered it's like having two heads. But when you collect yourself I hope you'll call me Allegra. And, by the way, these things make me as uncomfortable as they make you." She went back inside, leaving me alone with my clumsy self.

At lunch, Proctor and I sat on either side of our hostess, and I said how delicious the consommé was. "Actually, it's turtle soup," she said. It was difficult to eat the rest of the meal, with my foot so far in my mouth and the butterflies in my stomach. But I nodded and smiled and chewed as best I could, and I made what seemed to me an English teacher's joke—something feeble about cashing in Mr. Chips. Mrs. Marshall's frozen smile thawed into a real laugh—very musical—and I felt as if I'd done her a good turn. "Great chicken," I said when the veal chop was served, and she looked at me in proto-discomfiture until I shrugged, whereupon she got it and smiled a real smile again. Before dessert and after a trip to the bathroom, I made my speech: To afford the kind of diversity in our student body. All the way from catcher's mitts to calculators. Provide the brand of leadership that seems so sorely lacking in our nation. Instill the values, stem the rising tide of drugs. To defray cost of mandatory haircuts and install narrower and quieter ties (*Polite laughter.*) To pay for the polish Proctor uses for his brass blazer buttons and his bald bean.

This last I said to Dr. Morales in his cold, cluttered office the next morning as I lay on the slab-flat couch with the cervically inimical jelly-roll headrest. It was a chilly, drizzly day, the bad side of spring. I had already told him about Allegra Marshall and my high anxiety and various faux pas. "You did not really say this about the polish, Mr. Singer," he said.

"No—it's a joke."

"I have asked you to tell me what you said in your speech and first you drone like an old priest and then you become saracastic—sarcastic and rude, if I may say, since I, too, am bald. Why do you suppose you cry in fear before the hand?"

"Beforehand. Who said anything about crying?"

"These attacks of cramps and diarrhea—you are weeping like a frightened child, but since you are a man you must do it through your asshole. And I shall ask the questions here. Why are you so frightened of something so boring and contemptible, Mr. Singer?"

"If I don't know the drill here by now, I really should be ashamed of myself. It's *not* boring and stupid. I act that way only because I care about it so much and want so badly to do well, to appease the spirit of my dead mother, whom I magically think I must have killed when I was six, and to earn the respect of my father, who thinks I am a failure and wishes I had been a doctor like him, and to please you. Always to please you, of course."

"Again this same sequence—dull recitation with following it the scorn. Hohum and fuck you, is it not?"

"Well, I mean four years of—"

"No, it is thirty-two meenoose six years, Mr. Singer— twenty-six years of preventing yourself from genuine involvement in your feelings and your life. I swear to Christ that if Marilyn Monroe came to you with no clothes on and a wet pussy you would not know what to do with her. Now please listen to me. If you joke, I shall kill you and spare you the effort of this slow suicide. Is this school of yours a good school?"

"Yes. It could be—"

"Is it a good school?"

"Yes."

"Do your students respect you?"

"Yes." Satisfaction, as surprising as a twenty-dollar bill on the sidewalk, came to me with this answer.

"Tell me one important thing you have done for the school besides the teaching."

"Well—"

"It is dry, Mr. Singer."

"I'm helping to get scholarships for poor kids," I said, more proudly than I meant to.

"Good, there is feeling in your words at last. Anything else?"

"I'm convincing more people to apply, and now I'm helping to raise money. As of yesterday."

"Ah, your voice has fallen here. Why?"

"I don't know—the whole idea of raising money, being with rich people, glad-handing and putting on a show."

"*It is a good school!*" thundered Dr. Morales. "You are trying to make it better according to your convictions! Making a
speech is not selling eslaves or torturing cute lambs! A president of the United Estates has attended this school, three or
four *Nobelistas,* many professors and doctors, the director of the
Peace Corps, I believe, the head of Sloan-Kettering, the man who
designed—"

"How do you know all this?" I asked.

"I have looked it up. I should not have revealed this,
perhaps—it is bad technique—but just maybe you will take a
leaf from my tree, Mr. Singer. I am *interested* in my work. You
are my work. I am *interested* in you. And one more thing—if
there are rich people in the world, why should you not be among
them? You yourself are hardly from the road of tobacco. If there
is a rich young widow making goggle eyes at you, why should
you not fuck her, I ask you. Why should you not marry her,
when I come to think of it. Why didn't you mention how she
looked when you were speaking of her?"

"Less Marilyn Monroe than Ali McGraw," I said. "But
beautiful enough. Quite beautiful, in fact."

"In fact? I did not think it was in fiction. I do not know
who is this Alice McGraw."

"She's the one in *Love Story*—the girl who dies."

"Ah, yes. This is interesting. We must stop now, Mr.
Singer, but have you by any chance happened to notice the
corpses that have littered our conversation this morning like a
battlefield, as if it were. Your mother, the husband of the hostess, the character of this movie."

"Marilyn Monroe."

"Very good, Mr. Singer. You are quite right, I have
joined in this necrophilia. But it is *spring*, Mr. Singer. Time for
the new beginnings, for the birds to tweeter and among the
twigs to build their nests."

* * *

Dr. Morales's crude incitement concerning Allegra Marshall at the end of the session had not come out of nowhere. Near the beginning, when I mentioned her widowhood and the opulence of her apartment, I could feel him coming to attention like a setter behind me. I was surprised and annoyed to feel myself coming to attention the following week, when I was in the nurse's office at school, getting a Band-Aid for a wound inflicted by the staples that had interfered with my reading of "Hester Prynne: Hawthorn's Revolutionery Heroin." A little kid was lying on the cot looking green around the gills, and the nurse, a clinical type with a neurosurgeon's hauteur and the name Gladys Knight, of all things, was on the phone saying, "You and the babysitter probably have the same organism that George has, Mrs. Marshall, with the nausea and the vertigo. I'd bring him over for you myself, but George is the fourth incidence today, so I really should stay here."

I asked if it was Allegra Marshall she was talking to and she covered the phone and scowled at me. "This is important, Mr. Singer, if you don't mind," she said. "This child *and* his mother *and* the babysitter have all come down with gastroenteritis, and we're trying to figure out how to get him home."

"I met Mrs. Marshall last week. I'd be glad to take him home—I've got two free periods. Tell Mrs. Marshall it's me."

In another five minutes, George Marshall and I went out into the April sunshine and hailed a cab on West End Avenue, after a parting advisory from Miss Knight: "One of the other children had projectile vomiting." As we drove across the park, yellow with forsythia and daffodils, George sat still and regarded me. He was small for his age but built solidly, with blond hair and a turned-up nose with a few freckles sprinkled over it—he looked nothing like his mother. "My dad died," he said when we stopped for a red light at Ninety-sixth Street and

Fifth Avenue. "I know," I said. "It's very sad for you and your family." "My sister doesn't realize it," he said. "She's too little. Are you a teacher in the upper school?" I told him I was. "I thought I saw you," he said.

The taxi started up again, and George faced forward, looking sick and unhappy. His feet didn't quite reach the floor. Even though I'd never met this boy before, I knew for a fact that he believed that he had done something to cause what had happened to his family, and I wanted to reach over with both hands and shake the innocent truth into him before the guilt worked itself too deep into his heart.

George said he could go up in the elevator by himself, but the doorman said that Mrs. Marshall had asked me to take him upstairs, if it wasn't too much trouble. So up in the elaborately scrolled and paneled elevator we went. When the door opened onto the apartment's foyer, Mrs. Marshall was standing there looking very sick and forlorn herself, plain and ashen and lank-haired, so that the elegant dark-blue Chinesey housecoat she had on seemed as beside the point as the Aubusson on the floor and the modest Corot on the wall behind her. "I'm tired, Mom," George said, and he tottered away down the long hallway. "I'm going to lie down for a while."

"I'll be right there," Mrs. Marshall said.

"I hope your daughter's all right," I said. "The nurse told me your babysitter is sick, too."

"Emily is fine. And George's mother will be here in half an hour. She lives just over on Park. We'll be O.K."

"George's mother?"

"My husband's mother. My late husband's mother. Georgie is George Junior."

"Oh."

"It was nice of you to bring him home. Thank you."

"It was nothing. He's a sweet kid."

"Let me pay you for the taxi."

"Oh, no. That's all right." I looked over her shoulder at the living room, glowing with perfection in the morning light. "I know this is silly," I said, "but I wish there was something else I could do for you."

"Why is that silly?"

"I mean, I've only met you once, and——"

"Is it silly because I'm rich?"

"Yes."

"Ah——honesty. But it shows what you know." Tears were in her eyes now, and her nose looked more broken than distinguished, and she seemed skinny rather than slender and pathetic rather than tragic; and I felt ridiculous instead of gallant, and furious at Dr. Morales for his careless manipulations, and for regarding this woman so lubriciously and so lightly, like a personal ad, like a sitting duck. "I'm sorry if I've upset you," I said. "Don't worry about it," she said, pushing the elevator button.

"And I think you should be ashamed of yourself," I said to Dr. Morales the next morning, after telling him as calmly as I could what had happened with George Marshall and his mother the day before.

"I am," Dr. Morales replied. "I am truly ashamed." He rattled some papers around and cleared his throat a few times.

I sat up and put my feet on the floor and looked at him. He had a tax form over the yellow pad he used for taking what I assumed were scathing notes about me and his other victims.

"Filing late?" I said. "I hope you applied for the automatic two-month extension."

"This is against the rules, Mr. Singer."

"You mean the New York Psychoanalytic Society has an actual rule against doing your taxes during sessions with your patients? Why, that's positively draconian."

"I shall not explain myself to you, Mr. Singer. This is as forbidden to me as sitting up is to you. But God and Freud will pardon me, I feel certain, for occupying myself with other matters when a patient enters my office in an inappropriate rage, insults me further by thinking to disguise it, and then has the amazing condescension to tell me that I should be ashamed of myself, as if I were a four-year-old child who has deliberately belchèd during Communion."

"I would never have made such a fool of myself if you hadn't—"

"Had not what, Mr. Singer? Had not held a pistol at your head to force you to volunteer to take the boy home? Had not squeezèd your heart in the taxi to make you recognize his psychological situation and sympathize with him? Had not transformed you into Sharlie McCarthy and then like Edgar Burgeon thrown my voice into you standing there in front of the mother and to diminish her humanity on account of her wealth? By the way, Mr. Singer, will you please lie down."

"You want it both ways," I said, continuing to face him. "You want me to behave the way you think I should, and then when I try and then fail you disavow any part in the matter. 'My advice is to jump, Mr. Singer, but if you break your neck, don't blame me.'"

"Had not, in general, as I was saying, miraculously reached into your soul and poured into it the poison that you are convinced is so powerful as to threaten also anyone whom you might love. Like your mother, your father, like a woman. Like me. You are not Siva, Mr. Singer, nor Attila nor Hitler,

nor even Sharles Starkweather. You are not so lethal as you
wish to believe. Now please lie down."

"No. I don't feel well. I'm going home."

"You know, I truly *am* ashamed that after four years of
our work together you can still busy your mind with any
amount of anger at yourself and at me to ignore what is really
going on in your life—for example, the possibility that from
the start this woman has taken some interest in you, and that
this was why I tried gently and humorously to encourage your
interest in her."

"*Gently?*"

"Why else would a person divulge within five minutes
of meeting someone the highly intimate knowledge that she was
in analysis, as you divulged it to her also—why else would she
say this if she did not feel immediate trust and confidentiality?
And why else would she have asked you to accompany her son
in the elevator if not because she wished to see you again, and
being in a very unattractive and weakened condition, what is
more. Now please do lie down and try to address these matters."

"No, I really do feel ill," I said. "I'm leaving."

"So now the regression and withdrawal will be complete."

I called in sick and spent the rest of the day in or very near the
bathroom in my apartment. From time to time I hazarded a walk
into the living room to watch TV. I would doze on the couch,
wake up to a soap opera or a game show, whose gaudiness the
flu rendered almost hallucinatory, get up and turn it off. And
before stumbling toiletward again, I once or twice looked
around my place and took stock. In January, as my responsibilities grew at school, I had through an effort of will upgraded
my domestic situation. I discarded the bricks and boards and
sofa *trouvé* and card table, and the bottom half of a bunk bed

sold to me by the building's gaunt Croatian super for thirty-five dollars, and the dieseling vintage refrigerator, which I called the Serf of Ice Cream—another English teacher's joke—and replaced them with Door Store merchandise and new appliances. A captain's bed, a blond wall unit or two, a big, round, tan hooked rug in the living room, an oak table with a chrome base, even a Zurbarán print and a Magritte poster—that kind of thing. All in all, it had become a decent bachelor's place on the eleventh floor of a nice building on West End Avenue—plenty of light and a nice breeze in the spring and summer—just around the corner from Coventry. Rent-controlled, which you could still get back then, especially on the fringe of a bad neighborhood. But so what? It was still a pocket of isolation—especially in illness, when you'd like to be able to call on someone—and I felt like a penny in the pocket. Whatever progress I'd made was in baby steps, or in a marionette's artificial, hinged gait, with Dr. Morales pulling the strings. I felt far less desperate than I had four years earlier, but the absence of desperation is not life.

The flu subsided. I took a longer, deeper nap, looked in listlessly as Thurman Munson and his teammates braved chilly April conditions at Yankee Stadium, ate a little chicken soup, drank a lot of water, stayed on my feet, barely, in the shower, and collapsed onto my bed into an even deeper sleep, which lasted the night.

I felt much better in the morning but couldn't face the red-letter discussion looming in my Advanced Placement class or the concluding negotiations over *A Separate Peace* in my regular junior courses, to say nothing of playing pepper with the baseball team in Riverside Park after school, so I called in sick again and read and dozed on the sofa. I was brought out of a semi-dream, in which Dr. Morales lobbied the halls of Congress on behalf of Cuban cigars, by the ringing of the doorbell. It hadn't rung in so long that I'd forgotten when the last time was. I opened it without using the little burglar scope or asking who was there. What can anyone do to me, after all, I said to myself in the self-pitying aftermath of my stock-taking and influenza.

It was Allegra Marshall, well beyond influenza and its aftermath—looking very beautiful once again, in fact, if nervous.

"I'm sorry, I should have called," she said. "I know you're sick, but you live so close to the school that I thought I would just stop by. And then the doorman said he didn't need to announce me or anything."

"It's the super," I said. "My friend the super."

"So here I am. I hope I'm not disturbing you."

"I'm much better," I said. "It's O.K. Is George all right?"

"I took him back to school yesterday, and I asked for you and they told me you were out sick. And when they told me you were out again today I felt even more guilty. You probably got this from George, or maybe even from me."

"Oh, it's going around."

"But that isn't why I was looking for you at school in the first place," she said. "I wanted to apologize for being so rude to you the other morning. Here you had done me this kindness."

"I was rude first—worse than rude," I said. "You caught me out. I asked for it."

"Well, I'm sorry anyway. Now I really should leave you alone."

She turned away and started back toward the elevator, and as she did I heard that insinuating voice, which had already installed itself in my mind, say, "Now, Mr. Singer, I ask you—what do you wish this woman to do, take out a full-page advertisement in the *New York Times*?" I drew a deep breath and said, just as she was about to push the "Down" button,

"Wait, um, Allegra, as long as we're apologizing." She turned again, to face me. "I wasn't really doing you a kindness. I offered to take George home so I could see you. It was just an excuse. And my analyst sort of put me up to the whole thing anyway."

"You mean you *didn't* really want to see me?"

"No, I did, I probably did, or I would have, but this doctor of mine gets himself in the middle of everything, so it's hard to tell. He egged me on. He said *you* were interested in *me.*"

"He was right."

"What?"

"He was right."

"He was right?"

"He was right."

II–Mother's Day

They wanted to have children right away, but she didn't get pregnant. The specialist she saw couldn't find anything wrong. Still, she and her husband had sex by the chart, she took hormones, they went on tense "relaxed" vacations. None of it worked. At length, her husband said maybe he was the one with the problem—she had to give him credit for that. The specialist he saw, who wore a bright-red toupee, said "Whee" when he looked through the microscope at the semen sample, and the subsequent, more scientific assay found nothing wrong. Now they had both no one and each other to blame. It was an open field. It's like a poison in a well that you're both drinking from, Allegra told me. They kept trying to conceive a child but meanwhile adopted a baby boy through Spence-Chapin. They gave up on biology, and on sex, a couple of years later, and a few years after that, in the midst of growing strain and louder

silence between them, which they managed to hide from the
Spence-Chapin social worker, they adopted another baby—a
girl this time—in the hope that this would somehow solve their
problems. Three months after that, her husband was diagnosed
with pancreatic cancer, and three months after that he died.
Their parents were friends. She had known him all her life,
through Brearley for her and Coventry for him, Radcliffe for
her and Yale and Wharton for him, summers at Sag Harbor,
winters skiing out West. They went out with other people
from time to time, but nothing came of that. They thought
they were comfortable with each other. They got married when
she was twenty-three and he was twenty-five. The comfort
seemed to evaporate overnight. Even without all the reproductive trouble, there would have been trouble, she was sure. She
should have learned something from the way the dark skinny
boys with the scraggly beards and the banjos and their protest songs à la Phil Ochs attracted her in Cambridge. She
should have gone to graduate school in English at Berkeley
and thrown herself into the free-speech upheaval out there.
She should have done a lot of things. Until her husband died,
she felt as though her life had been written down before she
was born, in a novel so boring and predictable that even the
writer realized it and put the manuscript in some drawer and
left it there. Now she had despair to add to the tedium. No
one would come near her in her grief. Or maybe she pushed
them away. And she *was* grieving—you can miss someone you
don't much like, she had discovered. This was depressing all
by itself. Men stayed away out of propriety, and just as well,
in most cases. Her family and her husband's family seemed
afraid of her. She loved her son and daughter so much and so
feared what would happen to them if she couldn't give them
what they needed that she felt it almost guaranteed that she

wouldn't be able to. She sometimes had nightmares about having them taken away. Her husband had been a good father—she had to give him credit for that, too. As long as his long hours at Thomson & McKinnon, Auchincloss permitted. He hadn't had to work but he did, and that was really the only other thing she would give him credit for. Though she realized it was not a bad list and he was not a bad guy. Just the wrong guy. And she had found herself wondering, out there on the terrace when we first spoke, whether—dark and thin as I was and scraggly as my beard might be if I grew one—I played the banjo.

"Now I should leave you alone," she had said in the doorway after confirming Dr. Morales's conjecture. "I wanted to get another look at you—that's why I asked you to come up with George when you took him home. I could have just written you a note, after all."

"Well, would you like to come in?" I had said.

"Are you really feeling all right?"

"Yes."

"Then yes, I'll come in for a little while."

And that was when she sat down on my Door Store sofa and told me about herself. And then she asked me about myself. It got to be eleven-thirty, and I found I was hungry, for the first time in a couple of days, so I excused myself and went to the kitchen and wolfed down a bowl of cereal. When I went back, Allegra stood up and said, "I thought that talking to someone new or doing something different might help me out of this trap I feel I'm in."

"I'm flattered that you think of me as new and different. I feel more or less like the same old thing."

"I really should go now," she said, pulling at one of her cuticles.

"You don't have to."

"Then would you please kiss me?"

I went over to her and put my arms around her and kissed her. She tilted her head back a little and looked at me. She was so tall: eye to eye with me.

"Cheerios," she said. "Would you please really kiss me?"

I did my best.

"Good," she said. "Give me your hand." She took my hand and put it on her breast. She tilted her head back and looked me in the eye again, as if she were measuring something. "That feels very good," she said. "You don't know how long it has been."

"Yes, I do," I said. "But I think I can take it from here. I'm getting tired of people telling me what to do."

It turned out that she wasn't really directorial about sex but, as in that firm handshake when we met, just well mannered. "May I suck your cock?" she asked, with that unnerving look in the eye, and when I said "Sure" she said "Thank you." "Would you mind if we stopped for a second so that I can get on my hands and knees?" "Could you please hold my shoulders down?" "Would you put your finger in my ass." She sprinkled these courtesies among other, much more pre-verbal utterances, and the whole effect was wonderfully, almost overwhelmingly lewd. After a while, she didn't really have to ask but I let her every now and then anyway, for the pleasure of hearing her.

"Socialite widow Allegra Marshall, after copulating with prep-school pedagogue Jake Singer," I said, while we rested.

"What?"

"You know—those society-party pictures in the papers, I've probably seen you in them and had no idea who you were.

And now here you are. And you turn out to be a regular human being. So regular that you probably came over to the West Side just to use me. But if you did, I must say that I can't understand why women are always objecting to being used."

"After we fuck a few more times and then I tell you I don't care about you, you'll find out," Allegra said.

"Is that likely to happen?"

"The fucking? Oh, yes, I hope so. Right now, in fact, if you can, please. But I'll have to be discreet. I am a widow, you know. As for the rest, I have no idea. Maybe your analyst does. He seems very smart. All mine says is 'Why is that, do you think?' and 'What does this bring to mind?'"

"That sounds pretty good to me. I don't know why you need analysis—you're so direct."

"The closer I am to people, the more distant I feel, it turns out. And don't you think it's just a little bit strange for someone to tell all her secrets to someone she has had maybe fifteen minutes of conversation with before? And then beg for sex?"

"You didn't exactly beg," I said. "And anyway I don't think it's strange."

"Well, you should."

Three weeks later, after coaching third base in the varsity's last game, against Collegiate, I went down to Tiffany's and bought Allegra a silver-and-onyx bracelet for Mother's Day. She had discreetly come to my place again a week after the first time. And I discreetly had supper once at her apartment, late one night. She cooked some kind of chicken and I made some salad. Her kids were asleep. I dried the dishes afterward—I could hardly bear to use the dish towel, it was so exquisitely folded. I left just as the sun was hitting the tops of the buildings on Central Park West. Proctor told me I looked tired when he stopped by

my classroom to ask if I would say a few words at graduation.
He suggested I get some fresh air after school. Luckily, all I
had to do that day was give final exams.

"Mother's Day is Sunday," I said to Dr. Morales when
I lay down on the couch the morning after the trip to Tiffany's.
"Too bad I don't have one."

"It is indeed too bad, Mr. Singer. It is not funny."

"Well, at least I don't have to buy a present or anything," I said. "So, do you think Nixon will be impeached or
not?"

"For permitting you to employ him as a red herring, do
you mean?"

"For abusing his power," I said, as pointedly as I could.

"I don't know, Mr. Singer. Can we return to Mother's
Day? I know you were just being humorous, but here so sadly,
as you know, there are no jokes."

"Why should we talk about it? What's the point? I remember making a card for my mother when I was in first grade
in Bronxville, and she loved it. And then she died. Now I don't
believe in it—it's just commercial. I think that's probably because my mother is dead. Just bitter, I suppose."

"Remove the 'probably' and 'suppose.'"

"Well, so there you are."

"What about your new lover? She has children."

"So? I'm not one of them."

"I shall tell you what, Mr. Singer. I shall make a bargain
with you, not because I am feeling magnanimous toward you,
the good Christ knows, but because my heart goes out to this
woman, this poor woman who cannot have children naturally,
this woman whose husband has died, this woman who is trying
to fight her way out of depression and make changes in her life,
this woman who would be cut to the quicks if she could hear
you speak so coldly and callously about her, this woman who

has what suddenly appears to be the further misfortune of taking you into her bed. The bargain is this, Mr. Singer: Take the fee for this session and get your narrow and self-absorbèd ass off my couch and go to Tiffany's and with the money buy this woman something beautiful. And then give it to her. And do not come back here until you do."

"Free advice—a first for you," I said. "Well, even the analyst can have a breakthrough, I guess." I reached down to my briefcase, which was on the floor next to the backbuster, and took out the little blue box tied with a white ribbon and held it up over my head.

Dr. Morales was silent for a full minute. Then he said, "Why did you feel the need to tease me in this way, Mr. Singer? Could you not bear the idea that I have helped you to take such a step for once without having to get in the back of you and push?"

"I think you hit the nail on the head," I said. "When I went to buy this, I wouldn't have been surprised to find you driving the number four bus down Fifth Avenue, and when I went into the store I could hear you whispering, 'Now, don't be a cheapskates, Mr. Singer,' and the only thing that almost kept me from going ahead was knowing how much satisfaction this whole thing would bring you." In the middle of this I had started crying, though my voice didn't break. Tears just ran out of my eyes as if from a spillway.

"Think instead of the person who will receive this gift and how pleased she will be."

"We even came up with the exact same store. You know, I could accept help from you a lot more easily if you were less constantly critical of me, less sarcastic about it all, and if I didn't suspect that you were getting some kind of perverted kick from disparaging me and trying to run my life."

"I think this is the *only* way you can accept help, Mr. Singer. I think I am doing what is right. I do have my own life, you may be certain of that. I am not living through you or my other patients, much as you wish to believe it so."

"Are you sure?" I said. "Was there an ounce too much protest in there somewhere?"

I walked back to the West Side through Central Park, trying to calm down. The morning was soft and warm; flowers were everywhere. I heard a padding behind me and the next thing I knew I was flat on my face and someone was running with my briefcase. The next thing I knew, I was running after him and then catching up with him and knocking him flat on his face and taking my briefcase back. He got up and ran away. He was just a kid, a druggie in jeans and a black T-shirt, with a peace symbol hanging from a little chain on his narrow, sallow chest.

"He picked the wrong guy," I told Allegra, late on Sunday night. We were in her kitchen again, eating leftovers from the sumptuous meal the cook had prepared for her and her parents and in-laws that afternoon. She had a cook. She was wearing the bracelet I'd just given her, and she paid me the compliment of saying that getting through the day had been much easier because she could look forward to seeing me at night. It was also kind of her to be so enthusiastic about my present, I thought, when she probably owned enough jewelry to sink a yacht. I went on bragging. "He couldn't have known about my blazing speed or all-around athleticism, I guess."

"I did," she said. "Proctor told me when he told me about you before the dinner last month. Did you know that the white-haired man you were talking to, Alex Something—I forget his last name—gave the school a hundred thousand dollars the next week?"

"Yes, Proctor told me. How did you hear about it?"

"In the thank-you letter Proctor sent me. He said wasn't the school lucky to have you as a spokesman, and he thinks you have a brilliant future in education."

"What would he know about education?" I said. I ate a forkful of little potatoes as perfect as pearls. "You have a *cook*."

"You know, I can see where you could be a little scary."

"But you like me," I said.

"*And* I like you," Allegra said, standing up and taking my hand. "Will you come with me now?"

"Shouldn't we clean up first?"

"Leave it for the maid this time. I really can't wait."

"You have a *maid*."

Her bedroom was huge and looked like a chamber in an English country house, with a frayed but magnificent tapestry on the wall, a washstand in front of it, a vast mahogany wardrobe against the opposite wall, and a quiet Oriental rug the size of the Caspian Sea. The bed itself seemed a Yankee interloper; a thin and complex patchwork quilt covered it, and underneath was an off-white down comforter and pillows as yielding as fresh snow. I, too, felt like an intruder there, for all of Dr. Morales's reassurances. I folded my clothes into small dimensions and put them in a little pile on a wing chair with flowered upholstery. Then I put my wallet and keys and change in a tiny pile on top of the self-effacing clothes pile. I turned off the marble-based lamp that sat on a delicate little table next to the bed.

When Allegra came out of the bathroom, I could see by the moonlight pouring in the tall window from over Central Park that she had nothing on. She stood in front of me and turned the lamp back on and said, "Do you like me, too?" She was thin, but her breasts were full and her hips curved just widely enough to escape boyishness. It occurred to me that there is something to be said for motherhood without childbearing, and the luxury of my immediate material and sexual circumstances came home to me and seemed less like a stroke than an assault of luck.

"Yes, I like you," I said.

"If it's O.K., I'd like to get astride you," Allegra said.

"All right."

After this rearrangement, she leaned over and turned the light back on again. "Would you mind talking for a few minutes while we're like this?" she asked.

"Fine with me. You are like an erotic dream come true, you know."

"I swear I've never acted like this before. I wish you could stay with me in the morning."

"I wish I could, too," I said. "But there's your children, and the babysitter. And the cook. The maid. And my classes start at eight-thirty."

"I don't even know what a job is like. Is that awful?"

"Teaching is wonderful when it goes well."

"But you have to do it even when you don't want to."

"That's one of the good things about a job."

"That sounds puritanical."

"I think it's just middle class."

"I don't have to do anything I don't want to do."

"Of course you do," I said. "You have to take care of sick children even when you're sick yourself."

"That's love—it's different. Speaking of love—" she said.

"So this is love," I said when she was still again. To keep myself from coming I had been trying to think about how it would feel not to have to work. This beat my dusty old delaying tactic of mowing an imaginary lawn, even though in the middle of my reverie of wealth I felt Dr. Morales's influence seep into the room like swamp gas. *"Mr. Singer, I suspect and fear that you are about to open this gifted horse's mouth and inspect its teeth, is it not?"* I could hear him say. *"Can you not resist your impulse to piss on your good fortune?"*

"It might be," Allegra said. "I feel as though we would always get along well."

"But you don't know me at all," I was about to say, before Dr. Morales whinnied mockingly in my head to warn me away from honesty. "Would you mind if we turned the tables here again?" I said instead. "Because if it's all right with you I'd like to finish this off as if I were in control, pretty please."

Allegra laughed. "You're making fun of me," she said.

"Yes, but I really would like to do that."

"All right, turn me over now, and we can come at the same time. Let's watch each other, O.K.?"

"Sure," I said. "It would be a pleasure." And like an eight-year-old boy who has succumbed to wearing a tie for the first time, I silently added to the Dr. Morales inside my head, You win. I'll try to throw my lot in with this rich and interesting woman—who happens also to be a staggering piece of ass—and her wainscoted world. What would that world make of me, a neurotic school-teaching Jew without a Corot, Herreshoff, or nine iron to his name, I wondered—if it ever got to that point. Oh, well, I went on, I have nothing to lose. And I might have told myself that lie and forgotten about it and everything else for a little while if Allegra, holding me in her direct and at that point hectic gaze, hadn't said, "Jake, Jake, not yet, please" and I hadn't believed, for a split second, that she was begging me to cancel the calculating decision I'd just made. I did have something to lose, I realized then, as I tried to oblige Allegra—

whether more for fun or strategy I was suddenly no longer sure. In fact, some part of myself had just gone out the window and was hurtling down to the sidewalk below, although I couldn't put a name to it. "Now, Jake," Allegra said, and, just before ardor obliterated all further thought, I heard my indwelling Dr. Morales say, "It is your innocence that you have lost, Mr. Singer, and for that it is a high time."

Twentieth-Century Delphic Mysteries
Sheldon Roth, M.D.

Caught between birth and death, audacious humanity has labored ingeniously and endlessly at extracting meaning from life and relief from its inherent pain. A mosaic of cultural fashions—politics, philosophy, economics, religion, mysticism, art, and the Johnny-come-lately, science—has been popular in offering an existential nirvana. Our century, peculiar for its emphasis on the individual, has added another: psychology. The prime incarnation of the psychological solution is psychotherapy, a novel twentieth-century hands-on wrestling of Jacob's imagination with the angel of psyche.

A glance at psychotherapy reveals a daunting cross-sectional tangle of truth, fancy, and foible. The *Rashomon* trio of patient, therapist, and interested observers defies ordinary language; reasonable translation requires those extraordinary shamans of communication, writers. Each of this volume's nineteen short tales puffs an oracle of distinctive literary smoke from the artistic firing of kaleidoscopic matter. There is no story in this collection that could not be the basis of an intense seminar on either the theory or the technique of psychotherapy. Not only patients and therapists but also the uninitiated will find emotional resonance in these small mirrors held up to psychological nature.

As a therapist, I was gripped by each narrative as if I were listening to a patient in my office or a colleague detailing a therapeutic dilemma for consultation. I felt a range of emotions marked by pain, sadness, and longings to rescue and care for the protagonists, which included the often confused and confusing therapists. These dramas had the validity of everyday life, and they lingered in my thinking, rumbling about, bumping up against one another. I was surprised by the extent to which they functioned as acquired clinical experience and influenced my practice. On reflection, I realized that my surprise was a defensive reluctance to admit the realistic basis of art. Whether the packaging of these stories is fancifully humorous or grimly realistic, the authentic emotions evoked leave no doubt that these authors create out of firsthand experience. Consequently, these narratives cut a wide swath through the therapeutic field and depict many disturbing, dark, ironic twists and turns of fate. Therapy often flounders, or seems incidental but unessential to an ultimate resolution, or reflects bizarre and reprehensible behavior by the therapist. Tolstoy's profound observation hovers over all these tales: All happy families resemble one another; each unhappy family is unhappy in its own way.

Magic, Transference, and Transformation

All therapy that goes anywhere, and some that goes nowhere, partakes of the magical. People hope for transformation through a special relationship with another person: In everyday life this is usually a lover; in psychotherapy it is a therapist. Our unconscious safeguards a universal longing for revival of the magical mother and father of childhood to sprinkle fairy dust and wave a magic wand once again; under duress, this longing is awakened and enhanced. The magical aspect of the patient's transference (the characteristic manner of relating to people based on past experience) to the therapist is an ingredient of hope and softens the pain of seeking help. The dreamlike magical fantasy of Amy Bloom's "Psychoanalysis Changed My Life" and the fairy dust of John Updike's "The Fairy Godfathers" demonstrate two different fates for the alchemy of magic in psychotherapy.

"Psychoanalysis Changed My Life" expresses an almost universal wish in therapy: to be provided the opportunity to rescue the therapist. Rescue, restoring life, creating life, is a deep, nascent impulse stored in our unconscious. Countless myths, ancient and modern, from Moses to *Star Wars*, rest on this powerful urge. It is a displaced form of love and, in part, gives life to the wish to make the loved one forever grateful, appreciative, and bound to the rescuer. It is a talisman against loss. Connected to this wish is the belief that the grateful rescued person will grant us all that is in their power. Consequently, after Marianne rescues Dr. Zurmer, she is rewarded with the gift of her son as a lover. What patient, seeking a lover, has not wished that the generosity of the therapist would provide one?

Magic is just as potent in "The Fairy Godfathers" but is used as a therapeutically realistic stepping stone rather than a permanent residence. Oz's therapeutic dicta, however small, were a "celestial event" and "like golf on the moon; even a chip shot sailed for miles." Rhadamanthus, like the prophets of ancient civilization, inhabits an office that is a "cave of knowing." Tod and Pumpkin, between marriages, install a honeymoonlike, magical hope in these therapeutic ghosts in preparation for sustained love with each other. When the transition is accomplished, the psychiatrists are vaporized along with the transferences, and the couple is left with the dual realistic task of loving each other and dealing with their dimly felt terror. It is fitting that this story is short, because when measured against the longer time of enduring relationships, the honeymoon of romance or psychotherapy is always short.

Reversal of Figure and Ground: The Doctor Joins Alice in the Looking Glass

Transference is an unconscious, ubiquitous tendency to seek past experience in the present, especially lost loves or loves never attained. This tendency toward reproducing the past, whether actual or fantasized, becomes focused on the therapist. Particularly in lengthy psychotherapies, the transference as living history guides the treatment like an Ariadne's thread through the byzantine labyrinth of personality.

For the therapist, however, the transference is a two-edged sword. While revealing the dominant forces of a patient's nature, the empathic immersion in the living passions of the transference also brings a therapist close to a precarious emotional edge. Unconsciously as well as consciously, the therapist tastes and lives a multitude of roles and partial roles assigned by the patient's transference. Often in small ways, these roles are enacted with the patient before the dawn of full awareness. This role-responsiveness is a form of countertransference, and when used for understanding in order to advance treatment, it is highly desirable. This intense human relatedness is part of the pleasure as well as the pain of being a psychotherapist. However, if a therapist has a flawed personality, demonized by his or her own unresolved transferences, mayhem may result at this juncture. A number of these stories describe different angles of this catastrophe and detail its varied, but always sad consequences.

"Basil from Her Garden" reveals a therapist who increasingly joins the patient in a contrapuntal development of his own quandary over adulterous love. The therapist's thoughts and responses to the patient are cast in dialogue, joining the patient, reflecting on his life as the patient reflects on his own. The working machinery of the therapist becomes animate, organic, visible, and analyzable, like the patient's. Unfortunately, in this instance the therapist has gone no further than the patient toward resolving this conflict; therapeutic stagnation ensues. In some ways, the patient seems more advanced than the therapist because the patient is in touch with his erotic desires, relates to real people, and feels troubled. The therapist, by contrast, is more inhibited. In his erotic escapade, which is pure fantasy, he pursues admiration from a woman by spraying poisons methodically through her home, compulsively, room-by-room, and is primarily destructive, producing death. Although the therapist appears sillier than the patient—killing pests is trivial compared to adultery—one can argue that both behaviors primarily express rageful destructiveness. This absence of authentic Eros contributes to the relentless boredom that pervades the tale. The unconscious reigns in the narrative, and like its playground, the dream, it knows no barrier to the existence of opposites. Reversal occurs: Who is the patient, who is the therapist? Is there a patient? Is there a therapist?

A sublimated and contained voyeurism is part of a therapist's professional equipment. In "Samaritan" the therapist is a vulnerable voyeur, using binoculars in an effort to get close to people by magnifying them. This is a poor adaptation, however, as he cannot tolerate loss or mourning and ends sessions abruptly at key affective points, floating above life drugged on tranquilizers. His voyeurism also is not able to contain his gnawing envy of his patient, which degenerates to hate. The therapist's affective disability is a caricature of that of the patient, Mr. R, who leaves his session when painful feelings arise concerning his daughter and still suffers from an inability to mourn a lost dog. Similar to the therapist, Mr. R, who cannot connect loss, grief, and love, turns love to hate: "I started hating the dog." In a grotesque funhouse mirroring of the patient's derailed stance toward affects, the therapist also hates and ultimately turns murderous.

"The Psychopathology of Everyday Life" is good fiction, but it also reads like calamities I have consulted on in my practice. I found more realism than fantasy in this tale. It begins: "As my marriage deteriorated, I became increasingly distracted with my patients, drifting off into fantasy, confusing details and names. . . . I found myself identifying with the mistreated lovers of certain women patients. One, in particular." Yuri, the therapist, is thrown off-balance by his failing marriage; aggressive impulses and a need for power dominate his attempts to compensate. Baumbach's story captures the common, mysterious fusion of Eros and destruction. Yuri states: "We moved in these sessions between war and seduction, different faces of the same aggression." The sexual-boundary violation in this case portrays the need for power in sexual relationships that invade the therapeutic relationship. Aggression drives this romance more than love does: "I was unable to separate the sexual from the violent," he says, and "It gave me a sense of power and accomplishment." Hate breeds destruction. Blowback hits the therapist (what goes around, comes around); Yuri loses his patient-lover, and his therapeutic identity is shattered.

A patient-therapist personality match is a necessary condition for the progress of therapy. Without some essential similarity between the duo, a basis for authentic empathy is lacking. The two resemble the divided unfortunates in Plato's allegory on love, where the gods' jealousy and fear of the happiness of the two-bodied humans (he/he, she/she, he/she) descends in the form of an ax that severs them in two. The incomplete beings, grief-stricken, spend their existence seeking their lost half (thus, the variations of worldly love). Through the transference projected into the therapist, the patient seeks some lost aspect of him- or herself; the transference often seeks in the therapist a kernel or more of truth upon which to settle. In "Keller's Therapy," however, the psychopathic element of each party has unfortunate consequences; if you play with fire you are liable to be burned. Again, in both therapist and patient, unresolved grief melts down into destructive aggression, in this case, quite murderous. But, often enough, even a dedicated therapist (unlike Dr. Breen) is burned; therefore, trustworthy character is an important attribute of a successful psychotherapist. Pondering this occupational hazard my mind wanders at times to the old gypsy woman in the classic black-and-white Lon Chaney Jr. wolfman films, who counsels that "only the pure in heart" can face the dangers of evil. At heart, a therapist must have the best intentions toward a patient.

What can we make of all this psychological cynicism? Some of it is a highly astute understanding of the role-responsiveness and life-size humanness of the otherworldly therapist, taking him or her down to size in a metaphorical manner. These accounts tell an unconscious truth, if not always an exact, external truth. We must acknowledge, however, that instances of actual patient abuse are not uncommon in this professional world. Patients have been used inappropriately for financial, erotic, and political needs as well as more subtle psychological needs. Beyond these practical concerns, these accounts express a universal truth about all human relationships—transference is ubiquitous. People can use transference between each other creatively, maintain it, destroy it, or change it. Therapy merely borrows from life. In the cases of boundary violation, of singular importance are the roles of hatred and a drive for power that are often blighted offspring of the inability to mourn frustrated love.

The Mirror up to Nature

Therapy is a slice of life; the best of therapy reflects the best of life. The therapist merely holds the looking glass up to the patient's own nature, often tilting the glass to reflect the rest of nature that appears blurred or missing in the patient's image. Deceptively mundane, this approach has profound respect for the natural healing processes, buried by crisis and dormantly awaiting psychological focus. Many of the characters in these stories are baffled and sometimes exasperated by the simplicity of the "advice" given by the therapists.

In "Surprised by Joy," Harriet and Jeremy suffer under the protective blanket of depression rather than bear open grief over their lost child. The therapist makes some suggestions: "Keep a journal. . . . Crying helps. . . . Try going on a trip." This deft trio gives tiny angles of entry into the process of disentangling pathological grief, which, most briefly stated, is: Acknowledge (via the journal), bear (by crying), and put into perspective (through the trip). The therapist's role in this crisis is to stimulate latent adaptive abilities. Harriet dreams, and Dr. Benson points to the path laid out in the dream. He is backdrop, banal, and appears inconsequential to the bulk of the tale, which depicts the action of released mourning.

A variant on the advice to take a trip is found in "Slatland," where young Margit is overwhelmed by her understanding of her parents' unacknowledged marital strife. Professor Pine

368 *Sheldon Roth, M.D.*

suggests to her, "For every situation there is a proper distance."
Sometimes, he says, you need to rise above the earth to gain
perspective. Recounting to Margit how this floating technique
helped him as a child to cope with the fear of his mother's
death, Professor Pine culls out of Margit objectivity as an
adaptation to overwhelming affect. Later, as an adult, overwhelmed by lost love, Margit's objective capacity becomes
blocked, but with a short, reuniting visit with Professor Pine, she
recaptures her psychological skill. Many people use a brief visit
to a former therapist to regain some transiently lost psychological
skill, like a car getting a tune-up, or a slumping athlete turning to
a favored coach. Given the current weaving and bobbing of health
professionals—due to our contemporary belief that health professionals are interchangeable—the lifelong available therapist is
rapidly becoming an endangered species.

  Justified skepticism of simplistic advice (as opposed to
simple advice) is found in "Imaginary Problems." Doug, the
therapist, is not too keen on his work and is giving it up to
become an anthropologist. Undaunted by cultural context, the
proto-anthropologist psychotherapist suggests a ritual that is
tantamount to applying a Band-Aid to the gaping wounds of a
marital car crash. Interestingly oblivious to the bizarre cultural
prescription, Beth and Martin find their own way to healing
their mutual calamity.

The Children's Hour

Although an adult viewpoint dominates these stories, a few
penetrate the hazy past to the directness of childhood vision.
In "The Age of Analysis," Paul embodies the hidden disorder
of his parents' orderliness, a prophetic psychological voice that
precedes his father's flight from his mother. The snug world
created by his parents (both therapists) focuses their misplaced

interest on cases rather than on each other and Paul. Paul's raw and honest emotion is the only tonic for life in this deadened family and therapeutic scenario. The several analysts are text-book robots, not so much unfeeling as misguided. Like bureau-cratic shadows in a Kafka nightmare, their observations and advice are out of joint with the emotional needs of the family. Paul's unthinking, violent outburst is the most adjustive inter-vention in the narrative, but even that action gets misinterpreted and unappreciated by his analyst, Dr. Crewes (her name, like her thinking, suggesting a prosaic sock). Like many seemingly incomprehensible behaviors of children, Paul's actions match the situation; he does the wrong thing for the right reasons, while those about him do the wrong thing for the wrong reasons. I wish I could say this was a tale of pure fantasy, but I must con-fess that it describes situations that I have known.

"The Gentleman" is a complicated tale of parents, thera-pists, and therapy but mostly of childhood. Children have their own special interpretation of the therapeutic world their par-ents inhabit, which is at once foreign and familiar (because it is the parents'), magical and powerful, and closed to the deepest questions of their curiosity. Time is spent waiting while "Mom" pursues her periodic, mysterious business, but waiting time does not prevent the inexorable impingement of life on the innocence of childhood. This deft tale calls to mind the clarity and confusions with which adult patients remember their par-ents' therapies. Adults tend toward secrecy with children about their therapy, reproducing the cloak over sexuality and adult life. Children actively, bravely, and seriously ("We were seri-ous, serious to the point of solemnity") fill in the blanks with a mélange of fact and fancy, usually unknown to their parents. Like oil on water, the experiences of both child and parent are tightly proximate, yet ironically, are immiscible and inaccessible to each other.

Although peopled with adults, "Crazy for Loving You" is the childhood game of trading places and playing house. Bustling along, this story is a brief, riotous pastiche, conveyed with the frenetic energy and style of first-rate punk-rock music. This imaginative sampling of the world is commonly revisited in psychotherapy and expressed by "sibling" rivalry with other patients or desires to be the therapist. I once saw an adolescent in intensive treatment for many years, and he often entreated me to cast off my professional demeanor and let my hair down to him (although there was not much to let down compared to his flowing locks). One day, as he painted a glorious picture of what a great analyst he would make for me, I agreed. I hopped up, suggested he take my chair, and I slid onto my red leather couch. It felt good, relieving, cathartic, and I began to free-associate with my "former" patient, now sitting behind me, out of sight. After about twenty minutes I heard from my new analyst; he grunted and said, "Let's stop!" "Why?" I asked. Grunting again, he replied, "This is boring!" And that was the end of that.

Time, Change, Symptom, Character

Time frames relationships. On a forty-minute air-shuttle flight from Boston to New York City, I might do no more than smile politely at the person seated next to me. Yet on a six-hour flight from Boston to San Francisco, it would be most unusual if I did not strike up some rudimentary conversation and relationship with the person beside me. Some of these stories describe brief encounters with therapists over problems of discrete symptoms like depression. Other tales, despite their brevity, skillfully sketch years of therapeutic toil where the crucible is character, which, when alterable, submits only to the unrelenting wear of time and transference.

Time-limited therapy is exemplified by "If Only Bert Were Here," in which the consumer-patient gets a deal. "You feel better by Christmas, or your last session's free." The therapeutic technique rests on the principle of fighting fire with fire; grief over a dead cat (Bert) is pitted against impending grief of separation from the therapist. The ending sports a fascinating, bacchanalian feline funeral as mother and daughter, latter-day Long Island maenads, race through a backyard landscape, filling their forms with the spirit of Bert, thrashing nature with the daunting prowess of a tom. Having fulfilled this ancient ritual of grieving, their new life, coinciding with birth-filled Christmas, can then begin.

Therapy becomes limited by time in "The Whole Truth" because of the limitations of the patient: she is a liar. Psychotherapy is a fragile vessel that shatters without honesty. Truth alone will not order a disordered personality, but without it the situation is hopeless. This story captures the sad, repetitive behavior of those unable to profit from other people and for whom the impact of a therapist is like a mote in the wind. There are people who spend many years going from one therapist to another, just as there are people who spend their lives going from one person to another. A suspicious, deeply distrusting view of the world dominates their existence, along with an anger that fuels a defensive, protective, but distant interpersonal posture. I once knew a woman who for several months reported to her analyst dreams that were the dreams of a friend of hers who was also in analysis. She felt that her own dreams were uninteresting, and additionally, she wanted to see if her analyst's interpretations were as good as those of her friend's analyst. One day she confessed to her analyst (unlike the "she" of the "The Whole Truth"); he was furious, as well as hurt, and he pointed out her contemptuous motives. The patient was annoyed, also hurt, but stimulated to explore and master her characterological mockery. Like the Ariadne's thread of transference, honesty is another trustworthy guide in the stumbling complexity of treatment.

The Dioscuri of our fictional constellation "I'm Rubber, You're Glue" and "Influenza" sparkle with literary brilliance but also induce continual psychological eyestrain. How to understand these stories? After reading the first, I thought that Dr. Morales might have been correct in his understanding but wrong in his technique. Dispersing his well-advertised humility with a torrent of words and tauntingly baiting the patient with interminable interrupting, he did not seem the model of a listening analyst. The danger of such overpowering authoritarianism with a relatively passive person like Mr. Singer is that the patient submits sadomasochistically and follows orders. Of course, we could hypothesize that the transference-countertransference displayed was a necessary repetition of Mr. Singer's relationship with his alienated father and reveals the origin of his difficulties with women; he has identified with a woman-mistrusting father, now replayed by Dr. Morales. And since the second story leaps to the seventh year of treatment, we can imagine (with a large stretch of the imagination) Mr. Singer benefiting from an open, to-and-fro, rough-and-tumble, unbroken relationship with Dr. Morales, whose truths could be received in the spirit with which they were delivered. The fits, starts, and stops of characterological-dysfunction require endless adjustments. We can take this duo of tales as a précis of therapeutic relationships in which the participants are sufficiently well matched, despite seemingly overt blemishes, so that they can profit if they can endure. Of course, we are seeing this story through the pen of a man for whom intellectualized irony is a choice method for translating great sadness. Dr. Morales's version might have been surprisingly different . . . and then again, a reader of both sides might blend yet another version.

"Therapy was like puberty: you went through it and looked back only to marvel that you ever survived it," says the narrator in "Transference," by Peter Collier. Development is undulating; it not only occurs at its appointed time but reoccurs periodically in life as we are able to bear and consider what was unbearable at its origin: "To every thing there is a season, and a time to every purpose under the heaven." "Transference" reveals the value of a lasting relationship with a therapist who can catch up psychological threads ready to be woven long after the official completion of treatment. In this context, transference is enduring and awaits evolution. This tale unfolds the complex generational topography of a developing mind. While Adam considers his relationship with his recently deceased father, he is comparing it with his relationship to his own son, and further, with his past and present transferences to Dr. Fuentes. Reconsideration of the past often has multiple determinants, as in this story: external (death), internal (transference), interpersonal (fatherhood). Good therapy reflects life in its complexity and unpredictability. Both unfold like a possible postmodern form of painting: the oils are ever-applied, often worked wet-on-wet, and never completed.

Love's Labor Lost and Somewhat Found

"The Patient" surfaces the most powerful motive for treatment—love. Whether present or past, acute or chronic, real or fantasized, the aching pain of love taken away or never attained produces a suffering sufficient to endure the strange ways of the psychotherapist. Little else but the hope of finding love would allow anyone to endure such arcane frustration with another human being. Fiction will never finish its task of cataloging the incalculable varieties of mental havoc born of wrecked love. Also, because love can find many directions—self, lover, family, community, work, nature, God—its derailment may seem remote from a patient's chief complaint. "To Alexander's surprise, Dr. Kahmstetter did not pay much attention to the problem of his nose. He was more interested, it seemed, in the kind of people Alexander knew." Loss of love releases disintegrating, protective hatred expressed in symptoms. Alexander splits his world into "Ones," "Twos," "Threes," and "Fours" until he falls in love with a bright Four and begins to merge his splintered world—Eros is binding. True to life, however, Alexander recaptures a kernel of his distorted worldview when he discovers his wife is too threateningly real (good). His shaky self-esteem holds onto a psychological exit strategy in equilibrium with loving his wife, a trade-off that works. Especially with problems of a chronic nature, psychotherapy may provide satisfying outcomes, but basic vulnerabilities smolder silently, lying in wait for future opportunity.

It is hard for a psychotherapist to read "The Patient" without Freud's famous patient the Wolf-Man coming to mind. At one point, when Freud developed mouth cancer, the Wolf-Man developed a paranoid obsession about his nose and its imperfections. His love for Freud, threatened by the specter of cancer and his unconscious fear of abandonment by Freud, stoked a psychosis that was not abated until he fell into a replacement transference love with a woman psychoanalyst who took over the case for the ailing Freud. This issue of delusion, even if metaphorically applied to "The Patient," raises the question of psychotropic medications and their absence in these stories. Currently, medications are used to treat many clinical conditions, including acute reactions to external realities like the death of a loved one. For some people, the symptomatic relief obtained enables better use of psychotherapy, while in others, it closes off psychological inquiry. There is a wide range of valid and invalid applications of medications in psychotherapy. Although some of these tales date from a scientific cultural period of pure psychological determinism, prior to the discovery and acceptance of biological factors in mental disturbance, perhaps it is art that best explains why biology is not featured. The artistic creators of these tales seek out the struggling psyche, that ineffable entity that negotiates body, mind, and world in a sea of chaos. Each tale renders a universal truth of the psyche and lovingly strokes it into a narrative portrait, like a minimalist painting that isolates an essence, an essence that is primarily psychological. I can, however, envisage a future generation of psychotherapy-wise writers for whom psychotropic medications will be as indelible an experience as the analytic couch was in the past; we await their artistic synthesis.

Art and Psychotherapy

The quality of apotheosis or epitome that art lends to these stories imbues psychotherapy with a romantic mystical allure. The multiple dreams described, filled with primordial images like clouds, birds, black space, or dead children, further a mythical, unfathomable, otherworldly tone. Similarly, many narratives strike a humorous, fey, or whimsical pose. In practice, psychotherapy specializes in pain and is not funny. Although the ritual of treatment borders on the pompous, particularly in the classical psychoanalytic model, and begs for jest, this formality cannot explain all the humor. Perhaps it is an artistic translation of overwhelming pain into digestible experience. And maybe it also reflects the aggression aroused when dependence is stippled with guilt and shame; the tables are turned; it is the treatment and the treater that are Keystone Kop ridiculous.

Most commonly, however, psychotherapy runs along less dramatically in a workaday fashion, featuring pick-and-shovel factfinding, exploration, and much humanly understandable resistance to progress. In retrospect, though, a patient may remember therapy in a bottom-line manner similar to the apotheosizing quality of these tales. When recalling therapy, especially a long time later, people tend to have a summary affect that condenses mountains of therapeutic process: "I loved that guy!"; "What a waste of time; it burns me every time I think of it"; "I loved the smell in that office, it always relaxed me"; "I see his [or her] face looking at me and I feel confident again." To this summary affect, a few snatches of therapeutic dialogue persist. But even these dialogues are highly condensed and possess epitome characteristics. Thus, although misleading through impure reportage, art does polish, buff, and sharpen the experiential image of treatment. Beyond recognizing their experience, patients and therapists will savor its profound clarity.

If one story can be the apotheosis of these various apotheoses, then that story is "The Mysterious Case of R." The metaphor of this tale concerns art, but it also captures the essence of psychotherapy. It expresses an uncanny understanding that, like art, psychotherapy cannot be pushed. "To write without authentic inspiration . . . was hubris, hubris in the original sense, a sin against the Gods." If a therapist harbors an agenda for the patient, has goals for the patient that do not come from the patient him- or herself, then the therapy is doomed. Once Dr. Frimmle inflicts his wishes on his author-patient, both art and therapy vanish. Psychotherapy is nourished on the matura-

tional energy of a person's own hopes, loves, and frustrations—
the natural transference. Psychotherapy is the art of wooing
nature, not engineering or manipulating it. The art of human
relationships entails the same principle. So, too, the literary
Virgils of this volume provide an artistically natural history of
their experience, offering the reader freedom to (re)discover a
circle of their own psyche.

Notes on Contributors

Donald Barthelme is the author of nine story collections, including *Unspeakable Practices, Unnatural Acts,* and three novels, including *Paradise.* He was a frequent and long-term contributor to the *New Yorker* and won a Guggenheim Fellowship, a National Book Award, and a National Institute of Arts and Letters Award, among others. He died in 1989.

Steven Barthelme is the author of the short story collection *And He Tells the Little Horse the Whole Story* and has published fiction in the *Massachusetts Review, Yale Review, North American Review,* and elsewhere. His stories have won the Transatlantic Review Award and, three times, the PEN Syndicated Fiction Project competition. He teaches writing at the University of Southern Mississippi.

Charles Baxter's stories have regularly been anthologized in *Best American Short Stories* and the O. Henry award series. He is the author of six books of fiction, including *Through the Safety Net,* a collection of stories, and *Shadow Play,* a novel, as well as one book of poetry. Mr. Baxter is a recipient of the Lila Wallace–Reader's Digest Foundation Fellowship for Writers and the Michigan Author of the Year award and has received grants from the National Endowment for the Arts and the Guggenheim Foundation. He lives in Ann Arbor, Michigan, and teaches at the University of Michigan.

Jonathan Baumbach is the author of eleven works of fiction, including the novels *Reruns, Babble, Separate Hours,* and *Seven Wives: A Romance.* He published over sixty short stories in such publications as *American Review, Esquire, Tri-Quarterly,* the *Iowa Review, Partisan Review,* and *Boulevard.*

Lawrence Block is the author of forty novels, including *A Long Line of Dead Men, A Dance at the Slaughterhouse, The Devil Knows You're Dead,* and *When the Sacred Ginmill Closes.* He has also published under the bylines Chip Harrison and Paul Kavanagh. Last year he was named a Grand Master by the Mystery Writers of America, and he has been awarded the M.W.A.'s coveted Edgar Award three times. He lives in New York City.

Amy Bloom's collection of short stories *Come to Me* was nominated for both the National Book Award and the *Los Angeles Times* First Fiction Award. Her stories have appeared in the *New Yorker, Story, Antaeus, River City, Room of One's Own,* and other fiction magazines here and abroad. They have also been included in anthologies, including *Best American Short Stories 1991* and *1992,* and the 1994 edition of the O. Henry prize story collection. Ms. Bloom is a contributing editor for *New Woman.* She recently completed her first novel, *Love Invents Us.*

Peter Collier is the author (with David Horowitz) of *The Roosevelts, The Kennedys, The Rockefellers,* and *Destructive Generation: Second Thoughts on the Sixties.* He is also the author of a novel, *Downriver.*

Frank Conroy has worked as a jazz pianist, teacher, freelance journalist, and government employee and has been the director of the Iowa Writers' Workshop for the last nine years. His books include *Stop-Time, Midair,* and most recently, *Body & Soul.*

James Gorman is the deputy science editor of the *New York Times.* He is the author of *The Man with No Endorphins, First Aid for Hypochondriacs, The Total Penguin,* and most recently, *Ocean Enough and Time.* His work has also appeared in the *New Yorker,* the *Atlantic,* the *New York Times Magazine,* and other magazines.

Barbara Lawrence has worked as an editor at *McCall's, Redbook, Harper's Bazaar,* and the *New Yorker.* Now an emeritus professor of humanities at the State University of New York's College at Old Westbury, she has published criticism, poetry, and fiction in *Choice, Commonweal, Columbia, Poetry,* the *New York Times,* and the *New Yorker.*

Rebecca Lee is originally from Saskatchewan. Currently, she teaches writing at the University of North Carolina at Wilmington and is completing a book of short stories.

Stephen McCauley is the author of the novels *The Object of My Affection, The Easy Way Out,* and most recently, *The Man of the House.* Mr. McCauley has an M.F.A. degree in writing from Columbia University. He has taught writing at several colleges, most recently at Harvard. He lives in Massachusetts.

Martha McPhee is a graduate of Columbia University's M.F.A. program in writing. Her fiction has appeared in the *New Yorker, Redbook,* and *Open City.* With her sister, Jenny, she translated from Italian to English *Crossing the Threshold of Hope* by Pope John Paul II. Her first novel, *Bright Angel Time,* will be published by Random House in the spring of 1997. She lives in New York City.

Daniel Menaker is the author of two collections of short stories, *Friends and Relations* and *The Old Left*. The two stories in this volume are part of a novel, to be published by Knopf. "Influenza" was selected for the 1996 edition of the O. Henry prize story collection. Mr. Menaker was an editor at the *New Yorker* for twenty-five years, before joining Random House as a senior editor in 1995. He lives in New York City.

Lorrie Moore is a professor of English at the University of Wisconsin and lives in Madison. Her work has appeared in the *New Yorker, The Best American Short Stories,* and *Prize Stories: The O. Henry Awards.* She is the author of two collections of short stories, *Self-Help* and *Like Life,* and two novels, *Anagrams* and *Who Will Run the Frog Hospital?*

Francine Prose's most recent novel is *Hunters and Gatherers,* published by Farrar, Straus and Giroux. Her other novels include *Primitive People, Household Saints* (which was made into a feature film by Nancy Savoca, released in 1993), *Bigfoot Dreams, Judah the Pious, The Glorious Ones,* and *Marie Laveau,* as well as the collections of short stories *Women and Children First* and *The Peaceable Kingdom.* Ms. Prose is the recipient of a Guggenheim Fellowship, a Whiting Writers award, and the Pushcart Prize. She has taught at the Iowa Writers' Workshop and currently lives in upstate New York.

Sheldon Roth received his M.D. from the New York University School of Medicine. He was a resident in psychiatry and the chief resident at Massachusetts Mental Health Center, and he graduated from the Boston Psychoanalytic Institute. He is currently an assistant clinical professor in psychiatry at Harvard Medical School and a training and supervising analyst at the Psychoanalytic Institute of New England, East (PINE). He has a private practice in psychiatry and psychoanalysis, is engaged in teaching a broad range of mental health profession-als, and is the author of *Psychotherapy: The Art of Wooing Nature.*

Lynne Sharon Schwartz's most recent novel is *The Fatigue Artist,* published by Scribner. Her nine earlier books in-clude *Disturbances in the Field, Rough Strife* (nominated for a Na-tional Book Award), *Leaving Brooklyn* (nominated for a PEN/ Faulkner Award), and two story collections, *The Melting Pot and Other Subversive Stories* and *Acquainted with the Night.*

John Updike is the author of eleven collections of sto-ries, including *The Same Door, Pigeon Feathers, Museums and Women, Problems, Trust Me,* and *The Afterlife and Other Stories,* and sixteen novels, six volumes of poetry, five collections of nonfictional prose, a memoir, and children's books. He has received numer-ous honors, including the Pulitzer Prize, the National Book Award, and the National Book Critics' Circle Award. He lives in Massachusetts.

Permissions
Acknowledgments